Patricia Favier was born in New Zealand of French and English parents but has lived in many countries, including France, Canada and Britain. She began writing fiction and drama in her teens and after completing a degree in history, went on to become a journalist and local politician. She co-founded a book publishing company and was for many years its editor. She is also the author of numerous non-fiction titles, as well as a book for young children. She now lives in a small town north of Toronto, Canada with her husband and young daughter, where she enjoys writing, gardening and music.

A PRICE TOO HIGH

Book Two of The French Legacy Trilogy.

When beautiful American heiress Catherine de Lacy O'Donnell arrives in Paris to wed the Duke of Charigny, she has to deal with two unexpected problems: the French Revolution, which closes daily around her like a threatening cloud, and the arrogant disdain shown by her new husband. But far worse is the realization that it is the Duke's cousin, naval captain Christian Lavelle, who has stolen her heart. Her only chance of happiness is tossed before her like a gauntlet. She must decide whether to accept the challenge or deny it.

Books by Patricia Favier
Published by The House of Ulverscroft:

THE FRENCH LEGACY TRILOGY:
A MASQUERADE TOO FAR
A PRICE TOO HIGH
A TEMPTATION TOO GREAT

PATRICIA FAVIER

A PRICE TOO HIGH

Book Two of The French Legacy Trilogy

Complete and Unabridged

ULVERSCROFT
Leicester

First published in Great Britain in 1998 by
Robert Hale Limited
London

First Large Print Edition
published 2000
by arrangement with
Robert Hale Limited
London

The moral right of the author has been asserted

Jacket Illustration by Barbara Walton

British Library CIP Data

Favier, Patricia
A price too high.—Large print ed.—
(The French legacy trilogy; bk.2)
Ulverscroft large print series: romance
1. Social classes—France—History—18th century—
Fiction
2. France—History—Revolution, *1789–1799*—
Fiction
3. Love stories 4. Large type books
I. Title
823.9'14 [F]

ISBN 0–7089–4268–7

Published by
F. A. Thorpe (Publishing)
Anstey, Leicestershire

Set by Words & Graphics Ltd.
Anstey, Leicestershire
Printed and bound in Great Britain by
T. J. International Ltd., Padstow, Cornwall

This book is printed on acid-free paper

To my great-great-grandfather,
Joseph Favier, who fled Paris during the
Revolution and settled in Ireland

1

Paris, 1791

A cold, sleety rain began suddenly as a gust of wind ripped around the corner of the Rue Saint-Martin and into their faces. Christian Saint-Cyr Lavelle bowed his head against the stinging needles of icy water and cursed himself for a fool.

'Dammit, Fontenay, why do I give in to your lunatic notions? Even the Atlantic in January is friendlier than this!'

He glanced at his companion who was struggling to control the skittish horse upon which he was mounted. The creature was nervous, and Lieutenant Gérard Fontenay, at best an indifferent horseman, wasn't helping.

Captain Lavelle's own mount, aptly named Malavoir, was regarded as the ugliest stallion in the city, with a temperament well suited to his devil-black coat. He gave an impatient snort. 'Twas a sign his owner knew well: he wanted to run.

'Not here, you devil,' Christian muttered, yanking none too gently on the beast's mouth. 'You'll have us all killed.' He called to

1

his friend. 'There's an alley over there. It leads to the river and we can let them have their heads!'

'Aye aye, Captain!' Gérard sent him a mock salute, but Christian could see he was relieved to turn his horse out of the driving rain and let the narrow street afford momentary shelter.

They trotted along in silence, avoiding the piles of rotting cabbage and dodging upended barrels that stank of fish, for this was a poor quarter and with the turmoil of the past two years, no one much cared about cleanliness. Just surviving from day to day took effort, and the imagination of everyone was occupied with mightier things. The future of the king and the rights of the common man seemed so much more important than the state of the streets. After all, once the doors were closed and wine and bread brought to the table, such things assumed little importance.

Christian ducked as a bucket of water whooshed down from an upstairs balcony. The horse seemed to sense it a second before he did, and side-stepped neatly so that only his withers and his master's boots received a splashing. It scarcely mattered, with the rain and muck all around them.

As they neared the end of the street,

Gérard motioned to Christian to stop.

The sound that reached them was unmistakable. Men, mostly, and a few women, wearing the revolutionary cockade of red, white and blue, and carrying staves, burning torches and pitchforks. The oily flames blew wildly in the wind, casting strange shadows on the faces of their bearers.

'Damn rabble out for blood,' Christian muttered. He glanced around, but apart from retracing their steps, there was no other way to the river.

'They have no quarrel with us, Gérard. Let's go through.'

His friend turned to him, jaw dropping. 'Are you crazy, *mon vieux?* We may not be their prey, but — '

Christian spurred his horse into the mêlée, his friend's tutt-tutt just reaching his ears. He laughed. Gérard could be such an old woman sometimes. Perhaps it came of being married and having children — obligations he prided *himself* on having avoided.

The two naval officers entered the square side by side, causing a few eyes to turn and some comments to be hurled. Christian ignored them. He had no interest in the rabble's grievances. He only wanted to get home and into some dry clothes before he caught pneumonia. At least the rain had eased and the wind seemed less boisterous here.

'Captain, is this wise?' his companion muttered, as they became entangled in the fringes of the surging crowd.

Christian didn't answer. His eyes were searching over the heads of the rabble. ''Tis not us they are concerned with, Gérard — look!'

An elegant blue and gold carriage, reminiscent of something from the opulent days of the Sun King, stood halted in the middle of the crowd. The coach horses milled about, jittery from the press of bodies and clearly alarmed by the angry shouting. From his vantage point astride his stallion, Christian could see a dozen *sans-culottes* rocking the vehicle, bouncing it on its elegant springs.

He felt a pang of sympathy for the occupants of the carriage, then chided himself for it. They were not his concern. The Revolution had opened his world, laying a path of possibilities at his door. Such avenues had never existed when he had been a mere commoner in the noble House of Charigny. But now, with his reputation as one of France's most skilled naval explorers well established, the flames of the old order held promise for his future.

And helping aristocrats who were foolhardy

enough to venture out in their gilded conveyances was not on his agenda!

'*Capitaine*, this could get ugly. We must turn back!'

'I despise retreat, Gérard, you know that.'

Christian looked around, searching for a way around the crowd. But all the exits appeared jammed with a mass of noisy, unwashed humanity. He sighed, tugging his collar around his face and reining his fractious horse more tightly. Across the *place*, the men were working together now, encouraged by the shouting crowd.

'*Un, deux, trois!*' The berline bounced high on its springs, so high that two of the wheels momentarily left the ground. Another burst like that, Christian thought, and the thing would topple for sure.

Then, at the small window, he saw a face. Despite the distance — of some fifty paces — it sent a flood of dismay through him.

He stared over the heads of the crowd at that terrified gaze. Dark eyes set in a ghost-white face stared out, glancing wildly about until they came to rest directly on him. Christian felt speared. The woman looked straight at him, her expression pleading over the heads of her tormentors as though she knew instinctively that he would be the one to help.

Christian swore silently. Some of the crowd had noticed the two naval officers in their midst and he heard their shouts as they pointed. This was not turning out to be one of his better days.

He felt Gérard touch his arm. 'Don't think of it, Captain,' he warned, ever the voice of reason. He touched a hand to his hat as if to reassure himself that he still wore his revolutionary cockade. ''Tis not your fight.'

'She needs our help, Gérard. They'll tear her to pieces.'

His eyes scanned the crowd for the noisiest heckler, then he picked his target, shouting at a tradesman not too many paces distant who seemed to be something of a ring-leader.

'Who is this person and what has she done?'

The man cupped a filthy hand to his mouth and shouted, 'She is an enemy of the people, *citoyen*!'

'Why say you?' Christian knew he ran the risk of enraging the crowd against himself, but the man's arrogance irritated him. The woman, whoever she was, deserved better.

The tradesman laughed, egging on his neighbours. 'Why, citizen, if you can't tell that just by looking at her fine gold carriage, perhaps 'tis because you're one with her!' The crowd roared with laughter, turning now to enjoy this spectacle.

Christian glanced over their heads. The woman's face had disappeared behind the curtained window of the berline, but at least the monsters who had been rocking her vehicle had ceased for the moment and were watching him instead. He mistrusted their expressions.

It was impossible to tell if this was an organized event or merely a spontaneous outburst against a foolish aristocrat. He knew he must tread carefully, for his own sake, for spies were more common than square meals in Paris these days. Yet the fear on that woman's face haunted him.

He spurred Malavoir into the crowd, forcing the *sans-culottes* aside simply by refusing to make eye-contact with them. His stallion was tall and strong, as black as coal and with a face to match his ugly reputation. They let him pass. Gérard followed in his wake.

The captain kept his eyes on the curtained window of the coach. As the crowd's yelling subsided into muttering, the cloth twitched and she looked out.

Christian had known she was handsome, yet the face that gazed up at him through the rain pierced him to the core. Beneath the hood of her fur-lined cloak, chocolate-brown eyes thickly fringed with black lashes emphasized her pale cheeks, and her small pink mouth trembled slightly.

'Help me, please?' she asked, so faintly that he barely caught the words.

Malavoir forged restlessly beneath Christian's legs, but he held the horse in check, feeling a surge of anger at this bewitching woman.

'What can you possibly be thinking, *citoyenne*, to be out in such a contrivance? Have you no feeling at all for these poor people?'

He knew he was pandering to their baser instincts, but if he were to make a path for the woman's coach, he saw no other way.

'I say again,' he called loudly against the wind, so that those in the immediate vicinity could hear, 'are you a friend of the Revolution?'

There was a lull while she stared at him and Christian wondered if she understood what he expected.

He caught a glimpse of something in her eyes, or perhaps it was the tilt of her nose that made him raise his brows, but she answered with some asperity, 'I love freedom, *monsieur*, like all thinking people.'

The irony of her assertion amused him, given the opulent form of transport she chose. Around him, he felt a slight shift in the temper of the crowd and seized the moment.

'Let her pass, citizens, in the name of *liberté!*'

Before their leaders could decide how to respond to this, a gap opened before the horses, whose impatient milling about had kept many at a respectful distance. The coachman wasted no time and flicked his whip. In a moment the vehicle was plunging through the crowd and out into the side-streets.

'You're a total madman, Lavelle,' Gérard complained, as they took advantage of the resultant confusion to make their own retreat. ''Tis time you were back at sea.'

Christian grinned. 'Past time. For us both.'

They parted soon after, Lieutenant Fontenay to his apartment near the Louvre, and Christian for the elegant town palaces of the Faubourg Saint-Germain.

As he reached the wide boulevard skirting the river, he saw the berline again. Like a gilded cage on wheels it flew across the bridge over the Seine. And for one fleeting moment, the curtain flicked aside and he caught a glimpse of the bewitching face within.

★ ★ ★

Catherine allowed the heavy curtain to fall back across the window, shutting out the vision of the man on horseback staring at her from across the rainswept river. Yet even in the shadows of the swaying coach, she could feel his eyes upon her. Dark eyes, though perhaps 'twas only the stormy sky that made them seem so, for she was certain they were blue. When he had spoken those words, asking her if she were a friend of the Revolution, their eyes had somehow connected, as though he were speaking to her without words. She had understood instinctively. And yet he was a complete stranger.

She lay back against the padded seat, tugging her sable cloak tighter to ward off a sudden chill. Now that they were safe and speeding on their way, her mind dissolved into shock. What if that horseman had not happened along? That bloodthirsty mob would surely have turned the berline on its side, spilling herself and her maid into the jaws of who knew what horrors?

'Not long now, Miss Kitty,' the woman in the seat opposite murmured, reaching across to pat her mistress's hand.

Catherine forced a smile. 'I have a dreadful feeling about this, Martha, as though that mob was somehow a sign. We should have stayed in Philadelphia.'

The abigail harrumphed softly. Catherine noticed the heavy black rosary moving steadily through her hands, as it had done so often during their voyage from America. Poor Martha. She would follow Catherine to the ends of the earth, but that didn't mean she had to like it.

'You know what it says in the Bible,' her maid announced. 'Take care what you wish upon yourself, lest your dreams come true.'

Catherine pressed her lips together to contain a smile. 'I don't think that was the Bible, Martha. It sounds more like the Chinese laundryman who came on Fridays.'

Suddenly the coach slowed and they heard voices beyond the window, but mercifully they were not challenged again, and the iron-clad wheels continued along the heavily cobbled streets. But the distraction was enough to send Martha back to her beads with a vengeance.

Catherine sagged against the seat, wishing for the hundredth time that this journey would end. How big was this city, and why were there so many checkpoints?

And just who was that stranger? she wondered, her thoughts returning to the man who had effected their rescue. She could not forget the picture he made in that bleak place or the ease with which he held that

11

devil-black horse under control. He had saved her life. Of that she was certain.

At last she understood her hired coachman's warning: *Mademoiselle, to pass through Paris in a vehicle such as this is to offer your head on a platter.* At the time she had laughed. But that was when she had just stepped off the ship, with no experience of the turmoil she had since witnessed in France. How little she had understood the dangers!

Already, she was wiser. Already, she had seen the beast in the hearts of the people. And it had frightened her. She smoothed her hands over the cloak covering her knees, letting the silky fur trickle through her fingers.

She was not prepared. Her father had commented on the situation, but she had listened with only half an ear, so occupied was she with preparing for her departure for France. It had not seemed too significant — her childhood memories of the American Revolution were of heroic battles fought far from the protective walls of her home.

Despite the events of the day, she felt a thrill of excitement — and dread. For wasn't that how any young woman might feel when wild imaginings and cold reality suddenly became bedfellows in her life? It was a strange sensation that even when she had left Philadelphia and embarked upon her voyage across the wintry Atlantic, had not truly come upon her. Until now. She glanced at her maid, her fingers busy upon her rosary, her eyes closed and her lips moving in silent prayer. Perhaps Martha felt it, too.

For both of them, it was a wrenching change. One moment she had been plain Catherine de Lacy O'Donnell, rich but dull, her life devoted to nursing her mother; then Marguerite O'Donnell had given up her earthly struggle, and Catherine had found herself with no real prospects.

She sighed. A spinster. That was her lot in life. And it did not fit. It was not what she had dreamed of as a little girl, and it was certainly not what her beloved mother had desired for her.

Through all those years of bedside caring, Marguerite O'Donnell had taught her daughter two things: to believe in her dreams, and to speak French like a native. Catherine's mother had fallen in love with an Irishman who, while he had never been quite acceptable in English-dominated American society, had a great nose for making money. But she truly loved him and had stayed in America to share his life, though she never forgot her heritage. It was from her mother's lips that Catherine had learned about elegant balls, beautiful dresses and palaces full of kings and princes.

Princes! Catherine knew a fairy tale when she heard one, and yet those bittersweet dreams, spun on golden afternoons as her mother lay dying, became Catherine's reality, paid for by a lavish dowry.

It was not until after her mother's death that Catherine realized Marguerite's dreams had borne tangible fruit. Her father had told her of his deathbed promise to his wife: that he would arrange a marriage to a legitimate French nobleman for their daughter. She had been most insistent, even to specifying that it should be no lesser person than a duke.

Catherine had cried, clinging to her father, knowing as he did that the future could not atone for the past. But she had allowed him to write his letters, had not enquired as to his success until one day, as the first Pennsylvanian snows began to fall, he had brought her the news. Catherine de Lacy O'Donnell would become the wife of the Prince de Charigny's only son. A duke. Just as her mother had wanted.

She shook her head, still not comfortable with the image of herself as a duchess — much less as a future princess. She knew the arrangement her father had made had taken money — lots of it — and tried to focus on that fact to lend some reality to this strange dream. But she was equally certain that despite his promise to Marguerite, her father would have weighed the value of such a marriage carefully. The cost must reflect the gain. No fool, her papa.

She squirmed on the swaying seat, impatient for the journey to end. For the millionth time she wondered what her betrothed would be like. She slid her fingers inside her cloak and withdrew the gold locket she had worn since her father accepted her betrothal five months ago. Slipping her thumb under the tiny clasp, she opened it, as she had done a thousand times before, and let her eyes dwell on the miniature portrait of her future husband.

Catherine frowned. Surely, it could not be . . . ? Her fingers trembled as they held the tiny portrait, and she pushed aside the curtain to bring it into the light.

Her heart contracted for an instant, and then pounded so hard it almost stole her breath away. 'That man,' she whispered, 'surely it cannot be . . . ' Yet the likeness was unmistakable.

The man who had rescued her on horseback bore an uncanny resemblance to her fiancé.

*I am surely imagining things. There is some similarity, but . . . .*The nose seemed the same, the eyes also, but the chin of the man in the picture was a disappointment. She liked a strong chin in a man, and this was soft — one might even describe it as flaccid. And it didn't help that in the portrait he was dressed in the height of courtly fashion with an ash-white powdered wig. The man who rode that fearsome black stallion with such nonchalance wore but a simple greatcoat and top boots; *his* hair had been dressed with nothing more than a light dusting of rain.

She felt the carriage slow. *You are such a romantic, Catherine,* she scolded herself. *You've encountered only one gentleman since your arrival in Paris and your imagination has already decided that he's your betrothed.* She chided herself for such *naïveté* and tucked the locket resolutely away.

The berline lurched in a sharp turn, the horses responding swiftly to the coachman's barked command by pulling to a quick stop.

The beasts snorted in the damp air, then the footman's feet crunched in the gravel and the door was flung back. Beyond, Catherine saw wide doors open, spilling golden light across rain-slick marble steps.

'I believe we have finally arrived, Martha.' She squeezed her maid's hand and they looked at each other with a mixture of anticipation and dread.

Then Catherine accepted the lackey's arm, stepping out and following him quickly up the steps of the enormous mansion, with Martha close behind. So this is the Hôtel de Charigny, she thought, impressed beyond her expectations by the elegant façade and the lush gardens that she spied through wrought-iron gates beyond. It was a far larger house than any she had seen in Pennsylvania, with three storeys rising to a roof edged with sculptures depicting cherubs and satyrs. Rows of giant windows, that she mentally thanked God she would never have to clean, glowed softly through the rainy twilight.

She ducked into the shelter of the portico, wondering at her luck, wondering at her future.

How would her friends in Philadelphia feel if they could see her now? Would they still snigger about her, the not-quite-socially-acceptable Irish girl who was still unmarried at twenty-four? Catherine suppressed a sudden desire to giggle. Not any more. Now they would *die* for an invitation to visit.

A servant took her travelling cloak and led her across a broad white-marble foyer. She trailed him up a wide curving staircase carpeted in a deep red that set off the white stone of the balustrade and the polished brass trimmings sparkling in the light of numerous sconces. She stopped in surprise and looked about her. This was not quite as she had expected. She understood the Charigny estate had fallen upon very hard times, that the aristocratic establishment had been reduced to genteel poverty. Perhaps the Prince de Charigny was already spending her dowry. As she picked up her skirts to follow the servant, she couldn't help but wonder if it would be enough.

She was shown to her quarters and left in the care of Martha, who fussed about checking the linens and drawing the heavy brocade curtains. Catherine wandered about the little sitting-room in awe, trailing her fingers across the gleaming mahogany escritoire and admiring the fine artistry of two gilt-framed paintings of roses by the celebrated naturalist, Pierre-Joseph Redouté. A cheery fire danced in the grate and on the mantel above stood an elegant ormolu clock. She wondered at the size of the Prince de Charigny's debt that he would accept money from an American rather than discreetly dispose of such treasures. She poked her head through a door adjoining the salon, and her brows rose at the sight of the vast bathroom, lined from floor to ceiling in white marble, with a huge marble bath surrounded by urns planted with ten-foot palm trees.

Martha seemed less impressed. She pronounced herself satisfied with the housekeeping and proceeded to unpack their boxes.

'You'd best be making a good impression on these Frenchies, Miss Kitty,' she said, carefully withdrawing an elegant gown of white silk embroidered with red roses and sewn with tiny seed pearls.

Catherine eyed the gown, thinking it rather too fancy for the occasion, but then she touched her locket with her fingers and her pulse quickened at the thought of *him* seeing her in that confection.

'I shall wear that gown, Martha, and you must stop referring to our hosts as Frenchies. Remember, soon I shall be the wife of a French duke. I very much doubt that my husband will tolerate such insubordination.'

Martha's face fell at the notion she might be dismissed from her mistress's household, and she paled visibly. Catherine felt guilty, for she knew it was not badly meant.

'Pray, don't take it so hard, Martha. I shan't let them send you away, I promise.'

Martha blinked, but apart from lowering her eyes and attending to her work, made no further comment. Catherine sighed. Adjusting to their new life would be difficult for everyone.

A short while later, there was a knock at the door. Martha opened it.

A servant, dressed in plain black like all the others she had seen so far, bowed, looking past Martha to Catherine who was sitting on the edge of a *chaise-longue* and wondering when she would be summoned to meet her betrothed.

'Mademoiselle O'Donnell,' he said, emphasizing the last syllable in her name in a manner she had found quite charming ever since her arrival in France. 'If you will accompany me, please.'

Catherine took a deep breath and followed the man from the room and down the stairs, past numerous carved and gilded doors, until he finally bent to open a set. Stepping aside and standing stiffly to attention, he announced her.

Catherine tangled her fingers nervously in her ivory fan. This was the moment she had waited for, and yet now it was here, she felt nothing but panic. This place, this giant house with all its servants, was so alien to her. By American standards, she was wealthy, but this . . . this was something quite different.

She felt suddenly very small, very young,

and totally out of place.

The servant was waiting, looking at her with a touch of distaste that made it clear he was having much the same thoughts. Catherine met his glance, stiffening her spine. Well, maybe she wasn't an aristocrat, but she *was* engaged to the duke. If she was good enough for him, she was certainly not going to let herself be intimidated by his man.

She swept into the room, head erect, and the doors swung softly shut behind her.

At first, the salon appeared to be empty. She gazed in delight at the elegant harpsichord that stood beside the floor-to-ceiling windows, its glowing walnut veneer reflecting the light of a brace of candles resting on the lid. Through the still-open drapes at the windows she glimpsed a stone terrace, and the silhouettes of tall trees against the darkening sky in the garden beyond.

She turned to survey the rest of the room, instinctively drawn toward the fire crackling in the grate, and found herself staring straight into a man's face.

'Oh!' Catherine stood as if turned to stone. Her eyes widened in shock as she recognized the man who had rescued her from the crowded square that very afternoon. And he was staring at her, not in a friendly way, but with the coldest pair of blue eyes she had ever encountered.

'So,' he said, after a chill moment. 'It *was* you.'

Oh, dear Lord, Catherine thought. Martha had warned her about the curse of one's dreams coming true. Now she understood; for if this was her fairy-tale prince-to-be, he was not at all what she had imagined. This man was as hard as flint, and, if she was not very much mistaken, exceedingly angry.

2

Catherine gazed speechlessly at him.

Fleetingly, she compared his thunderous face with that in the locket she wore about her neck. The artist had done little justice to his subject; for in front of her stood as striking a man as she had ever encountered, tall and broad-shouldered, with an unmistakable air of command. His unadorned gentleman's clothes were plainer than she had expected and gave him a dangerous air, as though his magnificent surroundings and the wealth of her dowry meant less than nothing.

'I see that despite your stupidity you have arrived unharmed,' he said acidly. Catherine flinched, but she would not show the hurt, for she felt only gratitude to him for rescuing her.

'Thanks to you. I don't know what that crowd wanted of me, but 'twas indeed fortunate that you arrived when you did.'

His eyes narrowed for a second. '*Mamselle*, if you have no idea what happened this afternoon, you had best gather your belongings and return to America on the instant.' He ran a hand through his hair. 'Have you no regard for your own safety — or that of your servants?'

Catherine flushed, stung by his accusation. Her father had told her this suit was most eagerly awaited by both her betrothed and his family. How could her careless mistake have wrought such fury? Was he expressing a change of heart before they could even become acquainted?

'I care a great deal for the welfare of my servants, sir, and I apologize if I have given offence. I shall endeavour to do better — under your guidance, of course,' she added, watching him carefully.

He turned away, leaning one arm against the high mantel and staring down into the blazing fire. She noticed how very tall he was, and with his face averted she was at last able to steal a look unobserved. Her eyes flitted over his lean frame, broad-shouldered beneath his tan frock coat, and down to his strong legs as he reached a toe to push an ill-balanced log back into the nest of flames. He wore close-cut breeches of darkbrown twill and leather shoes that looked comfortable but scarcely new or in the height of fashion. His shirt was silk, but plain of lace and decorated with no more than a simple cravat. In fact, his clothing seemed not at all in keeping with his sumptuous surroundings.

'If you wish to hear my advice,' he said without turning, 'it's to turn that ridiculous carriage into scrap before it gets you into further trouble.'

'My berline?'

He pushed himself away from the mantel and rounded on her. 'Do you know nothing of the Revolution France has suffered these past years? I take it you Americans do gather the occasional morsel of news from Europe?'

'Certainly,' she replied, affronted by his sarcasm. 'Though I fail to see how your political difficulties have any bearing upon my transportation.'

He let out a short laugh, gazing at her with an expression that changed from incredulity to frustration and then to something she could not quite interpret. 'Those 'difficulties' could have cost you your life, *mamselle*.' He raised a hand and wiped it across his face. 'Perhaps you did not notice how few fine carriages are seen on our streets these days. They attract attention, and that is something no one can afford to do.'

'But, sir — ' Should she call him 'sir' or 'Your Grace'? she wondered in a panic, for this was not going at all well. 'Surely, things are not that bad. I was led to believe . . . ' Catherine's voice trailed off as she encountered the thunder of his scowl.

She looked away quickly. Unbidden, her mind filled with a vision of how she must have appeared to the poor people on the streets of Paris. He was right to chastise her. She had deliberately chosen the most opulent carriage she could find, wanting to make the best possible impression on her future in-laws. No wonder there had been so many to choose from, and all going for a song and a prayer.

She bowed her head, feeling suddenly very stupid. Her legs trembled and she glanced about, wondering if she could sit somewhere. 'I'm sorry,' she mumbled. 'I truly didn't think — '

She gasped as his warm fingers encircled her arm and his other hand pressed into the small of her back. He ushered her to a *chaise-longue*.

'Forgive me,' he muttered, more kindly than she had yet heard him speak. 'I was not considering the fatigue your journey has caused you. Pray be seated while I fetch some refreshment.'

Shaken by the strange sensations his intimate touch had wrought, Catherine sank wordlessly onto the chair and watched as he crossed to the sideboard and poured ruby wine from a decanter.

He returned with a glass. His fingers

brushed hers momentarily as he pressed it into her hands, creating a flash of heat where their skin made contact. Catherine stared at the wine for a second, wondering how the mere touch of his hand could cause her heart to leap about so wildly in her breast. Then he perched on the seat beside her.

Catherine scarcely dared breathe. He was so close she could smell the rainswept tang of his still-damp hair which curled around his collar and fell across his forehead. Her fingers itched to reach out and smooth it back, and she clutched her glass tightly in both hands to control them. She glanced up, feeling sad that their first meeting should have been so filled with acrimony, but where she had expected to read censure in those fathomless blue eyes she saw something gentler, something indefinable . . .

She raised her glass to touch softly against his. 'To the future,' she whispered.

She held her breath in the silence that was broken only by the crackling of the fire in the grate, hoping he might smile, that he might forgive, if not forget. But then he frowned, and a shuttered look marred his features once more.

He stood, turning from her and setting his glass down on a table so roughly that the contents splashed upon the marble surface.

Catherine set her wine aside, also untouched.

'Have I offended you?' she asked, bewildered by his abrupt withdrawal. 'I know I have a lot to learn about France and society, but in Philadelphia I was not considered witless. I think you will find me an eager pupil . . . ' Her stream of babble faltered beneath his icy glare. 'That is, if you would take the time to guide me.'

It was not the right thing to say. His brows drew together in a frown that could have stampeded an army.

'Why on earth should I wish to do any such thing? My dear Miss O'Donnell,' he went on, sarcasm making a mockery of the term, 'I have no intention of passing any more time in your company than good taste dictates. What you do or do not learn about society is of supreme indifference to me.' He leaned towards her, so she could be in no doubt of his sincerity. 'You may be buying yourself a title, but don't ever make the mistake of thinking you can buy me!'

Then he turned and marched out of the salon, letting the door slam behind him with considerable force.

Catherine sat stunned, staring straight ahead of her into the crackling fire, his bitter words making her ears ring as if he had physically boxed them. She felt numb, paralysed by the venom in his words.

She smoothed her palms across the heavy white silk of her gown, forcing herself to remain calm, to breathe in and breathe out until the trembling had passed.

Then she got up, replaced her wineglass on the sideboard and returned to her room.

★ ★ ★

Christian stormed out of the Hôtel de Charigny only to see his uncle's unadorned carriage turn into the boulevard. He leaned his back against the door with a sigh.

What a total *imbécile* he'd made of himself, he thought forlornly. And now here he was trying to run off like a knave. He watched as the carriage drew up and the Prince de Charigny descended, rather stiffly in deference to the rheumatism that plagued his left hip these days. Christian was fond of his uncle, who had been the only father he really remembered since his own parents died in the typhoid epidemic of 1764, when Christian was but five. And in those twenty-seven years he had developed the greatest respect for his foster parent's powers of deduction; he knew the little scene between himself and Dominic's bride-to-be would come to light sooner than Christian might like.

The prince hobbled up the steps towards him, leaning heavily on a silver cane. He stopped in surprise when he observed his nephew on the top step.

'Hmm,' he commented without preamble, as he resumed his climb. 'Are you leaving or arriving?'

Christian grimaced. 'I was leaving, but since you are here, I suppose I must be arriving again.'

His uncle gave him a puzzled look. 'Come into the library. I have some matters to discuss with you before the American arrives.'

'Miss O'Donnell is already here,' Christian answered, as they surrendered their coats to Gilles.

The prince raised his eyebrows. 'Where is she now?'

The man answered. 'In her room, sir.'

'Very well, then. Bring us some wine, Gilles, and let us not be disturbed. Come on, you young rascal,' he said to Christian, 'let's get to it.'

Over a glass of Madeira, Christian and his uncle discussed the most recent turn of events in the king's household, for the prince was closely involved in the fortunes of the monarch, although publicly he took no such stand. Once again, Christian warned him of the dangers, of the flood of spies who could betray him to the Assemblée at any moment. And, as usual, the prince waved a hand in dismissal at the suggestion.

'I am at the end of my life. If I cannot risk my neck, I can hardly expect anyone else to. But I thank you for your advice. Later, you must tell me what is happening at the Ministère de la Marine. I have heard that you might be sent to Brest to help train the squadron.'

Christian eyed his uncle speculatively. 'Your sources are good, as ever, Uncle.'

'So it's true.' He sat back in his chair and tapped a long unadorned finger on the top of his desk. 'If you get a frigate under your hands, lad, take my advice and run for America with her.'

Christian raised his brows. '*Comme un lâche*, Uncle? No, I am no coward and I do not care to steal a ship from my own navy.' He turned away, unwilling to admit that the idea had in fact crossed his mind during times of uncertainty. 'No. I want to take another expedition to the Pacific once things have settled down and I can't do that from America. They are not interested in scientific exploration.'

'There's always trade. Americans excel at that, so I'm told.'

'I have no interest in trade.'

'So,' the older man said after a moment of silence, taking a leisurely sip of his wine, 'tell me about my future daughter-in-law. Does she know how to behave? Is she fair of face? I trust I shall not have to behold the face of a hog's arse at breakfast for the rest of my days.'

Christian nearly choked on his wine. He turned away to hide a sudden smile, his mind captured by a pair of chocolate-brown eyes and a pert, upturned nose that tilted so enticingly. How could he possibly describe her, or the feelings she created in him when their hands had touched? Damn it all, she was engaged to marry his cousin.

'I fear she is not what you anticipated, Uncle.'

The prince's face fell. '*Nom de Dieu.* I knew 'twas a mistake.' He sighed heavily, wiping a hand across his brow. 'And yet, what choice did I have? The offer surprised me, given Dominic's state. But — ' He allowed himself a few well-chosen expletives before continuing. 'Once those *cahiers de doléances* were drawn up, the writing was on the wall, Christian.'

'Perhaps we should have refused.'

'Bah! And had the château burned and our holdings looted as that young fool Robert de Chambois did? He'd have done better for his

32

family's fortunes if he'd run to England with his parents. At least *we* bought some time.' He shook his head. 'No, you were right to advise me to make concessions.' He picked up his glass, twirling it slowly in the light. 'When I heard O'Donnell was looking to 'invest' as he put it, in a liaison, I snapped at the bait. Now poor Dominic will have to pay.'

'But you said it was for Dominic's sake — '

'Yes, yes. Not mine, certainly, at my age. Nor yours — you have your career and you've never asked me for a *sou* since you came here.' The prince peered up at Christian, a quizzical expression on his bushy brows. 'Damn strange that. Guess you got that from my sister, God rest her soul. Always was too damn independent — and look where it got her.'

Christian frowned, not wanting to rehash such long-buried memories. He turned the conversation back to the quixotic woman upstairs.

'Have no fear, Uncle. Mademoiselle O'Donnell is unusual, but easy on the eyes and most definitely a social butterfly. I fancy she expects life in Paris to be the same as it was before the Revolution.'

His uncle's eyebrows lifted a little, but he made no comment. Christian felt a renewed surge of frustration at the cupidity of the woman.

'She arrived in a carriage worthy of Cinderella and got herself mobbed in the Place Saint-Christophe. If I hadn't come along in time they would have torn her to pieces.' He ran a hand over his eyes to dispel the ghastly vision. 'Dear God, she came so close to arriving here in pieces with her head stuck on a pike . . . '

His uncle sat straighter, frowning. 'I trust you did not explain that to the lady.'

'Of course not.' Though the temptation had been real. 'But neither did I compliment her on her taste in vehicles.'

The prince guffawed, holding out his glass for his nephew to replenish. As Christian poured the wine, he had a sudden, horrible thought. Although he knew with sickening clarity what the answer would be, he forced himself to pose the question.

'Tell me, Uncle . . . *assure* me the girl hasn't come to France expecting to become a duchess?'

His uncle received the glass of wine, but held it before him without sipping it. With a rather sheepish expression on his face, he gave Christian a lopsided grin.

'*Au contraire*, dear boy. I very much fear she anticipates becoming a future princess.'

★ ★ ★

Martha answered the tap at Catherine's door, for her mistress had thrown off the white gown in disgust and was resting on the huge canopied bed, wearing a blue silk *peignoir*.

'Yes?' Martha asked, clearly forgetting that she had promised her mistress she would make every effort to speak French, now that this was their new home. '*Pardon,*' she said to the servant who stood stiffly at the door. '*Vous désirez quelque chose?*'

'*Mademoiselle* she is awaiting downstairs in the salon, miss,' came the answer, in passably good English.

Martha grinned at the footman, unable to resist teasing. 'Actually, *monsieur, mademoiselle* is resting from her journey, but she could be ready in a few minutes if you wish.'

The man blushed to the roots of his black hair and muttered something in rapid French that she was certain was less than complimentary.

'*Je m'excuse,*' Martha said, opening her eyes very wide, 'but I don't believe I quite caught that.'

He glared at her, then seemed to remember himself and straightened. 'Monsieur le Prince de Charigny commands to see Mademoiselle O'Donnell and meet her to his son.' With that

35

obscure announcement, he made an abrupt about-face and disappeared down the hall-way.

Martha closed the door, her shoulders shaking with laughter, and wiped her eyes on the hem of her apron. 'Oh, Miss Kitty,' she sputtered, trying not to giggle, 'these Frenchies do take themselves serious, do you not think?'

Catherine crushed a smile and did her best to look disapproving as she got up from the bed. 'Martha, you mustn't tease them. For all we know, our attempts at French may be even more comical. And apart from that,' she admonished, 'this is our home now, and we must show proper respect.'

Martha pulled a face.

'Martha.' Catherine gave her a warning look, and the maid had the grace to blush. 'Now, come and help me get ready. I must find something to wear for supper.' Her mind flashed to the painful interview she had endured earlier. She had no wish to earn that disdain again. She sighed. How could someone risk his own life to save a stranger one moment and then upbraid them so cruelly not an hour later?

'Why, Miss Kitty, you've only just dressed!'

'Exactly,' Catherine replied with feeling. 'And now I wish to dress again in something more suitable for a woman of sensibility.'

'Sensibility?' Martha echoed, clearly mystified.

'Do you not think me sensible, Martha?'

'Well, of course.' The maid was clearly flustered. 'Too sensible, if the truth be told. So sensible, in fact, 'twas a wonder you didn't accept your father's notion to marry Mr McBride.'

Catherine huffed. 'Amos McBride was a year older than my father, Martha! And an absolute stranger to water.'

The maid cocked her head to one side. 'You refused his hand in marriage because he couldn't swim?'

'Because he didn't wash, Martha!'

They giggled.

'Ah, well now. That's entirely different to be sure. I'm not sure but I got close enough to the man to smell him.' Martha crossed to one of the remaining trunks that sat by the window, as yet unpacked. 'Shall you wear your silver gown? 'Tis perfectly adorable and as fine a gown as anyone in the world would be seen in.'

Catherine gazed at the exquisite creation her maid was brandishing, trying to picture her betrothed's face when he saw her in that! It sparkled as pure gold threads woven here and there into the silvered silk caught the candlelight, and sparks shot from the diamonds stitched into the sweeping skirt, painting celestial patterns on the walls of the room.

She almost laughed. 'No, Martha. Somehow I think that will have to go the same way as the carriage we came in.'

'Miss?' Martha frowned. 'But it cost an arm and a leg, your father told me so himself.'

'And if I wear it, it might cost me my head,' she replied with asperity.

Martha stared at her mistress, clearly mystified by this sudden change of heart. Catherine was not about to explain. The contempt in those handsome eyes, his genuine anger at her *faux pas* in choosing the elegant berline over a more serviceable coach, was something she had no wish to incite again.

'Let's try something a little more demure,' she suggested. 'Perhaps the green velvet?'

Martha's brows shot up, and her mouth opened and then closed in silence as she encountered her mistress's level gaze. Shrugging, she fetched the heavy gown, smoothing out a few creases with her expert hands. It was an elegant gown, suitable for dining *à la maison*, with a generous white lace kerchief to cover the exposed neckline. It was not a dress to cause offence, even to the most exacting eye.

'It will do,' Catherine sighed, for she had spent so many months anticipating this night and the effect the Cinderella creation would have on her prospective in-laws.

Fifteen minutes later, as she stared at her reflection in the mirror, she felt suddenly rebellious. The green velvet made her travel-weary complexion look even paler than usual. Bilious would not be too strong a word. She turned away sharply. It would not do.

This first night, tired or not, she must begin as she planned to go on. She had not travelled across the great ocean to spend her life as a little mouse cowed by the first censorious glance. After all, she was an O'Donnell, and as everyone in Philadelphia knew, the O'Donnells were not easily intimidated.

'Martha, you were right. I had the silver gown made especially for this first evening with the prince and duke. If I am to show them I'm not just some timid colonial girl ready to crumble at the first hint of disapprobation, then I must start as I intend to go on. Bring me the diamond necklace and the ear-rings as well.'

Martha's grin nearly split her face in two.

'Shall we be putting the diamonds in your hair, miss?'

Catherine laughed at her maid's mischievous countenance. 'Everything we've got, Martha.'

★ ★ ★

Dressing in the silver gown was more of an ordeal than she had anticipated, for the fabric was weighted down by the precious metals woven into the heavy silk. Catherine gazed at her reflection in the dressing-table mirror as Martha slid the last of the pins into her hair.

'You've done me proud, Martha.'

The maid blushed, turning her pink Irish skin a violent red. 'Thank you, miss. I'm only grateful you chose the dress. You've no reason to be considering yourself a nobody, just 'cause they've got themselves those fancy titles. Your family has a name to be proud of, and no denying.'

Catherine reached up and patted her hand, smiling at the determined set of the woman's jaw.

'Don't fret, Martha. I'm quite capable of looking out for myself.'

'To be sure. But let's hope you won't have to once you're married and settled with ba — '

There was a firm knock on the door. Catherine's hand flew to her mouth.

'Goodness! They must think me so rude. How long has it been since the footman summoned me downstairs?' She leapt up from the *poudreuse*, and just had time to snatch up her fan before Martha opened the door.

Catherine smoothed the creases from her gown as she hurried across the room, an apology already forming on her lips. But the words died in her throat.

It was him.

Her eyes widened with dismay. She was so inexcusably late that he had felt it necessary to fetch her himself! Catherine felt the heat rise in her cheeks.

'I see you have at last completed your toilette,' he said dryly, his eyes travelling over her from head to toe. From the firm set of his mouth she knew she had dressed according to his expectations, but most certainly not to his taste. He himself wore a simple grey jacket with breeches buttoned below the knee. The notion that she totally outshone him caused her some embarrassment, which she quickly quashed. Had she not chosen this gown expressly to remind him of who she was and why she was here?

She would not be cowed and, as his eyes

finally returned to her face, she met his look evenly.

'Forgive my tardiness, sir. It was not my intention to keep you and your father waiting.'

He stared at her with what seemed like incredulity. Then he swore softly to himself, shaking his head.

'Believe me, *mamselle*, nothing could possibly inconvenience *my* father. I must speak with you before we join the others.' He looked pointedly at Martha, who was ogling the man as though he were some tasty morsel. 'In private?'

He held the door wide.

'Ah!' the maid said finally, bobbing a curtsy as she passed.

Oh dear, Catherine thought. If Martha was smitten with the man, she would have to listen to her singing his praises every waking moment.

He turned and closed the door behind the Irishwoman, leaving Catherine uncomfortably aware that she was closeted alone in her bedchamber with him. I must become accustomed to it, she told herself. It will be my life soon enough.

She straightened her back.

'No doubt you wish to apologize to me, sir, for your outburst in the salon? You made it perfectly plain that you had no desire to spend time in my company except as good taste dictates, and I — '

Catherine squeaked as his hand descended to her mouth, her words smothered by warm fingers that pressed against her lips. She could taste his skin, slightly salty with the faintest hint of wine, and her heart pounded beneath her bodice.

'Do you always chatter on like this? No wonder you get yourself into these muddles.'

Chatterbox! Catherine's face flushed with indignant heat.

He withdrew his hand and pointed her towards a *fauteuil*. 'Sit. I have something to say that I wish I need not. But since you are so ready to leap to conclusions, I have no choice.'

Catherine bit back the words of retaliation that flew to her lips and instead sat primly on the chair. She would not dignify his outburst with a response.

'Now, Miss O'Donnell,' he began, as he paced the floor in front of the fire. 'Kindly allow me to disabuse you of your misconceptions. You are here because of an arrangement between your father and Monsieur le Prince de Charigny that you shall marry his son, Dominic. Am I correct?'

Something in his look made Catherine's

heart miss a beat. She took a small breath. 'Is there some difficulty?'

His short laugh bore little warmth. 'There most certainly is.' He ran a hand through his tawny hair. She noticed that he wore it loose and short, allowing it to curl against his collar. It gave him a dangerous, almost piratical air.

He looked down at her, sighing. 'Our conversation this afternoon was not to my liking, and the reason for that has only just come to me. I hope you can forgive me.'

He stood in front of her, leaning down to pluck the folded silver fan from her fingers and lay it aside. Then his hands enfolded hers, and she was startled to feel callouses on his palms.

'How much did your father tell you about this arrangement, *mamselle*?'

Catherine licked her suddenly dry lips, her eyes searching his as she struggled to adjust to his warmer, more human side. The touch of his hands covering hers, warm and strong, set her nerves atingle and made coherent thought strangely difficult.

'I'm — I'm sure he told me everything I need to know,' she stammered. 'Although perhaps he could have been clearer regarding the Revolution.' She frowned. 'But then again, perhaps he did explain and I simply didn't listen. I am not much interested in politics, I fear.' She paused, realizing that she was chattering again. 'What precisely is your concern, sir?' Should she call him 'sir'?

His eyes were as blue as the sea, yet in their depths she sensed a storm brewing. He released her hands, fisting his own behind his back as he resumed pacing the carpet like a caged tiger.

'Forgive me if this sounds presumptuous, *mamselle*, but are you by any chance harbouring the impression that *I* am Dominic de Montaltier?'

Catherine's eyes grew as round as saucers, and she found herself utterly unable to breathe. What could he possibly mean?

He harrumphed. 'Damn. I feared as much.' He looked down at her, then resumed his pacing. 'Well, rest assured, Miss O'Donnell, you need not fear a lifetime shackled to one such as myself. I am nothing more than the poor cousin in all this, no trophy to be bought and sold at auction.'

Cousin! He was her betrothed's *cousin*! How could she have — ? But surely he had — ?

The blood drained from her face as she absorbed his words. She stared obdurately at him, too shocked even to reprimand herself for such monumental stupidity.

'It was my mistake,' he continued more gently. 'You seemed to know who I was and so I failed to introduce myself. That was inexcusable.' He extended the slightest of bows. 'Permit me to do so now. I am Dominic's cousin, Christian Saint-Cyr Lavelle. Just plain *citoyen*, these days, though in the navy I am still a captain.'

A captain? The man who had haunted her since they met — whose likeness she had worn in a locket about her neck for so many months — was a sea captain? Catherine stared stupidly at him, trying desperately to regain her equilibrium. All those things she had said to him, all that she had implied by her words — She blushed, the colour returning to her cheeks in a violent and oh-so-telling rush.

She stood up, picked up her fan, and drew in a deep lungful of air, but she could not bring herself to look at him.

'The fault — ' She cleared her throat. 'The fault is entirely mine, Captain. Perhaps, since we are to be related, we should put our previous conversations entirely behind us.' She saw his brows lift in surprise. Indeed, her outward coolness was unexpected even to herself, though she would never admit to it. She turned to the door. 'And now, I believe I have kept my betrothed and his father waiting longer than is respectable.'

★ ★ ★

Christian stared at the woman as she uttered these words, then ploughed past him like a frigate in full sail. He knew she would be upset, expected a tantrum of some sort, perhaps even to feel the slap of her palm across his cheek. God knew, he deserved it. But apart from a slight flush of embarrassment, she had taken his news without the slightest emotion.

He shook his head, dropping his arms to his side as he turned to follow her from her chamber. Was it just him? Had he spent so many years at sea in the exclusive company of men that he had lost whatever ability he might have had to understand women?

The fairer sex had never occupied much of his thoughts, he had to admit. He trailed the silver ship of a dress down the candlelit stairs and wondered what his cousin Dominic would make of this apparition, worthy of the infamous Marie-Antoinette herself. At least she'd had the decency not to powder her russet hair or resort to patches.

He caught up with her, offering his arm as they neared the lower landing. She hesitated and then laid her small hand on his sleeve. Even through the fabric of his coat, he could feel the warmth of her fingers.

She glanced up at him, searing him with dark eyes that caught the candlelight and shot sparks. She reminded him of another woman he'd known, a long time ago. He wasn't sure his orderly, well-planned life would survive another such as she, and he thanked God his uncle hadn't thought to marry him off to this heiress instead of Dominic. Dominic! She'd thought he was Dominic. Christian stopped, turning her to face him, just as they reached the library doors. That could only mean —

'*Un moment*, Miss O'Donnell! There is something else you must know, before — '

Too late. The footman had stepped up and swept open the doors, giving him no time to prepare her. No time to warn her that her dream was about to be shattered for a second time.

3

Something in Christian's voice made Catherine falter. She turned, wondering what else he could possibly say to disturb her on this trying day, but with no real desire to hear it. The man was impossible, having the effrontery to mislead her like that and then blaming it on her for making assumptions!

She had just opened her mouth to express these sentiments when the footman threw wide the doors to the salon. She had to content herself with casting Christian a glare, and then turned with real curiosity — and only a touch of disappointment that it was not he — to meet her real betrothed.

Head held high and the annoying captain's hand still gripping her elbow as though he owned her, Catherine entered the room.

'Mademoiselle O'Donnell!'

An older gentleman — Catherine took him to be perhaps in his sixtieth year — crossed the carpet and swept her an elegant bow. He was dressed in a modest jacket of deep gold with green breeches, his unpowdered hair in a queue. A single diamond sparkled in the lace at his throat.

She curtsied as Christian introduced him.

'Miss O'Donnell, may I present my *uncle*' — his slight emphasis was not lost on her — 'Joseph-François Saint-Cyr, Comte de Montaltier and Prince de Charigny.'

'*Enchanté*, Your Highness,' she replied, having opted for addressing him according to his highest rank. She blushed when he laughed.

'My dear, I am flattered beyond expression, but I pray you will address me simply as sir. I am not a prince of the blood, you know.'

Catherine looked quickly at Christian, hoping for some explanation, but his lips were pressed tightly together. He released his hold on her arm and turned away to pour himself a glass of wine from the decanter on the sideboard.

'Come, my dear, my son is waiting most anxiously to meet his bride.'

Catherine looked around her, wondering why he was not here to greet her himself. The prince led her towards the fire, and she realized with a start that another pair of eyes had been watching her ever since she had entered the room. On a small sofa beside the hearth, sat a man dressed in an opulent scarlet coat and purple breeches, with gold buckles in his red satin shoes and a huge diamond pin in the froth of lace that was his cravat. He wore a single patch below one eye, emphasizing the slackness of his face. Unlike his cousin, he wore his hair powdered and tied back, and his fingers, which he held steepled on his chest as she approached, were encrusted with rings.

Dominic's eyes as he watched her bore only a passing resemblance to the ocean blue of his cousin's. They were pale in comparison and bore a chill that she felt all the way to her toes. His features were similar, also, and yet they were not. The nose was not quite as straight, the brows less commanding, and his mouth was thin and pinched.

She held his gaze, acutely aware that he was examining her from top to toe, as though she were a horse at market. But slowly the ice in his eyes melted into something more resembling humour and Catherine felt some measure of relief. Her main discomfiture came from his refusal to stand up to meet her. She stole a glance at the prince, but he seemed undisturbed by his son's ill manners.

She stopped in front of her fiancé and stared at the soft, pale hand that extended itself towards her.

It was the prince who spoke. 'Allow me to present my son, Dominic-Joseph Torignac, Vicomte de Montaltier and Duc de Charigny. Dominic, I am delighted at last to bring you

51

your bride, Mademoiselle Catherine de Lacy O'Donnell of Philadelphia.'

Catherine placed her hand in her fiancé's, since that seemed to be what he expected. His fingers were slightly clammy, despite his proximity to the fire, and she felt a tiny shudder pass through her.

Alarmed at such a reaction, she gave him her brightest smile. 'I am delighted to meet you at last, sir.'

'Indeed,' he replied, his face devoid of emotion.

His eyes travelled over her attire. 'I must compliment you on your gown. So few people these days have the courage to display their wealth by means of their dress.'

Catherine frowned, puzzled by his tone. 'I — I wanted to make the best possible impression,' she responded, thinking of the way Christian had reacted. 'Does my choice offend you?'

'Not at all. It is a delight to the eye. As it was, no doubt, to the pocket of the dressmaker.'

Catherine swallowed. So he was mocking her after all. She rued the day she had ever allowed herself to believe in fairytales. How could she, a wealthy but ordinary American, have ever imagined that her father's money could buy her a place in this society? She had no idea how to behave, what to say, or even what to wear. And she was feeling ever more awkward as he continued to recline before her, studying her with that disinterested air.

Finally, he smiled, though it brought no warmth to his face.

'Pray enlighten me as to what enticed you to cross the Atlantic and abandon your cosy little colony.'

'Little col — ' Catherine caught herself before she exploded. She would not argue with her betrothed in the very first conversation they had ever held, even if that was precisely what she had done when she had mistaken Christian for Dominic. Obviously, getting used to French attitudes would take some study. She drew in a breath.

'America is no longer a colony, sir, since we had our own Revolution. And Philadelphia is not so small. Why,' she went on proudly, 'we even have our own stock exchange.'

She realized, too late, that her comment had only served to emphasize her plebeian origins. Dominic's brows rose and his pale eyes regarded her a little more coldly.

'I do not care to discuss trade,' he replied. 'Though since we have somehow ventured onto the subject, you might as well relate how your father made his fortune.'

Catherine felt herself colour under this

attack, but she straightened her back. From the corner of her eye she saw that Christian was watching her, obviously as curious as her fiancé to know how some lowly American *colonial* could have amassed sufficient wealth to make such a match for his daughter.

'My father is a ship owner,' she replied, ignoring both of them and turning to accept a glass of Madeira from a manservant.

'Indeed.' This from Christian.

'No doubt my cousin is vastly intrigued by such an occupation,' Dominic responded dryly. 'But then, he prefers the company of sailors and *putains* to that of decent society.'

'Dominic!' The prince spoke sharply to his son. He signalled to the manservants who stood impassively by the door. 'I think we should go in to dinner.'

Catherine stared at the two cousins, wondering at the obvious rancour between them. The room fairly crackled with it. She stood waiting for her fiancé to escort her to the dining-room, but he made no move to do so. It was the prince who took her arm.

'Come my dear. Brassart and Emile will tend to their master.'

As he led her to the door, Catherine looked behind her and saw to her amazement that the two servants were lifting her fiancé and carrying him as though they were some kind of human sedan chair. She turned away quickly, but not before she had caught a glance of sympathy from Christian. He raised his brows in an apology, but she turned back to the prince, determined not to embarrass herself further. So that was what Christian had wanted to tell her. No wonder he had quizzed her on how much her father had divulged.

A bitter lump formed in her throat as she realized that the father she had loved and honoured all her life could have so deceived her. How could he not have told her this? Was he so desperate to marry her to a title for the sake of his own business connections that he would throw her into the arms of a cripple? She blinked away the angry tears. Surely he knew that after years of nursing her own mother she yearned for a life free of sickness and incapacity. That he had deliberately sent her to become the wife of an invalid tore at her heart.

But at least everything made sense. Now she understood why a French duke would seek a bride from far across the ocean. He had made very sure that he found a victim who would not be too choosy!

Catherine knew that twenty-four was old to be in search of a husband. And in Philadelphia, she'd had few prospects. All the most suitable men were already married to girls younger than herself, and those who were not were either much older and widowed, with ready-made families, or so unprepossessing — like the odiferous Amos McBride — that marrying Liam Rafferty, her father's shipping clerk, had once seemed her only option.

Not that Liam was so bad. They had been friends forever, or so it seemed. But the affection she felt for him was sisterly rather than romantic. Being Mrs Rafferty just didn't excite her at all.

Catherine was seated to the right of the prince at the dining-table. Christian, to her discomfort, sat down directly opposite, while Dominic was deposited at the other end, facing his father. She kept her eyes down. She would not allow Christian to see her reaction to the discovery of her betrothed's physical disability.

She concentrated instead on the magnificent table, long enough to seat twenty and set with an immaculate lace-edged tablecloth made of the finest lawn. The cutlery was pure gold, exquisitely engraved with what Catherine assumed was the prince's coat of arms, and the china, which bore a matching pattern, was almost translucent in the light of three magnificent candelabra.

The first service consisted of a choice of soups and numerous appetizers. While it was being served, the prince explained that Madame Beaulieu, an old family friend, had been engaged to act as chaperon until the nuptials, but that she had taken to her bed today with a cold. Catherine acknowledged this courtesy, just as she wondered at the unmistakable snort she heard from her betrothed at his father's words. Clearly there were currents within this family that she must beware. She wondered if Christian might explain things to her on the morrow for, despite his disapproval of her, she felt he was at present her only friend.

She settled for the cucumber soup, but toyed with it, her appetite having mysteriously vanished. She felt Christian's eyes upon her and looked up, receiving a smile that was so unexpectedly sympathetic that she felt a sudden urge to cry. She looked down quickly and was grateful when he began to engage his uncle in talk about the government.

When the second course was served, she felt calmer and even managed to smile at Dominic as he recommended the roast veal marinated in cream. He himself ate little, she noticed, picking idly at the duckling he had selected from a platter.

The wine flowed, red and white and even a

pale pink rosé, which was new to her. Little by little, as the conversation ebbed and flowed, she began to relax and enjoy her exquisite surroundings, so fabulously sumptuous compared to life at home. This, when all unpleasantness was set aside, was just as her mother had described it to her.

But her betrothed was not. Her pleasure in finally arriving in this land of fantasy must be tempered with a firm dose of reality. She had captured part of her mother's dream, but the price was an invalid husband and a home in a city embroiled in revolution. And there was so much to learn!

To that end, as she allowed a servant to remove her plate and replace it with another in preparation for the arrival of a dish of juicy partridge, she took advantage of a lull in the conversation. Politics, it seemed, had been exhausted for the moment.

'May I enquire as to the usual entertainments in Paris?' she asked her future husband, who sat staring at her over his untouched capons. 'I have heard the theatre is excellent.'

He stirred to life somewhat. 'I don't much attend, but I'm sure we can arrange a visit if you wish.' His eyes locked on hers, and she caught the self-mockery in his tone as he added, 'As for other pastimes — as you can see, I am not much for balls and dancing, and there is precious little to do in Paris these days unless you are a favourite amongst the salon rats.'

Catherine flushed, stung by his rancour. 'I see. I would very much like to attend the theatre.'

The prince patted her hand. 'Then so you shall, my dear. Christian will take you around, won't you, my boy?' He glanced only momentarily at his nephew, not expecting any disagreement, and Catherine, catching sight of Christian's thunderous expression, had to suppress a giggle. The prince sailed on undeterred. 'Dominic feels a bit left out at these things, given his condition. Understandable of course. But that doesn't mean you have to stay locked up all day like him.'

'I wouldn't want to be any trouble,' she protested. 'I am sure Captain Lavelle has many important matters to occupy his time.'

That brought a guffaw from Dominic. Which in turn caused Christian to frown at his plate.

Catherine sighed. This would not be an easy house in which to reside. It seemed there was as much political tension within the walls as there was in the streets.

The prince, however, was either so used to the acrimony between his son and his nephew that he ignored it, or was blissfully unaware of the currents rolling across the dining-table.

'You should take her to meet *la petite bourgeoise*, Christian,' Dominic said suddenly, a faint smile on his thin lips. 'No doubt the ladies will have much in common.' He waved a hand in the air, and Brassart refilled his wine glass. 'Why, they can talk of babies and dresses and the latest manner of wearing the cockade.'

Catherine stared at him, wondering why such vitriol should be directed at her.

'Indeed, my cousin will be delighted to meet Miss O'Donnell,' Christian replied smoothly, without so much as honouring Dominic with a glance. Instead, he leaned forward across the table and spoke to her. 'Angé — Madame Fontenay — will enjoy your company. Her second husband, Gérard, is in the navy with me. We are plotting our next voyage to the South Seas together while we wait for the government to find some funds.'

'Alas,' interjected the prince, 'that is a most difficult task. The coffers are empty and the *assignats* become more worthless by the day.'

The two men lapsed into silence while the dishes were once again cleared. Within a few moments desserts were provided — a whole array of enticing compôtes and pastries, little tarts and sweet brioches, and then to her astonishment, ice cream. She made no secret of her delight in such a delicacy and the prince pressed her to enjoy a second dish of the delectable confection.

As she savoured the novel dessert, Catherine felt the skin on her neck prickle, and looked up to discover her betrothed's eyes upon her. Far from exhibiting embarrassment to be caught openly staring, Dominic merely smiled. It wasn't a warming smile, she thought, and she knew her answering smile faltered somewhat for she was unable to fully cover her uneasiness. That annoyed her, for she was not usually lacking in confidence.

The prince was also regarding her at that moment, but with considerably more friend-liness. Indeed, Catherine had taken an instant liking to the man. Despite her situation, he at least seemed happy to welcome her into his family.

'I beg your pardon, sir?' she asked, realizing her thoughts had led her away from the conversation at the table.

'Unnecessary, my dear. No doubt you are excessively fatigued from your journey. The question was merely one of idle curiosity. It can wait until the morrow.'

'Indeed, I am in perfectly good spirits, sir. I was merely thinking of something else.' She glanced back at Dominic and saw him smile into his dish of sweetmeats.

It was Christian who spoke. 'My uncle wondered how you came to speak such impeccable French, *mademoiselle*.'

'From my mother,' she said, addressing her reply to the prince. 'She was brought up in a French household until she was fifteen. She always spoke to me in French to preserve our culture, so she said.'

'And who then was her father?' the prince went on, selecting a delicacy from the dish before him.

'His name was Reginald de Lacy.' At the prince's raised brows, she continued, 'He was English, of course. His family were Normans who made England their home after the invasion.'

'An ancient lineage indeed, but hardly the source of your francophonic talents, I would have thought.'

'No, indeed,' she replied with a smile. 'My grandfather spoke scarcely a word of French. My connections are all on the distaff side.'

'Ah!' The prince touched his crystal goblet with one long finger and a servant immediately replenished his glass, then silently withdrew.

'My maternal grandmother was a lady

named Claire-Adrienne de Vaumont, although she referred to herself as Noailles.'

A sudden stillness overtook the room. For a second no one spoke, then the prince raised his glance from his wine and stared straight at her. Catherine's heart thumped painfully and she knew she had given more information than she had ever intended.

She lowered her gaze to her lap and fought uselessly against the bright colour that flooded her face.

The prince spoke softly to the servants. 'Leave us now.'

The door closed upon them with a gentle thud and still Catherine could feel the prince's gaze upon her.

At last he broke the silence.

'Your grandmother was a Noailles,' he said quietly. She looked up — for not to do so would only add rudeness to her sin — and nodded. 'Perhaps I mistake the family. May I ask who her father was?'

'Adrian-Maurice de Noailles,' she responded quietly.

'She was married to the third Duc de Noailles?'

Catherine could feel the avid curiosity of Dominic and the stiffness of Christian as they waited for her response. She looked up at the prince and shook her head gently.

'My great-grandmother was never married.'

There was silence in the room. Catherine stared at her hands. The prince seemed to be contemplating his port, Christian seemed to be suddenly very interested in investigating a dish of sweetmeats.

It was Dominic who broke the silence. 'My, my. So our little heiress has magnificent connections after all.' He laughed sourly. 'Pity about grandmama being a bastard. I suppose it's too much to expect that de Noailles actually acknowledged his little *progéniture?*'

Catherine looked up. She was who she was, but not by choice.

'It was a very long time ago. The marquis does not find the connection disturbing.'

Christian choked on his wine. 'Lafayette? You know Lafayette?'

She frowned. 'Certainly. Apart from the fact that since his marriage he has become a distant cousin, my father had many dealings with him when he was in Philadelphia.' She looked in confusion at the prince. 'I thought you were aware of that, sir. How could there possibly be any objections to my father's friendship with a man of such spotless and heroic reputation?'

The prince sighed, leaning back in his chair and raising his glass to the light. He examined the ruby wine in the glow of the candles, and seeming satisfied took a long sip.

'None whatsoever. He is, as you say, much admired. Though there are those about town who may wish their wives did not admire him quite so eagerly.'

Christian laughed. 'I hear they are calling him General Goldilocks now.'

'But his hair is red,' Catherine objected, confused.

That caused them to laugh even more. Dominic, she noted, was less pleased. 'Lafayette is lucky to have married into the de Noailles dynasty,' he replied curtly. 'For now he has the ear of the king and there are those who say he acts almost as his gaoler.'

The prince looked soberly at his son. 'I am sure it is not so bad, Dominic. The king will regain his power. Look at how a constitutional monarchy benefited England. France and her king will come through this, you'll see.'

'Constitutions!' Dominic almost spat the word. 'It is the king's weakness that has brought us to this — and that Austrian woman he married. If he were collecting the taxes as he should, there would be no debt and no need of *assignats*.'

Catherine's eyes widened as she listened to this, and she looked at the prince, catching the frown that flitted across his features.

'Take care, Dominic. These are troubled times and there are many ears in many corners.'

She caught a quick glance of understanding between Christian and his uncle, and wondered to whom he was referring. Could he suspect his own servants of spying?

'I beg your pardon, my dear,' said the prince turning to her. 'These are not matters you need concern yourself with. I shall call on Lafayette myself and make him aware of your arrival in Paris.'

'He knew that I was coming,' she replied. 'In fact,' she added, turning to Dominic, 'he has promised to stand in for my father at our wedding and give me away.'

The prince nodded. 'Very well, then I shall inform him of your safe arrival.'

Dominic chortled from the other end of the table. 'Does this mean he has explained to his in-laws that their ancestor was a philanderer?'

Catherine responded stiffly. 'I believe he is aware that since his marriage to the Vicomtesse de Noailles, we are related, however distantly. But I do not believe he has said more than that I am a cousin — of his.'

'How very chivalrous,' came the reply.

Catherine indulged herself in throwing him

a black look, but he seemed more amused than anything. She wished she could turn the clock back on the whole revelation, for it was a complication they could all do without. She blamed herself for not having been more circumspect. Perhaps Christian was right after all — perhaps she did let her mouth lead her brain.

'I apologize for airing this matter, sir,' she said to the prince. 'I had not considered the consequences fully.' She glanced at Christian, but his expression was unreadable in the flickering candlelight. 'I can only hope it will not endanger our arrangement.'

'Not at all, my dear. It was merely a surprise to us to hear that you have such . . . shall we say *elevated* connections. In the past such liaisons would have opened many doors for you — and they will today. The danger is that when you turn around, you may find those same doors locked behind you.'

* * *

Catherine did not fully comprehend all that had transpired over dinner, and she found herself still pondering it next morning. It was early, the late-winter sun not long in the sky, but the chance of the freedom to walk about in the magnificent walled garden was too tempting to resist. She partook of a little hot chocolate in her room, wrapped herself in her sable cloak and escaped into the shrubbery.

The white pebbled path crunched beneath her boots as she strolled through the rose garden and around an ornamental pond with a magnificent waterfall at its heart. The water cascaded through the mouth of a large marble fish and tumbled through fanciful little pools peopled with cherubim before trickling through stone leaves back into the pond. Sparrows and a pair of pigeons were making great use of this bounty, bathing in the shallow stone pools and drinking from the little cascades.

Catherine looked about her, stretching her stiff arms and breathing in the crisp morning air. She had scarcely slept all night, kept awake by a thousand thoughts, by all that was strange and new and by all that the future might bring. Not for the first time that morning, she found herself wishing her mother were here. Wishing she had someone who could understand how unfamiliar everything was. And how frightening.

She crossed the path that skirted the pool and settled on a wide stone bench beneath a chestnut tree. The sun still reached her through the bare branches, and she turned her face to it, closing her eyes to let the warmth soak into her skin.

'Lucky for you it's March,' said a deep voice. 'Can't have you turning as brown as a *matelot* on a ship.'

Catherine's eyes flew open. Christian stood there, looking down at her, one hessian-booted foot resting on the stone bench.

'I — I was just . . . ' She foundered for something to say, but whatever it was, it died on her lips. She gazed up at him, his face shadowed by the sun that lit his hair from behind like burnished gold. His eyes roamed her features, dwelling on her slightly parted lips in a way that made her tremble. She looked away, pulling her cloak more tightly around her.

'How did you find me?' she asked, wishing she didn't sound like a small child caught in some nefarious act.

'I saw you from my window. I'm an early riser myself.' He turned to watch as the last of the gardeners wheeled their barrows away at the end of the walk.

She glanced at them, frowning.

'Do they always tend the gardens this early?'

Christian shook his head. 'Usually they are gone by now. They do their work at night, so the gardens can be enjoyed during the day without disruption.'

Catherine sighed. 'Everything is so very strange,' she said, rather more wistfully than she had intended.

She started as he reached out and took her hand in his. The warmth of his fingers sent spirals of fire tingling up her arm, making her breath catch in her throat. She stood up and allowed him to tuck her arm beneath his and lead her towards the wooded walk that led away from the house.

Why did she react like this, when her sole purpose in being here was to marry his cousin? She chided herself for her girlish response. But for all that, it was difficult not to respond. He was a handsome man, tall and straight, with skin that was bronzed by a lifetime of sun and wind. The muscles beneath her fingers were corded with steel and brought her an image of him standing at the helm of one of his ships fighting to hold course in a storm. The images were not helping her reconcile herself to her future life as the duke's wife, and she put them firmly from her mind.

'I should know better,' he said after a moment. 'I have travelled around the globe many times and yet I forget how it feels to be a stranger in a foreign land. Especially one as restless as France these days.'

She nodded. 'It is not quite as I had expected.'

He looked down at her, his blue eyes clear now as he faced the light. 'And what did you expect?'

She turned away, laughing lightly to cover the awkwardness she felt at walking so closely by his side. 'I'm not sure, now. Less politics, certainly. I feel like I'm walking on glass most of the time. My mother certainly never prepared me for this.'

'Ah yes, your mother,' he replied. 'The granddaughter of the Duc de Noailles.'

Catherine stopped, forcing him to face her. 'Why is it so important? Is it because I am acquainted with General Lafayette, or is it just that my lineage contains a — a — bastard!'

She blushed furiously at having spoken such a word. But it only seemed to amuse Christian. No doubt he'd heard much worse at sea.

He stood with his hands on his hips, looking down at her. '*Mademoiselle*, you have a great capacity for our language but absolutely no conception of the importance of politics.'

She drew in an indignant breath. 'Are you calling me stupid, Captain?'

Her use of his title gave him pause, she was

pleased to note. He stared at her for a moment, then looked away, resuming their walk. Catherine hurried to match his long strides.

'I do not think you witless in the least, Miss O'Donnell. But there is so much you need to know if you are to avoid catastrophe.'

She laughed. 'That's absurd! You are completely mistaken, I am sure. I am here purely to become the wife of your cousin and a mother to his children. Nothing more.'

'Exactly my point!' He pulled on her arm, twisting her to face him. 'You are about to ally yourself to a family whose very existence may be dependent on their invisibility. And you bring them not only vast wealth with which they can foolishly continue their aristocratic lifestyle, but a connection to the king's protector. Do you not know that Lafayette has vowed to the people of Paris that the king will not leave?'

'Why should he want to leave? He's the king.'

He stared at her for a second, dumbstruck, and then shook his head. 'Oh, Catherine, how very little you understand. Come with me.'

He led her to an ivy-covered bower which sheltered a swing. Gently, he pushed her into the seat, then stood before her, holding the ropes in his hands, his legs planted squarely on the ground.

'The king is a virtual prisoner in Paris, though Lafayette denies it. He was brought here from Versailles and installed in the Tuileries with his family, but he is not trusted. He is watched day and night. The mob surrounds him whenever he tries to go out. If he does something foolish — and there are rumours that he will — Lafayette will be blamed. It will be seen as a conspiracy.'

'How could that possibly involve me?'

Christian ran a hand through his hair. 'It will involve anyone who is seen to be too close to him.'

'So you think it is unwise for Lafayette to attend the wedding?'

She saw a muscle clench in his jaw. 'If there must be a wedding, I don't suppose that will hurt.'

'Is there any reason it should not take place?'

He moved back from the swing, pulling it with him and then releasing it so she swung away. Catherine clutched at the ropes, not quite balanced.

'You must be ready for anything in France, Miss O'Donnell. You are aware, I trust, that my cousin's title is . . . er — '

'Yes?' she asked, wondering what new surprise he held in store.

'We use the term *ci-devant*, these days.'

'*Ci-devant?*' She looked perplexed. 'Former? Oh!' She frowned as realization dawned. 'But the prince made no mention — '

'No doubt he did not wish to disappoint.'

Catherine considered this information as she rocked on the swing. It would disappoint her father, perhaps even make him feel that he'd betrayed his wife. Her mother had been so determined that her daughter would marry into the French aristocracy; in her eyes, only that would avenge the wrong done to her family.

'So, I am not to marry a recognized duke at all, but merely one who was formerly a nobleman? How can nobility be dismissed summarily thus? Surely it is a birthright.'

'We are more concerned with the Rights of Man than the birthright of the aristocracy, *mademoiselle*.'

'You forget I am an American, Captain. I am passably familiar with the Rights of Man. General Washington himself spent time explaining such notions to me over a game of croquet, when I was younger.'

'I trust you defeated him.'

'Conclusively. He was too tall for the mallets.'

She threw him a teasing glance and he grinned back. The sight of him smiling at her, his eyes alight in the morning sun, created strange yearnings within her, but she had no desire to consider them. Not now.

'If we are to be cousins, Captain, you must treat me nicely.'

He stopped the swing and pulled her to her feet, trapping her hands in his.

'Are you so set on it, *mamselle*? Are you so determined to marry Dominic, even after his behaviour last night? He will not make you a good husband, you know.'

Catherine snatched her hands away, the previous moment's camaraderie quite spoiled. 'How dare you! I have spent weeks at sea and months preparing for this marriage, and I have only met my fiancé once. Even if he is not quite a proper duke any more, I am still his betrothed.' She turned and marched smartly away from him, back towards the house. He matched her steps effortlessly, increasing her irritation. 'It is obvious to me that you are jealous of your cousin. Why, the two of you fight like dogs. Why should I listen to anything you have to say about Dominic?'

'Because I know him. I have lived in this house since I was a boy.'

'Judging by your performance last night at dinner, you have failed to mature since,' she replied tartly, and then horrified at her own incivility, she stopped. Her hand flew to her mouth.

His blue eyes were filled with sparks of fire as he bent to her. 'You step too far, *mamselle*. I do not apologize for the ill feeling that passes between Dominic and myself, nor does it please me. But I give you fair warning that I will not stop trying to discourage you from making this marriage. My cousin will never make you — or any other woman — happy.'

4

Breakfast was an awkward affair. Of the prince and Dominic there was no sign, and Catherine's hopes of having the dining-room to herself for the quiet enjoyment of a brioche and a cup of chocolate were dashed when Christian entered the room not a minute behind her.

He nodded briefly but their eyes did not meet. She sat at the table with the morning sun streaming in behind her and watched as he helped himself to coffee from the sideboard. His movements quick and careless, he selected eggs from a silver dish and fruit from another, adding a croissant and bringing them to the table unceremoniously.

He glanced up as he picked up his napkin, catching her stare.

'My eating habits interest you, *mamselle*?'

She looked away, flushing. 'Not at all. I see you have a healthy appetite.'

'Many years at sea give one an appreciation of fresh food. I like to make use of it when I am able.'

She laughed. 'After my own experiences these past weeks, I can attest to that,' she replied. 'Too much salt pork and pickled cabbage. If I never taste another such morsel, I shall consider myself fortunate.'

'You get used to it,' was his only reply.

They lapsed into silence. Catherine toyed with her brioche, sipped at her chocolate. Turned to glance at the beautiful day beyond the windows.

Christian watched her unobtrusively as he ate. He felt stirrings of sympathy for her plight, despite reminding himself that it was she who was so determined to bring all this upon herself.

He sipped his coffee. It was black and strong with an aroma that reminded him of his most recent voyage to the Caribbean.

She kept gazing out of the window, turning her head so that he could see only the soft fall of sunlight on her cheek. It caught the russet tones in her hair and for the first time he realized that she was almost a redhead, not the brunette he had taken her for.

He frowned into his plate of eggs, thinking of another redhead who had nearly cost him his navy career. Although Léonie de Chambois had fallen in love with his commanding officer, Captain de la Tour, she had entrenched herself in his heart for many years. He smiled to himself. What a firebrand: unable to resist a dare, always reaching out to grab danger by the horns. It was a mystery how she had survived their voyage, and yet now she was a duchess with four children and a doting husband, safely away from Paris and all its upheavals. He would be a fool to say he didn't miss her — and her brother, Jean-Michel, who had been his closest friend for so many years — yet she no longer commanded his heart. No one laid claim to his affections these days, save the navy.

He looked up at Catherine. She should be away from Paris, too. This was no place for an *ingénue*. But he was certain she would never leave just because he said so; she had already demonstrated her contempt for his efforts to show her the folly of her forthcoming marriage. Perhaps Angé . . .

He pushed away his plate and stood. The abrupt move made Catherine jump. He stared into her upturned face. Her eyes were a rich brown, fringed with long curling lashes, and they melted something deep within him that Christian hadn't known was frozen. He didn't like those eyes; they were too disturbing. So he moved his glance to her lips. An unfortunate choice. They were pink and inviting, warm from her walk outside, and bore a tiny drop of chocolate in one corner.

He stared, mesmerized by that droplet. He

felt himself lean forward slightly, knew a sudden quickening in his loins at the thought of bending his head until he could lick the chocolate from her lips . . .

With a hand, that to his surprise shook only slightly, he reached out. Catherine stared at him, her lips parting slightly with shock as she felt the ball of his thumb rub softly across the corner of her mouth. Sparkles of fire tingled through her.

'You had chocolate on your lip.'

There was a gentleness in his voice she had not heard before and in her present state of loneliness and strangeness, it brought an ache to the back of her throat. She had not expected kindness.

She bent her head and wiped her mouth vigorously on her napkin. But although the smudge of chocolate had gone, the imprint of his thumb remained indelible.

'Thank you,' she replied unsteadily.

'If you are finished, I would like to take you to call on Madame Fontenay. Dominic never rises until after noon, and my uncle is already gone to the city, so I fear there is little to occupy you here.'

She rose from the table, relieved that some diversion presented itself, for she did not want to spend too much time alone with her thoughts today.

'I am ready.'

He glanced down at her blue morning gown. 'You will need to change. I take it you do know how to ride a horse?'

'Certainly,' she responded. 'I rode every day in Philadelphia.'

'Meet me at the stables when you are ready.'

She watched him stride from the room and wondered, not for the first time, how a man could be so tender one moment and so severe the next. It was as though he were drawn to her and then somehow repelled. What the reasons were for his abrupt changes of humour, she doubted she would ever comprehend.

★   ★   ★

A bonfire was burning in the courtyard near the stables as she let herself out into the morning sunshine a few minutes later. Two young boys were busily throwing pieces of wood onto the blaze, their laughing voices carrying in the still air. She took little notice as she crossed the cobbles towards Christian, who was tightening the straps under the belly of his magnificently ugly black stallion. But just as she neared the horses, something familiar caught her eye. She stopped short and stared at a piece of elegant oak, decorated with fine gilding, that one of the boys held ready to throw onto the flames.

She charged at the lad and snatched the piece of wood from his hand. 'Where did you get this?' she stormed, too furious to realize she had spoken in English.

The boy stared. '*Pardon, mademoiselle?*'

Flustered, Catherine repeated her question in French. The boy's eyes lit up with understanding and he indicated Christian with a stab of his thumb.

'*Monsieur le Capitaine,*' he said. 'He said we could make the fire instead of mucking out the stables this morning. It is good, *hein?*'

Incensed, Catherine strode across the courtyard to where Christian was now checking the saddle on a small white mare.

'How could you!' she stormed, when she was still several feet away. She thrust the wood under his nose. 'What is this?'

He continued his inspection of the saddlery, apparently unperturbed. 'I believe it used to be part of the door of your berline.' He turned to her, resting one hand on the mare's saddle horn. His lips bore a slight twist of amusement. 'But I think it might best be described as a piece of firewood now, don't you?'

Catherine shook her head in disbelief. 'You

destroyed my carriage? Just like that? As if it was just some old piece of useless detritus? As if' — she jabbed a finger into the front of his red riding jacket — 'as if it belonged to you?'

His brows rose a fraction. 'It was more than merely a piece of detritus, as you so elegantly put it, my dear Miss O'Donnell: it was a danger to your safety. And as for ownership, if I remember correctly you purchased the gaudy contraption for a song, *n'est-ce pas?* Did it not occur to you why that was?'

'I don't believe I take your meaning.'

He leaned forward and touched one gloved finger to her nose, as though she were a child. 'You bought the berline cheap because it had been abandoned by one of the *émigrés*.'

'Abandoned?'

'They could hardly take their coaches with them. There was scarce room enough on the ships for all the noble families who fled the Revolution. No doubt they have sold some of their jewels in England and America and bought themselves something more tasteful.'

Catherine sighed, tossing away the piece of wood. 'You are right. They would certainly not find something like that, even in a town such as Philadelphia.'

He smiled, holding out his hand to help her mount up. 'So you see, now you are relieved of all requirement for guilt. You need no longer berate yourself for having made such an advantageous purchase from the misery of some unfortunate.'

She knew he was joking, so she made no reply beyond giving him a black look.

As they rode out of the courtyard, the smoke seemed to mock her, spiralling up into the crisp morning like a signal to remind her of how much she had to learn. She drew her eyes away and followed Christian out onto the cobbled streets.

They followed the wide avenue past elegant buildings that were sometimes six storeys high, until they came to the Pont Royal, leaving the Faubourg Saint-Germain behind. They paused on the busy bridge to observe the river with its myriad little boats plying the waters, some carrying cargo, others simply fishing.

They passed to the other side, around the corner of the Tuileries, where King Louis and his family now resided, and through its beautiful gardens to the Rue Saint-Honoré. Here, street vendors bustled with their wares, darting between the wheels of cabs and carriages, shouting out the prices of their fresh-baked pastries and fritters, proffering flowers and oysters, brooms and candles — just about every kind of merchandise Catherine could imagine.

Christian purchased a posy of violets from a pretty young woman in a filthy skirt and handed them with a smile to Catherine, apparently oblivious to the flirtatious looks the girl was sending him. Catherine pinned them to her cloak.

'Thank you, Captain. They are lovely.' Then, as she pulled her little mare out of the way of a careering cabriolet, she laughed and said, 'Is there anything you can't buy in this huge city? Why I have never seen so many people in one place in all my life!'

He pulled beside her again, matching his larger steed's steps to the mare's. 'With almost eight hundred thousand souls to feed and house, it's hard to imagine Paris lacking goods of any sort.' He frowned. 'And yet,' he added, indicating a woman no older than Catherine, with a baby at her shrivelled breast and two more clinging to her ragged skirts, 'there is much poverty. There is never enough bread for the poor.'

She stared at the woman, who stood mute and with unseeing eyes, staring at the passers-by with one thin hand held out. Catherine reached into her pocket and withdrew a coin — a mere fifty sous — and dropped it into the woman's palm. Instantly the sightless eyes lost their vacant stare and brimmed with tears. They rode on, the woman's thin voice calling, 'Bless you, citizenness. Bless you!' behind them.

Catherine shuddered. 'We heard about the taxes and the high prices for food in the Philadelphia papers, but I had not realized it was quite this bad.'

'There is worse,' Christian replied grimly, but from the set look on his face, Catherine knew he would not explain. She began to realize how her elegant carriage must have offended the crowds when she arrived in Paris yesterday. Was it only a day since she had first met Christian across that sea of enraged faces? She shook her head in amazement. So much had happened, and she was quickly developing some notion of the unrest that gripped the country. She realized, though, she would not dare to voice such a thought, that she was actually grateful to Christian for having destroyed the berline. At least it would not haunt her with memories of her own stupidity.

They soon came to a small street near the Louvre and stopped in front of a row of apartments. Christian assisted her from her mare and handed the reins to the keeping of the concierge's boy. The concierge, an elderly man in a threadworn shirt, led the way up a flight of modest stairs to a heavy door upon which he knocked three times.

'*Quelqu'un est là,*' he told them in a guttural voice made scratchy with age, and took himself off, coughing into his sleeve.

After a moment, the door opened and a black maid ushered them inside, smiling warmly at Christian and eyeing his companion in silence as she took their gloves and cloaks. She led them to a salon and bobbed a curtsy at the door.

'*Merci,* Jeanne,' Christian said, as he indicated to Catherine that she should precede her.

Catherine drew in a breath, for she was always a little nervous at meeting strangers. She stepped inside.

Before she could so much as look about her, something small and squealing crashed into her, knocking Catherine off her feet. With a cry of dismay, she crashed backwards into Christian, feeling his arms wrap themselves around her as he sought to steady them both. For a second they teetered on the brink of gaining a foothold on the polished parquetry, but then both tumbled to the floor in an undignified heap.

'*Mon Dieu! Mes enfants, mes enfants,*' came a merry voice from inside the salon. 'What have you done?'

Catherine caught a brief glimpse of two small children as they rushed down the corridor, squealing with delight until a closed door signalled their escape.

Catherine looked up from her position on the floor and tried to smile at the vision of blue silk that stood laughing down at her. The woman had a riot of curling black hair that tumbled freely about her slim shoulders, and a sparkle in her eye that implied she knew exactly what part of Christian's anatomy was pressing into Catherine's back! She tried to get up, but couldn't, for her voluminous riding skirt was pinned beneath the captain's legs and his arms were wrapped tightly about her waist, pressed against the underside of her breasts. She felt a flush steal into her cheeks as she pointedly pushed his hands away and tugged at her skirts.

Christian grinned at his cousin. 'Another spectacular entrance, eh Angé?'

The woman pressed her fingers to her lips, but a giggle escaped nonetheless. 'You are too wicked, Christian. Must you always introduce your ladies to me in such dramatic fashion?'

His ladies? Catherine gritted her teeth and threw him a black look as she finally rolled free. He, irritating individual that he was, leapt to his feet and offered her his hand in an instant. She took it, since she had no choice, but once on her feet pulled away as quickly as she could to straighten her skirts and regain some of her equanimity.

'Where are those little urchins, Angé? I swear they get wilder by the day.'

The woman sighed. 'I fear it is true, my dear, but what can I do? I love them beyond distraction and they know it. Never fear, they will return once they perceive you have forgotten the warmth of their welcome.'

'I'll give them some warmth,' he said with feeling, casting an ominous glance in the direction of the closed door. 'On their little hides.' Then he grinned. 'Always assuming I can catch them of course.'

'Christian!' Angé remonstrated. 'Are you never to introduce me to this divine creature with whom you have been wrestling upon my floor? I am just dying of curiosity.'

'*Pardon, Cousine*,' he replied with a mock flourish. 'The sport was so distracting, I almost forgot my manners. Allow me to present Mademoiselle Catherine de Lacy O'Donnell, who is betrothed to my cousin Dominic. Catherine, this is my cousin — on my father's side — Mademoiselle Angélique de Fontenay.'

'Dominic's fiancée!' Angé clapped her hands. 'Why how romantic! You must tell me all your plans for the future. A beautiful wedding is just the distraction I need to cheer me up!'

Catherine smiled politely, wondering how much more bubbly the woman could get.

'That would be a pleasure, Madame de Fontenay,' she murmured.

'Oh, just plain Fontenay will do these days,' their hostess replied gaily, taking Catherine's arm and leading her into the salon. 'We have abandoned the old trappings and go about much more simply, as you will see. Beyond these walls, we are all mere citizens now, and if we are wise, we wear our cockades for all to see.'

'Cockades?'

'Do you not have one? Christian? What is this? How can this ravishing creature be safe upon the streets if she is not attired according to the principles of the Revolution?'

Christian opened his mouth to explain, but got no chance. Angé sailed blithely on as she led them towards the hearth where a cheery fire was burning.

'Please,' she said patting Catherine's hand, 'you must call me Angé, for I am no one of any importance. Christian and I, we are mere *bourgeois*, and happy to be so.' Her eyes sparkled as she squeezed Catherine's arm, barely pausing for breath before she launched into another stream of words. 'And you, so soon to be a duchess! Well, at least you would be if things were different. But we can

90

pretend, can we not? I find it makes everything seem so much brighter these days, *n'est-ce pas?*'

She led her to a chair covered with pink damask and pressed her to sit. Catherine's eyes widened with unspoken questions as she looked at Christian. He merely grinned and settled himself onto a *chaise-longue* that had seen better days.

There was a slight disturbance at the door and two small children entered the salon, their eyes darting warily about them.

'So there you are, you young *gamins*,' Christian said. 'Come here and take your punishment!'

Catherine's eyes widened as the children laughed and ran to him, wrapping their arms about him like limpets. Each duly submitted a cheek on which the captain placed a wet kiss.

'Hélène, Alexandre, come and meet Christian's friend — a lady who has come all the way from America to marry the captain's cousin, le ci-devant Duc de Charigny.'

The little boy, in black velvet breeches and a blue chemise, turned large blue eyes upon her and promptly stuck his thumb in his mouth. His sister, clearly the older of the two, pulled him boldly across the floor.

She dropped a little bob in front of

Catherine. '*Bonjour, mademoiselle*. My name is Hélène and I'm five. He's just a baby!'

Catherine's heart melted. The children reminded her of Jack and Libby, twins of her best friend, Amy, back home. Since they were born, four years ago, they had shown Catherine what life might have to offer if she were able to become a mother before she was too old.

And here she was, soon to be married. She reached out to the children and they ran to her, accepting her without question. Their trust touched Catherine and she gave them each a quick hug.

'I am delighted to meet you both,' she said, holding them at arm's length. 'Why, Hélène, you are surely becoming as beautiful as your mother. And you, Alexandre, I bet you look just like your papa?'

The girl was indeed the image of her mother — wild black curls surrounding a pixie face — but the boy shared only his mother's sky-blue eyes. His hair was straight, light brown in colour and framed a chubby toddler's face.

He stuck out his chest and pointed to himself with a podgy finger. 'I can fight with a sword. Do you want to fight with me?'

She repressed a smile. 'I'm not very skilled with a rapier, Alexandre, but perhaps later you can teach me.'

That appeared to satisfy the children and they ran off, talking in loud excited voices.

Catherine watched them go, smiling at the memories they brought back, and then felt Christian's eyes on her. For a brief moment their gazes connected and she felt that he was searching her soul. She looked away.

'Ah, *mes enfants*. They are so sweet, but sometimes . . . ' Angé threw up her hands in mock horror, grinning at Catherine. 'But you must think me remiss. No doubt you are longing for some tea.' She turned quickly to the bell pull to summon refreshments. She reminded Catherine of some exotic bird with her bright plumage and quick movements. 'Do Americans drink tea, Miss O'Donnell? Here we like to take tea with lemon, sometimes with milk, *à l'Anglais*. But we make it with nice hot water. I have never heard of anyone in France trying to do so with seawater, as I believe is the habit at Boston tea parties.'

The words were spoken with such a teasing lilt in her voice that Catherine laughed.

'Indeed, I come from Philadelphia, *madame* — *pardon*, Angé — where we make it a habit to use boiling water also.'

Another black maid, young and with an almost intimidated air, slipped into the salon to receive her mistress's instructions, casting a furtive glance at Catherine. Catherine noticed, however, that she sent a broad smile to Christian. Clearly, he was well liked in this establishment.

'I brought my servants with me from the Île de France,' Angé explained, seeing the unspoken question in her visitor's eyes.

'The Île de France?'

Christian interpreted. 'In America I believe you call it Mauritius. Angé lived there with her first husband.'

'Ah, indeed! My poor Monsieur Dumont. He traded with French India, you know. But the waters can be treacherous, as Christian has no doubt told you.'

'No, he has not,' Catherine said quickly, looking curiously at him. 'But our acquaintance is barely one day old.'

'*Quelle blague!* But that is famous! You have been in Paris so little? My, then we must become the best of friends, for I am certain you must be full of' — she looked at Christian with a twinkle — 'woman questions! What do you say, shall we send Monsieur le Capitaine away so we ladies may talk freely?'

Catherine laughed, for the woman's mood was infectious.

'Thank you, Angé, I would very much like

94

to be friends, but I could not presume. Besides, I rely upon Captain Lavelle to escort me safely back to the Hôtel de Charigny.'

But Christian was already on his feet. 'Perish the notion that I should stay where I am not wanted!' he said, the teasing light in his eyes making her breath quicken. ''Tis not far to my office, so I shall go and console myself with work. I shall return at noon.'

Angé smiled indulgently as Christian made his bow and departed.

'He's a good boy, don't you think? His father was my dear mother's brother — a most-talented musician, but sadly he died of the typhus when Christian was no older than my little Hélène is now. His mother too, poor boy.'

Catherine made no reply beyond the slight lifting of her brows. She could not begin to imagine ever choosing such a word as 'boy' to describe Christian Lavelle. He was a head taller than most men, with broad shoulders that looked as if he could lift an ox. She thought of the way his arms had encircled her and the heat that had flowed between them as they lay tangled upon Angé's parquet floor and the blood rushed to her cheeks. No, 'boy' was definitely not the word.

The little black maid returned with a laden tea tray and placed it before her mistress.

There were *petits fours*, pastries and fruits on porcelain dishes, and tea in a tall silver service elaborately carved with peacocks and other exotic creatures.

Madame Fontenay made Catherine's tea to her liking with a little milk and a touch of sugar and passed her the delicate Sèvres cup and saucer.

'May I tempt you with some *pâtisseries*? They are freshly arrived from the bakery this morning.'

Catherine lifted a hand. 'Thank you, no. The tea is quite refreshing and I breakfasted not long since.'

'Then you must tell me all about yourself, *mademoiselle*, for I am simply devoured by curiosity. How you come to speak our language so well, how it is that you are betrothed to Dominic . . . '

'Please, call me Catherine. I am, as you put it, a mere *bourgeoise* myself. It sounds strange to be treated so formally.'

'Ah, but soon, my dear Catherine, you will be a very great somebody. You will be the wife of the Monsieur le ci-devant Duc de Charigny.'

Catherine set down her cup. She felt as though she could talk to Angélique, much as she had been able to confide in her friend Amy at home.

'How well do you know Dominic, Angé?'

The woman's slender brows arched. She hesitated a moment, looking very directly at Catherine, who began to wonder if perhaps her assessment had been wrong.

'I have been introduced. I have even dined . . . once or twice, in his presence at the Hôtel de Charigny. What could I possibly tell you that you don't already know?'

Catherine sighed, uncertain whether to continue. But she didn't feel able to speak to Christian about such matters — he had made his opinion of her betrothal perfectly clear! And she had, as yet anyway, not a single friend in Paris apart from General Lafayette — and she could scarcely take such personal questions to him!

'I — I know very little of the duke. My father arranged the marriage through some business acquaintances . . . '

'I see. And there are . . . things you were not told, perhaps?'

'Indeed.' She glanced up at Angé and met eyes that were filled with understanding.

'I, too, have experienced an arrangement of marriage. My first husband, God rest his soul' — and here she blessed herself — 'was unknown to me until my wedding day.'

'He was? And — and how did you feel when you met him?'

'Confused. Pleased. Disappointed.' She shrugged. 'He was much older than I had expected, but he was a good man and in time I learned to love him. As much as a wife is expected to.'

Love. Catherine had not yet even considered whether she might in time learn to love the Duc de Charigny. Or have him love her. Angé sensed that she had not quite answered the question that Catherine had been reluctant to air.

'You were not told he was crippled,' she said succinctly.

Catherine looked up, shaken. 'How did you know?'

'Your face, my dear. You are not the blushing bride one might expect in a young girl about to marry a duke. And you are right: Dominic is no catch, except perhaps on paper.' Her eyes narrowed suddenly. 'Is that what your father sought for you?'

Catherine nodded, for there was little use in denial; Angé's skyblue eyes saw as clearly as a hawk on a spring day. That it was her mother's wish, rather than her father's seemed scarcely relevant, and Catherine certainly had no desire to relate once again the ignominious circumstances of her grandmother's birth.

'Bah! Then I am sorry for you. You will

have to find your excitement in some other quarter. There are many men in Paris, some of them quite amenable.'

'I beg your pardon?'

'Do not be alarmed, my dear. We cannot all marry for love. Some of us must marry for the convenience and prosperity of our families. It is the price of womanhood. A duty. But we must not let it bear us down!'

'I see,' Catherine replied faintly. 'So if one disliked one's spouse, one would simply find another man to . . . '

'Amuse oneself with?' Angé finished for her. '*Absolument.*'

Catherine shuddered. That was most certainly not what she had envisaged for herself. Catherine de Lacy O'Donnell had no desire to be a toy wife. She wanted a real marriage, a real home . . . and children like Angé and Amy had.

And one way or another, she was determined to get them.

5

The afternoon passed uneventfully for Catherine, who took advantage of the quiet house to rest and read a little.

She was sitting with her slim volume of poems in a small salon, decorated in blue and gold, whose windows afforded an excellent view of the garden. She looked up when Emile entered the room.

'*Mademoiselle*, your presence is requested in the library.'

She followed him willingly, wondering if at last she might talk with Dominic. She hoped that if they could get to know each other, it would set her mind at rest concerning their upcoming nuptials.

But it was not Dominic; it was his father who awaited her.

She curtsied.

'Come in, my dear. Pray be seated. Will you take some wine?'

She shook her head with a smile. 'I am not used to strong drink, sir.'

'Tea, then? Chocolate? Coffee?'

'Tea would be most welcome, thank you.'

Emile duly retreated with instructions to

fetch tea and Catherine sat primly on the edge of a gilded *fauteuil* with her hands folded in her lap.

The prince was looking somewhat tired, she thought, his frock coat cast carelessly across a chair and his hair dishevelled. But the twinkle in his eyes eased her fears.

'My dear Miss O'Donnell, I can't tell you how delighted I am that you are with us. It has been my dearest wish that one day Dominic would find a woman worthy of him, and I believe you are just that person.'

She flushed, wondering if he would offer such compliments were he privy to the disappointments that her first meeting with the duke had produced. However, she merely smiled.

'I am honoured to be connected with such a noble family, sir.'

He stared at her for a moment, then apparently satisfied by her sincerity, muttered, 'Yes, well . . . of course. But so are we. Your father has made quite a name for himself in shipping circles. I had many dealings with him myself in happier times.'

Her brows rose. 'You did? But — '

He waved a hand. 'Dominic doesn't know all that. He's never felt that the nobility should soil itself with business, but there are those of us who like to move with the times. A

101

little, at least. Nevertheless, I am concerned where all this republican fervour might lead.'

'It has been good for America, sir.'

He laughed. 'Indeed it has. But then old King George is as mad as a hatter! Anything would be better than to be ruled by such an *imbécile*.'

A maid entered, bearing a tea tray which she set down beside Catherine. She began to pour the tea, but Catherine smiled at her. 'Please don't bother. I can manage.'

Confused, the maid glanced at the prince.

He waved a hand.

The maid bobbed a curtsy and withdrew, still frowning.

'You know, my dear, you are in France now. The servants expect you to let them do their jobs. Surely you had servants in Philadelphia?'

'Indeed,' she replied, 'but only to do heavy work or the cooking. I am not accustomed to being waited upon every moment of the day.'

'Hmm.' He watched as she poured her own tea. 'I fear you will have to learn. Dominic is rather old-fashioned, as I'm sure you've noticed. He likes things in their place, the way they always were.'

Catherine felt there was another meaning to his words, and since she greatly desired to avoid falling foul of her betrothed, she ventured to follow her intuition.

'Are you suggesting that my fiancé will disapprove of my republican origins as much as my middle-class ways?'

The prince smiled. 'You have a quick mind, my dear. It should serve you well.'

His words, far from flattering her, made her heart sink. She watched as he got up, crossing to a small escritoire. Taking a key from his pocket, he unlocked the desk and withdrew a velvet pouch.

Catherine sipped her tea and set it back upon the table.

The prince returned to his seat near the fire, tossing the package by his side. 'May I be candid, Miss O'Donnell?'

'You may if you will call me Catherine,' she replied with a smile.

'Very well, Catherine. Tell me, now that you have arrived and made Dominic's acquaintance, are you content with the betrothal?'

She held her breath, for she had not expected such a forthright question, and she was uncertain how to respond. She tried always to be truthful, but there were times when that might not be the best course.

Her hesitation was not lost upon him.

'I see that you are not.'

'Oh, no! Indeed, that was not to be my answer at all!'

'Then why did you pause? Surely happiness is something that requires little thought. It either resides within us or it does not.'

'It is not that I am unhappy with the engagement to your son, sir. It's just that . . . ' She hesitated, unable to put her reservations into words.

He tipped his head slightly to one side, raising his brows. 'There are perhaps . . . unresolved questions?'

She smiled, her breath leaving her in a rush. ''Tis that exactly, sir. You see . . . that is, Christian tried to warn me, but . . . ' Oh dear, she was making an awful mess of explaining herself. 'It's just that I did not realize Monsieur le Duc had . . . physical difficulties.'

For a moment the prince merely regarded her impassively. Then he steepled his fingers on his chest and blew through them. '*Vraiment.*'

Catherine, alarmed that she would be thought selfish for expecting perfection, hastened on, 'I am not unfamiliar with such problems, you see. In fact, the reason I am not already married is that I have spent the last seven years nursing my invalid mother. And now that she is gone, I — ' She broke off, tears coming unbidden to her eyes. She sought a kerchief from her pocket.

'My dear Catherine, pray do not imagine that I criticize in any way your concern over this matter. I was fully aware of your devotion to your mother, for your father explained it to me in great detail.'

'He did?'

'Indeed. But you see, I drew a different — and clearly erroneous — conclusion from this. It was my belief that a person with the skill and understanding that you have demonstrated since you were sixteen would make you less critical than other young ladies faced with a husband who has, as you described it, physical difficulties. However, for all that, it was never my intention that you should agree to this marriage without the fullest knowledge of the situation. That, I fear, was a decision made by your own father, and one which I personally deplore.'

'Thank you,' she replied numbly. 'Perhaps Papa thought it would be best this way.'

'I believe he was mistaken.'

Catherine smiled wanly at him, grateful that he understood her position with such clarity. It gave her courage to pry a little further.

'May I ask you, sir, what is the nature of the duke's illness?'

The prince went to the sideboard to pour himself a glass of Cognac. He held the crystal goblet in his hands and slowly swirled the liquid to warm it, before inhaling the bouquet and taking a sip all in one smooth practised motion.

'When he was a very small child he became quite ill with a fever. I feared greatly for his life. He was all I had, you see. My dear wife, Anne-Elise, had given me a daughter, whom we named Hortense after my sister, but the babe died after only one day upon this earth. She was heartbroken, but then soon after, she gave me Dominic. Unfortunately, the birth cost her her life, and Dominic never knew a mother's love.' He glanced up at her and she saw the depth of sadness and loneliness that he had lived with, for it showed clearly in his eyes.

'I am so sorry,' she whispered.

He shrugged, returning to the sofa. 'It was a very long time ago. I merely tell you this so that you may understand some of my son's feelings. When he was spared from the grim reaper, I became very protective of him. Too much so, I am certain. And when it became apparent that he would always have the greatest difficulty in walking and that any exertion could make him ill, I indulged him. The illness has left his heart weak. If he becomes upset, or overtired, he is liable to the greatest difficulty in breathing.'

Catherine's heart sank. 'He has rheumatic fever.'

The prince's eyes narrowed upon her. 'You are well informed.'

'It is what killed my mother, though she contracted the disease after my birth.' She looked up at the prince, taking a deep breath and looking him squarely in the eye. 'I shall be able to care for your son, sir. As my father knew I would.'

The prince spluttered on his brandy. 'Indeed, you mistake me, Catherine! I did not arrange this marriage in order to obtain a nurse for Dominic. You will do no such thing. He has nurses and doctors enough! What he needs is a purpose in life.'

She frowned, not sure to what he was referring.

'What my son needs, Miss O'Donnell, is a wife and family.'

Catherine felt a great weight lift from her. 'But that is exactly what I myself most desire, sir! I have dreamed of nothing else for years. My mother and I often spoke of it, even though she knew she would never live to see her own grandchildren.'

He smiled at her, setting down his goblet and leaning forward to clasp her hands in his. 'You have made me a happy man with your words, Catherine. I have so wanted to see my son settled before I leave this world — '

'Sir! You are not ill?'

He returned to his seat. 'No more than any old man with a pain in his hip that plays up like the very devil when the weather is wet. I merely meant to imply that in these uncertain times — '

'I could make some ointment for your rheumatism, if you would like.'

'The devil you could? Well, that would be most welcome, indeed, my dear.'

She smiled, touched by his pleasure in so simple a thing. 'It would be no trouble.'

'Well, I have something to give you, my dear, so perhaps we shall be quits.' He picked up the velvet pouch at his side and passed it to her.

Catherine's eyes opened wide with wonder. 'What is this?'

'Something that has been in my family since the days the Charignys still lived in the Italian principality of Ciarini, from which we derive our name. I am not really a French prince, you see,' he confided, with a conspiratorial smile, 'but the inheritor of an Italian title. In France, before the Revolution, I was the Duke of Montaltier, an area in the high mountains near the border. Those lands I have given up, though I still have some claim to the principality of Ciarini in Italy.'

He stopped, smiling ruefully at her confusion. 'No matter. The important thing is that I want you to have these. They have been passed down from mother to daughter, but since I have no daughter, I believe they should go to you. Perhaps you will one day produce another heiress who may inherit the gems.'

Catherine unfolded the soft velvet gently in her lap. Inside lay the finest diamond necklace she had ever beheld, a long tear-shaped pendant on a delicate gold chain. Beside it lay two diamond ear-rings set to match. Her eyes misty, she looked up at the prince.

'They are truly beautiful, sir. I am honoured.'

*　*　*

And so Catherine's betrothal was confirmed. The prince announced that June 21st would be the date of the wedding, and that it would be held in the white marble chapel at the Hôtel de Charigny. Dominic refused to countenance being married by any non-juring priest who had assigned his loyalties to the state and renounced the authority of the pope. So for the sake of peace, his father had retained the services of Father Joubert, the family confessor.

Catherine was disappointed not to be married in a proper church, but there seemed to be little choice in the matter. She wondered what her mother might have thought.

She missed having her mother to talk to. Martha was a comfort, but it was not the same. So it was with much delight that Catherine accepted Madame Beaulieu's suggestion of a late-morning stroll in the gardens. The woman had recovered from the slight cold that had indisposed her the night of Catherine's arrival and had assumed her duties as chaperon eagerly. It was scarcely an arduous task, for she was seldom seen at supper and never at breakfast on account of her advancing years. But she had a keen wit and a motherly way about her and Catherine had liked her immediately.

They walked slowly, for nothing Héloïse Beaulieu did was ever hurried. She was dressed entirely in black, but to what purpose, Catherine had not discovered, for she knew the gentlewoman had been widowed for more than thirty years. She leaned on a cane and held Catherine's arm with her free hand.

'My mother and I used to walk like this,'

Catherine said. 'Until she was too weak to walk at all.'

Madame Beaulieu looked sharply at her. 'You have seen too much suffering, *petite*. A young woman like you should be nursing her babes at the breast, not tied to a sickbed.'

'Oh, I didn't mind. My mother was always my dearest friend. And 'twas she who taught me what I know of France.'

'So there are people over there who know French, *hein*?'

Catherine raised her brows. 'Many.' She tried to recall something Christian had told her of this woman's history. 'Do you not have a daughter in America?'

An expression of such profound sadness flitted through the old lady's eyes that Catherine felt momentarily alarmed.

'My beloved Marie. Such a beautiful girl, so spirited and loyal . . . ' Tears sprang into her eyes and Catherine led her to a stone bench so she could rest.

'Pray be seated, Madame Beaulieu. Shall I send for some refreshment?'

'No, no. I shall be perfectly fine once I rest a moment. Sit down, child. Would you do something for me?'

'Of course, *madame*. Anything.'

'Will you call me Nounou, as Christian does? I am not accustomed to all this *madame* business.'

Ah, thought Catherine. 'You were his nanny?' Small wonder her betrothed referred to the lady with such cutting sarcasm: Dominic clearly considered the woman no better than a servant, though the prince treated her with charm and courtesy.

'No, indeed. But he has been like a son to me since Jean-Michel took my beloved Marie away to America. And I lost Léonie to her handsome captain. Ah, *les pauvres petite*. How I miss them all.'

'Léonie?'

'I nursed all the Chambois children and they grew up with my Marie. Léonie and Jean-Michel are twins!' She raised her hands in a gesture of mock horror. 'Wild as the sea. Then there was their stupid older brother, Robert. He had his father's ways but lacked his wit. I think Madame la Duchesse had a difficult time when she gave birth to Robert,' she added confidingly. 'Georges, the youngest, I liked. Poor boy. He was lost at sea, you know.' She blessed herself. 'God is cruel sometimes, Catherine. He was cruel when He stole my daughter from me, but I am forgiving Him, bit by bit. Are you angry with Him, too, child?'

'Perhaps. I was angry while my mother was dying. But . . . ' She smiled wistfully, trying to

112

think about the future and not dwell on the past. 'But if it were not for my mother, I should not be here at all, about to marry Dominic.'

Madame Beaulieu sent her a sharp glance.

'What is it, Nounou? Have I said something?'

'*Rien du tout, petite.* Come, let us continue our walk and you can tell me about America. I wish to know everything about this place that stole my child.'

By the time the ladies had returned from the stroll, they had become fast friends, and Catherine had heard, with great astonishment, the entire story of Léonie de Chambois' amazing voyage around the world on a French naval ship — with Christian as her protector! This part of the tale disturbed Catherine for some reason, though she refused to listen to the little voice inside that whispered the word 'jealous'. Nevertheless, she could not avoid wondering how *she* might have fared cloistered aboard ship for so many months with him.

She listened as Nounou detailed why she had not gone to America with her daughter, nor responded to Léonie's entreaties to live with her in the south of France; how she had clung to her familiar Paris and the unfamiliar role of a gentlewoman elevated from servant status by the marriage of her daughter to a viscount.

They partook of a modest *déjeuner*, continuing their discussion freely, since Christian and the prince were out and Dominic was cloistered in his room. But no sooner had they left the table than Catherine was advised she had several visitors waiting in the salon.

Word had seemingly spread like a summer brushfire that the Duc de Charigny was betrothed, and half of Paris began to call. It was an odd experience. Catherine was quite used to the life of a lady, perfectly accustomed to receiving friends at any time of the day, but this was different.

Her callers were almost entirely ladies of the nobility. They came in twos and threes and entered the salon like ships on the ocean, ploughing across the Aubusson carpet with the feathers on their enormous hats flapping like sails in a storm. Catherine was exceedingly glad of Madame Beaulieu's company, though Nounou herself seldom spoke, seeming overawed by such company.

Catherine's visitors examined her through lorgnettes, or simply stared at her, blank expressions on their powdered faces as they searched for whatever it was their eyes so keenly sought. And when they found what they expected — whatever that might be — the corners of their carmined mouths pinched slightly. Whether this was from satisfaction or disapproval Catherine wasn't certain.

She offered refreshments and endeavoured to answer all their questions, none of them to anyone's satisfaction.

'Ah!' one dowager swathed in black silk proclaimed. '*Vous êtes une Americaine!*' As if that said it all.

The question Catherine dreaded most of all and which her many visitors seemed eager to ask, was 'And how, my dear, did you become acquainted with Monsieur le Duc?'

But at least that question, once answered, provided some relief. For the ladies, once realizing that they were devoting their precious time to investigating a nobody, soon took their leave and she was granted a few moments of peace until the next ordeal began.

This continued for three days, by which time everybody who was anybody had heard that the Duc de Charigny was marrying into the American business class, and that his fiancée, while quite pretty in her own rustic fashion, was of no consequence.

Once or twice, during some of the more difficult interviews, Catherine was sorely tempted to mention that her grandmother was a de Noailles. Their reactions would have provided her some much-needed entertainment. However, in deference to her position, she held her tongue.

She did manage to slip in Lafayette's name a few times, but that brought mixed responses. Some considered him a republican; others as the king's gaoler. One portly matron, swathed in layers of crimson silk, claimed Lafayette was so powerful nowadays that he controlled the royal family's every move. Why, he had even given a personal guarantee that the king would not flee France! Such arrogance!

Catherine was considering how to respond to this, when the doors to the salon opened and Christian entered. Their eyes met above the mountainous hats of the Comtesse de Bernier and her two homely daughters. A flash of understanding passed between them and Catherine sighed with relief as Christian crossed the carpet. He nodded at Nounou, who sat stiffly on a chair next to Catherine, and then turned to their visitors, executing an elegant bow.

'My dear *Comtesse*. Such a pleasure to see you. I trust Monsieur le Comte is recovered from his infirmity?' He bent over her hand, but Catherine noticed his lips did not touch

116

the woman's glove.

'*Monsieur le Capitaine*,' she replied, with an inclination of her head that caused the silk flowers on her hat to bob wildly. 'Your enquiry is most opportune. Indeed, my husband is feeling much recovered today, thanks to the ministrations of the inestimable Doctor LaJeune.' She turned her haughty eyes upon Catherine. 'You are acquainted with the doctor's methods, *mademoiselle?*'

'No, madame. I fear I am so recently arrived — '

'*Vraiment.*' The woman stared at her, momentarily losing her train of thought. 'I find your command of French quite extraordinary. Would that my daughters had mastered the English tongue in half so competent a fashion.' She raised her already elevated brows another notch and continued, 'As I was relating, Doctor LaJeune has his clinic on the Rue Saint-Louis. It is perfectly impossible to consider any other physician these days. His methods involve the use of electricity . . . '

At Catherine's blank look, she turned waspishly to Christian. 'No doubt, being a man of science, you could explain this to Mademoiselle O'Donnell, Captain.'

Christian nodded gravely, but Catherine saw one corner of his mouth twitch. 'I am familiar with the notion, *madame*. However, its use in restoring the body to a healthy balance eludes me. No doubt your husband, as a beneficiary of this cure, could fulfil that role better than I.'

The countess looked sharply at him, but Christian's expression remained carefully neutral. Catherine, who knew him well enough by now to catch the subtle gibe, suppressed a giggle.

'Are you acquainted with my daughters, Captain?' the countess asked in an abrupt turn of the conversation. 'My eldest, Bernadette.' The girl sent Christian a rather coquettish smile displaying a row of rotting teeth. 'She is prodigiously gifted at the pianoforte, you know; everyone is quite mad about her playing. And my youngest, Isabelle.'

This last was introduced with none of the fanfare of the first and Catherine felt some measure of pity for the girl. Christian dutifully bowed over their hands, then turned his attention to Catherine.

In response to his raised eyebrows, Catherine explained.

'*Madame la Comtesse* and her daughters have come to welcome me to Paris. It seems everyone has heard of my betrothal and is anxious to make my acquaintance. I have been overwhelmed by visitors these past three days.'

The countess drew herself up sharply, doubtless irritated to be thought one of a crowd. 'It is not my intention to be cruel, my dear Miss O'Donnell,' she said tartly, 'but 'acquaintance' may be somewhat too strong a term. Certain people who have something to gain from the conservation of their class are naturally curious. There is a difference.'

Catherine looked down at her lap, refusing to allow the woman the satisfaction of knowing the barb had hurt. She had put herself too far forward, despite the truth that in a few short weeks she would outrank this sharp-tongued woman. She was coming to realize how difficult it would be for her to gain any kind of acceptance into the noble ranks of her future husband. She felt Christian's hand rest upon her shoulder and took strength from its warmth. The Comtesse de Bernier, however, was not ready to relinquish her advantage.

'I am led to understand you are in some way connected with Monsieur de Lafayette,' said the Countess. 'I was not aware he had relatives in America.'

Catherine met her eyes and in them read a clear challenge that lay like a gauntlet between them. Christian squeezed ever so gently upon her shoulder, but Catherine's temper got the better of her. The woman was simply too irritating to ignore.

'Actually, *madame*, though I am myself unclear concerning the details, I understand the connection is through the de Noailles line.'

There was a shocked silence, during which only Christian's sharp intake of breath reached her ears. The countess's eyes widened momentarily, and then resumed their piercing assessment of her face. Her daughters sat as mute as ever by her side, listening to this exchange but clearly comprehending none of its meaning.

After a moment's awful silence, the dowager found her tongue. Her words fell softly into the void.

'There is, to my certain knowledge, *mademoiselle*, no *American* line in the de Noailles dynasty.'

What have I done? thought Catherine dismally. She felt like a canary who had invited a cat to dine. She drew herself up. 'I am not of American blood, *madame*. My family is a mixture of English and French.'

'O'Donnell is neither. Kindly explain.'

This was getting worse. Christian moved away, turning to poke sharply at a log in the grate with one toe of his shoe. Catherine could almost taste his anger.

'O'Donnell is, naturally, my father's name. His father was Irish by birth.'

'Hah!' said the Countess, as though she had finally unearthed some momentous secret. 'Pirates and blackguards, the lot of them.' She gathered up her fan, poked her youngest daughter with it and rose. 'Come along, girls. We have other calls to make.'

Catherine sighed with relief as the footman opened the doors for the party. But, at the last moment, the countess turned and waved the fan at her. 'You are not exactly ugly, *mademoiselle*, and if you are truly a blood relative of the Duc de Noailles and as wealthy as everyone says, then I for one would like to know what convinced you to marry the Duc de Charigny. And one way or another, I intend to find out!'

Catherine was astonished by this outburst. Others may have hinted at such a question, but no one had shown the effrontery to speak the words so openly.

Apparently, she was not alone in her thoughts. No sooner had the doors closed upon the Berniers, than Madame Beaulieu harrumphed loudly. 'Ignorant woman! So she is a countess. I have seen better manners in a night-soil collector!' With that, she gathered up her ebony cane and sailed out of the salon, her indignation having a most healing effect upon her arthritic hips.

Catherine turned to see Christian staring at her, his face thunderous.

'I'm sorry, Captain,' she said in a small voice. 'They were so very tiresome.'

He stared at her, his hands clasped tightly behind his back.

Exasperated by the tension of the past days, and by her own negligence, she jumped up. 'Why are they like that? Why, if they trouble themselves by coming to see me, are they so intent on belittling who and what I am? Is it some crime to marry into this family?'

Christian sighed. She was right, they had stepped beyond the bounds of propriety, and she was utterly ill-equipped to defend herself against the likes of Madame Bernier. He looked down at her, so small and cross, with her innocent puppy-brown eyes and her small mouth pressed tight with frustration. Did she have any idea how very appealing she was?

'You have broken the seal on Pandora's box, Miss O'Donnell,' he replied, more gently than he had intended a moment ago. 'Now the demons will out and all of Paris will be talking.'

'So let them. I am sick and tired of the whole business.'

'Your ennui is understandable. Let us speak no more of it. The Comtesse de Bernier is not much liked. Indeed if she is to concern herself with the reasons for *your* betrothal one must wonder what prompted her husband to choose her as his bride.'

'You seem to know the count well.'

'He is a member of the Assembly and highly regarded for one in the First Estate. Nor is he a fool, unlike his wife.'

Catherine frowned at him. 'For one who appears to command a great deal of respect among the nobility, you express somewhat acerbic opinions.'

He laughed. 'Not to their ears. To them, I am merely a naval officer who has brought some small glory to France. And my impure connections to the house of Charigny do me no disservice, either.'

She gestured with her hands, turning to gaze out the window at the now gathering dusk. 'I do not understand,' she said in a resigned voice. 'If you are the prince's nephew, then how can you be a commoner? You are not like me, connected by the thinnest of threads to an illegitimate line.'

He crossed to the window and stood slightly behind her so he could observe her features unseen. Her hair caught the last of the light, falling in soft auburn waves around her shoulders. He was pleased she had already adopted the new natural style. It made her look younger and emphasized the graceful line of her chin.

She turned and looked up at him suddenly, catching his examination. Their eyes met and became mysteriously entangled and Christian found he could not look away. He was aware of the softening of her mouth, heard her quick intake of breath and sensed the rapid rise and fall of her breast.

'How could your father let you come all this way, Catherine, and give you to such a man as Dominic?' he said quietly, almost to himself.

She whirled away from him, breaking the moment in a flash. After the difficult afternoon she had endured, she was in no mood to control her temper. 'I beg you would cease asking me this, Captain. I have given my word, that is why. And I believe that one's word, once promised, is as good as sealed. I would expect no less of you.'

'Indeed, you would have no less. But then it is not I you are marrying, is it?'

He stepped back as she flew at him, her fists curled into tight little balls. She thumped him in the chest in a most unladylike fashion and Christian felt an inexplicable urge to laugh.

'No, sir, I am fortunate it is not! And if we are to be cousins, I sincerely hope that you will get over this pompous tendency to mind my business rather than your own.'

'But you are my business,' he replied, grabbing at her wrists before she could inflict further damage. 'Dominic can't watch out for you, even if he wished to, and my uncle doesn't know you as I do . . . '

'Why you arrogant — Release me this instant!'

'Not until you promise to stop calling me sir or captain,' he replied, laughing. 'Cousins are surely at liberty to use their first names, even in your book.'

Catherine fell still, giving up the unequal struggle. He looked down at her with an odd surge of protectiveness towards this contrary creature. 'What would it take, do you suppose, Catherine, for you to realize the mistake that you are about to make?' And without a moment's thought, he bent his head and claimed her mouth.

She gave a little squeak but it was swallowed by his lips. Christian had only meant to kiss her for a moment, to tease her, but the touch of her mouth drove all such thoughts from his mind. She tried to pull away, then fell still like a captured bird as he brushed his lips gently over hers. He was stunned by the sensations assailing him. He deepened the kiss without having intended to and she opened to him like a sweet red rose. He lost himself in her embrace. His hands slid around her back, drawing her slim body close until her breasts burned against his chest, branding him.

Christian felt a surge of desire so great that he was forced to close his eyes against the pain. What madness was this? He, who had intended only to teach her a lesson, was being drawn into an abyss of need that was swamping his reason.

He released her abruptly and stepped back, filling his lungs and running his hands through his hair.

Her eyes were wide and staring and her lips moist from their embrace.

'*Nom de Dieu*, I'm sorry,' he said, cursing his voice for sounding so shaky. 'That was . . . That is, I . . . Oh, to the devil,' he said at last, and turning his back on that bewitching and utterly bewildered face, stormed from the room.

6

Catherine saw little of Christian after the scene in the salon, and had been kept busy with several more visitors and a few — rather too few, she privately thought — requests for her to call upon some of her new-found acquaintances. She saw Angélique almost every day, and between them they had replaced most of Catherine's American wardrobe in favour of the latest Parisian styles. Catherine welcomed the change, though it was at considerable expense, as the new styles were more relaxed and feminine.

There had also been visits to the best couturier in Paris in search of the perfect wedding gown. And there were many meetings with the staff of the Hôtel de Charigny, preparing for the event. Catherine had discussed the menu with the chef and sous-chef so many times, she thought she could recite every dish in her head, and there were to be almost a hundred of them. No expense was to be spared, the prince had said.

In such fruitful occupations two weeks had fairly flown by. Catherine's only regret was that she was no closer to establishing any kind of rapport with her husband-to-be than she had been the first night they met. Dominic remained aloof, never seeking her out and engaging in only as much social discourse as manners required.

So it was with some delight that on the morning of March 31st, as she was partaking of a solitary breakfast, she received an invitation for both herself and Dominic to attend a soirée to be given by Madame la Comtesse de Bernier.

Bernier? Catherine's initial pleasure was chilled by a sudden frisson of dread. Why should the *ci-devant* countess wish to honour *her* by such an event? They had hardly parted on the best of terms.

She thought back to their conversation and blushed as she remembered how she had taunted the lady with talk of a connection to the Vicomte de Noailles, General Lafayette's brother-in-law.

Christian told her the woman was not well regarded, but that surely did not mean she could not cause trouble.

Catherine slid the invitation back into its vellum envelope. She set it beside her plate and picked up her cup, sipping thoughtfully at the steaming chocolate before setting it down once more. Realizing she had lost all appetite for her brioche and plum conserve, she snatched up the invitation and ran from the room.

Perhaps this was just what she and Dominic needed, after all, to see and be seen by everyone as a couple. Perhaps it would help her to focus on her future life as his duchess and not to keep pondering her extraordinary and shameless reaction to Christian's kiss!

She paused as she reached the doors to her fiancé's rooms, certain she could hear talking. It seemed odd, for it was well known that *Monsieur le Duc* liked to sleep late and that he never tolerated being woken by a servant. Perhaps he was rising earlier than usual today. She hoped so, for she was too excited about the soirée to wait until the noon hour to share it with him.

Catherine knocked and listened. There was silence for a moment, then a soft curse followed by her fiancé's voice.

'Who the devil is that? Don't you know what time it is?'

''Tis Catherine, Your Grace,' she replied, addressing him in her usual fashion. She had discovered that Dominic preferred the old ways, expecting people to address him as they had done before the Revolution.

There was another curse, more muffled

this time, and much moving about, which Catherine took to be the work of his valet making him presentable. Finally he commanded her to enter and she opened the door, looking around in some bewilderment.

'Where is Brassart, Your Grace?'

'Brassart? What the devil would I want with him at this time of the morning?'

'I just thought — ' Catherine looked towards the closed doors that led to his private bathroom and salon and frowned. Perhaps she had been mistaken.

'Well, what is it that brings you here before the cock crows?'

She looked back at her fiancé, who sat propped up by a mountain of disarrayed pillows in a huge canopied bed, with the covers drawn up to his armpits. He wore no night-cap and she noticed that without his wig his hair was sparse and dark, not fair like Christian's. He seemed rather breathless, too, which no doubt was as a result of his attempts to tidy himself before admitting her.

'I — I merely wished to share some news, Your Grace,' she replied, crossing the floor to pass him the envelope.

'What's this? What do I care what you get up to? Or are you trying to rub my nose in it that you go about the town with that no-account cousin of mine?'

'No!' she cried, aghast at his inference. 'It's for us both — you and me. For tomorrow. I had hoped — '

'Huh,' he grunted as he perused the contents. 'Makes a change. No one seems to bother to invite me anywhere any more. Not that I miss all this nonsense. They're all boors and politicians, every last one of them these days.'

'So you'll go?' she asked, deciding the direct approach was probably the best.

'You're very keen.' He gave her a sharp look.

Catherine couldn't prevent a slight blush. 'I merely thought it was time we were seen as a couple,' she responded quietly, for she knew better than to excite a person in his state of health. 'As you say, I am most often seen in the company of Captain Lavelle or Madame Fontenay — '

'You're right,' he broke in. 'It's time I showed them I can still get about. Tell Brassart to arrange it.'

With that, he rolled towards the window and turned his back on her.

Catherine stood for a moment, staring at the brusque stranger she was soon to marry, and then, since he had clearly dismissed her, she retrieved the invitation and let herself out of the room.

Catherine saw no more of Dominic until they were leaving for the soirée next evening. Brassart and Emile carried their master through the chill, wind-blown rain to the prince's black coach and managed to get him comfortable. But the duke seemed breathless and fatigued and his pallor alarmed Catherine.

She climbed up, holding the hood of her cloak close to her face against the unseasonable storm and settled herself on the bench opposite. 'Your Grace, if you do not feel well — '

'Don't fuss, *mademoiselle*. I'm as well as I ever am. Where's my demmed father?'

At that moment, the prince came out of the house, and Catherine, mindful of his unequivocal statement that he did not expect her to be Dominic's nursemaid, made no further objection. But she watched the duke as the coach rumbled out into the wet night, only half listening to his father's pleasant ramblings on the state of the roads.

Her mind was otherwise occupied. It was concerning itself with the person seated across from her in the swaying coach, his features shadowy in the light of the swinging lamp. His eyes were closed in the gloom, so she was at leisure to truly examine her future husband for the first time. He was not uncomely. Neither was he handsome. Were it not for his petulant manner and his physical limitations, no doubt he would have been as eagerly sought after as any noble bachelor in Paris. But the reality was only too clear to her: Monsieur le Duc de Charigny was not considered a desirable husband in his own country.

And that simple truth worried her more than any other. Bar one.

She let her eyes rove over his body, noting that he was a little heavy around the waist, the result no doubt of lack of exercise. She wondered why he was so unwilling to walk; if it was the result of yet another affliction, or whether, as the prince had indicated, it was from being overly indulged as a child. Perhaps he merely chose not to.

Her mother had been weak, very weak in the last year of her life, but she had not been bedridden until the end. True, she seldom moved more than a few steps from her bed to her chair, or with much help from Catherine to the garden where she was able to while away a warm afternoon with the sun on her face and bird-song in her ears.

She wondered, as she gazed at the duke,

whether he was even capable of . . . fathering children.

The thought, even though it had not reached her lips, caused her face to burn. She knew that for most young women in her situation, the expectation of marital relations would spark curiosity, excitement, perhaps even a little anxiety. Catherine knew no such girlish sentiments. She knew only determination for the sake of the children she longed to mother. And dread.

But that was hers to endure, and she had long since come to terms with it.

The coach rolled to a stop and the door was thrown open. Catherine allowed the prince to hand her down and then waited as he followed. Brassart and Emile manhandled their master from the conveyance and up the wide stone steps, creating a minor sensation among the onlookers. Catherine wondered if it was that attention that Dominic craved, as she hurried through the rain.

The town palace of the former Comte de Bernier was smaller than the Hôtel de Charigny, but no less opulent. The salon was exquisitely furnished in soft blue and gold, with touches of ivory to lighten the effect. A huge and most welcome fire blazed in the grate. Above, on the ornate marble mantelpiece stood a gigantic ormolu clock, set off by a pair of Chinese vases. Other elements of chinoiserie decorated the room, adding an exotic flavour to the splendour.

The Comtesse de Bernier smiled coolly at Catherine as she arrived on the prince's arm, reserving her most disarming welcome for the prince himself. Catherine smiled at her daughters, Miss Bernadette and her younger sister Isabelle, who seemed already bored by the event, and was then introduced to the Comte de Bernier, whose eyes held none of the coolness of his wife's as he kissed Catherine's hand.

'My dear Miss O'Donnell. I seem to hear about you from every quarter these days. It is a great pleasure to finally make your acquaintance.' He looked at the prince. 'May I relieve you of this charming creature, sir, for I believe there are some here who are equally anxious to make her acquaintance?'

The prince released her with a smile and Catherine was led away across a room crowded with ladies in expensive gowns and gentlemen in their most brilliant finery.

'Now, my dear, tell me with whom you are already acquainted. Have you met Monsieur Barnave, over there?' He indicated a man engaged in a vigorous conversation with a younger man, who seemed to be contradicting him at every turn. 'That's Saint-Just stirring him up. Men of principle, both, but with rather opposing views on most things. Ah,' he said, as they approached a close-knit group gathered by the fire. 'Here she is, gentlemen. May I present Mademoiselle O'Donnell from America, soon to be Madame Montaltier and wife of the *ci-devant* Duc de Charigny.'

Catherine smiled as she recognized General Lafayette among the group. He came forward and took her hand to kiss it.

'My dear Catherine, how delightful it is to see you after so many years.' He turned to his companions and explained. 'When I last saw this beautiful woman, she was a mere girl at her mother's knee. Must be nearly ten years ago, now.'

'Nine, sir,' she corrected, withdrawing her hand. She noticed much change in him. Gone was the boyish awkwardness, overtaken by a maturity that spoke of his stellar success on both sides of the Atlantic. His brows were bushier, his forehead somewhat more prominent, but if his hair had begun to recede a little it had lost none of its distinctive Titian colour.

'Is it only nine? Good heavens, it seems a lifetime since I was enjoying your father's hospitality. I trust he is well?'

Catherine assured him he was, and

Lafayette then took it upon himself to introduce her to the rest of the gentlemen, as the Comte de Bernier was needed to welcome other guests at his post near the door.

'You are acquainted, I belive with Lieutenant Fontenay? A colleague of your soon-to-be-cousin, Captain Lavelle.'

Catherine smiled at Gérard as he kissed her hand. 'Indeed, I am sir. He and his charming wife have made me most welcome in Paris.'

'Where is Lavelle?' Lafayette asked. 'Is he not attending tonight?'

'I believe he will arrive later,' she replied, feeling her heart beat a little faster at the mention of his name. She turned as Brassart and Emile carried Dominic to a *chaiselongue* near the fire, though he never glanced her way.

The introductions continued, but Catherine scarcely took in all the names.

'If you will excuse me, gentlemen, I must see that *Monsieur le Duc* is comfortable.' She dropped a curtsy to the group and left them to their politics.

Dominic seemed surprised as she drew up a stool nearby.

'Are you comfortable, Your Grace? Is there something I may get for you?'

His eyebrows rose as he regarded her, but

his expression was benign enough. 'Pray don't trouble yourself, *mademoiselle*. Brassart is fetching me some wine.'

'Is that wise? Perhaps — '

'My dear Miss O'Donnell, if we are to live harmoniously in this arrangement of ours, you will kindly remember that I dislike being fussed over. I am quite capable of deciding what is best for me, thank you.'

Catherine drew in a breath. 'I do have some expertise in your condition, Your Grace. I nursed my mother through many years of convalescence — '

'Convalescence, you say! So you cured her, did you?'

She was stung by his words and felt the colour rise in her cheeks. 'My mother passed away last year. But I — '

'So. You think you'll do the same for me and get back the dowry your father has lavished on you.' His eyes glittered with a venom that brought despair to her heart. 'Well, enjoy your dream, *mademoiselle*. I have no intention of letting you poison me with your American potions.'

At that moment, Brassart arrived with a tray bearing a large glass of claret which he placed in his master's hand. Dominic held it up to the firelight and laughed low in his throat. 'The Duc de Charigny does not take orders from a little nobody, no matter how rich her papa is. If I wish to drink myself to death, I shall. And if I choose to live to a hundred, that too shall be my choice.'

Catherine could not suppress the rage engendered by his words, much as she knew he was deliberately trying to goad her.

'I do not know why you dislike me so, Your Grace. If you were against this marriage, you should have informed your father of your feelings months ago, so that we may all have been spared this charade. And as for your choosing to live to a great age, you certainly will not do so unless you get some exercise and stop pretending you cannot walk!'

And with that, she jumped up from the stool and went in search of Angé and a sympathetic ear.

★ ★ ★

The evening lost much of its fascination for Catherine from that point. Her attention was drawn frequently towards Dominic, for she was disturbed that they had quarrelled so publicly and with such venom, but he seemed perfectly at ease and did not want for company. On one such occasion she noticed him conversing with a tall, foreign-looking gentleman dressed entirely in black. She had not seen him enter the room and wondered who he might be, but as her thoughts dwelt upon his presence, she was startled to realize that she was being observed by him in turn. The man turned a pair of piercing dark eyes on her, raising his thin lips in a smile that sent a tremor up her spine. She felt herself flush red, dropping him a scant curtsy in reply to his acknowledgement, but she did not approach, and nor did he, she was grateful to see, for the man's eyes held some silent message that made her tremble, though she could not have said why.

She was relieved to find distraction in the person of the handsome young Saint-Just, who appeared at her elbow seemingly intent on grilling her on American republicanism and its constitution. Her relief was short-lived, however, as she found herself being regaled on the philosophy of the primacy of law. She even made the grievous error of objecting to his disregard for the opinions of the people, and as a result was forced to listen to his impassioned diatribe on the sovereignty of ethics. It appeared he was publishing a book as an outlet for his intense frustration at finding himself too young to be part of the *Assemblé*. Catherine secretly wondered how on earth such an opinionated young man would ever win election when the time came.

She was enormously grateful to be rescued by the prince.

He took her hand and laid it upon his arm as he walked her towards the adjoining supper-room. 'You looked as though you were going to faint if you heard the word 'constitution' one more time,' he teased her. 'I thought you might prefer some refreshments before the entertainments begin.'

Catherine cast him a warm smile. 'You are most observant, sir. Monsieur Saint-Just is an unusual gentleman, with very pronounced . . . beliefs.'

'He is also ambitious to the exclusion of all else. I would advise you to take great care in his company.'

Catherine nodded, but privately wondered if there was anyone in Paris — aside from Christian and Angé — to whom she might speak freely without fear of censure.

'It is not my intention to be in his company at all,' she replied.

After they had indulged themselves from the excellent supper-table, Catherine and the prince returned to the salon where the Comtesse de Bernier's eldest daughter, Bernadette, was to perform upon the pianoforte. Chairs had been set up in a semicircle so that guests might listen in comfort, and Catherine was glad of the respite from political talk.

Miss Bernier was quite a pretty young woman, until she smiled and displayed her rotting teeth. She gave a curtsy before settling herself upon the stool before a magnificent grand piano made of gilded and ebonized wood and painted in scenes depicting exotic birds. Catherine had never seen such an instrument, for her prized piano in Philadelphia had been a modest square one made of mahogany and beech.

Miss Bernier had chosen to display her famous talents with a complicated set from the German composer Bach, which impressed Catherine, for she knew how demanding the music was. Bernadette played it with cool precision but Catherine was left disappointed as she dutifully clapped her applause with the rest of the guests.

'You do not approve, *mademoiselle*?' the prince, who was seated at her elbow, whispered.

'Indeed, Miss Bernier plays with exceptional competence, sir.'

'But no soul?'

She smiled. 'I am being too harsh, if I make you think so,' she replied.

He winked at her. 'Indeed, I don't believe you are. Why don't you show us that pretty piece of furniture as it should be played?'

'I?' Catherine was aghast. 'Oh, sir, I could not possibly. In front of all these people!'

He patted her hand. 'My dear Catherine, I have heard you playing on the instrument in my house every morning, and it has never sounded better. What is that little favourite you always start with?'

'Mozart,' she replied, touched that he should have taken such interest. 'Sonata Number 15 in C major, if you wish to be exact. I was not aware you had such an interest in music, sir.'

'Indeed, it was a passion I shared with my wife, *mademoiselle*, and to hear you play brings back the happiest of memories.'

Catherine's eyes misted over as she saw the sweet sadness in his face.

'Won't you play, Miss O'Donnell?' he asked again. 'Just for me and my dear Anne-Elise?'

* * *

Christian Lavelle arrived later than he'd expected and bearing some disturbing news for his uncle. When he entered the Hôtel de Bernier it was so quiet he almost imagined he had confused the date for the soirée. Surely it had been for April 1st? But then he heard music and realized the entertainments were in progress.

He stepped quietly into the salon and leaned against the door, taking care not to disturb the concert. His eyes scanned the crowded room, easily finding Dominic lounging in his *chaise-longue* with a churlish expression on his face and a glass of wine in his hand. His uncle was sitting alone on the other side of the room, and Angé and her husband sat with General Lafayette and Monsieur Barnave, but of Catherine there was no sign.

He wondered why her whereabouts mattered so much to him. After all, she was not *his* fiancée. And then he noticed the pianist.

His heart beat a little faster as he absorbed the look of sweet rapture on her face as she played. The light from two huge chandeliers set her chestnut hair afire and turned her silk gown into an iridescent sea of green and blue with each subtle shift of her body.

He didn't know much about music, but he was pretty sure she was playing Mozart, and with such depth of feeling that the audience was mesmerized. Her fingers flew over the keys, colouring the air with dancing fire and sparkling dewdrops.

As the final rondo ended, Catherine paused, her head bent over the keys, her eyes closed. Then she straightened up and looked around at her audience with a gentle smile on her face that made Christian's heart ache. The whole room erupted with clapping — none louder than Saint-Just, he noted — and Catherine gave them a shy curtsy.

After that, an older woman whom Christian thought was the wife of one of the members of the National Assembly, sang to the accompaniment of a younger woman with bright red hair and a prominent nose, and after that two further sets were played by guests who entered bravely into the spirit of the evening and did not mind that their skills were by no means comparable to those who had preceded them.

At last it was over. Christian made his way across the room towards Catherine and his uncle, but he found it impossible to get close. She was surrounded by people congratulating her on her performance and issuing invitations for her to attend other soirées. She seemed quite overwhelmed by all the attention, and looked pleadingly at the prince, who seemed to be behaving as though it was no more than she deserved. Eventually, Christian reached her elbow.

'You seem to have made quite an impression, my sweet,' he teased. 'Did you throw yourself to the wolves, or did my uncle coerce you?'

'Cheeky braggart!' his uncle responded, then whispered, 'we were forced to endure the mechanical wizardry of Miss de Bernier and I couldn't resist letting Catherine show them how it should be done!'

Christian grinned. 'Letting, Uncle?'

At that moment, Saint-Just joined them. Christian inclined his head in response to his greeting, and withheld a sigh, for he certainly had no wish to endure a half-hour of the young politician's rantings.

'*Mademoiselle*,' said Saint-Just, taking her hand and kissing it with real passion. 'Your music is *ravissante*! Never have I witnessed such sweet ecstasy! Are all the young women of America so filled with honest freedom that their fingers can portray such purity of expression?'

'Trust you, Saint-Just, to find politics even in music,' responded Christian dryly.

The young man sent him a measuring gaze. 'There is only politics, Captain Lavelle. It is the guiding force of all life. And when France is free, you shall see how it can rule.'

They watched as he gave a stiff bow and turned away. Christian knew he had acted rashly, for one never knew when a fanatic might gain power — nor what he might remember of one's words to recall at a later date.

'That was outspoken for you, Nephew,' said the prince, eyeing Saint-Just's retreating back with equal distaste.

'*D'accord*. But what's said is said.' He turned to the prince. 'I have some disturbing news, Uncle. Mirabeau's illness has taken a serious turn for the worse. He has been asking for you but would entrust no one but me to bring you the message.'

The prince stared at Christian, a quick frown forming on his brow. 'That is indeed bad news. I must go to him at once. May I ask you to escort Miss O'Donnell and your cousin home safely, and to tell Monsieur le Comte de Bernier that I am unwell?'

Without waiting for an answer, he hurried from the room.

Catherine frowned. 'Who is this Mirabeau?'

'He's one of the most influential men in the Assembly,' Christian answered absently, for his mind was on the vexing question of why the great populist was so determined to speak with the prince. Christian had not known they were even friends, and the look on his uncle's face when he had imparted the news of Mirabeau's illness concerned him.

'Christian?' Catherine's hand upon his arm startled him.

'I'm sorry,' he replied quickly, forcing his

thoughts to the present. 'I fear that the man is dying, and it will be a sad day for France.'

'Who is dying?' Madame duRosier, whom Catherine had been told was formerly a viscountess, demanded, coming upon them so suddenly that Catherine jumped.

She saw Christian frown at his own thoughtlessness in speaking so freely in an open room, though why the illness of Monsieur Mirabeau should create a need for secrecy she could not comprehend.

Christian coughed. 'Ah, I heard — mayhap it is mere rumour — that Mirabeau's illness is worse.'

'*Vraiment!*' The former noblewoman lost no time in bearing the 'rumour' to the remainder of the guests. In fact, so efficient was she that Catherine wondered why people bothered to print newspapers at all. They could save themselves much expense by merely advising Madame duRosier of the news each morning.

She noticed that several of the gentlemen excused themselves soon after, notably Monsieur Barnave and the excitable Saint-Just. In minutes, all of Paris would know, without a doubt.

She was just about to enquire of Christian if they, too, could leave, for the hour was growing late and she was tired, when the

Comtesse de Bernier descended upon them in a cloud of perfume.

Catherine's heart sank when she saw the expression in the older woman's eyes.

'No doubt you think yourself mighty talented at the pianoforte, *mademoiselle*,' she huffed, without so much as a nod to Christian. 'Nevertheless, there is a good deal more to mastering such an instrument than fiddling about with Mozart!'

Privately, Catherine agreed, though she said nothing. Christian was not so polite.

'Indeed, Comtesse. I did not have the privilege of hearing your daughter play this evening, as I was inexcusably late. However, I found Miss O'Donnell's rendition quite peerless.'

The woman raised her brows. 'Indeed. And what, pray, is your experience of such matters?'

Christian coughed. He knew when he was beaten.

'Quite!' responded his hostess with apparent satisfaction. 'And now, young lady, I wish that you would answer my question.'

'Question, *madame*?' Catherine asked, genuinely confused. 'On what subject?'

'On the subject of your connection to Monsieur le Général Lafayette, of course. Don't think I haven't been giving this some thought. I have even spoken of it to the *vicomtesse* herself and she knows of no such — '

'Did I hear my name mentioned?' asked a deep voice, startling the little group. Lafayette stood at Catherine's elbow, regarding his hostess with a bland expression that told Catherine he had little love for the woman.

'Oh, *Monsieur le Général!*' the Countess said, suddenly all smiles. 'I was merely discussing Miss O'Donnell's amazing lineage. I hear that it is your wife's family to which she is related, after all. Silly me — I had quite assumed it was through you that she claims her bloodline to the de Noailles.'

Catherine glanced nervously at the general, who was gazing at her with a bland expression that made her distinctly uneasy. There was a moment's silence.

'I believe you are mistaken, *madame*,' he replied quietly. 'Miss O'Donnell is connected to the Lafayette family by a distant cousin who settled in America long before my father was born.'

'Oh, but sir, I was quite certain that Miss O'Donnell herself told me — '

Catherine jumped in before this whole situation became worse. 'Perhaps I explained myself badly, *madame*. I am sure I did not mean to give you any such mistaken impression.'

The Comtesse de Bernier's cheeks flamed as she sought in vain for a way to pry further. She glared at Catherine. 'It seems I have been the victim of an April Fool's joke, *mademoiselle*,' she snapped, without a trace of humour, then drew in a frustrated breath and whirled away from the group without so much as a nod to the general.

Catherine glanced at Lafayette and immediately wished she hadn't, for his eyes were frosty. 'I trust you have not played *poisson d'avril* on anyone else, Miss O'Donnell?'

'Indeed, no sir,' she replied, abashed. 'I'm sorry you had to be a party to that. It shall not happen again.'

'See that it does not,' he answered, and left them with a curt bow.

Catherine let out a breath. 'Oh, Christian, I don't think I can stand this. I feel like I am acting a role in a play and I keep forgetting my lines.'

He took her arm and guided her through the thinning crowd toward an alcove by the window, where they could talk undisturbed. Beyond the drapes she could hear rain pattering against the windowpane.

'Now do you begin to understand why it was a mistake to come here?' he asked, as they were seated on a bench.

'To Madame de Bernier's soirée? It was not so bad.'

He looked hard at her and Catherine knew her attempt at levity was a failure.

'To France, my sweet. If you have learned one thing it is that the people to whose world you aspire are terrified of losing everything to the Revolution. They have already lost their titles, their livery, their lands. And they most certainly do not have room in their shrinking world of privilege for a naïve young lady from the American *bourgeoisie*. They will never let you in, Catherine.'

She laughed lightly, annoyed that she sounded tremulous. 'Thank heavens in America we do not care to define people by their class. And we do not talk of any such thing as the *bourgeoisie*!'

She rose, but Christian's firm hand encircled her arm, pulling her back to sit beside him. 'You must go home, Catherine!'

She shook him off. 'Do you know what I think, Captain Lavelle? I think you are simply jealous of your cousin. I think you are trying to prevent our marriage in order to spite him.'

'*Au contraire, petite*, I am thinking of your sweet hide.'

'Nonsense! You have done everything you

can to prevent me from knowing Dominic. If you really wanted to help me, you would find a way for us to get to know each other.'

He was silent for a moment, staring at her with those deep-blue eyes, as fathomless as the sea. For the breadth of a heartbeat, she almost fancied he was going to kiss her and found herself holding her breath in anticipation.

Instead he shrugged. 'Very well. If that is what it will take for you to see the danger you are embracing, then so be it.'

7

Honoré-Gabriel de Riqueti, once the Comte de Mirabeau, died the next day, plunging the people of Paris into mourning. Catherine was touched by the depth of feeling that his sudden passing engendered, especially among the servants. Nounou took to her bed bemoaning the cruelty of nature to snatch away such a great leader at the premature age of forty-two. Catherine suspected the old lady's relationship with God had deteriorated once more.

For the few days after the man's death, there was talk of nothing else, but Catherine soon wearied of hearing him alternately praised by some and vilified by others. Her mind was occupied in trying to come to terms with the issue of whether or not she would truly be married if Father Joubert were to perform the ceremony in the Hôtel de Charigny chapel. Dominic insisted that a marriage, to be lawful in the eyes of God, must be conducted by a non-constitutional priest, not some political pastor at the whim of the government.

Catherine would have liked to discuss it

with the prince, but since Mirabeau's death he had scarcely been at home, seeming all-consumed with some unfinished business. She had heard him discussing the whereabouts of some important documents with Christian, but when she entered the room the discussion was suspended.

After mass on Sunday, Catherine approached Father Joubert himself on the matter of her nuptials, but he seemed merely embarrassed that the question be raised. Doubtless, he took his orders from the prince and was not in the habit of questioning them.

The following morning dawned brilliantly sunny and Catherine decided she would visit Angélique and seek her advice. She dressed for riding and was careful to pin a cockade to her hat before setting off in the company of the groom, Clonard.

It was a glorious spring morning, with the chestnut trees dropping white blossoms on the cobblestones, children playing in the small parks, and birds everywhere in joyful chorus. There were signs of mourning, too, for the passing of Monsieur Mirabeau — shops adorned with black crosses hung from windows and doors; black ribbons tied to horses' harnesses.

Madame Fontenay was delighted to see

her. 'Come in, my dear! The children have been at me for days now asking why you have not been to visit.' She took her arm and pulled her towards the salon, ever eager for the latest gossip. 'You have not been ill, I trust? I hear there have been cases of croup among some of the children. I have been keeping mine away from their little friends for the moment for fear of it.'

'Indeed, I am quite well, Angé. But I have come seeking some advice, and you are the only person to whom I can turn.'

'*Vraiment!*' Her friend's eyes sparkled. 'Then I am all agog! Tell me what troubles you.'

The black maid Jeanne brought tea and a platter of tiny gateaux, and they sat in a sunny nook that afforded pleasant views of the courtyard behind the apartments.

Catherine sighed. ''Tis about my wedding.'

'Oh, la!' Angé replied instantly, clapping her palms to her cheeks. 'You are not going to marry him after all! Christian will be so *content de soi* he will be crowing!'

'No, no, Angé. Indeed, you mistake my concern entirely.'

'Then you are still engaged to *Monsieur le Comte?*'

She nodded. Her friend's cornflower-blue eyes narrowed on her face.

'But you are not certain, are you?'

Catherine raised her chin. 'I gave my word.'

Angé sat back, waving her hands in the air so that the deep lace at her elbows caught the bright sunlight. '*Quelle sottises!* You gave your word, yes. But then you were safe in America dreaming of a handsome French duke who would sweep you off your feet and be the beau of the ball.' She leaned forward and patted Catherine on the hand. 'Tell me I am wrong. Tell me you are not disappointed in the hand Providence has dealt.'

Catherine sighed, picking up her delicate Sèvres teacup and taking a sip of the hot beverage. 'I cannot.'

'*Voilà!*'

'But that does not mean that I have altered my promise to my father, or to the prince.' She set the cup down once more. 'And it was my mother's dying wish.'

'Ah. *Ça, je comprends.* A promise made to the dying is not easily broken.' Angé tipped her head sideways, considering her friend closely. 'You have more spirit than most young women, my dear. And you will be good for the man, *sans doute.* Do you think he will be able to give you the children you desire?'

Catherine gasped at the audacity of the question, but laughed when she saw the twinkle in the older woman's eye. 'Perhaps

157

you should ask me that *after* we are married.'

'I heard what you said to him at Madame de Bernier's soirée, you know,' Angé continued blithely.

Catherine stared at her, dismayed. 'You did?'

'And I was not alone. You caused quite a stir, though everyone pretended not to hear. Gérard said you were a woman who could achieve anything, if you could make that man get up on his own two legs.'

'Oh, no!' Catherine's cheeks reddened with horror. 'How could I have said such a thing and quarrelled with him right there in front of strangers?'

'Strangers to you, perhaps, my love. But not to Dominic. I am led to believe that he was frequently seen at the gaming tables in his youth. But there was some scandal and he became a recluse, preferring to have his closest friends visit him at home. He is seldom seen about the city since the Revolution began.'

'What scandal?' Catherine asked lightly, feigning indifference.

But Angé was not fooled. 'La! You should know I do not like to gossip!'

At that they both laughed, and the moment passed. Angé's two children came in from their morning walk with their governess and squealed with delight to see Catherine, who was a favourite 'aunt' by now.

'*Tante Cat'rine! Tante Cat'rine!*' Alexandre cried, as he rushed across the room to leap uninvited onto her lap. Catherine hugged the squirming child, loving the sweet baby feel of him and the smell of sunshine in his hair.

'Have you enjoyed your walk, *petit?*' she asked.

'*Bien sûr!*' he replied. 'We seed the king!'

'You did?'

'Alex!' admonished his sister. ''Twas just a fine carriage.' She looked solemnly at Catherine, as though she were twice her five years. 'Alexandre thought it was the king because he'd never seen such a fine coach.'

'I see,' Catherine replied, winking at the girl over her brother's head. 'And how many horses did he have, Alex?'

His little face compressed in a frown of concentration, then he produced two chubby fingers on each hand and held them up to her. '*Comme ça.*'

'Only four?' Catherine smiled. 'Then perhaps your sister is right, *petit*. The king would surely have six horses to pull his carriage.'

The boy frowned. 'Is he so fat, *Tante Cat'rine?*'

They all laughed. 'Indeed, I have never seen the man, but I am told he has a prodigious appetite.'

'Me, too!' replied Alexandre, seemingly happy with this item in common with his sovereign. 'I'm starved!'

'Come, my darlings,' said Angé indulgently. 'If Tante Catherine has finished, I believe you may have some cakes from our tea.'

Catherine assured her she had, and the children retreated to the hearth with the platter of *petits fours*, no doubt wishing she would visit every day if the leavings were so good.

'Now, my love,' said Angé, in a quieter voice so the children would not overhear. 'Tell me what this great question is that so troubles you.'

Catherine grimaced. 'It seems the Revolution has made marriage a more complicated affair than I had realized.'

'It has made all of life more complex, but, God willing, when it is all over things will be a little better than before.'

'You really believe so?'

'Indeed I do,' Angé replied with some asperity. 'Perhaps the nobility will see they are no longer able to rule the lives of the majority, but must make a place for all.'

Catherine was beginning to question even

that, these days, but she was learning that it was politic to refrain from expressing her opinions.

'However that may be, I am at present concerned that the wedding we have planned may not be legal.'

'Not legal?'

'In the sense that God will recognize it, but the constitution may not.'

Angé looked thoughtful. 'Ah!'

'That's all Father Joubert, the family priest, would say when I spoke to him! 'Ah! Ah!' ' Catherine quoted crossly. 'Why can't he simply accept that whatever must be done must be done?'

'And what, pray is that?'

Catherine threw up her hands. 'That is precisely my problem, Angé. No one seems to know. Or if they do, they will not tell me.'

'*Quelle blague!* You had best tell me what you do know and then we shall consider what to do.'

So Catherine explained and Angé listened in silence, her dark head tilted slightly to one side.

At the end, she pressed her lips together. 'So if you are married by this Father Joubert, you will be married according to Rome but not according to the constitution of France, am I right?'

Catherine nodded.

'*Bien c'est simple*! You must marry in a church with a juring priest.' She shook her curls. 'I do not see the problem.'

'Dominic will not hear of it,' she replied.

'Ah.'

'Angé!'

'Oh, *pardon*! It is truly most vexatious.' She thought for a moment. 'Could you not perhaps be married twice? Would not that satisfy Dominic?'

Catherine stared at her, hope springing in her breast. 'Marry twice! Why Angé that is the oddest thing I ever heard of, but perhaps it is the solution. We shall marry at home with Father Joubert, and then have a quiet ceremony in a church with a recognized priest.'

'Will he accept, do you think?' Angé's brow was still troubled by thoughts of Dominic's opposition.

Catherine shrugged. 'Indeed, I wonder. Perhaps if I ask him very nicely . . . '

At that moment, the door opened and Angé's husband Gérard entered, followed closely by Christian, tall and striking in his naval uniform. She had never seen him dressed this way before, for he generally wore civilian attire for his job at the Ministry of Marine. Her eyes widened at

162

his brilliant blue jacket edged with gold, his broad shoulders swinging with gold epaulettes. His long legs were encased in red breeches and he wore a smallsword at his hip.

Gérard was similarly attired. The two men tossed their hats to the maid and crossed the carpet, their faces wreathed in smiles.

'La! You two are in good spirits this morning,' Angé teased, turning up her cheek for her husband to kiss.

Catherine quivered as Christian smiled at her, bending over her hand. His lips touched her fingers fleetingly, but still sent a trail of sparks up her arm. She felt herself blush and pulled quickly away, hoping he would not notice.

'Papa! Papa!' Both children left their play by the fire and ran to their father, grabbing him about the knees and almost toppling him to the floor.

'Whoa there, *mes enfants*!' He gathered them into his arms with one swoop and allowed them to plant sticky kisses on his cheeks, one each side.

'Hélène, Alexandre!' their mother admonished. 'You are making your father's fine clothes a mess. Pray set them down, Gérard. You spoil them.'

He did as she asked, laughing. 'Indeed,

dearest, if 'tis I who spoils the children, what is it you do?'

He wrapped an arm around her to show he was just teasing. Catherine looked at them enviously, seeing the easy openness of their affection for each other and wondering whether she would ever know even a tiny portion of such happiness.

She turned away, uncomfortable by the direction of her thoughts, and encountered Christian's pensive regard. He raised his eyebrows in a question she understood only too well. Drat the man! How was he able to read her thoughts so easily.

'So tell us this news you are so full of!' Angé demanded. 'Must we be kept waiting?'

Christian spoke up. 'Angé, may I present to you your husband, *Capitaine de vaisseau* Gérard Fontenay.'

'Captain!' Angé squeaked. She threw her arms about his neck and hugged him fiercely. 'Oh, dearest, I knew it would not be long!'

Catherine added her congratulations and Christian went to the door to call Jeanne to bring champagne. Soon, four glasses were filled and they were toasting Gérard's promotion.

The sparkling wine at so early an hour went straight to Catherine's head. Either that or having Christian hovering over her in such good spirits was affecting her brain, she thought.

'So,' Gérard said to his wife, 'now Christian and I can command sister ships if he can arrange it.'

Catherine looked at him. 'Are you expecting to return to sea, Captain?'

Their eyes met for a moment and she thought she saw pain in them, but it was gone in an instant. 'Of course,' he replied. 'We are navy captains, both, now. As soon as we can complete the financing, we shall take to the seas.'

Angé, Catherine noticed, also looked less than pleased by this news.

'How soon?'

Her husband shrugged. 'With things as they are, we cannot say. It could be a month or a year. There is so little money in the exchequer and the *assignats* are becoming worthless. We're hoping to get a mission to India, but even the Mediterranean would suffice.'

Angé sighed. 'I am happy for you, dearest,' she said to her husband. 'But such voyages will take you away from us for so long — I think I would prefer you remained captain of your desk at the Department of Maps.'

Catherine gazed into her glass to watch the bubbles mysteriously appear and shimmy their way to the surface, only to pop and vanish. Life it seemed, was becoming almost as ephemeral.

She felt Christian's hand upon her arm and started, spilling some of the wine.

'You are jumpy today, my sweet,' he teased, taking a white handkerchief from his pocket and brushing the drops from her skirt. 'I am returning to the Hôtel de Charigny now, if you would like to accompany me. I must see my uncle before luncheon.'

Catherine nodded. 'Thank you. I am ready.'

They took their leave and let themselves out into the lemony sunshine. It was warmer, almost balmy for the time of year and they rode in silence with the groom some yards behind, each caught up in their own thoughts.

As they reached the quay that ran alongside the Seine, Christian finally spoke.

'I have given some thought to your request,' he said, watching the fishing boats on the river.

'Which request is that?' Catherine asked.

'You charged me with jealousy and with interference between yourself and my cousin, I believe.'

She flushed. 'I — That was inexcusable. Pray forget it.'

'On the contrary, there was some validity in your accusation. I have decided to make amends.'

Catherine glanced at him curiously. 'Oh?'

'You expressed a desire for further acquaintance with my cousin, so that you might get to know him better?' She nodded. 'I have arranged for you to attend a ball together.'

'A ball!'

He continued to gaze at the river as the horses plodded along and she was unable to gauge his expression.

Catherine frowned. 'But surely a ball is rather a . . . challenge to Dominic?'

'Perhaps,' he said, turning at last to look at her. 'But perhaps for you he will choose to dance.'

Her heart quickened. 'Can he?'

He frowned. 'If he has the will, I believe he can achieve most things.' Catherine searched his expression, but could read nothing in those blue eyes. Then he turned away, leaving her wondering if he had meant to tell her a great deal more about her betrothed than merely that he was capable of walking. Perhaps if he could walk, he would also be able to —

She shut the thought out of her head, concentrating instead on steering her mare around a group of barrow boys and on to the Pont Royal.

'Who is hosting this ball?' she asked, as they neared the far side.

He laughed shortly. 'That's a secret.'

'A secret? But why?'

'Is it important?'

'I'm sure your cousin would think so.'

Christian merely shrugged and would not be drawn further on the matter.

They rode the rest of the way without speaking.

★ ★ ★

Christian spared nothing in his efforts to create the perfect occasion. He was damned if either his cousin or his fiancée could find fault in either the preparation or execution of his plan. Catherine had said she was tired of gatherings where people spoke of nothing but politics. She was determined that she wanted a chance to get closer to Dominic, to show him that she cared for him — this last he found hard to swallow, but he did, if only because he had vowed to do his utmost. He had promised to give them their chance at a ball. A secret ball. And that is exactly what they would get.

It galled him, nonetheless, he had to admit.

Why a woman of Catherine O'Donnell's sensitivities should throw herself away on someone as unworthy as his cousin escaped him. In all other ways, she seemed so sensible, so well educated, and not at all given to the false simpering of so many court ladies. Dominic was indeed a fortunate man, if only he realized the jewel he was receiving.

But the less Christian thought about *that*, the better for his peace of mind.

The date was set for mid-April, and the weather was as kind as one could hope. The day had submitted to a spring shower that brought forth a burst of new buds on the roses, and then the clouds had floated away and the sun had warmed the earth until it was redolent with the promise of summer.

When evening came, there was but a light breeze, and the clouds remained blissfully at bay, allowing the stars and moon free rein in the sky.

None of this was noticed by the participants in this strange adventure. Catherine came downstairs dressed in a new gown of deep-rose silk shot with flashes of midnight blue, a delicate black lace fichu fastened about her bodice with an emerald brooch and her hair unadorned except for a matching pin. As arranged, she met Christian in the library to await Dominic, hoping that this

169

night would see him at last enter the room on his own two legs.

Christian, still dressed in his street attire of grey breeches and coat with a plain white silk shirt and black riding boots, stared at her as she entered the room. My God, but she was beautiful. Her eyes shone like diamonds in her face, and she moved with a grace that any queen would surely envy.

'Have you spoken with your cousin?' she asked instantly. 'Will he dispense with the services of Brassart and Emile tonight, do you think?' Without waiting for his reply, she babbled on. 'Oh, I do so hope so. You know, Christian, this is most chivalrous of you to arrange such an evening.' She touched his sleeve with her ebony fan. 'I know you do not approve of my buying a husband — especially Dominic — but I am so happy that at last you are reconciled to the notion. I am sure it will work out if only we can come to some understanding before the event. Marriage is so sacred, do you not think so?'

At that, she tilted her face up to him and Christian was obliged to stare down at her exuberant features.

'I am sure you are right, *mademoiselle*. But I am the wrong person to ask.'

'Oh, fiddlesticks,' she responded lightly. 'You are always so pompous. Can't you imagine what it must be like to face a lifetime with another person, to make vows of chastity and obedience to that person that you shall keep for all of your days upon this earth?'

He stared at her, wondering how she could have lived four and twenty years without having bruised the perfect confidence with which she viewed the world. He turned away with a sigh.

'My cousin is late,' was all the reply he gave.

He saw her glance at the clock that ticked sonorously on the mantel. 'A little. I am sure he will be here soon. So tell me, Christian, who is hosting this famously secretive ball, and why would you not tell us until now? I have been racking my brains all week to figure out who is holding a ball, but not even Angé could tell me.' She sent him a mischievous look. 'Did you swear her to silence, too? Why, I declare it was most unmanly of you to interfere between a woman and her dearest friend.'

Christian shrugged. 'You will find out soon enough, if my cousin ever gets his breeches on. Dammit, where is the man?'

He tugged on the bell pull and paced grumpily until a man appeared.

'Emile, where is the duke? Why has he not come down?'

'I shall enquire directly, *Monsieur le Capitaine*,' the man responded, bowing as he left the library.

Catherine drummed her fingers on the table while she waited. It seemed like an eternity. Christian was pacing up and down, his scowl growing deeper by the minute. Then, at last, the door opened.

Her heart sank when it revealed no one except Emile again.

'Where is my fiancé?' she demanded, none too gently.

'*Monsieur le Duc* offers his apologies, *mademoiselle*, but he will not be accompanying you tonight.'

Behind her, Christian let out an expletive worthy of a seaman, which caused Emile to look nervously at Catherine.

'Is that so?' she responded tartly. 'Then I shall speak to him.'

Undeterred by the objections from the library, she hurried up to his rooms, knocked peremptorily and entered, to find Dominic lounging by the fire in his dressing-gown.

'What is the matter, *monsieur*?' she said sharply, refusing to offer him the courtesy of his favoured 'Your Grace'.

He looked up from the glass of burgundy he had been admiring in the light of the fire.

'Good evening, Miss O'Donnell. You are

looking most . . . expensive tonight.'

She ignored this. 'Why are you not dressed? Christian is waiting downstairs to escort us to the ball.'

'Ah yes, our little secret rendezvous.' He smiled at the wine and took a deep drink from the glass, holding it out at arm's length for Brassart, who stood in the shadows, to refill. 'I shan't be joining you, I'm afraid. My health, you know.'

'Your health!' she scoffed, stepping up to stand before him. 'Your health is the excuse of your life, is it not, *monsieur*? There is not the slightest impediment to your joining me at this ball, and you know that as well as I. And you do not need your man here' — she indicated Brassart — 'to carry you about like a babe. All of Paris is quite aware that you can walk if you choose. The melodrama is wearing thin, don't you think?'

'What *I* think, *mademoiselle*,' he replied with a glitter in his eyes, 'is that you had best cease your fishwifing and be off before I lose my temper.'

Catherine knew she was past controlling her tongue, and it felt too good to stop. 'You may well think such a thing, sir, but you had best remember there is four million *livres* riding on your acceptance of me. Unless you fancy a life in the poorhouses of Paris.'

For a second there was total silence. She heard Brassart draw in a sharp breath of surprise, for it was indeed, a huge sum of money, and by the look on his face, the actual sum was a surprise to her fiancé as well. She chastised herself — she had not considered that the prince might withhold such information from his son.

'Four million?' Dominic said slowly after a long silence. 'I should, I suppose, be flattered that you should value me so highly. Indeed, few people in France could afford such a sum for the most desirable connection, even assuming they could tell which that was, these days.' He stretched out his legs to the blaze, slowly swirling the last of his second glass of wine before downing it at a single gulp. 'But it does not change a thing. I have not the slightest inclination to join you this evening and subject myself to chill air and the undoubted displeasure of a thousand insects fornicating upon my person.'

'Insects!' Catherine almost choked. 'What on earth are you talking about?'

'Did my inestimable cousin not inform you? Oh dear. Well, he told me, since I refused to have any part of his silly plan unless I was in possession of all the facts.'

'Told me what, Your Grace? You're not making this at all clear.'

He smiled at her and the skin on Catherine's neck prickled.

'The ball — the famous, secretive ball — is to be in our very own garden, *mademoiselle*. It was to be just you and I, a cosy *pas de deux*.' He laughed, but his voice took on an edge that made Catherine uncomfortable. 'My cousin, you see, is a mere *bourgeois*, and does not share my sensibilities. *He* sees nothing wrong with spending the evening eating *en plein air* like a peasant. He forgets that a mere chill could kill me — or perhaps, that is what he hopes?' He raised his brows suggestively. 'So, *je suis désolé*, but I have . . . other plans.'

Catherine was speechless, and then she pictured it. An intimate ball, so they could talk without the encumbrance of others, without eyes or censure. It was perfect. She felt a rush of warmth for Christian that he should have been so thoughtful. But when she looked at her fiancé and saw him slowly consuming his third glass of burgundy dressed in a loose robe and slippers, and caring nothing for his cousin's thoughtful gesture, she felt a surge of anger.

'Has there been a time in your life, Your Grace, since the unfortunate circumstance of your birth and childhood illness, that you

175

have ever spared a thought for any person besides yourself?'

He looked up, clearly startled by her harsh words. 'I do not think you are in any position to criticize me, *mademoiselle*. But there is something you clearly have not understood about this marriage of ours. Being man and wife does not imply any automatic right of intimacy. It requires merely obedience from you. From me . . . ? I shall do as I please.'

'Just as you have always done,' she retorted acidly. Without a backward glance, she turned to the door and let herself out.

She found Christian standing at the bottom of the stairs, his face a black mask that matched her own feelings perfectly.

'*Monsieur le Capitaine*,' she said, placing her hand firmly upon his arm. 'I believe we have a ball to attend.'

8

Christian looked down at Catherine, her cheeks aflame and her eyes sparking with anger.

'I gather my cousin was not to be persuaded?'

'I have no desire to discuss the matter,' she replied, looking straight ahead. 'Kindly lead the way.'

As she was directing him towards the back of the house, he could only assume that Dominic had told all.

'Are you sure you wish to dine alone?'

'I shall do no such thing.'

'Then . . . ?'

'You shall dine with me. Come along. We must not disappoint the chef.'

Christian sighed. This was quite contrary to his intentions. He had planned to leave the betrothed couple to their own company and seek some solitude in a tavern. Being alone with Catherine under the stars was far too dangerous for his peace of mind.

'I regret that is impossible. I am not dressed for — '

'Nonsense!' she replied her eyes daring him

to contradict her. 'You look perfectly fine to me.'

Dammit, the woman was becoming as impossible as Léonie was when she was bent on something. He led her across the terrace and onto the walkway, where the sound of their feet crunching in the gravel seemed loud in the quiet night. He must have some flaw in his character that allowed him to be so easily bullied by not one, but *two* women! No wonder he spent most of his life at sea. At least there he could be free of them.

He chuckled when he realized that he had not even been able to keep Léonie off his ship.

'You find this situation amusing, Captain?'

He started, his thoughts having taken him away from the present. 'Not at all, *mademoiselle*. I was merely recalling a woman a long time ago who was as adept at manoeuvring me as you.'

He caught a glimpse of something in her eyes but it was too dark to be sure. She turned away as they reached the end of the path. Christian pointed across the lawn to where soft light dappled the grass from lanterns hung in the branches of a sycamore tree.

'Over there.'

They followed the light, which led them

through a short woodland path to a small clearing, hung with a dozen more lanterns gently swinging in the soft breeze. To one side of the clearing, beneath the spreading arms of a giant oak, was a table set with exquisite white linens and bearing a candelabra lit with half a dozen candles.

On the opposite side of the clearing, far enough away to afford the diners privacy, sat a string quartet. Their music filled the woods with the delightful strains of Mozart.

Catherine stopped dead. 'Oh, Christian!' She turned to him and he saw tears in her eyes. 'Did you really do all this just because I asked you? Even though you are against my marriage to your cousin?'

He smiled, feeling a strange ache inside. 'Come, let us at least have some wine.'

He helped her to sit at the small table and then sat opposite. The table was set with solid gold cutlery, Sèvres dinnerware, and crystal glasses rimmed in gold.

They watched in silence as Antoine, one of the kitchen servers, slipped from the shadows and filled their glasses with sparkling champagne, melting away again like a wraith. If he was surprised to see Christian rather than his cousin, he gave no sign. Catherine held up her glass.

'*Santé*,' she said softly.

They touched glasses and she took a sip, closing her eyes in ecstasy. He watched as she leaned back, letting her head fall against the upholstered chair, and stared up at the sky. Her neck was milk-white in the candlelight, her lips soft and red and curved in a blissful smile that stirred his heart.

'Oh, Christian, there must be a million stars out tonight. Did you arrange that, too?'

He crushed the warmth that swept through him at her softly whispered words, determined not to feel anything for this entrancing woman. As much as he wanted to prevent her marrying his cousin, he did not want to do so at his own expense. She must never transfer her intentions to him. He could not marry, had not the slightest desire to do so, and knew that if he were to fall in love, he would end his days blaming his love for the loss of that which mattered most to him in all the world — his career in the navy. No man could love two mistresses.

She looked up at him. 'Something is wrong.'

He shrugged, lowering his eyes to his glass. 'No. I was merely thinking that it is unwise of us to meet this way.'

'It was not unwise for me and Dominic.'

'You are engaged to Dominic.'

'But he would not come and you have

taken his place — as you have done so many times already. I am most grateful.'

Their eyes met across the table and Christian found himself unable to look away. Awareness flared between them, trapping him in a silken web that caused an unmistakable surge in his loins. He closed his hands around his glass, for he was certain they were trembling.

'Will you — ' she said, suddenly hesitant. 'Will you dance with me?'

He nodded, for speech was beyond him, and helped her up, guiding her into the clearing. The quartet immediately began to play a minuet.

Their hands touched, burned. She looked as stunned as he, though her dark eyes never left his face as the dance began. Slowly they turned, like moths circling a flame they knew would scorch, their eyes seeking one another out as they came once more face to face.

Catherine felt Christian's gaze, bright with sparks of fire from the lanterns, burn into her, searing her with its intensity. Each time they met in the dance and touched, her skin ignited beneath his. She couldn't stop looking at him. When she laid her hand on his arm she could feel the corded muscle beneath the cloth, feel the tension and hear his breathing, as laboured as her own. And then it would begin again. Turn, touch, lock eyes. It was as though they were the ones standing still, lost in each other's gaze, while the lanterns turned about them like a carousel dancing in time to the music.

She felt a pain somewhere near her heart, an ache of longing for this taciturn sea captain with his unexpected romantic side. If only life had been kinder. If only . . .

She sighed. There was no place for 'if onlys'. Whatever she felt for Christian Lavelle, it must remain locked away in her heart. For she must give herself to his prickly cousin, as promised.

The minuet ended and they returned to their table where Antoine was uncovering an array of mouth-watering dishes. Catherine laughed with delight at the delectable smells, for the open air had given her an appetite.

'What is this?' she asked Christian, pointing to a dish of something in a rich brown sauce. The aroma was heavenly.

'Truffles and wild mushrooms. They are one of Monsieur César's masterpieces. He will be mortally offended if we do not clean the platter.'

Catherine laughed. 'I have heard he is capable of crying if his diners fail to appreciate his art.'

They tasted from each of the six or seven

elegant dishes from the first service, then danced some more. When they returned to the table, Antoine presented a huge covered platter, lifting the silver cover with a flourish.

Beneath lay the largest lobster Catherine had ever seen, garnished with more truffles and an aromatic sauce.

'*Homard à la César, mademoiselle,*' he said as he set it before them. As if that wasn't enough, he brought further dishes of venison and rabbit, including a real treat — spring peas drizzled with golden melting butter.

'I'm not used to such sumptuous meals,' Catherine confided to Christian as they attempted to do justice to the dishes. 'Surely there must be vast amounts of food wasted?'

'The servants eat well.'

They laughed. Catherine gazed at him as she sampled a morsel of lobster, thinking how comfortable she felt in his presence.

'This is heavenly,' she murmured as she slowly savoured the shellfish. 'Christian, you must try some.' He was tackling a rack of venison, and shook his head, but she would brook no argument. She expertly eased a succulent morsel from its casing, dipped it in sauce and held it out to him across the table. 'Open your mouth, Captain!'

He laughed, but did as she bid, wrapping his lips around the fork.

'*Voilà*, was that not divine?'

He smiled at her across the table, while he obediently consumed the *soupçon*. 'Exquisite,' he replied when he was finished, and Catherine had the strangest feeling he meant something other than the fish. She blushed and looked away quickly.

'I do not think I can eat another mouthful,' she said, pushing her plate away.

'You have a healthy appetite for a lady.'

'I'm not accustomed to eating *en plein air*. It stimulates the palate.'

He was gazing at her again, his eyes almost black in the candlelight. 'So it does,' he replied.

'Perhaps a walk might make room for some of Monsieur César's dessert offerings?'

He stared at her with foreboding. 'What game are you playing, Catherine?'

He noticed her bottom lip quiver before she snatched up her glass and took a sip of wine.

'What can you mean? There is no game. We are simply keeping each other company, are we not, in a most pleasant manner?'

He gave her a warning glance but made no more response as he helped her from her seat. 'We can take the path here. It leads to the pond.'

'Pond! Why this garden is so immense, I

have not even discovered a pond during my walks.'

'Every self-respecting garden must have its little surprises, my sweet. This one is a little folly, complete with a whispering fountain of Cupid.'

He led her through the trees, beyond the range of the lanterns so that their path became increasingly dark, for little moonlight penetrated the canopy.

Halfway along, he stopped.

'You are shivering, Catherine.' He took off his frock coat and wrapped it around her, feeling a disturbing ache in his loins as she snuggled deep into its warm folds. That sensation was becoming all too familiar these days, at least when he was around Catherine. Her eyes shone up at him in the gloom, and although his own heart was pounding loudly in his chest, he was certain hers was, too. Perhaps it was the wine; perhaps it was the nightingale that began suddenly to trill from the treetops. Whatever the reason, Captain Christian Lavelle, for the first time in his life, found himself willingly doing something that was totally against his better judgment.

He took Catherine in his arms and kissed her. It was no ordinary kiss, no gentle test of feeling. He crushed her to him, wrapping his arms around her as though his life depended upon it, until her breasts pressed into his thin shirt, the chilled nipples scalding his skin.

'Oh God, Catherine,' he moaned into her mouth. 'How I have wanted this.' He kissed her deeply, as though starved for a taste of her. 'I have thought of little else since the last time . . . '

Catherine squeezed her eyes shut, pressing her body against his as she opened her mouth to the plunder of his tongue. His warmth seared her breasts, her belly, her legs where they touched his through the meaningless barriers of silk and velvet. There was no room for thought. No thought of stopping. She groaned as a sweet burning ache began deep inside, flooding her veins with languid warmth. Were he not holding her so tightly that she could scarcely breathe, she would surely collapse upon the ground at his feet.

His mouth roamed over hers, seeking her tongue, dancing with it, teasing the corners of her mouth. She answered him, tentatively at first and then with mounting passion that made her head spin with longing.

Slowly she became aware of something pressing against her. As her mind began to focus on the evidence of his need, reality returned, bringing with it fear long buried. She opened her eyes. Dark trees surrounded them, steel-strong arms surrounded her.

Arms that were strong, so strong —

Gasping, she pushed against him with all her might, shoving herself clear of him.

'No!' she cried, raising one hand to her mouth. Her breath was coming in short hard gasps. 'You must not, do you hear? You must never . . . '

With a cry, she turned from him, flinging off his coat as she grabbed her skirts in both hands and ran for the house.

Christian watched her go, cursing himself, cursing her, waiting until her sobs faded into the night. Then he bent to retrieve his jacket. He had frightened her, taken advantage of her vulnerability. He knew himself for a cur, but though he despised himself for his uncharacteristic lack of control, he could not be sorry for the kisses he had stolen. She had wanted them as much as he. Yet she was determined to give herself body and soul to one who was worse than he.

He sighed, slinging his frock coat over his shoulder. 'He will never love you, Catherine,' he murmured as he started back along the path.

Not as I will.

★ ★ ★

Sleep entirely eluded Catherine that night. She lay on her feather mattress staring up at the ruffles that hung from the canopy of the bed while the moonbeams on the wall turned into pale shafts of sunrise.

She blamed herself, for in truth no other person was in any way at fault. Not Dominic, for he was guilty only of disdain. Not Christian, for he had made no secret of his desire to subvert her marriage.

No, if Catherine de Lacy O'Donnell had been stupid enough to lose her heart to the cousin of the man to whom she was betrothed, it was she and she alone who had allowed it to happen.

She sighed, turning on her side to stroke the fur of Dominic's little dog, Bijou, who lay snuggled against her hip. Dominic may not care for her, but his dog did. Bijou had transferred his affections almost exclusively to her since the second day she had lived in this house.

His small brown eyes opened sleepily as she petted him, and he stuck out his tiny pink tongue and licked the back of her hand.

'What am I to do, Bijou?' she murmured. 'Your master does not love me. Christian wants me, at least for now, but only because he is jealous of his cousin. My father and the prince are depending upon me. And

Mama . . . ' Tears began to well slowly in her eyes, and as tired as she was she could not stem their flow.

The dog whimpered as a tear fell on him. He reached up and licked her cheek, and she hugged him like a child's toy, clutching him against her as she gave herself up to her misery.

Finally, when morning came, she slept, deeply and without dreams. When she finally awoke it was past noon and Bijou was gone, no doubt taken off for his morning romp in the gardens with one of the maids.

Catherine summoned Martha and indulged herself in a leisurely perfumed bath. She dressed in a simple gown of sprigged muslin with a wide blue sash, and while Martha was brushing out her hair, she looked at her in the mirror of the *poudreuse*.

'Martha, are you happy here?'

The maid paused, brush in hand while she considered this. 'I'm not sure, Miss Kitty. 'Tis not so bad, but I do miss Philadelphia, to be sure.' She resumed brushing and then stopped again, her head on one side as she studied her mistress in the mirror. 'Now, why would you be asking a question like that, miss?'

Catherine shrugged. 'I don't know, Martha.

It's not quite what I expected.'

'Well now, and isn't it exactly what you always said you wanted? Was it not yourself who was always bellyaching about how there had to be more to life than marrying the likes of Liam Rafferty?'

'Liam is a good man.'

Martha's mouth dropped open. 'Did you ever hear the like? Miss Kitty, there's none better, I'm sure. But you said yourself you'd as soon marry your own brother — if you'd had one. If I remember aright, he wasn't slow to ask you.'

'No, he wasn't. But nor was he what my mother wanted for me.' She sighed. 'Perhaps you're right — absence makes the heart grow fonder, as they say.'

Martha smacked the brush down on the dressing-table, coming around so she could face her mistress directly. 'Now, Miss Kitty, are you trying to tell me that you've changed your mind after all and you'll want to be sailing back across that accursed ocean to wed young Mr Rafferty after all?'

'No, of course not.' Catherine knew her answer was too quick and that Martha noticed. She caught the gleam in the woman's eyes. 'It's probably just the jitters. There's still lots of time for me to get used to Dominic.'

'Humph! A fine marriage that will be, if

you ask me! I don't mean to be above m'self, miss, but if you ask me that man's downright — '

'I don't ask you, Martha,' Catherine said severely before she could finish. 'This betrothal has been difficult for him and he hasn't had time to get used to it yet. I'm sure he will be perfectly reconciled to the notion when the time comes.'

Martha pursed her lips disapprovingly, but picked up the silver hairbrush and continued Catherine's toilette. 'Miss Kitty, you always were one to see the very best in folk, but I wonder if there's enough good in the duke for even you to find.'

'Of course there is, Martha,' Catherine replied with more determination than she felt. As she stared into the mirror at her own reflection, however, she wondered if perhaps there was only one course of action open to her.

A woman was born to her duty, after all.

★   ★   ★

Easter came and went, late that year in accordance with the vernal equinox. Catherine attended mass in the small chapel in the Hôtel de Charigny, in the company of the prince and duke — and Nounou, who seemed at last to have forgiven God for His recall of Mirabeau to the hereafter. Martha and Emile — with whom she appeared to be spending a great deal of time — were also present, along with a few other servants who were not at home with their families. The prince considered Easter the holiest of days on the calendar, to be a day of rest for all who could be spared, and those who had loved ones elsewhere in Paris had gladly taken advantage of their liberty.

The mass calmed Catherine, easing her troubled mind and helping her to face her future with courage. She did not look at her betrothed, but felt his eyes on her from time to time. Since the night of the 'ball' they had not spoken except at occasional meals when the prince was also present, nor had Catherine set eyes upon Christian, whose naval duties apparently kept him busier than ever.

It was a tempestuous month. On April 13 the pope had issued a bull condemning the civil constitution imposed on the clergy, and on April 18, the king and his family had attempted to travel to their palace at Saint-Cloud for Easter. The Paris mob took great exception to such action, since it seemed that the purpose of the journey was to celebrate mass with a non-juring priest.

Worse, the National Guard supported the mob against General Lafayette, refusing to obey his orders to arm themselves and protect the king.

Lafayette was publicly humiliated, jeered and whistled at, and utterly powerless to prevent the insults that were hurled at both the king and queen who sat impotently in their carriage amidst the mob.

The royal family gave up, returning to the Tuileries on foot. Lafayette, overwhelmed by his own impotence, resigned.

But resignation did not ease his troubles, as Catherine found out when the great soldier himself appeared at the Hôtel de Charigny soon after.

'I cannot remain at home,' he told them at dinner that evening. 'My house is constantly under siege and everyone in the street is kept awake by the drums and marching that goes on outside.'

'But why, pray?' Catherine asked in alarm. 'They can scarcely blame you for the actions of the monarch.'

'Indeed no, *mademoiselle*. They are begging that I resume my post. But what purpose could possibly be served? The king refuses to exercise his constitutional rights. He fears confrontation with the mob, but he has only to confront the Assembly and they would yield the point. No, if my sovereign will not stand against the factions, what role is there for me?'

He lapsed into a depressed silence and the meal continued with discussion limited to happier subjects and reminiscences of his time in America and his dear friend, George Washington.

A couple of days later, Catherine was able to report to Nounou — an avid follower of such goings-on in Paris — that he had relented and withdrawn his resignation. The National Guard, for its part, promised to punish those among its ranks who had so 'outraged the royal family'.

'I scarcely know how the poor man survived the fuss,' Catherine told the old woman as they sat on the terrace sipping tea. 'For when he returned to his offices, he was besieged by a huge crowd throwing flowers. He was forced to kiss a vast number of ladies, and even hundreds of national guardsmen, before they would allow him to pass!'

And so Lafayette's honour was restored. Paris breathed a little easier, and Catherine, too, for her nuptials were fast approaching and she did not want anything to mar them.

9

Catherine had not yet confronted her betrothed with the idea of holding a second ceremony to ensure their union was both official and blessed in God's eyes. In fact, she had delayed for fear of his reaction. Lafayette had heralded the idea, seeing it as quite fitting and proper, and armed with such support, she decided to approach Dominic.

It was early afternoon, a time, she had discovered, when the duke was generally at his best. In her efforts to create a greater rapport with him, she had taken to visiting him briefly each afternoon, to share the day's news or merely to enquire after his health. She would not be presumptuous enough to state that this had made them friends, but at least he seemed to tolerate her presence with equanimity, showing less inclination to mock her common origins.

So it was that on a sunny but still cool May afternoon, when Catherine returned from an invigorating walk in the gardens with Nounou, she took herself upstairs to his rooms to tackle the matter.

As was her custom, she knocked on the

door of his salon and entered, smiling at the valet who held the door for her.

'*Bonjour*, Brassart. Is *Monsieur le Duc* well today?'

Brassart inclined his head. 'Indeed he is, *mademoiselle*. He has been expecting you.'

Well that was progress, Catherine thought, pleased that her visits were making some impression.

Brassart announced her, and it was then Catherine perceived that she was not Dominic's only visitor. A tall gentleman of perhaps fifty stood by the hearth, one arm nonchalantly resting on the mantel. He relinquished his position and came forward to make a leg as she approached. Catherine frowned, racking her brains in an effort to place the man, for she was certain she had encountered him somewhere before, and she seldom forgot a face. Recall eluded her, yet the feeling persisted.

She allowed him to raise her hand to his lips, though his skin felt cold and slightly clammy like the lizards she had enjoyed catching in the woodpile when she was a child. She jumped when his tongue suddenly darted from his thin lips, licking her knuckles in a most abhorrent fashion.

'Sir!' she said, before she could stop herself. He merely smiled, with hooded eyes

196

that made Catherine's skin crawl. Suddenly, she recalled where she had seen this man: the Comtesse de Bernier's soirée.

She glanced quickly at her fiancé who was watching with a face absolutely devoid of expression. He waved a hand in the man's general direction.

'Mademoiselle O'Donnell, may I present Signor Gian-Paulo Cesare Boselli de Foscari. Foscari, my fiancée.'

Catherine stared at the tall Italian in his black clothes while she rubbed her hand surreptitiously on the back of her skirt.

'*Delizia, signorina,*' said Foscari, smiling lazily at her. 'I have heard so much about you from my very dear friend, here, that I am quite delighted to make your acquaintance at last.'

Catherine had not the slightest idea why Signor Foscari would be so pleased to meet her, but he certainly seemed to be. Then, to her acute embarrassment, he began to inspect her from head to toe, walking slowly around her as he did so. She jumped as she felt his fingers caress a lock of her hair where it lay upon her shoulder, and turned sharply, staring at him.

His smile broadened ever so slightly. Catherine glanced wide-eyed at Dominic, for something was not right here. She did not know what game he was playing, but it made her excessively discomfited. Her fiancé was gazing at all this with the same blankness of visage he had exhibited before, and Catherine's alarm increased. She looked about her for Brassart, but he had disappeared, leaving her alone with the two men.

'You are frightened of me, *signorina*.' It was a statement, not a question, but Catherine raised her chin defiantly.

'Indeed, I am sure I should have no cause to be, sir.'

'No, indeed you should not,' he replied, coming full circle until he faced her once more. 'You are very . . . alluring, my dear. No doubt you Americans live a more wholesome life than we poor Europeans. Your skin' — he reached out and stroked one bony finger across her cheek — 'is quite flawless. Remarkable.'

Catherine felt the blood freeze in her veins. She saw what he was doing, knew her only course of action was to turn and run from the room, yet her limbs had turned to ice. A plea formed in her mind — 'Dominic, help me!' — yet her lips refused to form the words. She stood, paralysed with fright as Foscari moved his hand to her shoulder and began slowly stroking down over the filmy muslin of her sleeve until he reached her bosom. She choked back a gasp of terror as the ball of his thumb came to rest on her breast and began stroking, ever so softly across her nipple.

Suddenly the door opened and Christian stormed into the room. Catherine sobbed with relief and crumpled to the floor, clutching her arms across her chest.

'Take your filthy hands off her, you damned cur!' Christian roared, pushing the man backwards with a punch to the chest that almost sent him sprawling. 'Dear God, I have a mind to take you out to the stables and run my sword through your black heart, but that would be too quick, too humane for the likes of you!

'And as for you,' he went on, turning on his cousin, who sat looking decidedly uneasy at last, 'you are no better than this *espèce de cochon*. Catherine is your fiancée, the woman who is soon to be your wife, yet you invite this — this scum into your house and let him paw her like the animal he is. When will you grow up and start being a man, Dominic?'

Catherine's sobs subsided, replaced by shock in the face of Christian's fury. The duke, at least, appeared embarrassed. For his part, Foscari remained clearly unmoved.

'You overstep yourself, Lavelle,' he interjected smoothly, 'if you think to intimidate me. I have been vilified by the best of men, but true art is not cowed by such vitriol.'

'Art!' Christian almost spat the word. 'You are no artist, Foscari. Just a twisted madman who puts his vile fetishes down on canvas and blackmails people with them.'

Catherine struggled to rise, but her knees felt like jelly. She smiled tearfully at Christian as he bent to help her.

'Are you all right, Catherine? If he hurt you, I will kill the man, no matter the consequences.'

She smiled at such gallantry. 'There is no need. I am perfectly fine, thank you, Captain.'

The Italian laughed mirthlessly.

Christian turned to him again. 'I give you one warning and one alone, Foscari: if you ever lay a finger on Miss O'Donnell again, I will kill you. Of that, you may rest assured.'

Without another word, he led her from the room.

There was a moment's silence after this departure. Dominic stared at the Italian, curious that he should take the threat so lightly.

'Don't tangle with him, Foscari. He is hot-headed and he's fought off many a pirate. Even were I able bodied, I should not like to raise his ire to that degree.'

'Ah,' replied the Italian, extracting a pinch of snuff from a silver box and inhaling it sharply. 'But then you are not me, *mi caro* Dominic.' He replaced the snuff box and drew a lace handkerchief from his pocket, waiting while the snuff did its job and then sneezing into it with great relish. He tucked the kerchief away.

'I must say I am quite taken with your little *borghese*. She suits my tastes rather well. But then, you have always known that my tastes were somewhat eclectic.'

Dominic's eyes narrowed. He knew Foscari was up to something, and he mistrusted the look in his eye.

'Yes,' the older man went on. 'I think I would like to have some sport with the young lady. Perhaps paint her likeness.'

'No!' Dominic almost surprised himself by the vehemence of his response. Perhaps he was beginning to care for Catherine after all. Or perhaps it was just the thought of her in Foscari's clutches.

'Ah, *mi amico*, I am sure you will change your mind. After all, we both have our little *segreti*. The difference is — ' he paused, casting Dominic a significant glance, 'I know your secrets from your own lips, whereas mine you know only by reputation.'

Dominic squirmed in his chair. 'What are you saying?'

'*Solamente* that if it were to one's

201

advantage to keep such a secret and not let it come to the notice of one's family — or one's rich little wife-to-be — then one might consider that worthy of some *favor speciale.*'

'What favour?'

Foscari smiled. 'Aha! I see we are already reaching agreement on this matter.'

'What favour?' Dominic reiterated, tired of dancing around whatever Foscari was hinting at.

He leaned over Dominic, so close that he could smell wine on his breath and see the gleam in his eyes. 'I want your wife, *signor.*'

He straightened, strolling slowly about the room, touching this and that with a laconic finger as he went. 'For a mere night or two, perhaps longer if her body proves as alluring to my brushes as to my other . . . senses. I am not greedy. And, given the presence of your irritating cousin, neither shall I be hasty. Sea captains, after all, do go to sea, no?' He stopped walking and turned to send Dominic a satisfied smile. 'I can wait.'

★   ★   ★

Catherine made her excuses to Christian and shut herself in her room, for she had no wish to listen to his tirade against Signor Foscari and how she must stay clear of the man. She

202

needed no encouragement on that score!

What did trouble her was that it was Christian Lavelle who should have come to her aid, while the man she was destined to marry had sat idly watching as the monster soiled her with his hands . . .

She shuddered folding her arms across her chest at the mere thought of those snake-like fingers touching her breasts. The very memory made her sick to her stomach. She drew a deep breath, forcing herself to be calm, to think sensibly. To cope.

When she felt a little better, she crossed to the window seat and sat looking out at the sunny spring garden, thinking how different it was from her father's garden back home in Philadelphia, and yet struck by the similarities. She watched as a pair of energetic swallows soared high in the sparkling sky, their beaks stuffed with twigs, and then folded their wings and swooped down in suicidal flight to disappear unerringly into their nest under the coping of the high garden wall.

She watched them coming and going, then turned her gaze across the huge garden, much of which was obscured by the foliage of the chestnut trees that grew as high as the house. Suddenly she felt claustrophobic.

She got up from her seat and searched out

her light woollen shawl, for the wind bore an edge despite the sunshine. She wrapped the shawl around her shoulders and left the room.

Just below the wide stone terrace that ran the entire length of the rear of the house, Catherine found a small stone bench, tucked out of the way of the wind and surrounded by a veritable wall of jasmine, now in full bloom. She settled herself in this little hideaway and leaned her head back, closing her eyes as the sun caressed her face. The scent of the flowers teased her nostrils like the most exquisite perfume and with her eyes closed she became aware of a thousand other scents and sounds around her — the high-pitched keening of the busy swallows, the gentle trickle of water from the formal stone fountain below the terrace.

She opened her eyes suddenly as she heard footsteps crunching on the gravel. Alarm skittered through her. She knew it was not Christian, for he had left the house when she shut herself in her room. And the prince was not at home today, having left on urgent business before breakfast.

She squinted, lifting a hand to shade her eyes from the sun. A man was approaching, and for one dreadful moment she thought it was Signor Foscari. But then she perceived that this person was shorter, broader and walked slowly with the aid of a stick.

She gasped.

'Dominic!'

It was indeed the duke. Catherine had never seen him so much as stand, so she was surprised to discover that he was much shorter than his cousin. But to see him walking — unaided — that was truly astonishing!

She ran to him, offering her arm. 'Your Grace!' was all she could say.

He stopped, breathing hard. 'You see, Miss O'Donnell, I am not as helpless as you thought.'

She felt her eyes fill with tears but blinked them back. 'Come, you will tire yourself. Let me help you to the bench.'

'*Tiens*! I am like a babe,' he grumbled, but allowed her to lead him, nonetheless. She settled him on the stone seat, debating whether to wrap her shawl about him, but deciding that might appear too forward.

He took a moment to catch his breath, then looked up at her, where she stood staring at him in astonishment. For once he was not dressed like a courtier, for he wore simple grey breeches and white hose with a jacket of dark green and no jewellery that she could perceive, except the large diamond ring he favoured on his right hand. Perhaps one day he might be persuaded to give up his powdered wig?

'So, I trust you are satisfied?' he said. 'Your reprimand was not without result, after all.'

'So I see. And I am truly delighted, sir. I am sure the fresh air and the exercise will do you only good.'

He made no reply beyond a slight harrumph beneath his breath. He gazed about him, feigning interest in the flowering jasmine. He tugged at the glossy foliage, then snapped off a twig and twirled it between his fingers. Catherine could see he wanted to say something, but she dared not hurry him. Finally, he looked up.

'Sit, Catherine. I have something to say to you.'

She perched herself on the other end of the bench, wondering at his sudden use of her name.

'If it is about Signor Fos — '

'It isn't, damn the man.' He glanced at her, then back to the twig he was worrying in his fingers. 'I — I . . . ' His voice trailed off and he threw the twig to the pebbled path with a frown. 'My cousin was right to say what he did. Foscari is a parasite. He likes to paint portraits of people engaged in . . . various acts. Sometimes he changes the faces to match those of famous individuals who might pay him handsomely not to display his works.' Catherine shuddered. 'But he will not bother you again, I am certain.' He glanced up, then uncharacteristically reached out and patted her hands where they lay tightly clasped in her lap. 'Christian is not the only one who can make threats, you know.'

Catherine gave him a wobbly smile. 'Thank you.'

Dominic sighed. 'You have nothing to thank me for, Catherine. I have done you no favour, agreeing to this travesty of a marriage. It is perfectly apparent to me that we are unsuited.' He gave a self-deprecating laugh. 'It would have been no small miracle if we had been otherwise, *n'est-ce-pas?* How my father ever thought to find a woman who could stand life with one such as myself — '

'Your Grace! Pray do not continue! There is nothing the matter with you except what you have created in your own mind.'

He laughed again, a short bark but with a hint of amusement at last. 'Indeed, *mamselle*, and what is that? A worthless invalid without even his own fortune to attract the bees to the honey pot? No, if I had been worthy of marriage my father would have found me a match right here in France a decade ago.'

Catherine did not know quite how to

respond to this, for the same thought had crossed her mind. 'You are not so old.'

'I'm thirty-five. Most men my age have sired a dozen brats by now.'

She flushed, but continued in his defence as bravely as she was able. 'I am sure you will ... father some of your own, sir. I have always greatly desired children, myself.'

She felt him study her averted face for a moment, and wished he would say what he had come to say and leave, for she was becoming acutely uncomfortable with this conversation.

She jumped as his hand closed over hers. 'You have such simple faith, Catherine. I wish life could be so straightforward.' He released her, leaning back against the bench and staring up at the swallows high above in the vast blue sky. 'But life is not so kind to us. It throws us chances and snatches them away before we realize what we have in our hands.'

'I don't believe I quite take your meaning, Your Grace.'

'I am letting you go, Catherine de Lacy O'Donnell. I am releasing you from your promise.'

Catherine's mouth dropped open. 'Our betrothal? You mean — Y-you do not wish to marry me?'

He stared up, watching the graceful birds

plummet again to their nest. 'What I wish? All my life I have had what I wish, is that not what you forcefully advised me? This afternoon, I believe Signor Foscari demonstrated the nature of one who is accustomed to always getting what he desires. I did not find it pretty.'

Nor did I, Catherine thought dryly. 'Then why, pray, did you not speak to him? Surely a word from you would have stopped — '

'Perhaps. But my cousin's opportune arrival made it unnecessary, I'm sure you'll agree.'

She fell silent, staring at Dominic as he sat on the bench, his eyes now closed against the sun as though he were basking without a care in the world. She didn't know what to make of it — or of him. She contemplated his offer and all that it would mean. Financial ruin for his family, surely, for hadn't that been the whole point of the betrothal, as far as the prince was concerned? Apart from creating an heir, of course.

She glanced at Dominic's inert form, wondering what it would be like to have him in her bed. The notion made her uneasy.

If she were to agree to this, there would be other things to face. She would have to return to Philadelphia, of course, alone and unmarried, as she had left.

Her father would be the laughing stock of the city, and she would be confirmed as an old maid who, for all her father's great wealth, couldn't even buy herself a husband! 'Twas not a pretty notion.

And what of Dominic himself? Would he continue as he was, living an idle and self-serving life — and a solitary one, for she had sensed his loneliness from the very first.

'I — ' she began uncertainly.

His eyes opened. 'I do not want your answer now. Tomorrow will be time enough. Or Sunday. It is of no importance.'

No importance? Catherine was speechless as she watched him get up from the bench and make his way stiffly back to the house, leaning on his cane but refusing her help. He disappeared through the French doors that led into the library.

Her thoughts were in a turmoil. Indeed, she scarcely knew how to begin to consider his offer. She paced up and down in front of the bench, her mind awhirl with all of it. Finally, she tugged her shawl tighter around her shoulders and hurried down the path past the fountain. The gravel was sharp under her satin slippers, but she was in no mood to care whether they would be ruined.

Once she reached the path that led through the trees, she began to feel calmer. She slowed her progress and looked about her as she walked, marvelling at the seemingly natural wood that had been so artfully created in the huge confines of a walled garden. She came to the clearing where she and Christian had dined and danced, and stopped, inhaling the rich aroma of fertile earth and new spring growth. Even now, it seemed a magical place, a place where on a quiet summer's night fairies would gather to dance and play. She laughed at such childish fancy and carried on, crossing the green sun-filled space and taking another little path that led deeper into the garden.

She stopped, recognizing the place where they had paused in the darkness and Christian had kissed her. That earth-shattering kiss, devastating to her senses, seemed to have happened but a minute ago. She pressed trembling fingers to her lips as the sweet memory brought tears to her eyes. She had panicked. The dark, she told herself. And the trees. The feeling of being out of control . . .

She looked up, gazing at the leafy canopy above her that had been so complete that night as to entirely block out the moon. Now it glowed incandescent green as the sun tried to reach the ground through the new-born leaves. She felt no fear of the place in daylight. In fact, it was beautiful.

To her right, a red squirrel scuttled in the undergrowth, making her jump. She walked on, and the little creature leapt to the trunk of a sturdy plane tree and scampered up to safety.

Soon, she began to hear the trickle of water and in no time at all found herself in a tiny glade, right in the corner of the garden. Water tumbled from what appeared to be a natural crevice in the ivy-clad walls that formed the far corner of the garden, trickling over mossy rocks this way and that until it fell at last into a natural-looking pool surrounded by tall reeds. Water lilies grew on the surface of the water, providing shelter to the myriad goldfish that flourished there.

Catherine thought back to that night and wondered what might have happened had she and Christian reached this idyllic place. That they would have kissed again, she had no doubt. But might not surroundings like this have created greater yearnings? Yearnings that might have led to something a great deal harder to forget, although Catherine knew she would never, if she lived to be a hundred, forget the feeling of his arms around her, or the way his lips had played upon her skin like the murmur of an enchanted breeze.

She felt herself grow warm at the memory,

felt a strange tumescence at the thought of what might have happened, and brought herself up sharply. She sat down upon a natural ledge at the pool's edge. It was just as well. She did not need the complication of Captain Lavelle's advances when she had Dominic's offer to consider.

She knew in her heart that if Christian were to appear right now, tell her he loved her and beg her to marry him instead of Dominic, that she would say yes. But that was a joke in the poorest of taste. She knew he despised her. Oh, she was not so much the fool that she didn't see he was attracted to her physically. But she was not that kind of woman. She had no interest in a short romance with a sea captain who likely did this sort of thing in every exotic land he visited.

No, Christian Lavelle had made his feelings quite plain. He didn't like Catherine, not for her wealth or her seeking of a title, nor for the fact that she had allowed herself to be betrothed to a man she'd never met.

She tossed a pebble into the pool, watching as the ripples swirled outwards, jogging the waterlilies. She had a choice now, a choice they'd thought already made and sealed. Why was it that everybody was doubting her resolve? At least her father had no such qualms. She had received a letter from him only yesterday, saying how happy he was that she had arrived safely and was soon to be wed. It was his heart's desire, and she knew he would be proud.

But the prince had asked her. Christian had demanded it, time and time again. And now, even Dominic was opening the door.

Did they think she would be unable to cope? Did they see something in her that she herself could not? Was there a weakness, perhaps, that made them believe she would be unable to handle herself as a duchess, even a 'pretend' duchess? Dominic had assured her that soon this revolutionary nonsense would be over and France would return to its familiar monarchy, so the cachet of '*ci-devant*' would no longer exist. After all, this was not America, oppressed by the rules of a government far away across the ocean. This was France with France's own Bourbon king.

She sighed. She may not be politically inclined, but she felt certain that even if the king were to regain control of France, things would never be quite the same again. And how would she, as an American duchess, fit into that scheme of things?

Perhaps they were right; perhaps it was folly to believe that she could become Dominic's wife; perhaps the sins of the past could never be rectified.

She stood up, staring at the little spring pretending to come out of the wall. The perfect little *trompe l'oeuil*, a trick of garden design to make a pipe full of water appear to be a natural wellspring bubbling forth from among the rocks. She only had one short life to lead — her mother had taught her that, both by her words and through her premature death. A marriage that appeared to be all that it should would surely be as convincing as the little pond. If she were to create the dream, would reality follow?

She brushed bits of moss from her skirt, feeling a little better, and turned back towards the path.

In her heart, she felt certain that with time, Dominic would become more responsive. With careful management on her part, and exercise, his health would surely improve. And who could say? Perhaps one day he might even learn to love.

★　★　★

She returned to her room. Martha was still out, having been given her freedom by her mistress to spend the day with Emile, so Catherine sat down at her inlaid walnut escritoire, took pen and paper and began a note.

Your Grace

While deeply sensible of the honour you intend in permitting me to reconsider my obligations, I find I have no desire to withdraw from our betrothal. Given the differences in our stations, I am, however, prepared to concede that it is you, sir, who may feel most constricted by our arrangement.

Pray be assured that should this be the case, I shall not stand in the way of a discreet withdrawal.

I remain

Your fiancée
Catherine de Lacy O'Donnell

10

Dominic did not reply. Catherine waited through an anxious evening, but he did not appear at supper, nor did he send word. She went out to a dull evening at the home of the American Ambassador, where talk was incessant concerning comparisons between the American and French experiences of revolution. Even Lafayette seemed bored. She persuaded the prince to take her home early on the pretext of a headache, and returned to her room out of sorts to find Martha waiting with a cup of chocolate and a strange expression on her face.

'Why are you looking at me like that, Martha?' Catherine asked wearily as she allowed the maid to help her out of her things. She tugged irritably at the pins restricting her hair, causing several to fly across the polished floor and skitter away under the bed.

The Irishwoman indicated the corner of the room with a tilt of her head.

Catherine raised her brows. Atop the small escritoire stood a heavy Sèvres vase filled with deep red roses.

Catherine frowned, crossing the room to take the card nestled within the fragrant blooms. She held it to the candlelight to read the words:

Miss O'Donnell.

Your offer is refused. We shall wed on June 21st and may God help you.

Catherine read it twice, then set it down. She could feel Martha's curiosity burning a hole in her back.

'He will marry me after all,' she said by way of explanation. 'We don't have to return to Philadelphia with our tails between our legs.'

'Miss?' Martha stared at her mistress, confused.

Catherine returned to the *poudreuse* and allowed her maid to begin unpinning her hair properly. 'You did not know that the duke offered to release me from my vow. I refused. Then I offered and now he too has refused.'

'Refused? Miss Kitty, you're not talking with the sense God gave a lamb. What are you saying?'

'Simply that I am to be Dominic's wife after all.' Catherine wondered why the news gave her no sense of relief. No feeling of any sort. Perhaps she was just tired.

'But is that not the reason we came all the way across that accursed ocean in the first place? Would you be telling me what this is all about, for I'm not following you, Miss Kitty.'

'Never mind, Martha. Let's just have a good night's sleep. There's a thousand things to do before the wedding, you know.'

Martha rolled her eyes.

★   ★   ★

Summer was in full bloom for Catherine and Dominic's wedding on June 21. She rose early, tired after a restless night and fearful of what the evening would bring once the vows were exchanged. For the hundredth time she found herself wishing her mother could be with her on this day. And that her childhood friend, Amy Cutler, could attend her. Instead, Madame Fontenay had agreed to perform this task, but while she was excessively fond of Angé, it was Amy whom she had known all her life, and Amy was the only person in all the world who truly understood Catherine's anxiety on this particular occasion.

She breakfasted sparingly in her chamber on hot chocolate and almond brioche. A little after nine, just as she was completing her toilette, there came a great commotion below.

'Run and see what it is, Martha,' Catherine

ordered the maid. She could not bear that anything should upset the day, for her feelings were so tentative and her nerves so stretched that she felt everything to be an omen — was the weather propitious, were the arrangements going without a hitch, was César content in his kitchen kingdom? So many details, so many things that could go wrong and render the whole event a disaster. With the pact between herself and Dominic so fragile, she could not bear that anything should threaten it now.

Her own feelings were doing that well enough already.

Martha returned out of breath from her excursion below stairs.

'Oh, Miss Kitty, 'tis the worst! The worst! May God have mercy on us all. What's to become of France?'

Catherine saw the fear on the maid's face and felt a shot of alarm. 'Whatever is the matter? Quickly, Martha, tell me the news.' She pushed Martha down on to the windowseat.

''Tis the king, Miss Kitty!'

'King Louis? What is the matter with him? He is not coming to the wedding, is he?'

'No, no! Oh, to be sure, there'll be war, now, Emile says so.'

'War! Martha,' said Catherine firmly, 'tell

me what you heard. All of it, from the beginning.'

'Well, miss, a messenger came from the general. He says he may not be able to come to your wedding after all.'

Catherine paled. A black omen, indeed. 'Why not? What has happened?'

'The king — and the queen, and the children — they've escaped!'

'Escaped? Martha, His Majesty is not a prisoner. Only prisoners can esc — ' Suddenly, the import of the woman's words sank into her mind. 'Oh, dear God. You mean they have fled? Martha, are you saying the royal family has fled France?'

The Irishwoman nodded, her eyes wide. 'In the night, so they say. And the general — you know he promised. He gave his word.'

Catherine looked down with a frown. 'You're very well informed, Martha.'

'I listen,' came the sheepish reply.

'To Emile, no doubt.' She turned away, holding her fingers to her lips as she tried to think what this might mean. If the king and his family reached Austria, there would indeed be a war. It was said that the royal houses of Europe were poised for just such an event, ready to strike at the heart of the Assembly and regain power for the Bourbons. It was certainly not good news.

'Help me finish dressing, Martha. I must speak with *Monsieur le Prince* directly.'

She found him in his study, in deep discussion with a man she did not recognize. Christian was there also, though he stood with his back to the room contemplating the bright morning beyond the open window. His hands were clutched behind his back, and his legs, encased in everyday breeches and black hessian boots, were spread. He turned as the prince greeted her.

'Ah, my dear Catherine, do come in. We are finished here.'

Without introducing his visitor, the prince escorted the gentleman from the room. Catherine raised her eyes in query at Christian, but he merely turned back to his study of the garden.

'So my dear,' said the prince, 'no doubt you have heard the news?' He continued as she nodded. ''Tis true, I'm afraid. Louis has gone and there is no trace of him to be found. Lafayette is incensed, as well he might be. I warned him 'twas foolish to offer his personal guarantee against such an event — now what can he do?'

'Does this mean he will not come to my wedding this afternoon?' she asked with some asperity, for she knew that Christian would snatch any excuse to see the wedding cancelled. He had made his opinion of the whole business abundantly clear these past weeks. 'The servants are saying that the king has placed France at risk of invasion — that there may be a war,' she said, with a glance in the captain's direction. She saw his hands flex behind his back, but otherwise he remained unmoved.

'They are right, so far as one can tell,' replied the prince heavily. 'In time, we shall discover the truth or otherwise of such a belief. Meanwhile, we have a kitchen full of magnificent dishes with hundreds more under preparation at César's hands as we speak. 'Twould be foolish to delay.' He grimaced. 'There is no word, no news. Until the king and his family are located, there is nothing anyone can do. Life must go on and we must hope that all this will end in a satisfactory manner. I shall send a message to General Lafayette myself, telling him of our decision to continue.'

Catherine smiled. 'Thank you, sir.' She hesitated. '*Monsieur le Prince*, have you — ?' She wasn't sure she wanted to voice her question in Christian's presence, but since he probably knew anyway, she continued. 'On the matter of the church wedding . . . ?'

'Ah, indeed. I have spoken to my son again, but I fear he remains adamantly opposed.

Perhaps, with things in such a state of upheaval, it would be wise to wait a few months. You will be married in the eyes of God, which is what really matters, and I believe the king may exercise his right of veto against the constitutional clergy, so — '

Catherine ignored the snort that issued from the captain. 'Meaning that our marriage before Father Joubert may suffice after all?' She brightened considerably at the prospect of so simple an outcome to such a thorny issue, for Dominic had so far refused to countenance a second wedding with a 'puppet priest' as he called them. 'But — '

The prince nodded, wiping a hand tiredly over his eyes. 'Yes, my dear, 'but'. It will all depend upon exactly where the king is and whether he can make good his escape. May God speed and help him.'

'He'll never make it,' came the gruff rejoinder from across the room. Catherine stared at Christian as he turned to face them.

'How can you say that, Captain? If he has managed to disappear without trace . . . ?'

'So far.'

'My dear boy,' said the prince, going to him and wrapping an arm about his shoulders, 'how did you become such an intolerable pessimist? The king will escape to Austria, everybody knows that, and then he'll return with half of Europe at his back — '

'Or not, Uncle,' replied Christian. Catherine saw a muscle clench in his jaw as the two men stared at each other in momentary silence.

The prince dropped his hand, and seeming suddenly much older than his fifty-nine years, turned for the door. 'I hope to God you are wrong, Christian. Dear me, how I pray you are wrong.'

Catherine stood, shocked by the depth of despair she had just witnessed. 'I don't understand,' she said to Christian, when the prince had gone. 'Why is he suddenly so afraid? Christian, explain this to me!'

He turned, as if surprised to still find her there.

For a moment he just looked at her, then he shrugged. 'The servants are happy. They hope Louis stays away. The nobility are afraid that he might not return and that they might actually have to make terms with the Assembly, but in their hearts they are hoping he will reappear at the head of a victorious invading army and put the whole country back to the way things were under the king's grandfather. Of course, in Louis XVI's case, it would be a return at the rear of the army. He wouldn't want to risk his own neck. Either way, it's a mess.'

'But . . . ' Catherine spread her hands, searching for the right words to make sense of it all. 'What if he has simply gone to Saint-Cloud as he tried to do at Easter? They would not let him go, so perhaps this was the only way.'

'If he were at Saint-Cloud, we would know.' He shook his head, resting one arm against the window and leaning on it. 'No. The king has taken his family and run for Austria, you may be sure of that.'

Catherine sighed. 'And on my wedding day,' she said, almost to herself. 'I knew something would go wrong.'

She turned for the door, but stopped when he called her name. She turned to find him looking back over his shoulder.

'There is something I wish to ask you.'

'Now? I have a great deal to do.'

He laughed, but it was a cold sound that made Catherine's skin prickle. 'As do I. But there is something I would ask you before you do.'

She crossed the carpet to him, stopping a few steps away, for she did not trust herself to get too close to this man. Her heart had shown itself for the traitor it could be around Christian Lavelle, and this *was* her wedding day. She wanted nothing further to distract her.

'So, you are afraid to come closer?' he taunted.

'Indeed, I am not!'

'Then show me.'

She glared at him, refusing to reply. 'You had something you wished to tell me, I believe. Pray be quick. My maid is waiting.'

'That's why she's a maid,' he replied dryly. 'So she can wait.' Christian felt his humour returning as he looked at her, standing there all defiant in her breezy yellow gown. It was made of some filmy cloth, muslin no doubt, and was adorned with tiny sprigs of flowers. A simple, countrified gown, more suited to a summer picnic than the library of a grand house like this. She wasn't even wearing her customary fichu, he noted, letting his eyes wander across the creamy skin above her bosom. And as for her hair, it fell like a cinnamon waterfall down her back, wave upon wave of heavy tresses that he just itched to run his fingers through.

'How shall I ever let you go, Catherine?' he surprised himself by asking.

Her dark eyes flashed dangerously and her pert little nose thrust itself even more into the air. 'You never had me, Captain, so your question is impertinent.'

'The devil it is,' he replied, reaching out at the same moment he decided to put that theory to the test. He grabbed her almost-bare shoulders and pulled her to him, surprised to find that she came willingly. But then he saw her palm fly at his cheek and lunged for it just in time.

'Let me go this instant!' she demanded.

'So,' he replied, feeling a wild anger where before there had been mostly amusement, 'you fancy yourself in love with my cousin, do you?'

'Of course.'

His brows lifted. 'Truly?'

She looked away, her eyes sliding to his shirt, which, in his haste at hearing the news about the king, he had scarcely buttoned. It hung half open, exposing a good amount of his chest. He was mollified to see her breath quicken as she gazed at his body. But then she glanced up at him, a brave little prisoner in his grasp.

'Perhaps I do not love him yet,' she answered, 'but in time I shall, I am sure. I intend to be a model wife and mother.'

'Mother! Not to Dominic's brats.' He released her, turning away, too disturbed by the notion of his cousin and Catherine engaged in the business of making children. Damn him for a fool. How could he have let this happen again? Had he not learned his lesson with Léonie de Chambois? Had he not suffered enough, standing by as she fell in love with their commander, even when she believed him to be no more than a simple naval officer — as Christian himself was? He had loved Léonie all his life, it seemed, since they were children. When she had married François de la Tour, Christian had resigned himself to the fact that he had lost the only woman he ever really loved. Until now. Somehow, this American beauty had stolen that special place in his heart, the place that Léonie had always inhabited.

And now here she was, in her turn, preparing to marry another.

He looked at her, surprised that his attack had not sent her fleeing from the room. Clearly she, too, felt there was unfinished business between them.

'You cannot marry Dominic.'

She opened her mouth, closed it and then opened it again. 'Captain Lavelle, you have been saying this repeatedly since the day we met, but not once have you deigned to tell me precisely why I should not marry your cousin!'

He drew a deep breath. It was now or forever hold his peace. 'Because you're going to marry me.'

'I — !' She almost choked. 'I'm *what!*'

He stepped up to her, closing the gap until

their bodies almost touched. 'You don't love Dominic and you never will. Nor he you, for that matter.'

'Indeed?' She stepped back, shaking her head as though she thought he'd gone entirely mad. 'And I suppose you do?'

He paced forward again, regarding her intently, for he could not bring himself to admit it had truly gone that far. 'Marry me, Catherine. Follow your heart.'

Damned if she wasn't going to argue that, as well, he thought. Christian didn't wait to hear another word. He swept her into his arms and brought his mouth down on hers, crushing the breath out of them both. She struggled for a moment and then with a little whimper her lips parted and he took the advantage, plundering the sweet recesses of her mouth with his tongue like a drowning sailor embracing a mermaid.

Dear God, but she was sweet. Her mouth tasted of almonds and chocolate and her hair smelled like summer flowers. He ran his hands through it, sliding down its length and letting the silken mass wrap itself around them both. He moaned as her slim body pressed against his. Her muslin-enclosed breasts pressed against the bare skin of his chest, sending a burst of powerful need through his loins unlike anything he'd ever experienced.

'God knows I want you,' he groaned into her hair, lifting the heavy tresses so he could plant a million kisses behind her ear and down to the creamy skin covering her collarbone, and then up again as she let her head fall back offering him the sweet torture of her soft neck.

In reply, she dug her hands into his shoulders, pulling him closer. His breeches were painfully tight and he held his lower body away from her, afraid that his obvious need might frighten her. But one hand slipped around to cup her breast, feel its warmth beneath his palm and the way the nipple hardened under his fingers. Her eyes flew open with shock, and she stared at him for a second, until her mouth sought his again, eager and hungry.

Catherine thought she would die. She felt tears squeezing under her eyelids with the exquisite pain of her longing for this man. How could such a thing be possible? How could any woman feel such hunger and passion?

She moaned as his fingers brushed slowly, rhythmically across the thin fabric covering her breast, bringing the nipple into aching arousal and creating a physical yearning deep within her belly that was so powerful her legs began to buckle.

She felt him support her, then lift her bodily and carry her across the room. She felt the rich embroidery of the sofa beneath her as he lowered her, but not once did his lips leave hers. His hand plunged into her hair once more, cupping the back of her head so he could deepen his kiss, stealing her breath, stealing her senses, while his other hand, gently at first and then more urgently, began stroking the length of her leg, pushing aside the filmy cloth in its path.

She gasped. His hand stilled. She looked at him, his eyes as blue as any flame, the hunger in his eyes utterly undisguised.

'Christian, you must stop,' she whispered, pressing a finger to his lips. 'Please, you must. For me.'

She saw him take a deep breath, tipping back his head to stare unseeing at the ceiling. He shook it, as though he were arguing with himself, and she felt her heart pounding like a racehorse, the physical power of her need urging her to take back her words, to reach for him and end it all here and now.

But she could not. He looked down, finally, staring at her, and then let his hands fall away.

'Don't do it, Catherine. In God's name, don't marry him.'

A sob born from sheer pain broke from her lips. 'I must.'

He stood up, but did not move away. She trembled as he stood over her, his shirt hanging loose at his sides where she had tugged it free of the waistband to explore the crisp hairs of his chest with her fingers. She ached to reach out and touch him again, to feel his muscles beneath her skin, but she curled her traitorous hands into balls and buried them in her lap instead.

'You are a fraud, Catherine. You and I both know that you do not have any feelings for my cousin. I have done all I can — I have even asked you to marry me, but doubtless I am no catch beside the wealthy Duc de Charigny, even if it is all *your* money.'

Catherine stifled a cry at the poisonous words. She pushed herself up from the sofa and ran from the room without a backward glance, unable to stem the tears a moment longer.

★   ★   ★

She ran up the stairs, ignoring the curious glances from the maids who were busy polishing and dusting in preparation for the evening's festivities, but as she neared her chamber, she knew she was not yet ready to

233

face the scrutiny of Martha McKendry, so she turned the other way, hurrying along the hallway until she came to one of the rooms that stood ready for visitors.

She let herself in, crossing to the windows thrown open to admit the clear morning air, and slumped onto the windowseat. With a sob, she lay her forehead on her folded arms and gave in to the misery that overwhelmed her.

When the last tears were shed, she remained thus, letting exhaustion have its way. Without really hearing them, she listened to the sounds of the morning, the calls of servants busy in the gardens and on the terrace below, where they hoisted oil lamps and garlands for the dancing. Their voices held a gaiety that contrasted strongly with Catherine's growing sense of doom.

Finally she lifted her head, wiped her eyes on the backs of her hands and gazed up at the sky, watching little feathery clouds dance by on the breeze. The swallows were back, their nest-building days finished now and the job of egg-sitting now requiring guard duty and fishing for insects. They swooped about the garden near the wood, snatching dragonflies in their sharp little beaks and then retreating to their wall to eat with relish.

Catherine shuddered, looking away from

the gastronomic delight of the birds. She sighed, knowing that there was no more time. She had a simple choice: to go and prepare for her wedding to Dominic, or to cancel it and, instead, plan her return to America.

And as for Captain Lavelle? His proposal — if one could call it that — was no more than a joke in the poorest of taste. Had it been anything else, he would not have had the effrontery to wait until a few hours before her marriage to his cousin. If he loved her, why did he not tell her so? And if he did not, why in the name of heaven would he torment her with such a proposal?

She shook her head as she eased herself up from the seat, stretching the stiff muscles of her back. She knew the answer to that — he offered for her only because he could not bear to see his cousin enjoy the fruits of marriage. Jealousy. How could it be so powerful that two cousins brought up side by side like brothers should deny each other what small happiness life might afford?

The brief respite from the upsets of the morning helped to quiet her nerves, though in truth she felt dazed as she re-entered her rooms and allowed Martha to fill the marble bathtub for her.

She lay back in the bath with the door into her chamber open, trickling her fingers through the scented water as she watched Martha in the other room bustling about, fussing over the tiniest of wrinkles in the moiré silk gown with its embroidered pearls and heavy gold lace at the sleeves. Martha chatted away in an amiable commentary about the gown, the weather, the preparations, and the king's disappearance, though Catherine only listened with half an ear. She scooped up a handful of water and held it, letting the fragrant liquid slide through her fingers.

She knew she had let loose a melancholy sigh, for Martha's prattle ceased suddenly. The maid poked her head into the magnificent bathroom and frowned.

'Miss Kitty, what happened downstairs this morning that's made you so solemn? To be sure, every girl's entitled to her wedding jitters, but — '

'I'm sorry Martha,' Catherine replied, sending her a quick smile. 'It's just this business about the king. 'Tis scarcely a good omen.'

Martha rolled her eyes as she came in and perched her hands on her hips. 'From what I hear, 'tis good riddance to the man — and his entourage.'

Catherine raised her eyebrows gently. 'I suppose I might feel the same way, were I in your shoes, but it's so dangerous — for everyone.'

'Dangerous? Huh! Living has been dangerous for the poor for a good many years if you ask me.' She cast a surreptitious glance at her mistress. 'Not that you would, mind.'

Catherine laughed. 'Oh, Martha, what would I do without you to keep me in touch with the common people? You must remember always to tell me things, won't you? Just because I shall be a duchess, doesn't mean I shall be deaf to the concerns of others.'

'Well and how could that be? A fine, educated, American girl like yourself.' She harrumphed at the very notion, and then frowned. Catherine could see something was troubling her.

'Come, Martha McKendry. Say it before it chokes you.'

'And what would I be choking on, Miss? I simply . . . well, I just wished to say . . . Oh, merciful heavens, Miss Kitty, I'm just going to say it and then bite my tongue. I don't believe this marrying with the duke is the right thing to be doing.'

She dipped her head, avoiding Catherine's eyes, and grabbed the silver dipper, filling it with bathwater and pouring it over Catherine's back. 'There now, I've had my say so I'll hold my peace.'

Catherine's jaw dropped. 'Martha!'

'No, 'tis all I wanted to say and I've said it. I'll not be drawn further.'

Catherine stood up, causing a rush of rose-scented water to pour over the edge of the tub onto the marble floor. She snatched up a towel and wrapped it around herself like a Roman toga, following her maid's retreating form into the bedroom.

'Martha, if you knew how sick I was of people telling me not to marry Dominic. And yet whenever I ask them why, do they tell me? Not a one. Well no more. Sit down this instant and give me one sound reason why I should not become the Duchesse de Charigny!'

Martha grimaced, but plopped herself onto the edge of the bed. ''Tis not me, miss. 'Tis what Emile has said that has me worried.'

'Servants' gossip?'

'Not gossip, miss! He knows, as God's my witness. 'Tis what he tells me.'

'Very well. Tell me what he tells you.'

Martha cast her eyes down. 'I can't.'

Catherine uttered a most unladylike exclamation and paced to the window and back, clutching the towel around her. 'Martha, how can I make such a decision if I have no information on which to base it?'

Martha looked up. 'He won't tell me what, exactly. Just that the duke has strange . . . friends.'

Catherine thought about Signor Foscari and frowned. 'So I've noticed,' she replied archly. Then turning back to her maid, she added, ''Tis not enough, is it, Martha? How would you feel if people kept warning you to stay away from Emile?'

Martha's eyes grew round as saucers. 'Oh, Miss Kitty, no one has ever said a bad word about my Emile, I promise.'

Catherine tilted her head to one side, considering the eager expression on the woman's face and the bright flush which had spread to her cheeks. 'You love him, don't you?'

The abigail mumbled something incoherent. Snatching up Catherine's satin wedding slippers, she began brushing off imaginary specks of dirt.

Catherine smiled. This she could deal with. 'Then you shall have him.'

'I beg your pardon?'

'You shall be married, Martha. As soon as today's festivities are over and things have settled again, we shall plan your wedding, I promise.'

For once, Martha was too overwhelmed to speak. Tears sprang into her eyes. Catherine was touched, ashamed that she never noticed the strength of the relationship between her maid and the footman. She might not be able to make a fairy-tale marriage herself, but she could certainly ensure that Martha and Emile had a chance at happiness.

She crossed to her small escritoire and rummaged through the drawers, finally withdrawing a small scroll sealed with wax and bearing the stamp of Patrick O'Donnell of Philadelphia.

'Take this with my blessing, Martha. Perhaps you and Emile can find a cottage suitable for babies.'

'Babies?' Martha set down the slippers and wiped her eyes with the corner of her apron. Her fingers trembled as she took the paper. Catherine watched, touched by the awe on her maid's face as she broke the seal, untied the ribbon and stared at the document.

There was pause. Catherine frowned.

'Miss? Have you forgotten I never learned my letters?'

Catherine chastised herself. 'Forgive me, Martha. 'Tis merely a bond. You can exchange it for money, though it's really too much to carry about with you.'

'Money? For me?'

'A wedding gift. It was part of the money I brought with me for our journey, but I didn't need it. Oh, never fear, Martha,' she added, laughing at the woman's concern. ''Tis not part of my dowry, I promise.' She wrapped her arms around her speechless maid and hugged her tightly. 'You have been the most wonderful and loyal companion to me, Martha, all through my mother's illness and after her death. How many servants would follow their mistress across the ocean to live in a foreign country in the midst of a revolution? Take the money, to please me. Use it to find some happiness of your own.'

'But — ' Martha kept staring at the bond, not quite able to comprehend what was being said. 'Are you saying you'll not be wanting my services any more, Miss Kitty?'

Catherine smiled a little sadly and began to unwrap her towel. 'I'll always want them, Martha, but what I want is not as important as what you should have. If you love Emile and he loves you, then you should be a family. Never fear, I shall speak to the duke once we are married. I shall be a duchess then, remember!'

Martha let out a bright spurt of laughter, dancing about the room with such joy that it made Catherine's heart ache. Why was *she* not as ecstatic on this, her own wedding day?

11

Midnight was long gone. The last of the guests had departed. The ruins of the giant cake, created tier-upon-tier by César and his pastry cooks, lay in silent testimony to the appetites of 200 guests. It had indeed been a gastronomic spectacle, made all the better by the scandal of King Louis and Queen Marie Antoinette's escape, for it seemed food and political conversation made good company after all.

Catherine was exhausted as she made her way up the marble staircase to her chamber. She marvelled that her new husband had actually managed to accompany her in the minuet, to the amazement of many and the applause of some. Otherwise, he had spent little time in her company.

As for Captain Lavelle, dressed elegantly in his naval uniform of scarlet, blue and gold, complete with a smallsword at his hip, he had been cool and courteous. They had scarcely spoken a word all through the festivities, yet she had felt his eyes constantly upon her. It was not hard to sense his disappointment.

Well, he had learned something about her

this day. He had discovered that Catherine de Lacy Montaltier, now unofficially known as the Duchesse de Charigny, was a woman of her word. She had made a vow to marry Dominic and she had kept it.

She hoped he would respect his new *cousine* for that much, at least.

She crossed the landing and the door to her room opened before she could even touch the handle. Martha beamed at her.

'Miss Kitty, why you look all out!' She drew her to the *poudreuse* and swiftly removed the diamond combs holding a small veil of spun gold that trailed down her hair. Catherine groaned with delight as the heavy weight was lifted from her head. She closed her eyes as she felt Martha sliding her fingers through her hair and gently massaging her tired scalp.

'I suppose I must call you *madame* now you're married,' Martha mused. ''Twill take some getting used to.'

Catherine made a face. 'I've been Miss Kitty for so many years, Martha, I think I might wonder whom you were addressing if you were to treat me so formally.'

Martha blushed with pleasure at her words. 'Very well,' she said. 'Miss Kitty you shall stay. Now, let's get you out of this gown, before you fall asleep in the chair.'

Catherine was only too happy to see the last of the heavy garment for one day.

'You must be tired, too, Martha,' she said sleepily. 'Did you see the cake? What a masterpiece. That César is a treasure.'

'To be sure, we all watched it taking shape, this past week. César says he'd like to open a restaurant, you know. He says folk are going out to those places now to eat and there's a good living to be made.'

'A restaurant? You mean he would work for himself, like an artisan?'

Martha nodded. 'Emile says it is an awful risk, but César says now that the *bourgeoisie* are getting more powerful and all — '

'Oh, Martha. No more politics, please. My head can't stand it.' She sighed as the maid unlaced her boned stays.

'Sorry, miss. I thought you should know, since 'tis yourself who's the mistress of the house, now.'

Catherine laughed. 'I suppose I am. But not until tomorrow. I'm far too tired to think about it tonight.' She wriggled out of her chemise and silk stockings, tossing the garters on the floor and yawning.

Martha clucked her tongue. 'You'd best not be asleep when *Monsieur le Duc* comes. 'Twould never do — first night, you know.' She winked at Catherine.

The new Duchess felt a frisson of fear, and swallowed quickly. 'Did you bring the cognac, Martha?'

'As you asked. 'Tis there on the bed table.'

Catherine glanced across the room and observed a silver tray with a crystal decanter and two voluminous glasses. She breathed a relieved little sigh. 'Thank you, Martha.' Then observing that her maid seemed puzzled, added, 'I thought we could have a private toast. To our marriage.'

'Of course,' Martha replied, though Catherine had a sneaking suspicion the woman saw through the lie.

She slipped into the white cotton nightshift adorned with blue satin ribbons and sat at her *poudreuse* again so Martha could brush out her hair and settle a matching frilled night-cap over her curls. She yawned.

'Enough, Martha. You are as tired as I am. Take yourself off to bed.'

Martha dropped the ivory hairbrush on the small table. 'Very well, Miss Kitty. Good night to you now.'

She turned to go and then uncharacteristically ran back, bending to kiss her mistress quickly on the cheek before scurrying off with her cheeks afire.

Catherine smiled. Martha was a good woman. She would miss her, but she was glad she had given her a chance at a new life. It was the one bright spot in an otherwise stressful day.

She wondered when Dominic would come, then found herself glancing at the cognac near the bed.

'You can do this, Catherine. There is nothing to be frightened of between a man and his wife.'

But she poured herself a good measure of brandy anyway, then ambled about the large room sipping it and fiddling with things. She found the small incense burner Angé had given her as a wedding gift and decided to light it. The exotic aroma of cinnamon and other rare spices rose up into the quiet air, making her feel quite heady. Then again, perhaps it was the drink.

Catherine glanced at the bed, knowing the time was near, and yet not ready to get in and lie there awaiting her new husband. She perched on the windowseat with her cognac and pushed the windows wide, letting in the sweet fragrance of the jasmine that bloomed far below. A night owl hooted from the trees and the moon twinkled periodically through the light clouds.

Paris seemed so quiet at night. During the day there was so much bustle and hustle, but at night, secluded behind the high stone walls of the Hôtel de Charigny, one could almost imagine oneself in the country.

She sat at the window for a long while, listening to the quiet sounds of the summer night, surprised to find that she had finished the cognac. Dominic was taking longer than she'd anticipated. She was sure he had seen her come up to bed, had expected him to arrive promptly and claim what was his, whenever he wished it, now that she was his wife.

She placed the glass back on the night table and climbed into the feather bed, disturbing little Bijou, who had been asleep there most of the evening. He licked her face sleepily and curled up on her legs as he usually did, unaware that soon enough his master would come and he would be relegated to the rug.

Catherine lay there, staring up at the soft candlelight caught in the golden tassels of the bed drapes. Perhaps she was mistaken. Perhaps —

Perhaps the duke expected her to go to him! She sat up, dislodging the dog, who grumbled and then resettled himself without a care in the world. If the dancing and all the excitement had tired Dominic, perhaps he would expect her to attend *him* in his room?

Catherine nibbled on her lower lip as she

pondered this question. Maybe he was just late. Or maybe —

The door opened quietly and Martha entered.

'Miss Kitty?' she called softly. 'Are you awake — ? Oh, I see you are.'

'What is it, Martha?'

The maid looked uncomfortable. ''Tis the duke, miss. My Emile says he's not coming.'

'Then I am to go to him after all?'

'No, miss. He said he was tired after all the shenanigans and needed his sleep.'

Catherine contemplated this and nodded. 'Indeed, with his health the way it is, he tires so easily. I can understand if he had no desire to . . . fatigue himself further.'

She dismissed the maid and lay back, feeling an odd sense of relief. She hugged Bijou and chastised herself for not having considered the delicate state of her husband's health. It had been a hard day for him, harder than for the rest of the company.

But she could not help feeling that had she married Christian Lavelle, she would not be spending the first night of her marriage alone.

She fell asleep with that thought.

★　★　★

The next day brought no relief, either for Catherine or the nation. There was still no news of the king, and the streets were in an uproar. Some wag had installed a sign on the gates of the Tuileries which read 'House to Let' and Lafayette was being accused of conniving in the escape. His pronouncement — that the royal family had been spirited away by 'enemies of the Revolution' and that all good citizens must help to find them and bring them back 'to the keeping of the National Assembly' — gave focus to the outrage. Soon, horsemen were leaving Paris by all the gates, searching the countryside for news of the vanished monarch. Lafayette was reprieved.

Catherine, however, was not. Dominic had not appeared for breakfast and when she enquired from Brassart was informed that *Monsieur le Duc* was resting.

Nounou, too, was still abed, so Catherine took the cabriolet and set off for Madame Fontenay's apartment, yearning for a friendly face with whom to talk over her disappointments. The little carriage had scarcely reached the river when it was obvious that being abroad in the streets during such an uproar was unwise.

She returned to the house and retired to her room to compose a letter to her dear friend Amy, losing herself for the morning in remembrance of life in Philadelphia.

Dominic did not appear at supper, either. Concerned for his health, Catherine mounted the stairs to his chamber and insisted that Brassart admit her. She found her husband reclining on a *chaise-longue*. At his feet, his young legs tucked up beneath him, sat a boy of not more than 14.

Brassart was fussing. '*Madame la Duchesse*, your husband expressly wished not to be disturb — '

'Nonsense, Brassart. I wish to see that he has not overtired himself, that is all. It is a wife's duty to have concern for the health of her husband, is it not?'

She crossed the large room, casting a curious glance at the boy, who scurried up from the Aubusson carpet and bowed, flushing red to the roots of his strawberry hair.

'Your Grace, I was worried that you have not ventured from your room all day. Are you ill?' She stopped before him, kneeling so she could examine his pallor and breathing more easily.

His brow darkened into a scowl that made her draw back. 'I have not ventured from my room, *madame*, because there is nothing to draw me from it. How I choose to spend my days is, I believe, my affair.'

She stood up, her face burning with embarrassment that he should speak to her so, and in front of others. 'I came out of concern, Your Grace. That is a wife's duty.'

'To hell with your duty, woman. If I needed a nursemaid, I would have called for one.' He waved a dismissive hand at her, turning his attention back to the trembling youth who had shrunk into the corner of the window. 'You are the lady of the house now, so go and play at châtelaine, but pray do not include *me* in your ministrations.' He turned to her as she stood rooted to the floor. 'You have what you came to France for. Be satisfied. 'Tis all you'll get.'

Catherine dropped him a bob of a curtsy and fled before the tears that were building behind her eyes could cause her further embarrassment.

She ran to her room, but by the time she reached it, anger had replaced despair. So, he had given her control of the house. Then she would take it.

She sat at her little writing-table and drew a sheet of vellum towards her. Dipping her pen in the ink, she began to compose a letter to Angélique.

My dearest Angé
Now that I am Madame la Duchesse I

find I am able to correct some of the improprieties that have existed in this household, the first of which is undoubtedly that you have seldom been invited here to sup.

As you are my dearest friend in all of Paris, I must insist that from now on you must come and go from the Hôtel de Charigny with all the freedom of an honoured guest.

To this end, I trust you will visit me tomorrow. I fear that the trouble over the king's disappearance means that my uncle and your cousin are never at home. Even dear Nounou is to take her leave now I am safely wed and is returning to her sister's house on the Rue Saint-Antoine, so we shall be two ladies all alone!

Your friend

Catherine

That night, though she waited and wondered whether Dominic might come to her, or perhaps summon her to his chamber, she was not surprised to find that he did not. She fell asleep, exhausted from the week's events, and slept dreamlessly for eleven hours.

When she finally reached the dining-room

on Thursday morning for her usual light breakfast, she found the prince there, looking as wearied as if he hadn't slept all night.

'What is it, sir? You are not ill?'

'No, indeed, my dear. Things have not transpired as I'd hoped they would.' He ran a hand over his brow. 'Ah, at times like this I miss the wisdom of Monsieur Mirabeau.'

Catherine had not realized they had been such friends. 'What has happened? Has the king been found?'

He sighed, lifting his coffee to his mouth and then setting down the cup, untouched.

'Indeed he has.'

Catherine felt gooseflesh rise on her neck. 'So has he crossed the border? Is there to be war?'

The prince shook his head. 'He was spotted at Varennes and stopped. Some perspicacious soul recognized him from his effigy on the fifty-livre *assignat*. The royal family is being brought back to Paris, under General Lafayette's orders, as we speak.'

Catherine was silent a moment, pondering the implications of this. 'The king is a prisoner, then.'

'It would seem so.'

She poured herself a cup of chocolate, but ignored the pastries on the dish before her. Her appetite had vanished.

For a few moments they sat on either side of the polished table, staring at the steam rising from their cups, but not touching them. Beyond the open window, from whence a warm breeze promised a stifling day, came the desultory call of a lark.

Finally the prince looked up. 'I am concerned for us all, my dear. I should have taken Christian's advice and joined the *émigrés* long ago. Now it may be too late.'

Catherine had never seen him so forlorn. 'But surely things are not so bad. Perhaps the king will have realized his error and will allow some compromise. He is still much loved by the people, isn't he?'

'I fear not. When he disappeared, he left a written declaration to the people complaining of all the things he has been forced to do and forbidding any of his ministers from signing orders or using the royal seal on any documents.' He shrugged. 'He has tried to steal out of France taking the power of government with him. The Assembly will never forgive that.'

Catherine stared at him, trying to absorb the enormity of the king's actions and how their own lives might be affected.

'I am certainly learning that this is not the same,' she said finally.

The prince looked up from contemplation

of his cup. 'As what, pray?'

'As America. 'Tis one thing to fight off the control of a foreign power over your own land; quite another to be at war with oneself.'

The prince smiled, reaching across the table to pat her hand. 'You are entirely right, my dear, but I fear I am depressing you unnecessarily. It's the waiting that has taken its toll on my spirits, I promise you, nothing more. First, three days of waiting and wondering where the king was, and now the wait while he and his family are brought back to Paris.' He got up from the table and Catherine followed, leaving her untouched breakfast. 'But you must not let it destroy the happiness of the first days of your marriage.'

Catherine resisted an ironic laugh and did her best to smile.

As they left the dining-room, a footman announced Madame Fontenay and with a cry of delight, Catherine ran to meet her friend. They hurried away like two errant schoolgirls, through the library and into the gardens to walk before the day became too hot.

'I have so much to tell you,' Catherine said, as they passed the fountain and took the path towards the wood.

'And I you,' Angé replied, retying the ribbon on her hat as they walked. 'There is such a bustle all over town, I took twice as long to get here as expected. And my dear Gérard is so preoccupied with his own plans at present, he has no interest in the king's activities! Can you believe it?'

'Indeed, 'tis hard to credit. It seems no one can speak of anything *but* the king's escape.'

Angé slid her arm through Catherine's. 'Ah, but for my husband, the sea has always held more attraction than anything else — even me, I suspect!' She giggled, sounding more like twenty than her actual thirty-one years.

Catherine stopped, turning to look directly at her friend. 'He is going to sea?'

'*Mais, bien sûr!* Surely Christian has told you? They are leaving this very afternoon. Gérard is captain of his own frigate at last, the *Puissance*, and he is to accompany Christian's *Liberté*. There are some other vessels. I forget the exact details. They are to escort some merchant ships bound for the West Indies.'

Catherine took a deep breath, her heart feeling such searing pain that she feared she would faint otherwise. She turned away and they resumed their walk.

'Christian had not told me, but then I have scarcely seen him since — ' Since he asked me to marry him, she thought forlornly. Since he kissed me till I was senseless in his arms . . . She touched a finger to her lips.

'Since the wedding', Angé supplied. 'Of course not.' She laughed. 'A newly married woman has . . . other things to occupy her time, does she not?'

Catherine blushed, wondering whether she could bring herself to tell Angé the truth about her non-existent marital relationship with her husband. But that would be disloyal to Dominic and it was early days yet. He had taken the longest time to even bring himself to treat her kindly. If she worked hard, surely she could regain his confidence and even his love. Secretly, she thought that could take years, but she had the rest of her life.

Putting the happiest smile she could muster on her face, she led Angé through the woods to the secret little rock pool. There was no point in worrying about the future, she thought. Life was to be lived and enjoyed, one day at a time.

*   *   *

The next evening, Catherine was surprised to find her husband seated at the dining-room table when she entered. The prince was there, too, clearly awaiting her to begin the meal.

In deference to the continuing uncertainty in the streets, they dined alone, though the prince announced that he would be going out after dinner to a gathering at the Jacobin Club.

They ate roasted veal *en croute*, and small squabs accompanied by fresh green salads from the kitchen gardens, while the prince related the day's events. Marat's efforts to incite the people against the king were bearing fruit, he explained, for over 30,000 had attempted to storm the National Assembly only to be turned back by Lafayette's National Guard.

'The king is expected to reach Paris tomorrow,' he went on, signalling to the footman to replenish his wine glass. 'So perhaps things will calm down. Monsieur Barnave is working hard at the Assembly to persuade them not to dismiss the king.'

Dominic snorted. 'They have no power to dismiss Louis. He is scarcely some *bourgeois* employed in a workshop, to be cast off when not required.'

Catherine flushed, looking down at her plate, for she was sure the reference was meant for her.

The prince frowned. 'The Assembly is the

law, Dominic. You must accept that. If we can create a constitutional monarchy out of all this mess, it will be a miracle indeed. If not — ' He sighed, picking up his glass and twirling it in his fingers. He glanced behind him at the attending servants who stood silent around the fringes of the room. With one hand, he signalled them to leave.

Catherine felt a sense of foreboding. She glanced uneasily at Dominic.

When the door had closed softly behind the servants, the Prince set down his glass and leaned forward over the table so he might speak without raising his voice.

'You must listen to me, both of you, for your own sakes. Things are getting more and more dangerous for us. I wish now that I had followed Christian's advice and left the country in '89, but since I did not, we shall have to take our chances.'

Dominic sat back. '*Nom de Dieu*, Father, you're letting the rabble's threats addle your brain!'

The prince ignored this. Catherine interjected. 'Are you saying we should leave France, sir? Where would we go?'

'Not to your damned republican colony, 'tis for sure!' Dominic answered.

Catherine kept her eyes upon the prince, who cast his son an impatient glance. 'You do not seem to understand the predicament we find ourselves in, Dominic. The country is so volatile, it would take no more than a spark to turn it into a tinderbox. No, I think you would both be safer in Italy.'

'Italy!' Catherine had not considered such a destination.

'We have lands there, in the High Alps. I am still a prince in Italy, even if in France I am merely a *citoyen*,' the prince replied. 'We no longer have our holdings in the south of France or the Loire, of course — '

'Since my devoted cousin persuaded you to sign it all away with the *cahiers*,' Dominic interjected acidly.

The prince sat back. 'Christian's advice was sound, Dominic,' he replied, not unkindly. 'We had no choice. If I had refused to sign the *cahiers* and return the land to the peasants, they would have taken it anyway. At least we were able to leave with our possessions intact.'

Which explained why the Hôtel de Charigny was so luxuriously appointed, Catherine thought, remembering how struck by this thought she had been when she first arrived.

For a moment there was silence, while each of them contemplated the future, and then Dominic spoke. 'Well, you may run if you wish, *mon père*, but I shall stay. I am not afraid of power-hungry lunatics like Saint-Just and Marat.'

Catherine gazed at her husband, knowing that despite everything, she could not leave without him. With a sense of impending doom, she said quietly, 'Then I, too, will stay. A wife's place is at her husband's side.'

⋆　⋆　⋆

There was no further talk of flight to Italy, for the next day the king was brought back to Paris in disgrace and put under guard in his old lodgings in the Tuileries Palace. Hundreds of public notices appeared throughout Paris proclaiming that any person caught applauding the king would be flogged and whoever insulted him would be hanged. Consequently, his return, witnessed by thousands, was greeted by eerie silence broken only by occasional bursts of '*Vive la Nation!*' Lafayette inspected the guard, then presented himself to the king for further orders.

'I seem to be more at your orders than you are at mine,' snapped Louis in reply.

Catherine witnessed none of this personally, but listened to Martha's recital of the details in the privacy of her rooms. Privately,

261

she began to wonder if the prince was not right to suggest that she and Dominic take whatever chance they could and flee to Italy. After all, they were newlyweds. What would be more natural than for a newly married nobleman to show his ancestral homeland to his bride? But she knew better than to broach the subject, for the whole upsetting business of the king's betrayal had clearly shaken the Duke's confidence. Dominic, it seemed, was finally coming to understand that the Revolution was real. Not only that, but there had been rumours in Paris about his lack of interest in her, and that his uncle had 'sold' him to an American heiress to restore the family fortunes, knowing that his son would never make a proper husband. The gossip hurt Catherine, for it put the worst possible light on the matter and made her the dupe.

To make matters worse, Catherine had not even spoken to Christian before his departure for the naval academy at Brest. He and Captain Fontenay had left early one morning, and all Catherine had heard was that he sent his best wishes to her via his uncle.

Perhaps it was for the best, she thought sadly, as she wandered in the rose garden enjoying the heady scent of the summer flowers. The season was hot, though not as humid as she was used to in America, and she was spending as much time as she could out of doors. Occasionally she went riding, but that was not always possible, and she never ventured out without her groom.

She stooped to inhale the spicy scent of a lavender-tinted rose. She had too much time, that was the problem. Although she saw Angé every few days, and regularly visited other ladies about the town with whom she had struck up an acquaintance, she had little to occupy her. Dominic she saw rarely, and never once had he expressed the slightest desire with regard to physical relations. And Nounou had returned to live with her sister in the Rue Saint-Antoine, now that her charge was safely married.

Catherine plucked the sweet-smelling rose, pricking her finger on a thorn. She wandered off down the path, licking the drop of blood from the wound. If only she could have children her life could take on some purpose. But if she were to become a mother, she would have to find some way to entice her husband into her bed.

She lifted the rose to her nostrils, teasing them with the sweet scent as she took her now favourite path through the trees to the secret little pond at the far end of the garden. How would she ever summon the enthusiasm to seduce her husband, she thought sadly, knowing that if it were Christian Lavelle she was hoping to bed, that question would never arise. The memory of his lovemaking was still so fresh in her mind that she needed only to be in the room where he had first kissed her, or sit on the sofa where she had shamelessly run her hands over the bare skin of his chest to relive the tumultuous passion being near him had brought.

But now it was too late. She had followed her head rather than her heart, just as he had accused her of doing. Now, she was married to his cousin.

12

July's weather began as hot as the passions of the people. Scorching winds desiccated the country and the people's nerves as well.

The heat, however, appeared to cause no discomfort to a certain Italian gentleman who fancied himself the creator of a new art form — the depiction of ladies in all manner of erotic acts, designed to amuse and titillate those with pockets deep enough to purchase his canvasses. Indeed, Signor Foscari felt himself to be in the greatest of spirits as he made his way up the cool marble staircase of the Hôtel de Charigny in Brassart's wake.

He stood back, allowing the valet time to announce him, and then passed through the gilded doors to *Monsieur le Duc's* private sitting-room.

'My dear Dominic,' he said, making a leg and giving the duke his most engaging smile.

'What the devil do you want, Foscari?' Dominic grumbled, from his customary seat on the *chaise-longue*. He had one hand wrapped around a small brown-and-white fluffy animal, which Foscari took to be the sort of undersized dog most favoured by ladies, and was languidly feeding the mutt from a dish of *petits fours*. He watched distastefully as the duke pushed the creature to the floor and brushed crumbs from his crimson frock coat.

'Don't you ever open a window, Dominic?' Foscari asked, raising a scented handkerchief to his nostrils. He crossed to the casement and without asking permission, flung the long windows wide. A hot breeze instantly enveloped the room.

'*Grâce à Dieu*, Foscari, you're making the heat worse.'

'Better to be hot than airless, *caro amico*,' he replied. 'For myself, I like the heat. I find it — invigorating.'

'Pray let me guess,' retorted Dominic dryly. 'It reminds you of Italy.'

'*Esatto!* But my dear friend, why so glum? This is surely not the face of a happily married man.' He waved his handkerchief about him airily. 'Where is the lovely *signora* today? Preparing layettes, perhaps, for the new *bambino*?'

He saw Dominic scowl and felt a burst of triumph. So, he had discovered his secret — and with such consummate ease!

Feigning genuine concern, he perched on a *fauteuil* close to the duke, from whence he could observe the slightest of reactions. 'Tell me, dear friend, confess all to me, your great admirer. Things are not well between yourself and the lady perhaps?' He sat back, pretending to think while he enjoyed the deepening scowl on the duke's face. 'Perhaps . . . perhaps the lady is too . . . shy, shall we say?'

Dominic's reaction was masked as he leaned down and placed a tiny crystal bowl of water on the floor, clicking his tongue to the dog. The pampered creature came eagerly, his soft pink tongue darting out daintily to drink.

Foscari indulged in a touch of snuff while this cosy little scene transpired, and then decided to launch his final volley.

'Rumour has it,' he said with deceptive softness, 'that your wife, the very beautiful Signora Catarina, has found solace already.'

At last he was rewarded. Dominic's brows drew together sharply. 'What the deuce are you talking about, Foscari?'

'Merely a rumour, *amico*. And after all, now that the captain has sailed away in his little boat, what harm can it do? She is here. He is there. Who knows, perhaps a hurricane will catch him and he'll go to the bottom, at the helm — a hero to the end. Now there's a comforting thought, wouldn't you say?'

The duke was turning purple. Most gratifying.

'Did you come here to repeat the prattle from the gutter you so love to inhabit, Foscari? Well, now that you have, Brassart will be pleased to show you out.'

Dominic lay back on the *chaise* and closed his eyes, his breath coming in tortured gasps.

I must have a care, Foscari thought. It was an irritating fact that one must be cautious not to over-excite the sickly duke, lest his condition prove suddenly fatal. And anyway, fishing was more entertaining if one's prey remained alive and wriggling upon one's hook.

'I shall depart upon the instant,' he said gravely, 'should my presence cause you the least discomfort. But I would not wish to be precipitate.'

Dominic's face seemed to have regained its customary pallor. 'Ah, of course. You have not yet said what you really came for, have you?'

Foscari inclined his head in assent. 'I shall be brief and to the point, in deference to your distressing fatigue, Your Grace.' He raised his handkerchief to his face, fanning it idly to ward off the heat. 'These are dangerous, difficult times. And . . . expensive ones. I fear I have rather stretched my personal finances. Which leaves me, as I see it, with two options.' He waved the kerchief in the air. 'One, I could create some new pictures,

268

which, given their subject, might well raise their price considerably to the ardent collector. Or, two, I could perhaps be persuaded to preserve my canvasses for an alternate use, away from prying eyes. For a fee, you understand.'

The duke's mouth opened and closed. He glared at Foscari, but seemed unable to decide how to respond. Confusion was a promising sign.

The Italian continued. 'It is my understanding that your lovely new bride brought with her from America a considerable fortune. Now that you are safely married, it is, after all, no longer within the lady's demesne, but yours, to spend in whatsoever manner you deem appropriate.'

The room was silent for a moment, only the flapping of a curtain tassel against the window breaking the hush.

Then the Duc de Charigny raised his head, looked at the door and bellowed, 'Brassart! Get this vermin out of the house!'

Foscari was disappointed, but took care to hide it as the valet burst into the sitting-room.

'My dear Dominic, you don't want the girl, so what harm can there be? She'll only get restless, left to her own devices. Women can be such a trial if you don't keep them on a tight leash.' He leaned over the duke so the servant would not hear. 'And I am really quite good with virgins.'

Dominic was incensed. 'You are talking about my wife, Foscari, and the relations between me and my wife are none of your affair. Get him out of the house, Brassart, and instruct the servants that should he call again, they can borrow one of my father's rapiers and run him through — with my blessing!' He cast one last scathing look at the Italian and turned away.

Foscari's features turned puce with rage, but he controlled himself. He seldom lost control. 'I will leave you, Charigny,' he said smoothly. 'But do not underestimate me. Believe me when I vow you shall rue the insult you have done me today.'

★   ★   ★

The heat was drier than summers in Philadelphia, but came with an incessant hot wind that seemed to blow through one's head leaving a kind of craziness behind. Catherine knew that if she did not escape the house and occupy her mind with some distraction, she would go mad.

All morning, her thoughts had been occupied with Christian. She wondered if he was standing on the deck of his frigate enjoying a cool ocean breeze. She tried to imagine him there, dressed in his favourite working clothes, enjoying the game of outwitting the English privateers that flourished in the Channel, preying on unwary French ships. She felt no anxiety for him. It was unthinkable to her that he should fail at any task he undertook.

Yet he had failed to prevent her marriage to Dominic. She clenched her fists on the sampler she was pretending to work on and stabbed the needle through the fabric. If it were so important that he would offer for her himself, why had he not simply told her why he was so opposed to the match? At first she had considered it mere jealousy, but now she was not so sure. It was a riddle that she was still no closer to solving.

The morning of her wedding came unbidden into her mind, as it so often did these days. With nothing to occupy her time except some very undemanding domestic matters, she found herself reliving that heated encounter with Christian time and time again, in exacting detail: the feel of his tongue plundering her mouth like a honey-starved hummingbird; the scalding touch of his fingers stroking her breasts . . .

She tossed the sampler onto the table and crossed to the window, dabbing her

271

perspiring forehead on the sleeve of her blue muslin gown.

She would go riding, down to the Bois de Boulogne, where the trees would offer some protection from this accursed wind and heat.

She changed into her summer riding dress, eschewing the hat in deference to the temperature, and ran downstairs.

In the stables, she found one of the grooms giving water to a huge black stallion — Christian's mount, the evil-looking beast named Malavoir. It certainly suited him, she thought.

The man dropped the bucket and bowed to her. '*Madame la Duchesse* desires to ride? I shall saddle your mare instantly.'

She didn't remember seeing a blackamoor in the stables before. She smiled at him. 'What is your name?'

'Zamore, Your Grace.'

'Well, Zamore, I would like you to ride with me. I never go out alone these days. And — ' She turned and looked at Malavoir, standing motionless once more, his huge head hanging listlessly in the heat. 'I believe I would like to ride Captain Lavelle's horse.'

The groom's black eyes widened. 'Your Grace? Oh, no, Your Grace, he is too big for you. He is too fierce. Only the captain can ride this horse.'

Catherine was astonished. 'Are you saying he hasn't been ridden since Captain Lavelle went to sea? Why that's perfectly ridiculous. Saddle him this instant, Zamore. You may take my mare.'

For a black man, Zamore's skin managed to pale quite nicely at this news, but he was too polite to argue further. In silence, he saddled the horses and handed her up, though she could feel his apprehension.

They rode out through the gate in silence, Catherine finding Malavoir quite a handful, but not a wicked beast. Her father had owned a horse that was truly evil and she had tried on several occasions to tame the creature, to no avail. After a particularly nasty fall, the animal had finally been put down.

She experimented with Malavoir, finding that his responses were headstrong, but no more so than many a stallion. By the time they had reached the Bois de Boulogne, she concluded that the creature's reputation sprang from his looks and size rather than any ill-breeding.

'Oh, blessed relief,' she said to Zamore as they entered the shade of the forest. She looked at him and smiled. 'No doubt this heat does not trouble you.'

'No, Your Grace. I am from the Île de

France and we are much accustomed to the heat.'

She tipped her head to the side, considering him. 'Your French is excellent, Zamore. May I ask how you came by such fluency.'

He grinned, his teeth making a white slash in his ebony face. 'Madame Dumont taught me.'

'Dumont?' Catherine frowned, then comprehension dawned. 'Ah! You mean Madame Fontenay?'

He nodded. 'When her first husband was still alive, I was her slave.'

Catherine frowned. 'I did not know Madame Fontenay kept slaves.'

'Oh, not now, Your Grace. She set me free many years ago.'

'And you stayed with her?'

'Of course. She was the best. She taught me to read and write — '

'Yet you are a stable hand?'

He shrugged, turning away. 'I like horses.'

They rode in silence for a while, keeping to the edges of the paths where they could enjoy the cool, green canopy. There were many nobles out riding, presumably with the same notion of escaping the heat. Catherine smiled and nodded at one or two, and stopped to speak briefly with Isabelle, the younger Miss Bernier, out riding with her maid.

A few minutes later, the trees thinned around them and through the forest Catherine espied a lake where small boys were sailing little boats and dogs were frolicking in the shallows, chasing sticks.

'Oh, look, Zamore! Let's give the horses a drink.' She spurred Malavoir into a canter. From behind her she heard the blackamoor's impassioned plea.

'*Non, Madame la Duchesse. Grâce à Dieu, non!*'

But it was too late. The stallion had seen the water and suddenly Catherine had a horrible feeling she might have misjudged Christian's horse. She pulled back on the reins, commanding him to stop, but the great beast pounded through the trees, ignoring all her efforts to control him. His enormous hooves tossed up great chunks of earth as he went, Catherine found herself bouncing high in the uncomfortable side-saddle, acutely aware that the giant's stampede had attracted the attention of everyone within earshot.

Malavoir reached the water and, with a devilish snort, plunged into the depths, rider and all.

'Oh lord,' Catherine sighed, as the creature proceeded to wade blissfully into deeper and deeper water. She could hear Zamore calling to her from the shore, and saw her little white mare standing up to her fetlocks, drinking. Zamore was wading out to her, but she waved him back.

'Don't trouble yourself, Zamore. He'll come out when he's . . . Ah!'

Malavoir, apparently, liked to swim. He lurched out of his depth, stroking strongly for the other side of the pond. Catherine, whose muslin gown formed a balloon of air, floated right off the saddle and into the pond. The air, naturally, chose that moment to leave her skirts, and she found herself treading water with several yards of sodden cloth clinging to her legs.

Fortunately, it was not far to shore, and swimming in the cool water was the most gloriously refreshing experience she'd had all day. By the time she reached the shallows, where many gallant hands, Zamore's among them, were reaching out to assist her from the water, she was giggling.

She stood on the edge of the pond, amid the horrified gazes of the ladies and their escorts, and the unabashed scrutiny of the intrigued children, with her blue muslin sticking to her like fur to a drowned cat. Bits of pond weed were stuck to the cloth, but she ignored them, watching the great beast that had put her in such a predicament calmly swim to the other side of the pond and climb out, side-saddle still attached to his back like a leather mantilla. He shook his massive head and then turned, staring back at her across the lake.

'I see what you mean, Zamore. Captain Lavelle's beast does rather have a mind of his own.'

But as July progressed, she continued to ride the great creature, keeping him well away from sight of water, for it was this that was truly his undoing. In all other ways, he was a spirited and challenging mount, and Catherine came to respect his independence.

The days dragged by. People went out less and less to the theatre or to soirées, and balls were virtually unheard of. So she visited her small circle of acquaintances, tried to recover the kernel of a relationship that had been developing between herself and the duke before their marriage, and generally tried to interest herself in the activities of the house.

Of the prince, she saw little, and when they did encounter one another at breakfast or dinner, she was struck by how weary he looked, and how agitated, though she was unable to discover the source of this tension.

She missed having Christian around to converse with. Not until he had disappeared from her life did she realize how greatly she had begun to depend upon his opinions and his ready conversation.

Then, one day in the middle of the month, she began to feel the first real stirrings of unease.

With Zamore at her side, she had set out on horseback — her favoured means of transport in the warm summer days — to pay a visit to Miss Bernadette de Bernier, with whom she had struck up a friendship. She would visit the de Bernier ladies from time to time, happiest when she discovered that the lady of the house was absent and she could while away some time in walking about the rose garden that dominated the Bernier property, or playing duets upon the pianoforte with Miss Bernadette.

On this particular morning, there were more people than usual in the streets, and Catherine and Zamore kept to the narrower routes, coming upon the Hôtel de Bernier from a side street, to the sounds of artisans wielding hammers.

Catherine reined in her mount in surprise, staring at the workmen. They paused in their activities, glancing somewhat uneasily at her great black horse.

'Whatever are you doing?' she called.

'Boardin' 'er up, *citoyenne*. Keep out the riffraff.'

'Boarding up the house? But why? Where is

278

the *famille Bernier?*' She was beginning to feel very uncomfortable, asking questions so openly, but so great was her surprise, that she had not thought to be more circumspect.

The workman to whom she had addressed her question, pushed his red cap back on his stringy hair and squinted up at her. 'They friends of yours, *citoyenne?*'

Zamore touched her arm. '*Madame,*' he whispered, carefully avoiding the use of her title in front of such a man, 'we must be away.'

But Catherine was not to be cowed. 'I know of these people, *citoyen,*' she replied, putting as bland an expression upon her face as she could muster. 'Have they moved?'

'Moved?' He spat on the ground. 'More like fled the country with their tails between their legs like the rest of them *émigré* dogs.'

Catherine felt herself pale at his words. Zamore tugged on her reins, his urgency unmistakable. 'Come, please, *citoyenne,*' he said.

She glanced at him, shaken to the core. 'Of course. We must be about our business.' She turned Malavoir, glancing back at the workman as they continued along the street, as though that particular residence had not been their original destination. She saw the man pick up another long board ready to attach it to the once-elegant front door, and turned her eyes away. She reached a hand to her bonnet as if to reassure herself that her Revolutionary cockade was securely in place.

They turned at the corner and stopped.

'Zamore,' she said, her agitation evident, she knew, 'what does this mean? Can what that man said be true?'

The blackamoor shrugged. 'Look about you, *Madame la Duchesse.*' He waved a hand, indicating the row of elegant town palaces facing them.

Catherine inspected each one carefully as they rode slowly along the wide boulevard. Why had she never noticed before?

'Half of them are empty, Zamore. More than half.' He nodded, but made no reply, and they continued in silence, noting the number with tightly closed windows.

Occupied houses did not have all their windows closed and shuttered in July, Catherine thought, realizing with a jolt that much of fashionable Paris was becoming a ghost town.

'What is to become of us, Zamore?' she said sadly. 'Are we all to become ghosts, too?'

Instead of returning home, for Catherine was in so melancholy a mood that the thought of shutting herself up in the Hôtel de Charigny was quite repugnant, they followed the once-elegant boulevard towards the Pont Royal. A visit to her ever-cheerful and optimistic friend, Madame Fontenay, would brighten her spirits.

'What is that commotion?' Catherine asked, looking about her as they neared the river. There were soldiers everywhere, National Guardsmen by their uniforms, and two of them galloped up the street, their expressions tight and angry.

'Messengers,' Zamore said, keeping his chestnut close to Malavoir's flank in case the big horse took exception to being jostled.

A smartly dressed *bourgeois* hailed the riders. 'What news, *citoyens*?'

As they passed, they called out to anyone who would hear, without once slowing their horses' stride, 'A riot at the Champ-de-Mars. Many are dead!'

This created great consternation amongst those in the street, and soon crowds had gathered as shopkeepers and artisans came out into the street to seek more information.

'What is happening, Zamore? Why would people be gathered at the Champ-de-Mars?'

'We must go, Your Grace. It might not be safe on the streets.'

'Very well.' Catherine knew she was attracting attention to her giant beast, who was well known around these streets. They made their way home by the smaller avenues, with Catherine wondering when the city would ever settle down. It was more and more like living in the midst of a war. Which in a way, she supposed she was.

When they were clear of the crowds, Zamore explained. 'The Cordeliers Club was organizing a massive petition against the reinstatement of the king, Your Grace. Everyone was to come to the Champ-de-Mars to sign today.'

'And the National Guard was there,' she said to herself, though she saw him shrug from the corner of her eye. 'Will this never end, Zamore?'

He made no answer. They rode through the wrought-iron gates of the Hôtel de Charigny, clattering over the cobblestones of the courtyard towards the stables.

At supper that evening, both the prince and Dominic were present, much to Catherine's surprise. Clearly, the prince had something he wished to discuss, though on this occasion he waited until the meal had been dispatched and they had retired to the salon.

Catherine played on the pianoforte while her husband and father-in-law enjoyed the cellar's best cognac, then the prince dismissed the servants.

'Come, my dear,' he said. 'Your playing is

superb as always — a reminder of far happier times.'

Catherine frowned at his tone, but took the seat at his bidding, declining his offer of a brandy.

'Very well,' said the prince. Setting down his glass and clasping his hands behind his back, he began to pace slowly back and forth before the empty fireplace.

'You may recall, both of you, our discussion of a few weeks past concerning the possibility of removing our domicile to the High Alps.'

Dominic, reclining on the *chaise-longue* with his brandy glass in hand, snorted. 'Not Italy again, Father!'

The prince regarded his son thoughtfully for a moment, but made no reply.

'I cannot divulge all I know, for to do so would be to put you both in danger. But I can say this: today's events at the Champ-de-Mars have made me realize how very powerful these new factions are becoming. I am told some of the leaders have gone into hiding — demagogues like Marat and Desmoulins — but the unfortunate business will only make them more powerful, even while they remain hidden from the public eye.'

Dominic yawned widely. '*Nom de Dieu, Papa*, the king has been reinstated and the wretches are just poor losers. It will be forgotten in a week.'

The prince shook his head. 'I don't think so. Lafayette gave them fifty new martyrs today.'

Catherine gasped. 'Fifty people died? I had not realized . . . When the soldiers said — '

'You were there?'

'Oh no,' she assured her husband quickly. 'I had gone to visit the de Bernier sisters, and some National Guardsmen — messengers I believe — came galloping past towards the Tuileries. They said some people had died, but *fifty* . . . ?'

'You should not be abroad in the streets,' Dominic said coldly.

'I had Zamore with me,' she replied, flushing at his tone. 'And I wore my cockade.'

She realized her mistake too late. Her husband's expression blackened and he threw his glass, cognac and all into the empty hearth where it landed in a crash of breaking glass.

'Damn it, woman, you are an aristocrat now, not the wife of some *bourgeois* undertaker! No wife of mine is to wear one of those . . . pernicious devices!'

'But Christian said it was the only way to be safe in — '

'Christian! It is not Lavelle who is your lord and master. You are married to me, *madame*, and I'll thank you to remember your wedding vows. If I say you are not to wear a cockade, then you shall not, do you hear?'

This outburst had expended his breath and he lay back upon the *chaise*, struggling to draw air into his lungs. Catherine did not go to him, but sat and watched while he gasped for life-giving breath.

The prince glanced at her and shrugged, and she drew some comfort from the knowledge that he sympathized with her position. He poured a glass of water from a pitcher on the side table and carried it to his son.

'Drink this. You must not get yourself excited about things that do not matter, Dominic. It is not safe for Catherine to be out in the city unless she wears the cockade.'

'Then let her stay indoors,' he retorted, wiping his brow and casting her a venomous glance.

'Exactly,' replied the prince. 'Now at last you are coming to understand our predicament. We are slowly becoming prisoners in our own country.' He poured another cognac for his son and placed it on the *guèridon* beside him.

'I am getting old and the gout is affecting my leg more and more. Without Christian here, I do not feel I can look after you both as I would like.'

Dominic's eyes narrowed. 'What are you saying, Father? Are you in some kind of danger?'

The prince shrugged. 'We are all of us in danger, simply because of who we are.'

Catherine clasped her hands tightly in her lap. So there *was* a reason he had been so out-of-sorts lately. 'My husband is right, sir. Perhaps it would be best if we were to understand your situation a little more clearly.'

But the prince shook his head, turning to gaze up at the heavy painting that hung on the wall. It depicted an elegant lady in a swing made of silk ropes entwined with flowers. Around her, small perfectly coiffured dogs with bows in their collars, played with children in silks and lace. Another world. Another lifetime.

'If you do not go now,' he said, without turning to look at the duke and duchess, 'it may not be possible to leave at all.'

Catherine paled. 'What do you mean sir? We have given no offence, done no one harm.'

Still he did not turn. 'But the sins of the

father may be visited upon the son, is that not what God warns us?'

She glanced at her husband, noticing that this conversation was not sitting well with him. He looked flushed and there was a pale line around his mouth. His breathing was deeply laboured.

'Your Grace, are you ill? I must send for Brassart at once.'

She ran for the door. Talk such as this may well be necessary, but it might also be the death of her husband.

She saw the duke safely to his room and gave him a potion that the doctor had prescribed to help him sleep. His attack on her for showing outward sympathy with the Revolution had been cruel, but from his point of view, justified. She knew his belief in the monarchy was absolute, if misguided, and she had not dared to defend herself by informing him that his father also never left the house without the red, white and blue upon his hat.

She sat by his bed until he had fallen asleep, watching the fine lines around his mouth ease and his colour improve. When she was satisfied that he was in no danger, she instructed Brassart to have someone sit with him at all times, and returned to her own rooms.

It was late. A heavy moon hung over the

garden, bathing the trees in colour-sapping light. An owl hooted mournfully and fell silent, leaving only the distant murmurings of the city to break the silence.

She looked around her luxurious chambers, remembering how she had felt when she and Martha had first arrived here only a few months before. Now it seemed like a prison. She had pictured herself in love with her new husband, perhaps preparing for the birth of her first child, proud of her swift success in producing an heir, her days busy with layettes and nursery planning.

Instead, she found herself a married woman in a society where her few friends were fast disappearing, confined to a house in which her only companion — aside from the prince and the servants — was a husband who showed not the slightest interest in her company.

It was like living in a shadow world, where the past had somehow slipped through her fingers, and the future had not yet arrived.

When — indeed, if — it did, what would it bring?

13

There was so much commotion on the streets that for a few days, Catherine did not dare to venture from the house, but finally she ordered the small carriage to be brought round so that she might visit her dear friend Madame Fontenay safely, keeping behind its curtained windows to avoid any unpleasantness with her husband over the wearing of the cockade.

Nevertheless, in case of need, she tucked the rosette carefully into her reticule. She had learned from the first that it was wise to be prepared in Paris. She arrived at the apartment near the Louvre at the same moment that one of the maids was returning from an expedition to the *pâtisserie*, and they entered together, the maid taking Catherine's coat and bobbing away as Catherine said she would announce herself.

She let herself in to the sunny salon and was surprised to discover her friend seated upon the windowseat surrounded by books and with a black maid sitting on either side of her.

Angé's cheeks flushed scarlet when she saw

Catherine, and she shooed the girls away, clutching books to their chests.

'Pray, don't stop,' Catherine objected. 'I am perfectly content to wait until you are finished.'

'No, of course not, my dear. We were done for the day anyhow.'

The blackamoors scurried away. Catherine stared after them.

'Are you teaching them to read, Angé?'

Her friend laughed a little self-consciously. 'Among other things. I find them most eager pupils.' She waved to a pair of love seats positioned near the open balcony. 'Come, dearest. Let us have some cool refreshments and talk. 'Tis an age since I saw you.'

'You have not been coming to visit me very often,' Catherine chided her.

'I am afraid of encountering your husband. He does not approve of me, you know.'

Catherine sighed as she settled herself on the pale-blue sofa. 'He can be something of an ogre, I know, but he is seldom out of his rooms, unless he goes out altogether. You need have no fear, especially if you visit in the mornings, for he never rises before noon.'

'Then I promise I shall come tomorrow! Now, shall we celebrate?' She tugged on the bell pull and then dropped down onto the opposite seat.

A maid appeared almost at once and Angé asked her to bring champagne and *petits fours*. Catherine's brows rose.

'Champagne at this hour? In honour of what, do tell?'

Angé smiled conspiratorially. 'My husband had been ordered home.'

Catherine paled. 'So soon? But I thought they would be gone — ' She blushed furiously and began again. 'I thought Gérard would be gone for months and months. Has something happened?'

'Indeed, no!' Angé laughed, her girlish voice tinkling, and clapped her hands. 'I knew you would be pleased. And, before you ask, Captain Lavelle is returning also. They are, at last, to mount a voyage to French India and must come home to prepare. The first of the funds have been approved — is that not famous? I had a letter from Monsieur Thévenard, the Minister of Marine, this very morning.'

The wine arrived at that moment, suspending the many questions that were forming on Catherine's lips. It was as well, she thought, for her mind was awhirl. She knew she should feel no more than cousinly affection and concern for Christian's welfare, but deep down she was aware of an altogether different set of emotions. Her heart was beating a little faster, the day seemed suddenly a little brighter, and some of her anxieties concerning their possible flight to Italy seemed to pale. But India? If he sailed away to India, she doubted they would meet again, for a few years at least, or maybe, never. That sombre thought cast a sudden pall over her short-lived happiness.

'Catherine, my dear! Whatever is the matter? You look positively morbid.'

Angé pressed a glass of wine into her hands and, despite the early hour, Catherine sipped it eagerly. She avoided her friend's eyes, trying desperately to collect herself.

Angé leaned back against the sofa and studied her friend.

'Something is troubling you, dearest. Tell me all, quickly now, before it burns a hole in your happiness.'

Catherine sighed. 'My store of happiness is scarcely big enough to excite a blaze, I'm afraid. 'Tis nothing. Your news startled me, that is all.'

'Indeed 'tis not all.' Angé plucked the glass out of Catherine's hands and took them in her own. 'Look at me, Catherine. We are friends, are we not? There is nothing you cannot tell me, nor I you.'

Catherine looked up, touched by the genuine concern in her friend's blue eyes.

'Very well. The truth is, I have missed Christian, and I am glad that he is returning. But when you speak of a voyage to India, I wonder if we shall ever meet again, and if he does not visit from time to time, how shall I ever bear it? What shall become of me?'

This melancholy thought caused tears to fill her eyes and she covered her face with her hands and wept, unable to stop the flood, no matter what Angé thought of her. But, far from condemning her for such an outburst, Angé wrapped her arms about her, rubbing her back and murmuring words of encouragement.

When Catherine finally had herself under control, she accepted the voluminous white silk handkerchief that Angé pressed upon her, wiped her face and blew her nose.

'Better, dearest?'

She nodded. 'What must you think of me, Angé, for putting on such a scene. What should a newly married woman care if her husband's cousin goes to India or Timbuktu?'

Angé's eyes gleamed. 'Aha! Perhaps this is the root of the problem, do you not think? Consider this,' she continued, as she once again pressed the champagne glass into Catherine's fingers. 'A young girl marries a man chosen for her, sight unseen, by her father. She marries him because she must, but she does not love him. Instead, she has fallen in love with his handsome cousin — '

'Angé!' Catherine was appalled, looking over her shoulder lest one of the servants beyond the door might be eavesdropping. 'I have done no such thing! We are friends, nothing more. I miss talking with him, and listening to him while he speaks of far-off lands he has visited and — '

'*Quelles sottises!*' Angé interrupted. 'You are in love with the captain. And he with you, if I am not very much mistaken.'

Catherine gasped. 'No! That cannot be. He condemns me for what I have done. We quarrel about Dominic every time we meet . . . ' Her eyes grew round as she stared at the smug expression on her friend's face. 'Angé, you must not say these things. Nay, you must not even think them. I am married to Dominic, and there's an end to it.'

Angé selected a tiny marzipan-covered cake from a silver dish. 'Very well, if that is your wish. But I do not believe Dominic is making you happy — that would be too much.'

Catherine was about to argue that point as well, but she sighed. 'Yes, indeed it would.' She toyed with the stem of her glass, twirling the sparkling wine without really seeing it. 'He does not care for me. He never seeks me out. I try to visit his rooms every day, but it seems only to remind him that his father sold him for thirty pieces of silver.'

'La! He does not think so little of you, surely?'

Catherine nodded. 'Whenever I displease him he takes pleasure in reminding me that I am merely rich, whilst *he* is noble.'

Angé's retort was certainly not one to be spoken in polite company, but Catherine was becoming accustomed to her blunt manner of speaking and took no offence.

'When I agreed to this marriage I did so because I believed that for my part I would gain a husband eager for an heir, and that I would be certain to become a mother quickly. I do love children so, and I am not young any more.'

'You are scarcely old,' Angé replied sharply. but then her voice softened. 'Are you saying Dominic does not wish for children?'

Catherine set down her glass and went to stand at the open balcony, staring down at the garden below. Angé's little ones were there, playing ball in the shade of a large sycamore tree with their nanny.

She turned, leaning her back on the railing and looking straight at Angé. 'My husband does not come to me at night.'

Her friend's brows rose slightly, yet she

seemed barely surprised. They stared at each other, no words necessary to convey further meaning. After a few moments, Angé fell back against the sofa and sighed.

'Christian was right. He should have stopped you.'

Catherine felt that old fury at these veiled references to her husband rise anew. 'I asked him why I should not! I asked you, too, if I recall. Yet you declined to tell me. Christian even offered to marry me himself if I would abandon his cousin, as though I were some worn-out shoe to be cast to the poorer relation.'

Angé sat up sharply, her voice bubbling with delight.

'Christian asked you to be his wife?'

'On the very morning of the wedding, right after we heard the news about the king's disappearance.'

'*Fascinant!*'

'Not to me. How would you have felt if such a thing had happened to you?'

Angé smiled slowly. 'If I loved the man and did not love my betrothed — ' She gave a silvery laugh. 'That would depend.'

'On what, pray? Could there be a greater unpleasantness to be endured on one's wedding day?'

'That would depend, *chérie*, on whether

the match was necessary — as you say yours was.'

Catherine sat down, frowning at her friend. 'I do not believe I follow you, Angé.'

'You could always take him as your lover.'

'My lov — !' The word came out in a horrified squeak. Catherine clamped a hand over her mouth.

Angélique raised her glass. 'It is perfectly acceptable these days, dearest, especially when one's marriage bed is not to one's liking. Affairs can be very advantageous, if one arranges them in an appropriate manner.'

There was silence in the salon for a few moments. Catherine felt dazed. She stared stupidly at her second glass of champagne, reaching for it with shaking fingers. She took a sip, feeling the ice-cold wine slide down her throat. It did nothing to cool her blood, so heated was she by the very *notion* of taking Christian Lavelle as a lover!

'Such a thing is impossible,' she said at last.

'In Philadelphia, perhaps. But this is Paris.'

Indeed it is, thought Catherine. 'Do you speak from experience, Angé? I can scarcely imagine you engaging in any such . . . activity.'

Her question was enormously impertinent, but so was her friend's suggestion, so Catherine felt no compunction in asking.

Angé merely laughed. 'Indeed, no. You see, I met my second husband within a very short time of coming out again after my year of mourning, and we have been so deliriously happy ever since that I have felt not the slightest inclination to wander. Besides,' she added without rancour, 'I am not a member of the nobility, as you are. We *bourgeois* are far more strait-laced. It's one of the things that so irritates the aristocracy.'

'I am a *bourgeoise* too,' Catherine objected.

'Bah! You are a duchess. Now you can follow whichever set of practices amuses you. If you choose to play by their rules, no one shall condemn you for it.'

'Oh, this is all so silly. I am astonished that we should even be discussing such a thing. After all, if I were to take Captain Lavelle' — it seemed safer to use his title in such a context — 'as a lover, then I would in all likelihood create a child. And since my husband chooses not to consummate our marriage, how pray would that be explained?'

'You would tell him, I suppose. These things are usually done quite openly, you know. Lafayette has several mistresses. He even writes to his wife, who is friends with them, and asks after their health when he is away.'

'Never!' Catherine was aghast. She shook her head, staring at the silver dish of pastries in front of her. 'I could never do such a thing. It would break Dominic's heart. You know he hates Christian. To tell him that Christian was the father of the Charigny heir would be too cruel. 'Twould be the death of him.'

'That would solve the problem, of course,' Angé replied airily. At Catherine's shocked expression, she laughed. 'Come, my dear, I am teasing. No doubt you are right. The only other way is to persuade your husband that your charms are worth exploring. Perhaps he will enjoy it once he — '

'Angé!' Catherine's cheeks burned. 'Please, I think we should speak no more of this.'

So for the remainder of the visit, they discussed the abrupt departure of the de Berniers and Catherine learned the melancholy news that while the ladies had escaped successfully to Spain, Monsieur le Comte de Bernier had been captured and was under arrest at La Conciergerie, the large prison housed in the Palais de Justice where many nobles suspected of treason were held.

She returned home deeply saddened and with a great deal to ponder.

*   *   *

August began hotter than ever and, as Catherine partook of her solitary breakfast, she found she had little appetite. She had slept poorly, her mind whirling with all that she and Angélique Fontenay had spoken of so openly the day before. She toyed with a crisp apple that she had peeled, cored and quartered, but could somehow not bring herself to eat. She pushed the dismembered morsels slowly around on her plate, trying to keep her wayward thoughts from revolving — as they had done all through the night — on the notion of taking Christian Lavelle to her bed.

Catherine sighed. It was no use. The more she tried not to think about it, the more traitorous her thoughts became. She could think of nothing else, in fact. Visions of his broad, muscled chest under her fingers had played through her mind so many times that they had begun to embellish themselves with a life of their own. She clearly recalled a dream in which she had wantonly torn the shirt right off his chest, only waking in a sweat when she dreamed she was doing the same with his breeches.

She blushed now, even to think of it. Thank the Lord she had awoken in time!

The door to the dining-room opened and

Emile announced Madame Fontenay and her children.

Startled, for she had not been expecting them at such an early hour, she jumped to her feet.

'Angé! What a surprise!'

Her friend sailed into the room looking a picture in a white muslin gown with a broad blue sash and bonnet to match. Behind her came Alexandre, in little blue breeches and matching jacket, clutching his sister's hand. Hélène, too, looked a perfect little lady in her buttercup-yellow dress and flowery bonnet. The children seemed nervous, perhaps because the house was new to them and rather finer than they were accustomed to. But when they saw Catherine, they ran to her, arms outstretched. She hugged them tightly, enjoying the feel of their sweet little bodies in her arms.

'I am so glad to see you all,' she said, as she sat them at the table and pushed a plate of *pâtisseries* towards them. The children tucked in eagerly, although no doubt they had eaten a scant half-hour before.

Angélique cast them an indulgent smile. 'Do not forget to leave room for our picnic, my little ones.'

'That sounds like fun,' Catherine said wistfully. 'Where will you take them?'

'Not them: us,' replied her friend airily. 'Go fetch your bonnet. I don't want to waste a moment of this gorgeous day.'

'But . . . ' Catherine tried to think what plans she had made for this day. Nothing came to mind. 'Very well,' she said laughing. 'I will be but a moment.'

She ran up to her rooms, her step lighter than it had been for days. A quick glance in the cheval mirror told her that her sensible grey silk morning dress was quite the last thing she would want to wear for a picnic *sur l'herbe*. She rummaged through her gowns.

'Aha!' She snatched a light summery gown *à la mode créole* cut from palest apple-green lawn and embroidered with clusters of tiny pink blossoms. The simple drawstring neck-line would be cool on even the hottest day. She shrugged into it easily, and leaving her long hair loose, settled a large straw bonnet decorated with apple blossoms on her head. She picked up her cockade, contemplated attaching it to the hat, but jammed it into her reticule instead.

Satisfied with her reflection in the mirror, she skipped downstairs to collect her friend and the children.

They were ready, the children looking quite satisfied with their extra breakfast, and the dish of pastries entirely cleared.

Angé had hired a small coach for the day, in deference to the children, and they rumbled along the cobbled streets towards the Bois de Boulogne, crossing the Seine at the Pont de Louis XVI and into the Faubourg Saint-Honoré. The Champs Elysées was as busy as ever with Monday-morning activities, but there were no open signs of discontent after the 'massacre', as it was being called, at the Champs de Mars.

The forest was cool and green after the heat of the city and the children leaned out of the coach windows, with little regard for their mother's admonition to take care, pointing out possible spots for their adventure.

Finally, the vehicle rolled to a stop at the end of a long promenade. Several other coaches and cabriolets were parked there, showing they were not the only Parisians to think of this as a fine refuge from the summer heat.

They left the coach with instructions for it to return at four, and followed the children along a path through tall oaks and birches. They were near the river, but looking for a quieter spot, and chose a clearing beside a small stream that flowed down a short distance before joining the Seine. The children arrived first, running like wild things around the little grassy enclave whooping with delight. Alexandre had already stripped off his jacket and shoes and was running barefoot in the grass.

The women laughed, neither of them finding it in their heart to scold the boy.

They set down the picnic basket Angé had furnished, and spread a blanket on the grass at the base of a huge beech tree.

'This is heavenly, Angé,' Catherine said on a sigh as she settled her back against the tree.

Alex ran up. '*Maman*, may I catch a fish? I brunged my pole Papa gave me.'

'Brought,' corrected his mother, as she dug the tiny two-part pole from the depths of the basket. 'Here you are. Hélène, will you help your brother, dearest?'

The little girl responded in her usual way to her responsibility, by taking over entirely. They sat at the edge of the water giggling and chattering far too loudly for any fish to come near them. But then, Catherine thought, catching a real fish was not truly their purpose.

The two women sat in companionable silence, listening to the children's chatter.

'They will be back on Sunday,' Angé said, lying back on the blanket and staring up at the bright blue sky overhead.

Catherine's heart did a sudden jolt, but

she kept her voice disinterested. 'Who will?'

'Our captains.'

'Our — ?' Catherine gasped, her face flushing mercilessly. 'Angé! He is not *my* captain. I have a duke, *you* have a captain.'

'You could have one too, dear heart,' replied her friend, rolling over and resting her chin in her hands. Her blue eyes danced with merriment.

Catherine regarded her sternly. 'You make him sound like some prize to be bought and sold, Angé. Don't you know that's the very thing that most maddened him about my marrying Dominic?'

'That was different.'

'In what way, pray tell?'

'That was marriage: I'm talking about love.'

Catherine blushed, turning her gaze to watch the children at the water's edge. 'I do not make the distinction.'

They were silent for a while, each occupied by their own thoughts. A red squirrel taking advantage of the tranquillity chose that moment to scamper to the ground, snatch a fat beech nut from the forest floor and dash back up into the branches, where he sat, flicking his tufty ears and chattering while he inspected the morsel.

'You know, Catherine, sometimes you are

305

so stuffy. Do you not think that a life spent without love would be a terrible waste of God's gift?'

'What I think,' replied Catherine acerbically, 'is that a life spent in adultery would be a life of sin.'

Angé sighed. 'You Americans can be so prickly.'

'You French can be so *risqué*.'

'There is always confession.'

'There is always abstinence.'

They glanced at each other, then burst into laughter. The children, hearing them, came running back to complain that the fish were just not hungry.

So the fishing rod was abandoned, and a game of *cache-cache* ensued, with little Alexandre taking the first turn at hiding while the ladies feigned not knowing where he was. After a suitable lapse of time, while everyone pretended to be searching in vain for the boy, his sister found him and the game became more demanding.

It gave them quite an appetite and, even though it was barely noon, they were soon opening the picnic baskets and sharing out the delectable dishes within.

Catherine sat back after they had eaten, holding a glass of white wine in her hand. 'You know, this is the most perfect day

I've had since I arrived in Paris. You are a genius, Angé.'

'*Maman* and us have the best picnics,' Hélène said proudly. 'Except when Papa is home. Then we go boating, too.'

'Sometimes,' Angé added.

'When will Papa be back?' asked Alex, as his mother attempted to wipe blackberry conserve off his hands and face.

'Next Sunday, dearest,' said his mother, kissing his sun-gold hair.

'Will he stay home this time?' little Hélène asked wistfully.

Angé prevaricated as she finished wiping the children's faces. Catherine's eyes narrowed as she saw a telltale touch of colour stain her cheeks. Angé turned to tuck the cloth back into the picnic basket, taking much more care than the task necessitated.

'I'm not sure, darling. You will have to ask him when he gets home, won't you?'

The children, apparently satisfied, ran away to play at the river's edge with a toy boat that their father had made for them. It had tiny cloth sails like a real frigate and he had painted the name on the bow: the *Puissance*.

Catherine tipped her head on one side, considering her friend's curious response.

'Why do you not want the children to know about the voyage to India? Surely they will need to be prepared for such a long absence.'

Angé avoided her eyes, busying herself with the platters and remnants of the meal. '*Bien sûr*. But it will be months before he's ready to leave, so . . . '

'Angé.' Catherine reached out and stilled her friend's hands. 'Look at me. What are you hiding?'

The older woman flushed. '*Rien du tout*. It's just that . . . ' Her voice trailed off.

Catherine was troubled by her friend's evasiveness. She lay back against the tree, finishing the last drop of wine in her goblet.

There was something Angélique was not telling her, of that she had never been more certain. As to what it might be, Catherine had a feeling, but she could not quite —

'Oh, saints preserve us!' she said, sitting up suddenly. The clarity of her realization took her breath away. 'You are fleeing France!'

Angé gave a little cry of dismay, and the dish she had been holding spun from her grasp.

She stared at Catherine, who read only too clearly the truth of the words in her eyes, though she tried quickly to veil them.

'How did you guess?'

Catherine sighed. 'Never fear, Angé. Your secret is as safe as the grave with me. Everyone seems to be either leaving or

308

contemplating it. Why, just two weeks ago I went to visit the Bernier sisters to find the family gone.'

'So I heard. Also that the count was arrested and has been brought back to Paris.' Angé shuddered. 'What is to become of him?'

'The servants say he will be executed, but I don't know,' responded Catherine sadly. 'I did not realize that coming to France might mean becoming its prisoner.'

'Your father should never have sent you.'

Catherine shrugged. 'We did not know how bad things were. But you, Angé — surely you and Gérard have nothing to fear? The Revolution will not endanger your lives as it will mine.'

Angé retrieved the upset dish and wrapped it in muslin before placing it back in the hamper. 'It was my idea,' she said quietly. 'I want my children to grow up in an atmosphere of freedom and happiness. Paris is becoming more and more poisonous. There is no way to escape the politics.'

'But where will you go?'

They paused in their conversation as an elegant lady on horseback and her beau rode past on the bridle trail not far from where they sat. The ground shook with the sound of the horses' hooves.

When they were gone, Angé continued,

though she kept her voice low. 'I am hoping my husband will smuggle us aboard his ship and we may return to the Île de France. I do so miss the beaches and the flowers and the exquisite birds.'

'It sounds wonderful, but wouldn't he be in great trouble if he knowingly allowed stowaways on his vessel?'

Angé sighed. 'Indeed he would. But what other way is there?'

What indeed, wondered Catherine.

There was a sudden wail from Hélène at the water's edge. Something in the child's voice set Catherine's heart to pounding. She and Angé sped across the grass to where the child stood crying and waving her arms.

To their horror, they saw that little Alexandre had fallen into a deep pool under the overhanging bank and was being dragged into the centre of the swirling stream. The wide River Seine flowed swiftly past at the very next bend. If he were carried that far, he would surely be lost.

'Alex!' cried Angé, her voice cracking with fear.

They could see the little boy's head, but he kept slipping below the surface. His little boat, which he had no doubt been trying to retrieve, floated a few feet in front of him, bobbing and turning in the fast-moving water.

Catherine kicked off her shoes and tore off her bonnet. She slithered down the bank, which was treacherously wet, and slipped into the river, gasping at the coolness of the water on her sunwarmed body. Her heart was racing. She longed to call out to the boy, but resisted. She would need all her breath if she were to swim against the encumbrance of the skirts tangling her legs. She could hear Angé and Hélène screaming for help on the bank as she struck out in the direction she had last seen the boy's head.

Quickly she reached the spot, for the current was strong and her gown worked like a sail. But she could not see him. She trod water, looking about in panic. Then she heard a choking little cry that tore at her heart.

'*Maman!*'

He was near the final bend in the stream, dangerously close to being swept into the Seine as the tributary emptied itself into the larger waterway. But he was caught behind a half-sunken log.

With a prayer of thanks, Catherine struck out again, grabbing both boy and branch as she drew even with him.

She wrapped one arm around him, his head upon her shoulder, well clear of the water. Tears of relief filled her eyes and she hugged his little body close.

'You are safe, Alexandre. Do not cry. Tante Catherine has you now.'

The child clung to her neck, his tiny chilled fingers clutching her hair for dear life.

Catherine kissed his cheek, and taking care to ensure her skirts were not entangled in the branches of the half-sunken tree, struck out for the bank.

Crossing the river to where his mother and sister waited was dangerous, for the Seine was perilously close. Before they even gained the bank, strong arms reached down and plucked them to safety. Catherine smiled at the two gentlemen who had come to help, allowing them to assist her from the water.

Angé grabbed her child from Catherine's arms and clutched him to her. 'Oh my darling baby,' she sobbed, weeping tears of joy.

Catherine thanked the strangers, but refused further offers of help. She shook out her drenched skirts to cover her ankles, noticing that the men had also ruined a fine set of clothes.

She and Angé had been so preoccupied, she thought with remorse. So embroiled in their own concerns they had failed to watch the children properly.

She sat on the grass, squeezing the water

from her drenched hair and skirt and getting her breath back. If anything had happened to Alexandre . . .

How *could* she, who so longed for a child of her own, have been so careless . . . ?

She watched Angé cradle her son with one arm and her daughter with the other, hugging them fiercely and rocking back and forth, her eyes tightly shut. It was impossible not to feel a stab of envy. But with Dominic as her husband . . .

Angé looked up.

'I owe you my life, Catherine.'

Catherine flushed, embarrassed by the intensity of her friend's expression. 'Indeed you do not. 'Twas nothing. But you must teach him to swim.'

Angé's eyes were wet with tears. 'No matter what happens in life, Catherine, the love of a mother for her child is so powerful, so precious that there is *nothing* to equal it. You have saved my life because you have saved my son.'

14

Sunday was too hot for riding, so after letting the horses stretch their legs in the Bois de Boulogne, Catherine and Zamore returned to the Hôtel de Charigny earlier than usual. She was tired, having found sleep impossible the night before, and was glad to return to the huge town house.

They rode in through the wrought-iron gates and across the cobbled courtyard. Something in Zamore's manner as one of the stable boys reached up to hand her down, made Catherine glance up.

A tall man stood half in, half out of the shadows at the stable door, watching them. His head was tipped quizzically to one side and a slight smile twisted his lips.

'Christian!'

She leapt off her horse and ran towards him, only realizing at the last moment how that might seem. She stopped just in front of him, heart pounding.

'I see you are back, *Capitaine.*'

'I see you are riding my horse, *madame.*'

She laughed. 'He needs his exercise. And he is not so bad, so long as one stays well

314

clear of the water.'

His brows rose. 'Dare I ask how you came by such intelligence?'

She grinned. 'The hard way. Ask Zamore. He is my witness. Although — ' she added, anxious not to get the blackamoor in trouble, 'he did try to warn me.'

'He has my sympathies,' replied Christian dryly. 'No doubt you took as much notice of him as you usually do of me.'

She flushed and looked down, certain he was referring to another matter entirely. Suddenly she noticed that he was favouring one leg quite heavily, and that he leaned on a crutch that was tucked unobtrusively into his armpit.

'Captain, you are hurt!'

He shrugged. ''Tis nothing that won't heal.'

'But I understood you were merely assisting the new head of the squadron at Brest. How did you come by such an injury?'

Christian looked down into her brown eyes, brimming with real concern. He wondered how to answer, whether to tell her that his own inattention during battle had led to a stupid error — inattention caused by memories of her that seemed to intrude upon his every waking moment.

He chose not to. She, after all, was hardly to blame for his overactive desires.

'We ran into a couple of privateers intent on helping themselves to our cannons. I disabused them of the notion, but not before they toppled my mast and me with it.'

Her skin took on an unmistakable pallor at his words, and he saw her hand reach out to him, then hesitate as if she were uncertain she should touch him. He took her hand and pressed it to his lips, feeling the quiver in her fingers even through her cotton gloves.

Neither spoke. Christian was suddenly aware that Zamore's dark eyes were upon them. No doubt the other stable hands, while assiduously intent upon their duties, were watching, too.

'It's Sunday, lads,' he said, giving them a quick smile. 'Be off with you till nightfall. I will see to the horses.'

They touched their caps and scurried away, all except Zamore, who stood tall and stared at his master.

'I shall rub down the mare and Malavoir,' he said.

'You will go and enjoy a swim in the river, or I will personally drop you in it,' replied Christian calmly. 'I shall tend to the animals.'

Zamore's eyes flashed, but he finally nodded, giving Catherine a quick glance as he left.

'He is a wonderful man,' she said quietly

316

once they were alone. 'I think you should find a better place for him. Do you know he can read and write?'

'Of course. I taught him to use an astrolabe, too.'

She turned to him, eyes as round as moons. 'You did?'

'When I brought him back to France with me. He was eager to learn everything he could.'

'He is wasted as a servant.'

Christian resisted the inclination to laugh at her earnestness. 'Utterly.'

She seemed surprised. 'If you agree, then why do you employ him as your groom?'

He shrugged, turning away and hobbling towards the bucket that one of the men had left on the stone floor of the stable. 'He wants to be a sailor, but the navy is not ready for that.'

He picked up the bucket in one hand and tried not to splash its contents as he hobbled across to Catherine's white mare. Curse that damn sea brigand's black heart. This stupid wound was making him feel like a damn fool.

An instant later, he felt her fingers close over his as she drew the rope out of his hand.

'Let me do that, before you break your other leg.'

He watched as she swung the wooden

bucket and plopped it down in front of the horse, who was cool enough to drink her fill now.

''Tis not broken. It got in the way of a piece of wood that was hit by cannon fire.'

She turned, looking straight at him with none of the vapid air of most ladies.

'A splinter, in other words.'

He shrugged. She studied him for a moment, then said, 'I shall look at it later and see if it needs dressing. Did you have stitches?'

He laughed aloud at that. 'If I say no, I suppose you'll get out your darning basket! No thanks. I'd as soon have my ship's surgeon attack it with his own weapons of torture.'

She pulled off her gloves, tucking them into the pocket of her skirt, and then rubbed the horse's nose, before moving to the next stall and doing the same for Malavoir. The great beast lowered his head for her as though accustomed to the fact that she could not reach behind his ears, where he had a special sweet spot.

'Contracting gangrene, so I am told, is also torture. But seldom survived.'

He grunted, mesmerized by the way her hands moved over the horse's broad black skull. The dopey creature was as infatuated with the woman as he was, which almost made Christian jealous. What he wouldn't give to have her do that to him . . .

'Captain?' She was standing right in front of him and he'd been too absorbed to listen. 'I said, would you like some refreshment?'

He would, but not the kind she had in mind. He groaned silently. What was he thinking? She was Dominic's wife now!

He shook his head, turning away. 'I'll rub the horses down. You go into the house. No doubt I'll see you at supper.'

Catherine stared at him, puzzled by the way he had suddenly withdrawn from her. Clearly his wound was significant, yet he seemed to discount it entirely. She watched him collect the brushes he needed and lift the rail to let himself into Malavoir's stall.

'No! Christian, you mustn't. What if he moves suddenly? He could crush you.'

She grabbed his arm and felt him stiffen. For a second, neither moved. She saw a muscle twitch in his jaw.

'Please?' she asked, more gently this time. 'Perhaps if we bring him out into the aisle, then we could both rub him down without fear.'

She breathed a sigh of relief as he nodded, then stepped in front of him to bring the horse out herself, for she worried that he might not be able to move quickly enough in the face of any sudden side-step on Malavoir's part.

Once he was tethered and happily munching on a bucket of oats, they began to groom his coat, unable to converse with the horse between them. They repeated this procedure with the smaller mare, and this time, they could at least see one another across the horse's back.

Still, silence hung between them. There were so many things Catherine wanted to say, but couldn't, and once or twice he seemed about to launch into a conversation and then fell silent.

She glanced across at him as she worked. He looked wonderful. His light-brown hair was tipped with gold from the sun and his skin was bronzed and healthy. His simple white shirt lay open at the neck, exposing a deep 'v' of sweat-slick golden skin. Her fingers itched to feel it, her tongue to taste its saltiness. Appalled by her own audacity, she lowered her eyes and concentrated on the white horsehair in front of her face.

'Catherine,' he said at last, leaning on the mare's back and staring solemnly at her across the space. 'If we brush this creature much more she's going to be bald. I believe I need to talk to you.'

Catherine's heart beat a little faster, but she

smiled, tossing the brush on the wooden bench behind her. 'I'll put her back in the stall.'

Now there was nothing left to keep them in the dusty stables, with its comfortable smell of hay and dried oats, yet Catherine was loath to return to the house.

'Why don't we walk in the garden?' Christian suggested.

'But your leg . . . ?'

'Is fine, so long as we don't go too far or too fast.'

They followed the little path that ran through one of the kitchen gardens and gave out directly onto the edge of the wood. It was cool and shady there and Catherine sighed, tugging at the strings of her bonnet.

She jumped at the sound of his voice beside her ear. 'Take it off. I like to see your hair loose.'

She continued to walk along the gravel path, but did as he asked, loosening the ribbons so it hung low on her back then laughing awkwardly as she felt his fingers twine in her tresses. Angé's words came back to her, full force — *you could always take him as your lover.* She stopped, turning to face him. Carefully, she covered his hands with her own and removed them from her hair.

'I am your cousin, now,' she said quietly.

He stared down at her, his blue eyes tinged with grey. 'I would have had it otherwise, Catherine. You know that.'

'No!' Her eyes filled with tears. 'That was unworthy of you, to offer for me on my wedding day. It was a cruel act.'

He turned away and she could see by the tension in his shoulders that her words had wounded him deeply, yet she could not bring herself to feel pity. It was she who was the injured party.

He turned back, his expression regretful. 'I never meant it so. I had tried to make you reconsider your betrothal, not because of my cousin, but because — '

'Because?'

'Because ... I thought you deserved better,' he finished lamely. Catherine turned away, for the melancholy in his face was breaking her heart. She walked on, pondering the hopelessness of their situations, and hearing Angé's words echoing around and around in her head: *Take him as your lover ... take him as your lover.*

How could she even begin to ask him something like that? How could any woman? Surely making such an approach was a male preserve?

She glanced at him, struggling along beside

her with his crutch, trying to pretend it was nothing. But the lines on his face were clearly etched and she knew it was causing him considerable pain.

'I think we should go back. Would you like to wait here while I fetch a sedan chair?'

'God forbid!' he replied. 'If you don't mind, I should like to rest at the spring.'

Catherine nodded; then, as it was still some distance further, tentatively reached out her arm and wrapped it about his waist for support.

He stilled, their eyes meeting for a heartbeat, and then he wrapped his free arm about her shoulders and they continued on their way, hips occasionally brushing as they walked. Catherine's heart was pounding, not with the effort of taking some of his weight, but with the touch of their bodies and the warmth of his arm where it lay on her shoulders. It would be such a small thing, to turn and bury her face in his chest, to feel his arms enfold her and to enjoy, if only for a moment, the sweet safety of his embrace.

She steeled herself against such fancies, forcing herself to concentrate on supporting him as they reached the end of the garden and the tiny waterfall. She eased him down onto the stone ledge beside the pool, then stepped away and found a spot for herself at a safe distance.

He noticed, she was sure, but said nothing.

The glade was cool and quiet, with dragonflies hovering over the trickling water in search of insects. A small frog croaked once from the rocks and fell silent.

'How are . . . things with you and Dominic?' he asked at length.

Catherine's head shot up. She opened her mouth to assure him that all was perfectly fine, but something about his expression made her change her mind. She shrugged. 'We have an understanding.'

'Concerning what?'

Catherine bent her head over the pool and trickled her fingers through the crystal water. 'Is that any of your concern, do you think?'

'None,' he answered quietly, 'except that I care for you both, though you probably don't believe that.'

She looked up. He was watching her with such an enigmatic expression that Catherine could *almost* read something in his eyes. But not quite.

She brushed the droplets of water away on the skirt of her apple-green gown. 'I believe you.'

'So?'

She shrugged. 'He . . . ' She wasn't sure

how to phrase it. 'He makes no demands upon me.'

She saw by the flash of emotions across his features that he clearly took her meaning, but his tone remained bland. 'Perhaps time will help.'

'Perhaps.'

For a few moments there was silence. A dog barked somewhere beyond the walls and a crow alighted on the top of a pine and began cawing before flying off again. Catherine knew that she would have no better time to explain herself to Christian, perhaps even to broach Angé's adulterous suggestion, but she couldn't seem to find the words. Suddenly, he led the way.

'I hear you are quite the heroine, by the by.' She looked up, puzzled. 'Gérard tells me that you saved his little boy's life last week by leaping into the river after him.'

She shrugged. ''Twas nothing. The child slipped on the wet grass while trying to retrieve his boat.'

'The Fontenays do not seem to think it was nothing.'

'They are lucky to have such beautiful children,' she said wistfully.

'Is that your hope, too?'

'Of course, but — '

'But?'

'My husband . . . '

She could not go on. Saying the words hurt too much, made the emptiness of the life before her too terrible to face.

'Come here,' Christian said softly, reaching out to draw her into his arms. She went willingly, thrilling at the feel of his strong arms around her as he pulled her to sit on his good knee.

She couldn't look at him, for her feelings were too raw, so she buried her face in his shoulder, feeling the pulse that beat strongly there and breathing in the essence of his skin.

His fingers wove through her hair, sliding under it to tilt up her head so he could look at her.

God, she was beautiful. Her wide, brown eyes were dark with emotion and her pink lips softly parted as though inviting a kiss. He felt the powerful tug of need that being this close to her always seemed to bring, but held himself in check, for he had enough guilt already where his cousin's wife was concerned.

And yet . . .

'I want to kiss you,' he said softly, unable to lift his eyes from her lips.

Her voice was as soft as a whisper of wind. 'And I you.'

Her invitation blew his scruples aside like

gossamer in a storm. He lowered his head, brushing his mouth lightly over hers. 'Like this?'

She nodded, her eyes closed, but he felt her body pressing a little closer to him and moaned with the response it provoked in him.

He slid one hand beneath her chin and raised her face to his, sweeping his lips over hers and then, as they parted in welcome, covering her mouth hungrily, letting his tongue search out hers until they were plundering each other's senses with wild abandon.

The kiss lasted until they both ran out of air. Christian set her away from him so he could look into her eyes, seeing a heat of desire there that surely matched his own.

Dear God, what was he doing? This was his own cousin's wife of less than two months! The same woman whose very memory had caused him to almost lose a leg, and yet here he was again, inviting — nay begging — for more trouble.

'Catherine, we cannot do this. This is not how cousins behave.'

'I know,' she replied in a small voice, 'but what choice do I have?'

He frowned. 'About what, pray?'

She grasped him by the arms, her entreaty now unmistakable. 'Christian, please. This is hard for me. I was not brought up to think like this, but — '

'What the devil are you talking about?'

She jumped up from his lap and began to stride across the glade in front of the pool, twisting her hands in front of her. Her straw bonnet, its daisies bobbing wildly, bounced about on the back of her neck where it hung on its ribbons.

'You must understand that when I entered into this betrothal, I desired only a family and children I could devote myself to. My mother had her hopes for me, and my father his own reasons for desiring this marriage, but for my part — '

She stopped, looking directly at him. 'Christian, if I cannot have even a child of my own to love and cherish, what purpose do I serve in life? Am I to have nothing to fill my days? What about me? What of *my* desires?'

Christian was losing the thread of this conversation, and he wasn't sure he wanted to steer it back to what was really troubling her. Yet she seemed to require an answer. 'You are afraid Dominic won't give you an heir?'

She flapped her arms at her side, her face scarlet. Christian understood, and he could see her pain. He knew how much she desired a family and he cursed himself again for not having done more to prevent her marriage.

'Catherine, 'tis not your fault. There is no shame in wanting a child. Look at all the joy Angé's children have brought her. I remember she was afraid that she, too, would never have children when her first husband died so soon. But then she met Gérard and — Well, you know the rest.'

''Twas her idea.'

'Idea?' He frowned. 'What was?'

She stared at him, beet red, then mumbled something and dashed away towards the trees.

'Catherine! Catherine, come back!' Oh, damnation, he thought, heaving himself up from the rock and grabbing for his accursed crutch.

To his surprise, she returned, stopping directly in front of him like a recalcitrant child, staring down at the tips of her shoes. A rush of words tumbled from her lips.

'Christian, I would like for you to become my lover and be the father of my children.'

His mouth opened, shut and opened again, but not a word came to mind. He stared down at the top of her head, watching the sun bounce red lights off her auburn curls, and all he could think about was standing on the deck of that stupid corvette thinking about making love to her while a cannon exploded amidships.

Finally, she looked up. There was not a trace of remorse in her eyes for the extraordinary words that had just passed from her lips. She seemed to be simply waiting.

'You're very sure of yourself,' was all he could seem to say.

'You seemed to like kissing me.'

'*Like*!' he exploded, causing her to jump back uneasily. 'Of course I *liked it*! But that doesn't make it right. Dear God, do you know what you're asking? There is a little more to making babies than stealing a kiss now and then.' He ran his free hand viciously through his hair. 'You expect me to sneak about at night behind my cousin's back, jumping into his wife's bed? More than that, you can stand there calmly and ask me if I would father my cousin's children under his very nose, as though you were asking me to pass you a bowl of cherries? Have you utterly lost your mind, woman?'

She made a small strangled sound, but he barely noticed.

'Goddammit, Catherine, you have bewitched me into many things since you first landed yourself in the midst of my life, but not this. I have some pride, you know, some principles. Obviously you do not!'

At that, she came to life, turning her back and fleeing through the trees with her skirts billowing behind her. He could hear her sobs all the way to his heart.

★   ★   ★

Catherine sent Martha away and spent the remainder of the afternoon lying on her bed with the bed curtains drawn, indulging in a fit of remorse and self-pity. She knew it was futile. She could never take back the shameful request she had made of Christian, and he rightly despised her for it. She felt as though she had lost her only real friend, apart from Angé.

And soon Angé would be gone, and Christian would no doubt return to his naval duties, and here she would be, the motherless wife of an uninterested duke, friendless in the midst of Revolution.

Such thoughts should have driven her to tears, but even that relief was denied her. She lay dry-eyed, clutching Bidou to her like a child's toy, her cheeks burning with the humiliation of the scene at the pool.

By the time Martha returned to help her dress for dinner, she had begun to hope that perhaps Christian would change his mind, once he'd had time to consider the notion.

The trouble was, she truly didn't know if she could accept it if he did agree. She seemed to be caught between two demons: the mortal sin of adultery versus the natural instinct of motherhood. If she did not commit the first, how could she ever fulfil her destiny in the other?

★　★　★

Christian poured himself a second cognac. He knew it was foolhardy to be drinking so much before dinner, but his leg was hurting like the devil and his conscience was no better.

He'd considered having a tray sent to his room and avoiding coming down to supper altogether, but Catherine would probably do that herself after the scene in the garden. There was not much point in them both hiding away, and anyway, he wanted to see his uncle and catch up on what had happened in Paris since his departure.

He swirled the brandy in the glass, letting it catch the candlelight. The strong spirit was almost the colour of Catherine's hair, yet it lacked the rich hue of her tresses, especially in sunlight.

Perhaps if he got drunk he would be able to blot today's entire episode from his mind. God knows, he needed to. All he'd been able to do all afternoon was think about how tantalizing her offer had been. Until she had actually voiced such a fool notion, he had been able to control his imagination — most of the time.

Now it was all he could do not to go up to her chamber this very moment and agree to the preposterous proposal. What would she do if he did, he mused? Would she fall into his arms?

He laughed down at the cognac, still untouched in his glass. She'd probably faint!

What had made her say it? How could she have made such an offer when she must know how impossible it was? Dominic was his cousin, his only cousin — almost a brother to him since the day his parents had died. Just because they were not close . . . How could Catherine believe his morals were so lax he would stoop to betraying his own family?

He sighed. Léonie would never have done such a thing. But then, her feelings for him were entirely fraternal. Despite everything, he was certain Catherine's affections went deeper.

He wandered to the open windows of the salon, where the day's warm breeze was cooling now. The scent of rain hung in the air, and the sun had set with no tinge of red to promise a fine day on the morrow.

The door opened. He turned, expecting his uncle, only to find Catherine staring at him. She was dressed in a demure blue dimity gown with a white muslin fichu tucked in at her waist. Her hair was tied back in a simple blue satin bow, leaving a few tendrils to curl about her face.

She looked wonderful.

Innocent.

Desirable.

Forbidden.

He swallowed hard.

'Would you like some wine?' he asked finally.

She nodded but did not speak, crossing the salon and sitting with her back to him.

He poured a glass of Madeira and handed it to her, then retrieved his brandy and stood by the mantel, wondering what on earth to say. There were so many thoughts in his mind that he could decide on no single course.

He'd lost his taste for cognac, anyway. He set the glass down.

'How is your leg?'

'What? Oh! It's fine,' he lied.

She gazed at him steadily and he looked away.

'Has the doctor seen it?'

He didn't want to talk about his damn leg. ''Tis fine,' he grumbled.

The wind gusted suddenly through the open window, bringing a sharp smattering of raindrops. He hobbled towards it, but she jumped up quickly and pulled the sash down before he could. She remained where she was, looking out into the rain-swept dark. He could see her face reflected in the glass as he stood behind her. His arms ached to reach out and take her by the shoulders, but he made no move. *She's your cousin's wife*, he kept telling himself.

She was looking at him in the darkened glass. Her voice, when she finally spoke, cracked with emotion.

'I am sorry for what I said.'

He stared back. 'As am I. I spoke more harshly than I should.'

'It was a stupid notion.'

'Yes.'

She looked down, then turned and slipped past him, careful that not even their clothes should touch. She resumed her place on the chair, folding her hands in her lap.

Christian's leg ached abominably. He sat on the *chaise-longue* and stretched it out before him, looking at her as she waited dejectedly for supper to be announced.

Finally, he could bear the tension no longer.

'I am not without feelings, either, you know.'

She looked up. 'I did not think otherwise.'

'Yet you repeatedly insisted you had to marry my cousin, whom you did not love nor even much like, and when I asked you to be my wife, you — '

'You asked me on the morning of my wedding! Your purpose was merely to stop the marriage.' He stared at her, for he had never seen her quite so angry before. 'How can you have the effrontery to assert that your intentions were anything but dishonest?'

He was shocked that she saw his proposal that way, but, since there was nothing to be done about it now, it scarcely mattered. If that was her opinion of him, then so be it.

'So now you think you can have both of us. Dominic for his title and me for . . . ' His voice trailed off. He couldn't bring himself to say lovemaking, not to her face. 'You do not know me nearly as well as you think, madame, if you would consider for even one minute that I would betray my cousin.'

Her cheeks were scarlet. 'You make no secret that you dislike him.'

'I think he could have made himself a better man, but that is merely my opinion.

Apart from Cousin Angé, he and my uncle are the only family I have.'

She turned to the *guéridon* beside the chair and picked up her glass. He noticed that her fingers trembled slightly.

'Would your kisses have been less impassioned had you not planned to seduce me, Catherine?' he asked quietly, causing her to spill some of the wine on her skirt.

She glared at him, set down the glass and drew a handkerchief from her pocket. 'You will excuse my confusion, Captain,' she replied acidly, as she stabbed at the droplets on her skirt, 'but my memory remembers the incident differently. It seemed *you* were the one trying to seduce *me!*'

He grimaced. 'If so, it was only because — ' How could he tell her that he had been unable to think of anything else for weeks while he was away? That would hardly discourage her advances now. And discourage her, he must. He sighed. It seemed he was destined to get himself entangled with other people's wives. First Léonie and now Catherine.

'Pray, think no more about it,' she said haughtily, as she tucked the handkerchief away. 'I shall find someone who will be only too pleased to oblige me — Angé tells me such arrangements are perfectly common in

Paris. I am certain I shall have no difficulty choosing someone to my taste.'

He gasped, then bit back an angry retort as the door opened and the prince came in.

They went straight in to the dining-room, Christian seething over her callow words. But at least now he had the real measure of the woman. First opinions were often right, as he had so frequently observed. This American was simply out for what she could get. She'd had no qualms about marrying an invalid for his title; now she thought to snap her fingers and get any man she fancied into her bed.

But not Christian Lavelle. She had chosen the wrong man.

The prince, fortunately, seemed unaware of the tensions that ran high between them as they sat down. He first grilled Christian on his injury, then on the naval port of Brest. They talked of preparations being made for d'Entrecasteaux's voyage to the Pacific and of the clumsy vessels he had been allocated for this perilous journey. The navy's title of 'frigate' did nothing to make the refitted store ships into useful vessels for the task ahead of them, and Christian was not slow to express his foreboding regarding what this might mean for his own future command. Money remained a contentious issue.

But although the prince asked many

questions, Christian had the impression it was more for the sake of form. His uncle seemed to have no more than half an ear for the conversation, and Catherine seemed entirely absorbed in the meal, though she appeared to do more playing with her food than actually putting it in her mouth.

Eventually, he could stand it no more.

'Uncle, is something troubling you?'

The prince looked up from his barely touched dish of ice cream and wild strawberries. They shared a glance, then the prince looked at his daughter-in-law.

He sighed, setting down his silver spoon. 'Perhaps you can help me persuade Catherine and Dominic that it would be best if they left France,' he said, 'for I have been unable to budge them. Things are quiet now, but still the king is under guard and has not agreed to sign the new constitution. The fanatics are pushing for a republic and the return of all émigrés from abroad — to what purpose I can only shudder to think. It is not safe, Christian. If they are to go, it must be soon.'

Christian glanced at Catherine, but she was toying with a small bunch of grapes, plucking them slowly and dropping them one by one onto her plate.

'What can I do?'

The prince shrugged. 'Persuade your

cousin. I have suggested he go to Italy. At least there they will have a place to call home.'

Christian grimaced. 'If memory serves, I do not believe Dominic has a very high opinion of Italians.'

'Better that than Frenchmen out for his blood.'

Catherine's head came up. 'What can you mean, sir? Have you not made every concession asked of you? We have offended no party — why should any of us be in danger?'

The prince looked away. Christian had the uneasy feeling there was something he was not telling them. Perhaps he would ask later, when he could speak to his uncle alone.

'You are not, my dear,' he said sending her a smile. 'I am merely being cautious. If you are to start a family, it would be best to be somewhere safer, that is all.'

Christian saw Catherine's cheeks redden, but she avoided his eyes and excused herself from the table, claiming a headache.

When the door had closed upon her, the prince spoke again. 'When I heard you were coming home so soon, I was hopeful that we could effect their escape right away, Christian, but since you are wounded, it will have to wait. No doubt I am fussing unnecessarily.'

340

Christian wondered about that. 'I hear de Bernier has been arrested.'

The prince nodded. 'There are others, as well.'

They contemplated the sorry state of things while they drank their coffee and the rain pattered on the shutters beyond the windows.

'And you, Uncle?' Christian said later. 'Will you go with them to Italy?'

The prince looked at his nephew with a sadness that struck Christian to the core.

'No, dear boy. I believe I may have to entrust their safety to you.'

15

Christian was fully occupied for the next few days with his work at the Ministry of Marine, despite the ache in his leg. The doctor had dressed it and urged him to change the bandages regularly, but he had been lax and he was paying the price by Thursday. So when a sharp knock came on his office door at noon, he was in no mood to be pleasant.

'*Entrez!*' he barked, not even turning from his charts to see who it was.

'*Monsieur le Capitaine Lavelle?*' enquired a young voice. Christian turned to see a young street urchin, dressed in rags, holding a note that had once been on clean white parchment.

'What is it, boy?'

'I have a message for you, *citoyen.*'

Christian reached into his pocket and withdrew a coin which he tossed to the ragamuffin. 'Give it here, then, and be off.'

The child was only too happy to oblige. Christian broke the seal, which was unstamped, and unravelled the paper. It was from his uncle.

'Meet me at the Conciergerie,' it read, and

was signed simply 'J-F'. Joseph-François, the prince's first name.

Christian muttered a curse, grabbed his crutch and hobbled from the room, calling out to his clerk that he would not be back that day.

The Conciergerie! The medieval prison in the Palais de Justice. The note did not say the prince had been arrested, yet Christian could think of no other explanation.

He reached the street and hailed a cab, ordering it to the Île de la Cité. Although it did not take long, with his anxiety and every jolt of the vehicle searing his leg, it seemed an age.

He was escorted into the high-vaulted Salle des Gardes and presented himself to the gaoler, an unkempt individual with rotting teeth and a clutch of heavy keys tied around his corpulent waist. Christian resisted the temptation to raise a kerchief to his nostrils.

'I am here to see Citoyen Charigny,' he said, eyeing the *sans-culottes* who stood at one side of the large room holding evil-looking pikes in their hands. They looked as if they would like an excuse to use them.

'And whom might you be, citizen?'

'Lavelle.'

'Lavelle.' The man stroked the grimy stubble on his chin. 'I've heard that name before. Now where . . . ?' Finally, it came to him. 'Eh, you that navy captain? I got a nephew in the navy.'

'Is that so? May I see Monsieur Charigny?'

'*Monsieur?*' The gaoler spat a large globule of mucus into the dirt on the floor. 'When they get in here they're just plain citizens, like the rest of us.'

'Citoyen Charigny,' Christian repeated, beginning to lose patience. He reached into his pocket and withdrew a gold louis. 'Perhaps this will help. No doubt your wife needs a new dress.' She'll need a new husband if you don't hurry up, he thought.

The man pocketed the gold greedily. It seemed to improve his mood. 'Indeed sir, always happy to oblige. Follow me.'

He led Christian along a series of dark corridors until finally he stopped, selected one of the keys at his belt and inserted it into a lock, swinging the heavy wooden door wide.

'You got ten minutes,' he said, locking him in.

'Christian!'

His uncle enveloped him in a hug, but Christian was alarmed by the feebleness of the embrace. He held his uncle at arm's length and studied him in the weak light of a high barred window.

'Are you ill, Uncle? Why are you here?

Never fear. I shall have you out before the day is over.'

The prince shook his head sadly and pointed him to a chair. 'Sit down, dear boy. Your leg is still not healed. Let us have some wine. At least they allow me some of the comforts of home.'

Christian's brows rose as he looked about him. The room was reasonably clean, had been whitewashed once, perhaps in the days of the king's grandfather. A small bed stood against one wall, and there was a stool as well as the chair on which he now sat. The prince was pouring wine from a pewter jug at a small wooden side table, over which was mounted a shelf containing a candlestick and a tinder-box.

Not exactly 'all the comforts of home', he thought as he accepted the wine. He'd had more luxurious appointments during his days as a lieutenant on his first voyage to the Pacific.

They sipped at the wine, which was rough but drinkable.

'So, Uncle, what are you charged with?'

The prince sighed. ''Tis a long story, Christian. Yesterday, perhaps not entirely by accident, an iron chest was discovered in the Tuileries. Not by a member of the king's party, unfortunately. There were papers in there that I have been attempting to locate since my friend Mirabeau passed away. I had no chance to speak to him privately before he died, so I was not able to ascertain their whereabouts.'

'What are these papers, and why should they concern you?'

'They involved discussions we were having for the restoration of the monarchy. Mirabeau was being paid handsomely for his work, but the real nature of it was a secret. Until now.'

'And you?'

'And I was foolhardy enough, in the beginning, to add my voice to some of those notes.'

Christian swore under his breath. He stared at his uncle. 'So now they are arresting you because Mirabeau is already dead. Not only that, but he was buried in the Panthéon as a great man!'

'There is talk that his body will be exhumed.'

Christian shook his head. 'What are we coming to, Uncle? Is this where Louis' inaction has led us, to suspicion and intrigue, men who change from being heroes one moment to traitors the next?'

The prince shrugged. 'We never knew where it would lead, nor do we now. If the king refuses to sign the constitution . . .'

Suddenly, something his uncle had said came back to Christian. 'Wait, you said when the papers were discovered you thought it was not an accident. What did you mean by that?'

'I'm not certain myself. I heard the name Foscari mentioned, but I have never met such a person, nor had any dealings with an Italian of that na — '

'*Merde!*'

'Christian?' His uncle frowned. 'Do you know this man?'

'Not really. No, Uncle, 'tis nothing. But perhaps I can find out what it means. If we could prove the papers were forged — '

'They were not.'

There was silence for a moment, then Christian set down his goblet on the floor and took his uncle's hands. 'Tell me what I can do.'

'For me, nothing. I am at the end of my life and my health is not what it was. I have done what I wanted and seen my son married, though I would have liked to see a grandchild or two before I die.'

Christian thought of Catherine and her desperation for the same event, but forced it from his mind.

The prince went on, 'You must promise me, Christian, that you will get them out of France. I have never asked you to do anything for me in your life, until now. Please. Can I trust you to get Dominic and his bride to safety?'

Christian felt a dead weight settle on him, but how could he refuse? 'Of course, Uncle. I shall get you all out.'

The gaoler knocked on the door and they heard the key being inserted into the ancient lock.

'Not I, dear boy. You have no need to — '

'You are entitled to a trial, Uncle!'

'The trial will take too long!' His uncle's voice was demanding now. 'Do not wait, Christian. Promise me!'

Light from the hallway spilled into the small room. Christian hugged his uncle tightly and picked up his crutch. 'I shall send you some things before nightfall, Uncle. God keep you.'

Then he left the cell, not looking back as the sound of the key grating in the lock cut him off from the only father he could remember.

★ ★ ★

They gathered in Dominic's rooms, sending the servants away. Word had spread to the house before Christian had even arrived, and he found everyone in a dither. He did his best to be reassuring, but his uncle's valet, especially, was badly shaken.

Dominic was stunned. He had taken such a bad turn when he'd heard the news that Brassart had persuaded him to rest in bed. Now, Christian and Catherine sat on either side of him on the deep feather mattress.

'How could they do this?' Catherine cried, her eyes wide with fright. 'He has never expressed a harsh word to anyone.'

Christian sighed. 'He knows he is in great trouble. Mirabeau, clearly, is the lucky one. He at least is dead and doesn't have to face his accusers.'

'The king will help him, surely,' said Dominic, though he sounded as shaken as Catherine by the events of the day.

'There is nothing he can do. He is still a prisoner himself, at least unless he chooses to sign the constitution.'

'He could pardon him!'

'Dominic, your father's crime is not against the king! It is against the people.'

At that, the duke lapsed into moody silence. Catherine felt for him. Until now, he seemed to have been able to ignore the unpleasantness of the Revolution and hide away from its realities. But no more.

She reached out a hand and laid it atop his. 'He will have a fair trial, Your Grace.

There is still hope.'

But his look told her he didn't believe that any more than she did.

'Your father made me promise to get you both out of France,' Christian said in a low voice, clearly fearful that there could be eavesdroppers at the door or in the adjoining rooms. 'I shall have to obtain travel documents for you. Meanwhile, you must say nothing of this to anyone, not even your own personal servants. Is that quite clear?'

'Are you saying I cannot even trust Brassart?' Dominic was indignant.

'Trust no one. We must speak of this only where there is no chance of our being overheard and we must continue with our normal daily routines as though we have every intention of remaining in Paris to stand by the prince until his trial. That must be our publicly stated goal.'

Catherine took a deep breath, for there was a lump of fear forming in her chest. 'Who may we take with us?'

'No one.'

Dominic spluttered. 'I must have Brassart! I cannot possibly manage without him.'

Christian looked sternly at his cousin. 'You will have me and you will have your wife. Between us we can provide whatever you need. In the meantime, I suggest that you start getting some strength into those atrophied limbs — without exciting comment from the servants. You will need whatever strength you can garner.'

For once, his cousin did not argue, but Catherine saw that he was deeply troubled.

'Did my father ask to see me?'

Catherine saw a flash of dismay cross Christian's face, but it was gone when he replied, 'Of course he did, Dominic, but he also thought it would be safer for you not to visit him. Your face is not well known on the streets and, given our predicament, that is an advantage. We must keep it that way. You too, Catherine,' he said, addressing her directly for the first time. 'You must cease your rides with Zamore. Receive visitors as usual, and go about as you normally would, but use a carriage and keep the curtains drawn.'

She nodded.

'Go now, Catherine. Gather the servants and reassure them that the whole business is nothing but a misunderstanding. I need to speak with my cousin.'

She looked quickly from one man to the other, their resemblance so strong and yet their personalities so different. Perhaps this whole frightful business would bring them closer together. She could only hope some good might come of it.

When the door had closed behind Catherine, Christian's manner changed abruptly.

'Very well, Cousin. Now that we are alone, perhaps you can tell me about Signor Foscari's role in all of this.'

Dominic's shock was evident, which mollified Christian a little.

'What can you mean? How could Foscari be involved in . . . ' His voice trailed off and he lay back against the covers with a weary sigh. 'Oh *nom de Dieu*, I threw him out.'

'He came back?' Christian felt anger growing, but tamped it down deliberately. It was important to discover the truth, and he would get nothing out of Dominic by threatening him.

'Once you were gone, he thought he would be safe. I had Brassart throw the weevil out and tell the servants to run him through if he tried to return.'

'Did you, be damned?' Christian's estimation of his cousin rose a notch, something it hadn't done for a long time.

'But he vowed he would get even.'

'It seems he found the perfect way.'

'But how? What contacts would Foscari have at the Tuileries?'

'Money is all the contact you need these days, Dominic.'

'Does my wife know of this?'

Christian winced inwardly at the sound of 'wife' on his cousin's lips. 'No. She has no need to know. It would only make her more fearful.'

There was a moment's silence, then Christian felt his cousin's hand on his. 'Will they execute my father?' he asked, his voice barely above a whisper.

Christian grimaced. 'Not if I can help it, Dominic. The trouble is, he has refused my help. He cares only for you and Catherine.'

'But you will help him.'

They looked straight at one another, brother to brother, sharing the pain without words.

'You have my word.'

★ ★ ★

There was nothing to be done that night, though Christian sent Zamore with a package of books, food and cognac to the Conciergerie for his uncle. He himself was exhausted, and fell into bed without undressing, succumbing to sleep almost instantly.

He was awakened when the blackamoor came to rouse him, confused to find himself still in his boots and breeches when the sun was high in the sky, and not pleased to find Catherine at his bedside.

'Undress him, Zamore. Cut off his boots if you must.'

Christian tried to sit up, but his head felt woozy. 'Damn. What the hell did I drink last night?'

'Very little, if I recall,' Catherine said crisply. 'You are ill. Lie down and be silent.'

'Be si — ' He glared at her as the big black man pressed him to the pillow. 'Zamore, get your hands off me!'

'No, sir. You must do as *madame* says.'

'The hell I will! Who do you work for, anyway?'

'You, sir,' came the quiet reply, as the man wrenched the boot off his good foot.

Christian grabbed the hessian and threw it across the room. 'Then leave me be! I can dress and undress myself.'

Zamore took hold of the other boot and pulled. Christian screamed.

'Cut it.' This from Catherine.

The blackamoor took a wicked-looking dagger from his own boot and neatly slit the leather, exposing an ugly swollen calf and foot. He then proceeded to slice through the fine calfskin of Christian's best pair of breeches.

'You don't do things by halves, do you, *Madame la Duchesse?*' Christian ground out through clenched teeth.

'I may be an *ingénue* in French society, Captain, but after years as a sickbed nurse I know more than I ever cared to about medicine. And one thing I have learned is that being faint-hearted is the worst thing one can be.' She stared at the grimy, sweat-stained bandage encasing Christian's thigh, then nodded at Zamore, who used his knife one last time to sever the muslin and lay open the wound.

It was bad, but not gangrenous. 'You are lucky, Captain. With a thorough cleansing and proper dressing every few hours, you may yet walk on two legs for a few more years.'

'Where the hell's my doctor?'

Zamore grinned, displaying a row of white teeth. 'She's right here, sir.' Christian groaned.

Catherine worked quickly, laying towels beneath the leg to protect the bedding, stripping off the old dressings and washing the torn flesh. It had clearly begun to knit together, but in places breaks had appeared in the barely formed scar and malodorous fluids were seeping out. The whole leg was swollen and red and his skin was hot to the touch.

'I am tempted to lance it,' she told him

brusquely, satisfied by the flicker of alarm in his eyes, 'as a reminder to you to take better care of yourself in future. But I think a good cleansing and a poultice I learned from the Delaware Indians will do as well. I am not much keen on revenge.'

'The Indians! From what I've heard, they have some interesting methods of torture — I trust this is not one of them.'

She made no reply, though a faint curve touched her lips. Instead, she sent Zamore for boiling water and muslin bandages. When he had gone, she leaned over the bed so he could see her. 'Christian, I am going to make you well, so you can keep your promise to your uncle. If you die, we shall be trapped here, so don't imagine I am doing this out of the kindness of my heart.'

He smiled. 'Does this mean you're going to pamper me?'

She spluttered, jumping off the bed as though burned. 'You are quite the most impossible man I have ever known!'

'Yet you asked me to father your children.'

She whirled away from him, her face burning. Grabbing a crystal decanter, she poured him a hefty glass of cognac.

'Drink this!' she ordered sharply, avoiding his eyes.

'I haven't had breakfast.'

'Good. The less there is in your stomach, the happier I shall be.'

She was right, too, for once she started work on his leg, he tossed back the brandy and was grateful.

★   ★   ★

She gave him a draught of something when she was done, and the next he knew the sun was coming up again. God, had he slept an entire day away?

He sat up sharply, then groaned, clutching his head. Gingerly, he lay back on the pillows waiting for the room to stop spinning.

'You are awake,' came a soft voice from near the window.

'Catherine?'

She crossed the room, her pale-yellow gown like a ray of floating sunlight as it approached.

'What was in that potion you gave me?'

He heard her laugh. 'All manner of things you need not concern yourself with. Are you feeling a little better?'

'I'm not sure.'

Then he felt her fingers descend on his brow, the palm of her hand press against his forehead, cool and soft.

'That feels good,' he murmured, closing his eyes.

'Your fever is almost gone. Let me check your leg.'

He watched, fascinated by the professional detachment with which she lifted the sheets and exposed his leg, seeming unconcerned to be so close to — He stifled a gasp as her fingers pried around his thigh, prodding the edges of the wound.

She stilled, frowning at him. 'Does that hurt?'

Christian laughed. 'No.'

'Then why . . . ? Oh.' She blushed, deeply and — to Christian's way of thinking — in a most gratifying manner.

She tugged the sheet down quickly, but although it covered him it was precious little to disguise the effect her touch had produced. He watched her as she crossed to the window and picked up a shawl that had fallen to the floor from the windowseat.

He frowned. 'Have you been here all night?'

She wrapped the shawl around her shoulders, hugging it to herself, and nodded.

He didn't know what to say.

'You were . . . not well,' she muttered. 'I thought it best that I be here in case I was needed.'

'Catherine — ' He reached out a hand. She stared at it, and for a moment he thought she would refuse to approach him. Then she sighed, crossing to the bed and taking his fingers awkwardly in her own. 'I'm sorry for what has happened between us since my return. I don't want it to spoil our friendship. We shall need to rely on each other soon enough.'

'Will we go as soon as you are well enough to travel?'

'Sooner, I hope.'

But she shook her head, making her russet curls bob and sway down her back. 'We will not move from here until you are completely fit. Dominic is weak — he will need your strength.'

Christian looked at her, with her chin jutting out in determination. She looked like she would have enough fortitude for them all.

'Another day or two,' he said, 'and I'll be ready.'

'Five at least,' she countered.

'Three.'

They settled on four.

★   ★   ★

But it was not to be. Christian's leg took a week to be rid of infection and left him limping for several days more. While he was thus indisposed, Catherine sent a note to Lafayette asking him to visit. She and Christian dined with him, and even Dominic made his way downstairs in the interests of persuading the general to intercede on the prince's behalf.

The response was noncommittal, but Catherine felt that was better than nothing.

With their planned escape imminent, she turned her attention to other matters that had been set aside during all the upheaval, commencing with Martha and Emile's wedding. They were married by a juring priest in the little church of Saint-Bénédict, with all the servants from the Hôtel de Charigny in attendance, as well as Emile's considerable extended family. Afterwards, at a party Catherine had organized to celebrate the event, they were married again by Father Joubert, to satisfy Martha's stringent religious convictions.

It was a joyous event, providing a much-needed change in the generally sub-dued tone of daily life that had prevailed since the prince's arrest.

The happy couple, having already used Catherine's generous gift to secure a small farm outside Chantilly, left soon after to begin their new life.

Catherine hugged Martha goodbye on the front steps.

'Thank you for all you have done, dear friend,' she said tearfully, kissing the Irishwoman on the cheek.

'Oh, Miss Kitty, 'tis I should be thanking you. If you had not given me and Emile this gift, we would never have stood a chance — '

'Fiddle,' Catherine replied, teary-eyed. 'Love will find a way, isn't that what they say?'

Martha harrumphed. 'So they do, and best you not be forgetting it, neither, Miss Kitty!'

Catherine laughed. 'I'll do my best, Martha.'

She watched as they climbed into the rented carriage. Their meagre belongings were already strapped to the roof, ready for the journey. Catherine envied them — how simple it all seemed, to marry the man one loved and go somewhere to start a new life, a family of one's own. Not for them the dangers of fleeing the country in secret.

Martha leaned out of the carriage as it began to move. 'I shall name my first babe after you, Miss Kitty!' she called. Christian, standing just behind Catherine, laughed. 'They had better hope 'tis not a boy, then.'

They stood, long after the servants had gone inside to return to the wedding feast, watching as the coach rumbled away towards the river.

When it turned north and was at last out of sight Catherine looked about her, noting that the front doors were closed and they were alone on the steps.

'Christian,' she said in a low voice, 'I know we too must leave soon, but we cannot go and leave the prince in gaol. We must do something to help him.'

Christian shrugged. 'I have done what I can. I have spoken on his behalf to everyone I dare to hope might have some influence over his release.'

'With what result, pray?'

'None. So far.'

She was silent a moment. 'You do not believe in his innocence.'

'How can I? He has told me himself that the documents are genuine.'

'And yet you have said he was betrayed.'

Christian shrugged again, avoiding her eyes. Catherine frowned, wondering why he would not tell her.

'Why do you not trust me, Captain?'

He seemed taken aback. 'Of course I do. How else could I contemplate what we are planning?'

'Then tell me what else you know about my father-in-law's arrest.'

'Nothing. There is nothing to tell.'

He reached for the brass doorknob, but she stayed his hand. 'Who was it that betrayed him?'

She held her breath as she waited and, for a moment, wondered whether he might refuse to answer. Finally, he sighed.

'I do not know for certain, but I believe it was Foscari.'

Catherine gasped. 'That Italian? The one who — ?' She shuddered, remembering the feel of his fingers on her body, the gleam in his eyes that still turned her stomach when she thought of it. 'But why?'

'Because, my sweet, he came back when I was away and Dominic had him thrown out. Wounded pride is a great incentive to revenge, and Foscari is an extremely vain individual.'

They went inside, but Catherine was in no mood to rejoin the revellers in the servants' hall after Christian's revelation. She retired to her private salon to sit in her favourite window nook and think about what Christian had told her. Then an idea came to her. She rang the bell, and when a young maid appeared, asked her to send up Zamore.

The blackamoor listened to what she told him and left without a word, promising to return by nightfall.

While she waited, she occupied herself in making adjustments to a few of the clothes she had secretly removed from Martha's things when the maid was packing her belongings. She had tucked some pretty cottons and muslins in their place, so Martha could make some new clothes for herself.

The clothes were somewhat large for Catherine, and she wanted them to fit comfortably. Who knew for how long they would need such disguises?

Zamore returned near midnight, tapping softly on her door and apparently not surprised to see her still fully dressed and waiting for him. Catherine listened to his news and bade him good night, but she did not go to bed.

She spent several hours making lists and notes from some of the books she had brought with her from America. Then, exhausted, she burned all the notes in the fireplace and stirred the ashes, falling into bed as dawn was beginning to pale the eastern sky.

Catherine slept later than she intended and came down for breakfast next morning after ten. Due to the late hour and the warm sunshine, she decided to take her refreshment on the terrace, and in so doing encountered her husband already up and taking some air.

'Your Grace!' she said, surprised and delighted to see such improvement. He was sitting in a cane chair, wearing a simple white chemise and no wig.

Catherine stared at her husband, having seldom seen him without his wig. His hair was receding rather sharply from his fore-head, she noticed.

'Good morning, my dear,' he said, apparently amused by her astonishment. 'The sun is quite pleasantly warm. Pray, sit with me.'

She accepted his offer in silence, waiting while Brassart, who appeared from the dining-room doors like the shadow he liked to emulate, brought her a cup and saucer.

She glanced up at him. 'I believe I should like tea this morning, Brassart.'

'Very good, *Madame la Duchesse*,' he replied, disappearing like a wraith in search of the pot.

'You are feeling well today, Dominic,' Catherine said, watching him carefully.

'It's an uncommonly promising day, my dear,' he replied, passing her a news sheet which lay open on the table before him.

'What is this?'

'Examine it yourself.'

She picked up the sheet, which was one of

those published by the more moderate groups in the city. Still, she had not known her husband concerned himself enough to bother with such things.

'There!' Dominic's finger pointed to a passage outlined in black.

' 'His Majesty the Emperor and His Majesty the King of Prussia — ' ' she read aloud. 'Whatever is this?'

'It is called the Pillnitz Declaration. Pray, continue.'

Brassart brought a silver teapot, poured her tea and left the pot on the table. Catherine resumed reading, saying some parts aloud and skipping others.

' ' . . . declare jointly that they regard the present situation of the King of France as a subject of common interest to all the sovereigns of Europe . . . and that in consequence they will not refuse to employ . . . the most effective means . . . to assist the King of France . . . '.' She looked up at Dominic with a frown. 'What does that mean?'

He indicated the paper, so she read further, scanning the comments about the rights of kings and the well-being of the French nation and then reading aloud, in astonishment, the last portion: ' ' . . . they will give their troops appropriate orders to act'. Dominic, is

Prussia going to war with France?'

He smiled. 'So it seems.' He looked about him, then waved to Brassart who was tidying things at the sideboard in the dining-room. 'Fetch *Madame la Duchesse* some eggs. Poached.' The servant bowed and retreated to the kitchens.

'But I don't want eggs, Dominic! I am perfectly content with my usual brioche.'

'But I am not content to have Brassart's ears flapping,' he replied, then pointed to the news sheet with one finger. 'Don't you see, we shall not have to flee after all. The monarchies of Europe will come together and invade France, restore Louis and put down these vagabonds once and for all.'

Catherine looked dubious. 'But a war? Do you not think that might make the situation even more precarious for your father? After all, he will be seen as having actively supported such a plan. As will we.'

Dominic looked a little concerned for a moment, but then shook his head as if to banish such thoughts. 'He will be vindicated. You will see.'

Catherine was not so sure. 'I do not see any such happy outcome, Your Grace. Even were the invasion to succeed, it would take weeks, perhaps months. In the meantime, the *sans-culottes* will be looking for scapegoats.'

She shook her head. 'I am truly sorry not to share your optimism, but I believe your cousin is right. We must keep to our plan.'

Moments later she excused herself, meeting Brassart with the eggs as she left through the dining-room, explaining that she was not hungry after all.

She returned to her room and, mindful of Christian's warning that they should not show their faces on the streets any more than was necessary, she summoned a maid and ordered the small carriage. Dressing quickly in one of her plainest gowns from her days in Philadelphia, she bundled her hair beneath a large straw hat that shaded her face, and left the house.

She took the carriage to the Marais, a district she seldom visited, for it was not popular among the well-to-do, and ordered the driver to take her to an apothecary's shop she had heard of.

Catherine hurried inside, made her purchases as quickly as she could — buying a number of items, including some which she would have no use for — and returned to the carriage.

She was home within the hour.

★ ★ ★

Contrary to Dominic's belief that the *sans-culottes* would be cowed by the thought of Europe invading France to restore the monarchy, he was dismayed to discover that they welcomed war. Instead, they believed that France would defeat all the remaining monarchies of Europe — even England's — and create liberty for all, as they had done in France. Robespierre made impassioned speeches against such notions, but the idea of war seemed refreshing and inevitable to the poor.

Suddenly, the tables were turned, and with it, the duke's opposition to fleeing France began to dissolve.

Christian came to his room the night after the Pillnitz Declaration, and told him to prepare. He was to bring nothing — no clothes, jewels, no possessions that could identify him. Worse, he left a set of garments that Dominic was supposed to wear — the dowdy black dress of a provincial lawyer. Dominic was mollified that he need not pretend he was a peasant.

He sat for some time after his cousin had departed, staring at the garments. He looked around his salon, with its priceless paintings and ornaments, rich furnishings and gilded mirrors.

Leave it all, Christian had said. Dominic

snorted. 'Twas easy for him to say — he hadn't been born to it as Dominic had. This was his life, his heritage, the essence of what made him.

How would they live? If they escaped, how should he provide for himself and his wife?

A sudden flood of bitterness when he considered her family's wealth next to his own threatened to overtake him, but then he had a thought. The money. Her enormous dowry. Perhaps some of it was still in the house. He knew his father had already exchanged some of the bills and made investments with others, but might not the remainder be at their disposal?

Dominic took a candle and let himself out of his room, making his way slowly down the stairs, for he was still unused to such manoeuvres on his own. He opened the door to his father's study and closed it softly behind him, setting the light on the desk. For a moment he listened, then when he heard no sound from the sleeping house, he set to work.

16

The next day being Sunday, Catherine attended mass in the little family chapel at her husband's side, and then breakfasted lightly, for her nerves would allow nothing more. Making her excuses, she went to her room, dismissed her new maid and spent a few minutes in preparation.

Then she summoned a carriage, requesting Zamore as her driver, snatched up a covered basket from the small table beside the door and ran downstairs.

It was raining lightly and the streets of Paris were slick, but a light sun shone through and Catherine peeked out at the rainbow that hung over the magnificent cathedral of Notre-Dame in the distance. Perhaps it was a good omen. The carriage stopped and Zamore handed her down.

They entered the formidable prison of La Conciergerie, Catherine clasping her basket tightly, feeling a horrible sense of doom. She wondered whether she had the strength to do this, whether it might not be better to leave things in the hands of Fate.

But, as they entered the high-vaulted Salle

des Gardes and came face to face with her father-in-law's gaolers, she put such timidity from her mind.

She explained who she was and asked to see the prince. Her basket was taken, none too politely, its contents emptied on a broad wooden table and picked over thoroughly. She was left to repack the cakes and meats and breads while they watched suspiciously, no doubt annoyed to have found nothing. Then she was ready. She and Zamore were escorted through the long damp corridors.

It was like entering a tomb. The prison was surely the most oppressive edifice she had ever entered and, were it not for the love she felt for the prince, who had never shown her anything but kindness, she would never have set foot in such a place.

She swallowed, forcing herself to breathe in and out slowly, lest the close space overwhelm her. She must be strong.

The gaoler unlocked a heavy door and they were admitted.

'Half an hour, *citoyenne*,' he exhorted, as he locked it behind them.

Catherine saw the look of astonishment on her father-in-law's face as they entered.

'My dearest Catherine! And Zamore! Pray, what is that nephew of mine thinking that he would send you to visit me in this frightful place?'

He hugged her, tears in his eyes. He looks so frail, so beaten, Catherine thought with dismay. And yet, that would do no harm.

'Christian did not send us, sir. We are here at my sole bidding.' She glanced at Zamore. 'In fact, the captain would be most displeased with me were he aware of our visit.'

The prince frowned. 'I think you had better explain, my dear. Pray, be seated. Would you like some wine?'

'No, truly, there is no time.' She passed him the basket. 'These are for you. I fear they are the last we may bring you.'

The prince's eyes gleamed for a moment. 'So, he is keeping his promise after all.' He glanced at the blackamoor and Catherine saw his concern.

'It's perfectly all right, sir. You may speak freely in front of Zamore. I have told him of our plans. Now,' she continued, taking both men by the arm and pushing them gently, 'you must both turn your backs for a moment.'

'Turn — ? Whatever are you doing, dear child?' muttered the prince, but he did as he was bid.

Catherine lifted her skirts quickly and fumbled beneath her petticoats, untying a string from around her waist and slipping out a small bundle bound in cloth. She dropped her skirts, straightening them hurriedly.

'You may look now,' she said, 'but do not speak. I have much to tell you and little time before the guard returns.'

The prince's eyes widened, but to her relief he sat on the bed and watched in silence as she unrolled her package and removed two small vials. She explained their use, making him repeat the instructions twice so there could be no mistake She explained Zamore's part, too, so that both should understand.

'Will you do this?' she asked the prince. 'I know there is a most terrible risk, but 'tis the only choice I had.'

The prince spread his hands wide. 'I — I don't know what to say. I have the greatest trust in you my dear, but so drastic a risk . . .'

'The danger will be less if you are careful, sir. On no account confuse the bottles, and remember how to dispose of them properly. Do it tomorrow, immediately you hear the bells of Notre-Dame calling people to the noonday mass.' She grasped his hands as they heard the guard outside the door, his heavy keys clanking at his waist as he searched for the one to the prince's cell. 'Don't be afraid.'

The prince kissed her hands, then hugged

her again. He grabbed the package she had left and slid it quickly beneath the thin mattress on the bed.

There was no time for more. Catherine took one final look at her father-in-law, knowing it would be her last, and fled the room, tears spilling mercilessly from her eyes.

She had herself under control by the time they reached the carriage. Zamore drove them home again and, as he handed her down at the door, she smiled.

'Thank you Zamore. I shall never forget your part in this.'

'I do not like doing this without my master's knowledge.'

'I know. But he has other things to think about, as I explained. I shall tell him as soon as we are safe, fear not.'

'Very well, *madame*.'

'Look after him, Zamore,' she whispered as she ran up the steps.

If the blackamoor heard her, his face showed no reaction.

★　★　★

Catherine spent the afternoon playing the piano, since it was too wet to venture out. Dominic had come downstairs on his own, as he was now doing regularly, and sat listening and fiddling with a pack of cards. It was the most companionable afternoon they had ever spent, though Catherine was rather too anxious about the prince to enjoy it fully.

At four, Christian appeared, the tea tray not far behind. She dismissed the maid and poured the beverage herself.

'Your leg seems a great deal better,' she commented, as she passed him his cup.

'Good enough,' he commented, giving her a sharp look as though daring her to even think about checking the wound to see. She pressed her lips together in amusement.

Christian set the cup down and leaned forward. 'We go tonight,' he said quietly.

Catherine gasped, spilling some of her own tea in the saucer. Tonight? But she had told the prince her plan had to be carried out on the morrow! How could she leave now? She set down her cup, heart pounding.

Christian continued, his voice a low murmur. 'There is no moon, and the rain will giver us cover. Be ready to leave at midnight and make your way together to the Rue de Bourbon. There are some warehouses there and it should be quiet. I shall meet you there.'

'And then where do we go?' Dominic asked. Catherine noticed that he was short of breath. She laid a hand on his arm.

'To the Port de la Grenouillère. A boat will

be waiting.' He grimaced. 'I trust neither of you gets seasick.'

'I shall prepare some powders,' Catherine replied quickly. 'Just in case.'

Christian nodded. 'I have your papers. Take them now and bring them with you.'

Dominic frowned as he looked at the identification papers his cousin handed to him. They were thoroughly dog-eared as though they had been used for years. 'Joseph Torignac!' he said, surprise on his face. 'That is my middle name. How did you come by these?'

Catherine looked at her own. 'And Margot Torignac,' she added. 'Is this a coincidence, Christian?'

He laughed. 'Indeed that would be rather too much, don't you think? No, they are forgeries. I thought it would be easier for us to remember who we are if we had names that were already familiar.' He looked at Catherine with an apologetic shrug. 'In your case, I felt it best to give you your mother's name. De Lacy was too obviously English.'

'I am amazed,' she said, staring at the papers. 'Why they look as though they have been used for a lifetime.' She looked up at him. 'And who are you, Christian? Are we to call you Wizard?'

'I took my father's name. Georges Saint-Cyr. It will do.'

'Hmm,' Catherine said considering this. She studied him, her head to one side. 'Do you think he looks like a Georges, Dominic?'

Her husband did not answer. He did not seem to find any of this amusing.

★   ★   ★

Catherine clutched her dark cloak around her, pulling the hood more firmly over her head to ward off the light rain that continued to fall. Despite the mild August temperature, she was shivering.

Beside her, leaning his back against the granite wall of a grain warehouse, Dominic coughed. She glanced at him, wondering how he would endure the journey on which they were embarking. He looked so alien, dressed in the slightly tattered black clothes of a provincial lawyer. His hair, which he still wore long, was unpowdered and tied back in a queue, and his hands were entirely bereft of jewels.

They started as footsteps sounded behind them.

'Come,' said a low voice which Catherine knew to be Christian's. Without a word, they followed him, his dark cloak flapping open despite the rain. He led them down a short street and out onto the Port de la Grenouillère which ran alongside the Seine.

There was little activity at this time of night, as Christian had predicted, but in deference to the lack of moonlight, the city lanterns were lit, glowing softly across the dark waters of the river from the road beside the Tuileries. The oil lanterns also cast their golden glow to illuminate the Pont Royal, but Christian led them to a set of steep granite steps beyond reach of the lights. He took his cousin's arm firmly and they began to descend towards the river.

No one spoke. Catherine, about to follow, caught a movement from the corner of her eye. She turned, her heart pounding in her breast. There was something in the shadows of a doorway opposite the bridge. She stared, holding her breath in terror. Nothing. Perhaps she imagined it. Turning in response to Christian's soft call from below, she hurried down after the men, chastising herself for such foolish imaginings.

Before they reached the bottom of the rain-slick stairs, they heard the clip-clopping of hooves on cobbles and froze as a pair of horses pulling a cabriolet passed over the bridge. Then all was quiet again, and they continued their descent.

As they neared the water's edge, Catherine heard the gentle slapping of waves against a hull. A small boat waited, indistinguishable from the thousands that daily plied up and down the river. Silently, Christian handed her in, then she turned to help Dominic. The deck rose and fell gently, but the movement was entirely foreign to Dominic, who clutched the side for support, making the boat rock abruptly.

'It's all right, Your Gra — Joseph,' she corrected herself. 'Come under the canvas and sit.'

She led him inside the little covered cabin, whose roof was a rudimentary oilcloth awning. She was grateful for that much, for the steady rain was becoming heavier by the moment.

They sat on a wooden bench and Catherine folded her husband's cloak over his knees. 'Soon, we shall be safe. Christian will get us out of the city, you shall see.'

She wished she felt as confident as she sounded, but she knew she must appear untroubled for Dominic's sake, lest he become ill with the anxiety of it all. She heard the ropes being thrown on the deck and felt the boat sway slightly as Christian pushed it out into the stream. He did not raise the sail, but allowed the current to carry them towards their destination. With the rain, the river was swollen and unusually fast, and she could see the captain manning the small tiller with ease as he steered the boat into the fastest water.

She gazed out through the opening in the canvas, holding her breath as they passed under the lights of the Pont Royal, but then darkness swallowed them again and the rain wrapped itself like a blanket all around. The smells of fish and tar and wet hemp ropes filled their nostrils.

The boat glided down the Seine, passing under more bridges. Once, she heard Christian exchange a greeting about the weather with another boatman, but for the most part they slipped past silent ships moored along the high walls without incident.

She was just beginning to relax, when she saw lights ahead.

'What is that?' Dominic asked. She had thought him asleep, but obviously he was as awake as she.

'I think it may be the checkpoint at the gates of the city,' she answered.

'We'll never get through,' he replied. 'What possible reason could we have to be found skulking out of Paris in a stinking tub like this in the dead of night?'

Catherine squeezed his hand. 'Christian will find a way.'

But she prayed, nonetheless. On the shore, they could see guards with muskets. They were shouting and waving their guns, and her heart sank, but suddenly she noticed that their attention was occupied elsewhere. She pressed her eye to a hole in the canvas. Another boat, larger than theirs and brightly lit with lanterns, lay between themselves and the guard post. On its deck stood three fishermen, clearly the worse for drink, with several women dressed in the most appalling clothes — if one could call them that — that Catherine had ever seen. The women, whose breasts had completely tumbled from their scant bodices, were dancing about and calling lewd comments at the guards.

She pulled back from her peephole, embarrassed to have witnessed such debauchery, and sat frozen while Dominic asked her what she had seen.

She stared straight ahead. 'Nothing,' she lied. ''Twas too dark to see.'

The darkness hid her blushes, and she sat waiting for the pounding in her ears to stop. Suddenly, she realized that all was quiet once more. Quickly, she put her eye to the hole. Nothing.

'What is it?' her husband asked, clearly offended that she was not sharing her observations.

'Dominic, we're through. Christian did not stop at the post!' She got up, causing the boat to wobble. 'Wait here.'

Without waiting for his response, she left the little cabin and edged her way along the tiny deck to the stern.

Christian smiled as she approached, his teeth a gleam of white in the dark. He had cast off his cloak and wore only a white shirt, open at the neck and with the sleeves folded up over his forearms. His hair looked dark and was stuck to his head by the rain that ran in rivulets down his neck.

'Worked like a charm, eh, my sweet?' he said with a grin.

Catherine stared back up the river, now curving away from the city walls and their guard post. 'You arranged that!' she said incredulously.

'How else could we get through? Cost an arm and a leg, but it was worth it.'

Catherine sat down on the tiller seat and stared at him.

'Thank you,' she said quietly. 'I should have known you would not have overlooked the guard post.'

He sobered, looking down at her. 'I told

you I would get you out of Paris and I meant it.'

She did not know how to reply. She stared up at him, his feet planted wide, his broad shoulders facing the dark river ahead. So safe, so dependable. He had always made her feel this way, she realized.

She laid her hand over his on the tiller.

'You seem to spend your life rescuing me,' she said softly.

'You seem to spend your life needing to be rescued.'

They laughed quietly.

'I must go back to Dominic,' she said. 'How far do we go on the boat?'

'Not far. The river turns north soon and we are going south. We shall leave the boat at a small village not far from here and take a wagon to Versailles.'

'What kind of wagon?' Catherine wondered if he expected them to ride with pigs or hay.

But Christian merely laughed quietly. 'You'll see. Don't worry, there'll be plenty of room to lie down. You may even get some sleep.'

Catherine relayed this news to Dominic, who seemed mollified, for he was clearly fatigued by all the excitement.

Christian was true to his word. Within the hour they disembarked from the little boat and found themselves on the outskirts of a small village. Next to the little jetty where they left the vessel, sat a heavy wagon and two horses.

'*Nom de Dieu!*' Dominic said, when they saw this contraption.

'Christian, is this what I think it is?' Catherine asked.

'Georges,' he reminded her. 'We must use our assumed names now. You must begin to think of yourselves as Citizens Margot and Joseph Torignac of Poitiers.'

'Very well — *Georges*,' Catherine said with emphasis, 'is this a hearse?'

He shrugged, giving her an apologetic look. 'I said there would be plenty of room to stretch out.'

Catherine giggled. Dominic glared at the two of them, but made no demur. They climbed into the back of the sombre wagon and Christian threw in some blankets. Surprisingly, it was not so uncomfortable, and soon the rhythmic bumping and swaying of the conveyance rocked them into fitful sleep.

Dawn was breaking when the cadence beneath the wheels changed. The cobbles of the streets of Versailles woke them instantly, and they sat up. Soon the hearse stopped and Christian opened the doors, his finger to his lips. They climbed out stiffly and found themselves in the courtyard of an inn.

'Go inside quickly and order breakfast. Speak to no one. I shall return shortly.'

Catherine watched as he leapt back onto the box and whipped the horses. The hearse was gone before the noise woke the innkeeper, and they were able to explain that they needed breakfast while one of their horses was reshod.

Apparently, such an occurrence was not unheard of, for the portly innkeeper, rubbing sleep from his eyes, seemed in no mood to enquire further. He led them into a small parlour, stoked the fire into a desultory blaze and ambled away to rouse his wife to cook for the travellers.

By the time they had finished their meal, Christian had returned. Catherine was amused to see that he had changed his clothes and was now dressed like a groom. He had shaved, too, and no doubt had a meal himself. She marvelled that he should find all this subterfuge so simple, and not for the first time since their journey began did she thank God for that.

In the still-deserted parlour of the inn, Dominic, having clearly recovered from the fright of leaving Paris, demanded to know their route to Italy.

Christian looked hard at his cousin, for he knew he could deceive him no longer. Equally, he knew Dominic would not be happy with what Christian had in store.

'You are not going to Italy,' he replied, holding up a hand to still the volley of objections that his cousin was about to loose. ''Tis what the authorities will expect. They will be looking for you on all the eastern routes.'

Catherine paled. Her eyes searched his face, but she did not question him. He hoped she would be happy with his decision. After all, he had made it without once asking their approval.

'I am taking you to Bordeaux,' he said, finally. 'Perhaps from there we can find a ship going to America.'

Catherine leapt up from the table. Her eyes held a gleam. That gave him answer enough.

Dominic was horrified. 'America! You have lost your mind. I shall certainly go to no such place.'

Catherine turned to him. 'But Dom — Joseph, Georges is right. No one will think of Bordeaux. We shall be safe there.'

'I will agree only if you can obtain passage on a ship bound for Italy,' came the determined response.

And from that position, he would not be budged.

For the moment, Catherine and Christian acquiesced, for to argue the point seemed futile at so early a stage. Who knew what they would find when they reached the Gironde?

They continued their journey that day in a diligence that rumbled ponderously on its way from stage to stage. Conversing, except in small talk was impossible, for they never had the coach to themselves. Indeed, at one point Catherine counted sixteen people and two chickens crammed into its compartments!

They left the diligence at Chartres and travelled by means of a modest carriage that Christian procured for them, complete with a young driver who could return the vehicle when they had finished with it. The price of 15 *livres* a day was highway robbery, but he badly needed rest, so he parted with the money willingly and settled down to sleep as they made their way towards the Loire.

Catherine tried to sleep also, as her husband, who was increasingly wearied by the journey, spent most of his time doing. At least she had no need to make conversation, but she found sleep impossible. The ridiculous pillow Christian had that morning insisted she wear beneath her dress so people would think she was with child, was hot and made her skin itch in the late-summer heat. And she was nervous, more anxious than she would have admitted. She felt more vulnerable swaying along the unfamiliar countryside than she had in Paris where she had friends and a home.

She jumped as she felt Christian's booted leg press against hers, but when she glanced at him he was quite asleep. She sighed, wishing he were awake and she could talk to him, for she always found him reassuring. But he needed rest, for he'd barely slept since the night he'd spirited them out of Paris. How he had managed everything so well, she could not imagine. The false documents and passports he had somehow acquired had not once been questioned. And he had brought an extra set for himself, for in Versailles he had changed his identity from fisherman to that of a minor government official from Paris, escorting his ailing brother home to Poitiers. She leaned over, delicately lifting a lock of sandy hair off his forehead where it had fallen in sleep. In a way, she supposed it was the truth. He *was* employed by the government. It was harder to picture her husband as an ailing provincial lawyer, though, despite his simple black clothes and lack of adornment. Whenever she looked at

Dominic, she could see only a pampered duke, out of his element, looking with disdain upon those around him whom he considered so socially inferior to himself that they were unworthy of the slightest attention.

She sighed. He was not an easy man. She wondered what her father would think when they arrived in Philadelphia.

If they did.

Suddenly there was a shout and the carriage stopped.

Christian was instantly alert. '*Qu'est-ce que c'est?*'

Catherine looked out, for the small windows bore no glass and were uncurtained. 'A post-house. Oh dear, 'tis a guardsman.'

'I shall see to it.'

But before he could descend, the gruff features of a man in his thirties appeared in the window.

'*Vos papiers!*' he barked. 'Where are you headed?'

'Poitiers,' Christian replied calmly, handing their documents to the soldier. 'My brother here is suffering from rheumatic fever. He came to Paris to be treated by Doctor Lajeune, but he is too ill to travel home alone, so I am escorting him and his wife.'

The guardsman stared at Catherine, who looked back as calmly as she was able. His glance fell to her stomach, and his demeanour softened.

'There's a fine inn at Châteaudun, *citoyenne*,' he said, returning the papers to Christian. 'The beds are clean and you can rest there.'

'You are most kind, sir,' she replied. Dominic, she saw, was stirring, and she did not wish him to awaken too quickly, lest he use one of their real names by mistake. 'I am quite hungry. Will it take long to reach this place?'

'*Pas du tout!*' He indicated the high-walled castle rising from the trees behind him. 'It's the Chien Gris, just past the château. Can't miss it.' He stepped back and called to their young coachman, 'Drive on!'

'What the devil . . . ?'

'It's all right, *Joseph*. 'Twas just another guard post. We are safely through.'

Because they had no wish to create suspicion, they did indeed stop at the Chien Gris, taking some refreshment before continuing to Blois on the banks of the Loire.

They remained there for the night, setting off again soon after daybreak.

They reached Poitiers with no further difficulty, spending their nights in various hostelries, and changing their identities completely as they ventured into Poitou, lest they encounter someone local who might be suspicious. In Poitiers, Christian dismissed the carriage and obtained another with him acting as their driver. The next day they crossed the long flat plains and marshes of Charente and entered the Gironde.

The carriage rumbled off the road shortly before Blaye and through a pair of magnificent gates.

'What is this place?' Catherine called up to Christian, as they rolled up a long weed-infested drive that had clearly not been used in a while.

Christian frowned. Something was not right here. 'The Château de Beligny,' he replied. 'A friend of mine lives here.'

Or did, he thought, staring at the magnificent edifice as they approached. The four-storey building seemed much as he remembered, though he had not visited in years, but the grounds seemed neglected, the house cold.

He halted the coach in front of the château and stared with foreboding at the broken glass in many of the colonnaded windows of the ground floor. The front doors themselves hung open, and no sound came from within.

Catherine and Dominic climbed from the coach and stood on the gravel driveway staring at the place.

Christian jumped down and strode up the steps, pushing aside the heavy door. Inside, the place was overrun with vermin. Vines were beginning to invade the rooms through the gaps in the windowpanes, their tendrils gaining a foothold on the shutters.

He turned and left.

'Who lived here?' Catherine asked quietly.

'The Duke and Duchess of Béligny,' he replied.

'Ah!' Dominic said, with a sharp glance at him. 'The famous explorer and his irrepressible wife, Léonie.'

Catherine turned wide eyes to Christian. 'Léonie? The one Nounou told me about?'

He glanced at her. 'The same.' He cast the empty house one final look and turned his back on it. 'Come, we cannot stay here. We must find lodgings.'

They skirted Blaye and took the road for Bordeaux, where Christian deposited them at an inn before disappearing to dispose of the carriage.

He returned later that night to find Dominic asleep upstairs and Catherine sitting by the fire in a small parlour, for though it was only September the nights already held a touch of autumn chill.

She poured him some wine, and he accepted it gratefully.

'Are you hungry? I can ring for some food.'

He shook his head. 'I have eaten. You may stay here for the night, but tomorrow we must find a safer place for you. I have to return to Paris.'

'Paris!' she said, then dropped her voice, realizing they could be overheard. 'I thought you were going to find us a ship to America?'

'I will try. I have enquired, but there is nothing in port right now, so we must be patient. When I hear of something, I shall arrange the necessary documents, but meanwhile you must be careful. There is much unrest on this side of the river.'

'How long will you be gone?'

He looked at her. She looked so forlorn, her eyes dark with fatigue. He reached out a hand to cup her cheek, wishing he could take her in his arms, but knowing that he must not.

'I shall return as soon as I can, Catherine, never fear.'

She rested her cheek in his hand for a moment, then put on a smile that was patently false. 'We shall be fine.'

He dropped his hand, for touching her disturbed him. 'I have spoken to someone who knows of a cottage in the country. You could be safe there if you stay indoors. I will return or send word when I can. I must see my uncle and tell him what has become of you — ' He stopped, noticing that her cheeks were suddenly aflame. 'Have I said something to upset you?'

'Not at all. 'Tis simply rather warm in here,' she said, putting her hands to her cheeks. Then she stared at him. 'How can you return? Surely they will know you disappeared with us. You will be arrested!'

He shook his head. 'As far as anyone knows, I have been in Brest with the squadron. I shall be quite amazed to find my cousin and his wife gone.'

She looked dubious. 'Will they believe you?'

'I hope so.'

She stared at him, her eyes dark in the firelight. 'Oh, Christian, how shall I bear it without you?'

Without a moment's thought, he drew her into his arms. She laid her head on his shoulder and clung to him, her silent tears trickling down the open neck of his shirt. He just held her, stroking her back and letting her give vent to her fears, for she had held all emotion within her since they left Paris, and he was glad she could release it at last.

'You cannot return to Paris, Christian,' she said at last through her sniffles.

He reached down and eased her face away

from his shoulder so he could look into her tear-stained face.

Her eyes were wild with fear and he felt a stab of alarm.

'Why? Catherine, what are you trying to tell me?'

She gulped. He passed her his handkerchief and she wiped her eyes. 'It's . . . '

'What, Catherine?'

She sighed tearfully, blew her nose and perched on the edge of the worn horsehair sofa near the fire.

''Tis your uncle. He is dead.'

Christian felt a terrible pain slam into his chest. 'What are you saying?'

But she was already shaking her head. 'No. Not dead. At least, I hope not. But they will think so. Oh, Christian, I would have told you everything, but there was no time, and I made Zamore promise — '

'Zamore! What has he got to do with this?' He shook his head. 'Catherine, you are making no sense. Pray begin at the beginning.'

So she did, unfolding the most extraordinary account of bottles of poison and —

It was too much.

'Are you saying that you staged his death? That the prison guards would think him dead when he was not?'

She nodded.

'And when was all this to occur, may I ask?'

'The day after we left Paris. I had not known we would leave so soon. I thought that your grief and Dominic's would be truly convincing if you did not know 'twas all a plot. Then we could have disappeared when everyone assumed us to be on our way to inter the body — '

'God, Catherine, how could you plan such a thing and not share it with me?'

She bowed her head. 'I'm sorry.'

He came to her, wrapping her small trembling body in his arms and holding her close. 'Dear God, my sweet, if the guards had caught you — It doesn't bear thinking of.'

'I was very careful,' she mumbled into his shirt.

He felt her arms insinuate themselves into the folds of his shirt, her fingers warm through the thin fabric. Her head lifted towards him and she stared up at him, her lips slightly open and her eyes wide and dark.

He felt the hunger within, and struggled not to respond to her sweet face and pliant body, but he knew he was lost. With a groan, he lowered his face and covered her mouth with his own, his lips claiming hers in a way they seemed destined to do. He slid a hand into her hair, lifting her face to his and tipping back her head to give him greater access to the sweetness of her mouth. She wound her hands around his neck, pulling him closer to deepen the kiss. A tiny sound of joy escaped her lips and he plundered her mouth with his tongue, tasting her like the sweetest wine that ever was.

His body was betraying him. He knew that. He felt her shift against him, her hip grazing his erection and causing a stab of desire so fierce he thought he would explode.

'God, we must stop!' he groaned, pushing himself away. She lay in his lap, looking up at him with a dazed expression. His breath seemed choked in his lungs and he knew that if they didn't stop now, he would make love to her right here on the parlour rug.

'Christian, I don't think I can bear it if you go.'

'I must. Now we have nothing to do but wait, I would go mad being always so near to you and never having you.'

They stared at each other for a long moment. Then Catherine spoke.

'You could have me. You know that.'

He leapt from the chair, dislodging her roughly in the process. 'I cannot. I am not proud of my weakness for you, Catherine. Kissing you is bad enough. I will not betray my cousin by taking his place in your bed. Not now, not ever!'

He saw the shock on her face and knew himself for the *âme damnée* that he was, but he could do nothing to soften the words. Why did he have to be the one cursed with what his cousin mockingly called his 'bourgeois morality'? Why couldn't he just accept her invitation and bed the wench? God knew, he wanted to so badly that he could almost taste it.

He stared at her as she turned back to the small fire and sat on a chair, her back straight as a spar.

'Forgive me,' he said softly.

He left the inn and went out into the night, planning to return to the port and find a vessel that could take him to Brest, for he did not wish to return to the capital by the same route he had just travelled. But as he entered the street, a shape moved out of the shadows towards him.

'*Monsieur!*'

He turned at the sound, wary of thieves and vagabonds in this part of the town. He could not see the face of the man who approached, and reached to his boot where out of habit he kept a small dagger.

'*Non, monsieur.* 'Tis I, Grimaud. From the *Astrée.*'

Christian grabbed the man's elbow and pushed him back against the wall, pulling back the hood of his cloak.

'Dear God, so it is!' he said in a low voice, recognizing the old sail maker from his service in Hudson Bay. 'How did you know 'twas me?'

'I was waiting, sir. My boy saw you at the waterfront today. Said he was sure 'twas yourself, Captain.'

'Come.' Christian said, looking about him anxiously. 'Walk with me.'

The two men hurried along, Christian allowing the man to lead him, for his knowledge of Bordeaux was not great and he had not visited in some time.

Eventually, they entered a small dirty street where piles of garbage attracted rats and other vermin. Undeterred, Grimaud led Christian to a door and ushered him inside.

They entered a small room, ripe with the smell of tar and canvas and the sharp tang of hemp. Piles of cloth lay on every surface.

'My workshop,' Grimaud explained. 'Mostly I repair sails for the fishermen. There's not much call for aught else these days.' He lit a candle, pushed away balls of twine and awls with the back of his beefy arm and placed it in the middle of the worktable. 'Sit, Captain. I'll be brief.'

Christian pulled up a stool.

'The reason my boy thought to tell me about seeing you was 'cause we'd been talking about you just this very morning.'

Christian frowned. 'Why would you do that?'

'Well, sir,' said the old sailor, 'I can't think of no easy way to tell you, but . . . the National Guard is looking for you.'

'Go on,' he ordered grimly.

'They're going to hang you for treason.'

17

Christian stared at Grimaud, trying to make sense of his words.

'They want to hang me for treason?'

The sailmaker shrugged. 'I know you, Captain. You were the best officer I ever served with, and I would again, given half a chance. But they say you and your cousin's American wife spirited your uncle out of gaol under the very noses of the National Guard, pretending like he was dead when he wasn't.' He scratched his head. 'Did you really do that, sir? I've been racking my brains trying to see how 'twould be possible, but I can't figure it myself.'

Christian grimaced. 'I didn't believe it, either.'

'So 'tis not true, after all, sir! I'm mighty relieved to be hearing that. I shall tell that fellow — '

Christian's head came up sharply. 'What fellow? From whom did you hear this?'

Grimaud looked surprised. ''Twas an Italian, I think he was. Forget his name. Reckons his own master was wrongly accused of murdering the prince, but then he made

402

'em dig up the body.'

'And?'

Grimaud shrugged. 'Wasn't one. Coffin was empty as a pisspot, if you'll pardon the say-so.'

Christian sighed with relief. That much, at least, was reassuring. But having Foscari on their tail was not. Briefly, he described the Italian to the old sailor, but he shook his head.

'Nah. Don't sound like him. He was much younger'n that. A servant, too, I reckon. Can still smell 'em ten leagues away.'

So, Christian thought, as Grimaud fetched wine and pewter mugs, Foscari had his spies out. No doubt he had seen through Catherine's little deception and planned his revenge. A pity the charge against Foscari hadn't held. If he remembered correctly, the so-called painter had been imprisoned under a *lettre de cachet* in his youth for poisoning his first wife. It would have fitted together rather well. He wondered whether Catherine had somehow found that out and planned it so. He would have to ask her.

Grimaud returned and Christian, deciding he had no choice but to trust the man, explained their predicament.

'You'd best not leave them in that inn,' Grimaud said when he was finished. 'That

Italian fellow was questioning everybody. 'Tis only a matter of time before they figure it out.'

'I have nowhere else to take them. There is a cottage in the countryside I know of — on the other side of the river past Blaye — but I have to see it for myself first. I must know that they will be safe there.'

'You meaning to leave them?'

'I was planning to return to Paris.'

Grimaud shook his head and refilled Christian's pewter mug with more of the dark red wine. 'You can't do that, Captain. They'll have you quicker than a monkey up a tree.'

Christian frowned into his wine. 'You're right, old friend. At least for now I must stay away.' He knocked back the drink and stood. 'Thank you for your friendship. You have likely saved my life, Grimaud, and I shall not forget it.'

'Wait!' Grimaud hurried to the door as Christian swung it open. He closed it again. 'Your cousin and his wife, they can hide here for a while. I have a cellar beneath my shop where they would be safe if they were quiet during the day. Once I close up for the night, I can send food in and you could move about.' He shrugged. ''Tis no luxury, but they would be safe.'

Christian considered this, but knew he had

no choice. 'Thank you. I shall bring them before dawn.'

★ ★ ★

Dominic was burning with fever when Catherine woke him early on Saturday morning. She debated taking the risk and leaving him where he was, but the fear of Foscari's spies snapping at their heels spurred her on.

She mixed some powders and fed the potion to him, then Christian helped him dress and carried him downstairs. Getting the duke to the sailmaker's shop was more difficult, but Christian fetched Grimaud's wagon and Dominic was able to lie on a piece of canvas. Catherine lay beside him, clutching their meagre belongings and her precious stock of herbs and medicines. Christian threw an old sailcloth over them.

The cobbles jolted them at every move, but finally the wagon stopped. Without a word, Catherine slid out from her hiding place and ran inside. Already, Grimaud and Christian were carrying Dominic into the shop.

'Lead the way,' Christian said.

They followed Grimaud down a set of stone steps into a small two-roomed space beneath the shop. It had been swept clean, but the walls were damp, for they were not far from the river. In the corner was a cot with a thin straw mattress; beside it, a table on which stood a washbasin, pitcher and towel. On the other side of the room, stood a larger table bearing a basket of food, a jug of wine and some stoneware mugs. The second room held a pallet of straw laid directly on the flagstones, but nothing else.

''Tis not much. I'm sorry,' said the sail maker. 'If you hear three knocks, you'll know 'tis safe to open the door. Otherwise, you must be silent, or else . . . ' He flushed, rubbing the back of his neck awkwardly.

'Please, Monsieur Grimaud,' Catherine said, touching his arm. 'We know you and your family are taking a very great risk for us. We will not put you in any danger, I promise.'

He smiled at her, rather sheepishly. 'I'm not worried about any such thing, citoyenne,' he said. 'Captain Lavelle saved me from drowning up there in the accursed frozen seas of Hudson Bay. An eye for an eye, that's what the Bible says.'

Catherine smiled at his inverted reference as she watched him climb the stone steps. She heard Dominic moan, and turned to find Christian helping him onto the cot in the corner.

'He is so hot, Catherine,' Christian said as

he removed his boots. 'What ails him?'

'I don't know,' she said, coming to his side. She felt his forehead and he cringed from her touch.

'I am so cold,' he whispered.

Christian frowned. 'Cold? He's damned near an inferno.'

'Take off your cloak and wrap him in it,' she ordered, doing the same with her own. Dominic's eyes were clouded with pain and the sedative she had given him, and she was alarmed by the sudden onset of his condition.

'Is that warmer, Your Grace?' she asked, but he made no response, having drifted off to sleep.

They heard footsteps on the wooden floor above them and exchanged glances. How many hours must they stay quiet now? Catherine wondered. She looked down at her husband, then motioned to Christian. Close to his ear she asked, 'Has Dominic ever suffered from tertian fever?'

'I don't believe so,' he replied in a low voice. 'But the marshes of the Charente are well-known for their malarial airs.'

She sighed. 'Perhaps I am wrong. We shall see.'

They turned and looked at the duke, his brow beaded with sweat and his breathing laboured.

Catherine got up and quietly poured some water into the wash bowl. Taking the cloth, she dipped and squeezed it.

Christian eased the cloaks off him, so his body might cool while he slept and Catherine bathed his face, dipping and redipping the muslin until Dominic seemed more relaxed, his sleep more natural.

Christian took the cloth from her and tossed it back in the bowl. 'You look exhausted,' he said. 'Lie down and sleep. There is nothing else to do until dark.'

Catherine nodded. She stood up and stretched the kinks out of her back and neck, then walked quietly through to the next room, taking her cloak with her.

She lay on the mattress, covered herself with her cloak and tried to sleep, but the sharp straw kept poking her and she tossed and turned. She stared up at the ceiling, noticing the cobwebs that hung between the heavy beams. A faint light from the tiny grille high up on the wall illuminated the sticky threads black from years of soot and grime.

She lay quietly, trying not to feel the jabs of the straw. Trying not to contemplate how small the cellar was, or how much it reminded her of the prince's cell at La Conciergerie. Trying not to let claustrophobia come to call.

Her legs began to shake. She clenched her fists under the cloak and breathed as evenly as she could manage, making herself think about the wide green fields of the Loire Valley they had passed through, with its ambling rivers and fairy-tale castles. She fell asleep to the steady rocking of an imaginary coach.

Christian sat in the other room on the foot of his cousin's bed watching Dominic's face as he slept. He knew he, too, needed sleep, but the cold stone floor did not entice him, and he dare not disturb Catherine. The pallet in the other room was wide enough for two, but that did not mean he trusted himself to share it with her.

He rubbed a hand over his face. As soon as it was safe, he would go out and find that cottage. They could not stay here. Dominic needed a doctor. Christian needed to find his uncle.

His head shot up as he heard a sharp cry from the other room. With a glance of concern at the workshop over his head, he hurried to the door.

Catherine was having a nightmare. Her hands were clenched in her cloak and she was fighting it, pushing it away from her as though it were attacking her.

He grabbed the cloak and pulled, but she

cried out. Christian clamped a hand over her mouth, and she tried to scream into his fingers. In desperation, for he was sure the workers above would hear, he clasped her to his chest and began to rock her like a babe.

'Catherine, Catherine, wake up! 'Tis just a dream. Wake, do you hear?'

Slowly, her struggles faded, and she went limp in his arms. Breathing a sigh of relief, he laid her back on the pallet.

Her eyes flew open. 'Christian!'

He pressed a finger to her lips. 'Hush! You had a dream. Go back to sleep now.'

But her eyes were wide with fright. 'I — I can't! Oh God, Christian, where are we? Are we going to be buried alive in here? How will we ever get out?'

Alarm coursed through Christian. He had encountered a few sailors with claustrophobia, terrified of being below decks in a storm. Left to their screaming and babbling, they could soon spread their fear to others and create chaos. But here, entombed in this tiny cellar in fear for their lives . . .

He clutched her to him again, rubbing her back like a child while she trembled and sobbed. 'Don't be afraid, Catherine. We shall leave here soon, I promise. There's a little cottage in the country near Blaye, on the Duc de Béligny's estate. I shall take you there tomorrow and you will be perfectly safe. I promise.'

He didn't know what he was burbling, but his words seemed to soothe her and she stopped trembling and fell asleep in his arms.

Carefully, he laid her down on the mattress, but when he tried to remove his arm from her shoulders, she cried out, and he stopped.

Ah well, he needed the sleep himself. He eased her across the pallet and lay down beside her, cradling her head on his shoulder.

In a heartbeat, he, too, was asleep.

★   ★   ★

Something woke him. He lay in the dark and listened. Then he knew — it was the lock turning in the sailmaker's workshop door. The work day was over at last.

Beside him, Catherine's breathing was deep and even where she lay with her back to him, curled up like a kitten. He rolled off the mattress and tiptoed to the other room to check on his cousin.

Dominic was still sleeping, too. His forehead felt cool and he seemed relaxed.

Christian turned as he saw Catherine standing in the doorway. She smiled, her chocolate-brown eyes sleepy and her hair tumbled about her face.

'Thank you,' she said softly.

'For what?'

'For stopping me from getting us all arrested. I'm not very good at being locked up.'

He shrugged. 'It's understandable.'

She crossed to her husband and checked his temperature.

'He's better,' she said. Then, looking up at Christian she explained, 'I was accidentally locked in the root cellar when I was a little girl. I've never been able to stand small dark places since.'

'You don't have to explain.'

'Did you mean what you said? About the cottage?'

He nodded. 'We can't risk staying here. Dominic seems better, but if he should need a doctor we could scarcely explain our presence in this tomb.' He glanced at her ashen face. '*Pardon*. Poor choice of epithet.'

There was a knock on the cellar door, followed by two more. Christian hurried up the steps and slid back the bolt.

Grimaud hurried through, closing it behind him. He carried a candle which he set on the table.

'I have bad news, my friends,' he said, his voice cracked with worry. 'There is to be a

412

house search in this district tonight. I do not know if it is you the authorities are searching for, or whether they are simply giving themselves something to do to satisfy their Revolutionary fathers, but they must not find you here.'

'We shall go at once,' Christian said.

Catherine ran to gather up their belongings and make the rooms look untouched.

'But your cousin, Captain?' asked Grimaud. 'Is he well enough to be moved?'

'He is better. The fever is gone and he has slept all day. But he cannot walk.'

'You shall have my wagon. I have a sail I must deliver down river tonight, so I shall take you myself. It will not be very comfortable, I'm afraid.'

'We do not care for comfort, *monsieur*,' Catherine said quietly. 'Only for our lives and yours.'

'Then we shall go as soon as you can be ready.'

Grimaud was right — it was not comfortable, nor was it fast, but at last they came to a crossroads and stopped.

Grimaud came around and lifted the tarpaulin. 'I can take you no further, lest I am challenged. My way is west now, but the cottage you seek is just beyond that copse. There is a stile at the end of the field.'

Catherine scrambled off the wagon, and helped Christian to get Dominic down. He was wide awake and seemed greatly improved, to her relief, though he had not stopped grumbling since he awoke.

'Thank you, sir, we will always be grateful,' Catherine said, kissing the old sailor on both cheeks. He blushed.

'Think nothing of it, *madame*. May God keep you.'

They crossed the quiet country lane and let themselves into the field, hurrying across its open space as quickly as Dominic could manage. He grumbled his way over the stile and then insisted upon sitting on a log to rest once they were under cover of the trees.

After a few minutes, Christian lost patience. 'Dominic, either get up and start walking, or I shall throw you over my shoulder and carry you.'

Complaining at every step, the duke did as he was bid and they finally reached the far side of the wood. It was pitch dark now, but a bright harvest moon illuminated the little cottage that stood not far from the trees, adjoining a field.

'Wait here,' Christian said, indicating a grassy spot beneath a large oak. 'I shall make sure there is no danger, first.'

Catherine watched as quickly he crossed

the open space and disappeared into the cottage. Clearly, it had not been used in years, for roses that had once climbed the trellis, now almost covered the windows, and where there had been a vegetable garden grew ten-foot hollyhocks entwined with runner beans, all thoroughly gone to seed. But its very air of abandonment would be a blessing. She could not dare domesticate the scene. That would expose their hideaway in an instant.

Christian returned quickly and they helped Dominic into the house. He was clearly exhausted.

There was little furniture, but it would suffice. Catherine laid her basket on the dusty table and quickly made a makeshift snack for their meal. They were all hungry and sat on the hard wooden chairs, looking about them as they ate.

Afterwards, she and Christian explored the upstairs and discovered rudimentary beds with no mattresses, their ropes hanging slack with overuse. Christian set to work to tighten them and they spread out their cloaks on one so that Dominic at least could rest.

Catherine was not tired since she had slept most of the day, so she set to work cleaning the inside of the cottage. They might at least be comfortable for however long they must remain there. Christian went off in the moonlight, promising to return, but not telling her where he was going. At dawn he was back, bearing some empty pallets, a few towels and a sack containing a few tin plates and cups.

'Where did you get all this?' she asked.

'At the château. The servants had clearly looted the place, but they took the duke's belongings, not their own. I can collect a few more things tomorrow night. Meanwhile, I shall fill these covers with clean straw if I can.'

★ ★ ★

After two weeks, the little cottage in the Gironde was becoming a dreary prison. The October rains were falling, and Catherine shivered as she stood at the small kitchen window peering out through the vegetation that half-obscured her view. Not that there was anything much to see, for the rain pattered on the dirty glass and blanketed the world beyond.

She stared out into the gloomy afternoon, wondering where Angé was, and how Martha and Nounou were faring. She felt most vulnerable when Christian was away from the cottage, as though his very presence somehow kept them safe. She always felt safer with him around.

She was about to turn from the window, when she caught a movement through the misty rain. He was back! She raised her hand to tap on the glass when something about the figure disturbed her. It was a man, for certain, but he was not approaching the house. He wore a heavy cloak that shadowed his face and he was staring straight at the little dwelling —

Catherine stepped quickly away from the window, heart pounding. Her mind flew back to the apparition near the Pont Neuf the night they made their escape from Paris. Could this be the same man?

She tried to look out again, without going closer to the dirty glass, but he was gone. There was nothing to be seen but grey mist and steadily falling rain.

Had she imagined it?

She turned from the window to face the shadowy room, rubbing her arms against the sudden cold. The grate stood empty, pinging now and then as drops of rain found their way unmolested down the draughty chimney. Christian would not allow them to light the fire, lest someone see the smoke and word get out that there were strangers in the cottage. Perhaps someone already had? She glanced uneasily at the window again, wondering if her imagination was playing tricks.

Bah, it was probably some simple traveller wondering whether to choose this abandoned cottage to shelter from the rain. If that was the case, she was only grateful he had chosen to move on in search of more inviting lodgings.

She pulled her thin woollen shawl closer around her shoulders and glanced at Dominic, who was lying on his bed against the far wall of the room. They had moved him down here so Catherine could watch him more easily, for his health had caused alarm. The tertian fever had run its course, she hoped, for he had gone more than four days now without a recurrence. But she was greatly concerned by the rash on his chest and legs. She had prepared various salves, but nothing seemed to help.

When the weather cleared, she would go into the fields and see if she could find some new herbs to replenish her store. Her knowledge of medicines was considerable, but she wished they could take the risk of calling a doctor to her husband.

'For the love of Heaven, find something to occupy yourself, Catherine,' Dominic grumbled, from the bed where he lay propped up with straw-filled pillows. 'Bring the cards. We may as well play until the girl comes.'

'The girl' was Giselle Luchon, an intelligent and pretty ten-year-old whom Catherine was teaching to read and write. In exchange, Giselle ran messages for them and, more importantly, brought them their only cooked food of the day, which her mother prepared at her own fire. Madame Luchon, whom Catherine had never met, was the widow of a navy carpenter who had served on several voyages with Christian, and he trusted her implicitly.

'Very well,' Catherine said, fetching the worn pack of cards from the mantel. She dragged a rough wooden table, covered with a length of cloth, close to the bed and pulled up a chair for herself.

They played at piquet. Catherine had never liked the game, and found her attention wandering.

She jumped when the door opened.

It was Christian, soaked to the skin. Catherine chided herself for being so edgy.

'Nothing today, I'm afraid,' he told them, as he took off his cloak and hung it over a chair to dry. 'There's naught but fishing boats in the harbour, though they say there might be a vessel on its way to Antwerp any day now.'

'Antwerp!' Catherine's voice held a note of dismay.

'There'll be others,' he said, his voice gentle. 'I know the waiting is hard, but we have no choice.'

Dominic threw down his half-finished hand and snorted. 'Of course we have a choice. We can take a carriage to Narbonne and find a boat to Italy.'

Catherine's heart sank. 'But Your Grace,' she said, for she had returned to calling him by his title when they were alone, since it seemed to soothe him, 'you are not well enough to travel by coach.'

'Then I'm not well enough to travel on, some leaking tub across the Atlantic.'

Catherine exchanged a pleading glance with Christian.

He took a chair, turned it backwards and sat astride the seat, facing his cousin. 'Dominic, now you are stronger, there is something you must know. About your father.'

Catherine saw her husband frown, and felt some alarm. She and Christian had decided not to tell him about the prince, for fear of upsetting him when he was ill. She dreaded his reaction.

'Perhaps this is not the time?' she said gently, hoping to dissuade Christian. 'Giselle is expected — '

'Tell me,' Dominic interrupted, paying no heed to her.

Catherine retreated to the window.

'He is no longer in prison,' Christian began. Ignoring his cousin's gasp of surprise, he went on quickly to explain the circumstances of his disappearance. Catherine felt her cheeks flame as he recounted her involvement in this, but she remained with her back to them, staring out into the rainy afternoon.

When he got to the explanation of the two vials and Zamore's part in removing evidence of the trick, Dominic exploded with rage.

'How dare you! Your stupidity has made us all criminals! Now my father will never clear his name. How do you even know you did not kill him with your evil witchcraft?'

Catherine turned, gasping. 'Alchemy is not witchcraft!'

'Shut up, Dominic,' Christian said brusquely. 'Your father is not dead. The ruse worked just as Catherine planned.'

'How can you possibly know that?'

Catherine wound her fingers into her shawl and pulled it tightly across her chest. Indeed, even *she* did not know that. The dose of digitalis she had given him should have been just enough, but with his age, it could just as easily have been lethal. There was no way she could be sure, though she had not dared tell the prince that. Her deepest fear was that she had given him too much.

Christian answered his cousin. 'Because I am told that there are spies looking for him — and us — all across France. 'Tis why we cannot risk travelling to Italy — they will expect that.'

The duke scoffed. 'So your plan did not fool the guards after all.'

'At first it did,' Christian said, casting Catherine a sympathetic glance.

'Zamore was there,' Catherine said quietly. 'He was to pronounce him dead and scare the guards into thinking they would be to blame. The doctor Zamore sent them for had been well paid to confirm the death and remove the body with all haste. Meanwhile, Zamore was to remove the vial containing the potion he had taken and draw their attention to the empty bottle of arsenic.'

'So the death certificate would state that he died of arsenical poisoning,' Dominic mused. 'How much of my father's money did that cost you?'

Anger flared in Catherine. 'It was *my* father's money, Dominic.'

They stared angrily at each other for a moment, then Catherine turned away. How could she ever have thought she could soften his attitude? He had always hated her, from the very start.

'The plan went perfectly, it appears,' Christian continued, ignoring the tension in the chilly room. 'Until a rumour started that it was not suicide. A story began to spread that Signor Foscari had poisoned your father.'

Dominic gaped at him, then laughed. 'How very fitting. I trust they arrested the blackguard.'

'Indeed they did. But he demanded the corpse be exhumed.'

'Pray, continue,' Dominic said, clearly intrigued now by the tale.

'There was none.'

'No body?' Dominic looked at his wife, his eyes holding a glitter of mockery. 'So, the clever sorceress forgot something after all.'

'You could scarcely expect me to ask someone to be buried on your father's behalf.'

Dominic shrugged. 'One can buy anything with enough of one's father's money,' he replied slyly.

That was too much for Catherine. She grabbed her cloak and stomped out of the house, not caring that it was still raining or that the mud was splashing into the wooden sabots she was wearing. She strode away to the woods, where at least she could have some respite from the weather while she calmed down. She gave a moment's thought to the possibility of someone watching the cottage, but dismissed it out of hand. She was just highly strung these days. The waiting was driving her to delusions.

She had not been out more than a few minutes when she heard footsteps in the thick carpet of leaves. Heart in her mouth, she turned. It was Christian.

'Don't let him get under your skin like that, my sweet. I have explained that there is no hope but to try for America. I think he will agree, for he is as frustrated by our incarceration here as we are.'

Catherine took deep breaths to calm her jangled nerves. She trailed one finger down the silvery bark of a birch tree. 'Will it be much longer, Christian? I am losing my wits here.'

He shrugged. 'That is in God's hands, I fear. Come inside now, it's cold enough without a fire to warm the cottage. If you get wet, you could catch your death, and then who would care for Dominic?'

She snorted inelegantly, but turned to follow him. 'He doesn't seem grateful for the care. He prefers Giselle's company to mine.'

She felt his palm press against her back as he guided her beneath a low-hanging branch.

His hand felt warm and sent a shudder of heat coursing through her chilled body.

'He has never been an easy man, Catherine.'

She was thankful he at least refrained from adding 'You knew that when you married him'. It was an adage that ran punishingly through her own head often enough.

Giselle was there when they returned, her heavy basket containing fresh bread and a rich cassoulet of beans and sausage of various kinds. Dominic seemed a little taken aback by the humble offering, but hunger won over style and he joined the others in devouring the meal with relish. By the time they had finished, darkness had fallen and the evening was cold and damp.

They readied themselves for bed, Catherine giving her husband an extra blanket, though it meant she had only her cloak for warmth, and then they retired, for lighting candles was almost as dangerous as a fire might have been.

The night was still, the rain having ceased and the wind gone. But the clouds lay heavily over the sky and there was no glimmer of light as Catherine lay in her narrow cot under the eaves, curled in a tight ball against the chill, with her cloak wrapped around her. She thought about finding a ship and returning to

America, wondering how her father was and whether he had the slightest notion of the disaster that had embroiled his daughter. She knew he would be mortified, for he cared deeply for her. He would blame himself for sending her on such a mission. He always did when his own optimism blinded him to reality, as he had found to his cost a few times in business. Nevertheless, it was his optimism and his keenness to take risks that had led him to make his fortune in the first place. It was one of the things both Catherine and her mother had most admired about Patrick O'Donnell, for he could always find brightness in the darkest situation.

Catherine fell asleep trying to think of the silver lining in her present cloudy circumstances, but no dreams came.

When she awoke, stiff from her unnatural position all night, the sun was streaming in through the tiny casement and a lark was spiriting its glorious song through the bluest of skies.

She hurried downstairs to see to Dominic, but found him still sleeping, so she attended to her own ablutions, then prepared a simple breakfast of bread and preserves Giselle had brought from her mother's larder. She wondered if Christian was still asleep, but a look at the hook by the door showed that his cloak was gone.

Dominic awoke in a foul mood, which dampened Catherine's spirits despite the beauty of the morning. She helped him outside to the spider-infested convenience, keeping a keen eye out for anyone lurking around the cottage or the woods behind, but seeing nothing. Then she settled him back in his bed, plumping the pillows so he could sit up.

She took down her ointments and a piece of clean muslin.

'How is your rash this morning?' she asked.

'I don't have a rash.'

Catherine looked up. 'You had quite a nasty patch yesterday.'

'Well, I don't today.'

She sighed. 'Very well. I shall bring you some breakfast.'

While he ate, she opened the door and sat on the step to enjoy the sun on her face and arms. Hearing a crash, she turned. Dominic had pushed his tin plate to the floor and was clutching his stomach.

'Your Grace!' she said as she leapt up. 'What ails you?'

'Damn you,' he ground out through clenched teeth. 'You mean to poison me, too. Well, you won't do it, I tell you . . . aah!'

Catherine flushed. 'I did not poison your father, and I certainly would not poison you.' She pulled gently at his arm, but he shrugged her off. Sweat was beading his forehead and he was gasping for breath. Catherine felt a streak of real alarm. 'Do you have pains in your stomach?'

'You . . . know I do!'

Catherine ignored that and went to the small basket that held a few herbs and the ointments she had prepared for his rash. She frowned. 'I do not have the right medicines for this. I shall have to go out.'

'Don't waste your time,' he said, as the last paroxysm passed. He lay back against the pillow, slowly regaining control over his breathing. 'Whatever you try to feed me, I shall have none of it.'

Catherine stared at him in horror. How could he believe she was trying to poison him?

'I know what you want, Catherine de Lacy Montaltier. Don't think I don't know what you and my cousin get up to when I'm asleep.' Catherine gasped. 'You're so good with sleeping potions, aren't you? Good enough to give yourselves all the time in the world to fornicate with that *bourgeois* fool under my very nose. Well, you may have taken my title, *madame*, but

428

I have your money!'

Catherine's hand flew to her mouth. She saw him smile as her cheeks flamed. "Tis a lie! I have never — Christian is an honourable man — '

He laughed unpleasantly. Catherine turned away, trembling. Could her attraction to his cousin have been so transparent? Had he somehow guessed that she had entertained exactly that thing he was so cruelly accusing her of?

But she had only asked. Not done. There was a world of difference. She calmed herself, wiping her hands on her cotton apron. She would not honour his accusations by arguing the point. Dominic would believe whatever he had a mind to. She could — she would — do nothing to disabuse him.

'Your Grace,' she said coolly, going to his side to sit upon the bed. 'You are my husband. I have done nothing to betray you, no matter what your fevered brain makes you believe. I cannot force you to believe me if you choose otherwise, but as your wife I can help you. Whatever you think of my miserable attempts to help free your father, I am trained in the medicinal arts, and I can ease your symptoms.'

He shook his head.

She persevered. 'Do you not see that if we

could just get to America, things would be so much better? You would be quite comfortable there, and we have very competent doctors. Perhaps . . . ' She swallowed hard, feeling a flush steal into her cheeks. 'Perhaps they could help you with your . . . problem. So — so that we might . . . ' She could not bring herself to say 'consummate our marriage', not after his vile accusations concerning Christian. 'So you might perhaps have a son — an heir?'

He laughed. 'So that's your plan, is it? You think some half-wit colonial physician will put everything to rights and you shall have your dearest wish — little brats to suck at your breasts.'

Catherine stared at him, speechless. He continued, clearly invigorated by his own vitriol. 'You presume to believe that I would actually *like* living in a backwater such as your precious Philadelphia with its petty little Puritans and its 'stock exchange'. No, no — don't tell me, my dear Duchess, for 'tis too tempting to guess the role you envisage for me — ah! I have it, I shall spend my days bouncing the little brats on my knees and wiping puke off my breeches!' His face took on a purple hue. 'And for this, you wish me to sail across a dangerous ocean in some accursed fishing bucket?'

18

Catherine was spared an answer. At that moment, Christian returned, tossing his cloak over a chair and setting a small bottle on the table.

He glanced from Catherine to his cousin, and raised his brows to her. 'Are you being difficult again, Dominic? I've brought you some cinchona in case you should get the ague again.'

Catherine smiled gratefully, for she was almost certain her husband had suffered an attack of tertian fever and that it would return. She placed the bottle on the mantel.

'I have need of some fresh herbs to make a salve,' she told him. 'Could you sit with your cousin while I go out?'

Christian frowned. 'It would be better after dark. 'Tis not safe during daylight, even for me.'

She shook her head. 'They must be picked as soon as the morning sun has dried the leaves, or their potency will be low.'

Dominic snorted from the bed. 'You see, Cousin? I told you she's a witch.'

Christian rounded on him. 'You are lucky

she is so knowledgeable, or you might be dead by now. Pray keep your vitriol to yourself.'

The duke was silenced, but not subdued. Christian ignored him and turned to Catherine. 'I shall come with you, but first I shall fetch Giselle to sit with my ill-tempered cousin. Perhaps she can improve his mood.'

He returned promptly with the girl, who seemed content to draw up a chair at the duke's bedside and take out a bunch of corn husks she was fashioning into a rough kind of doll. As Catherine took up her basket and followed Christian out the door into the sunshine, she could hear Giselle chattering on about the things she and her mother had been doing that morning. She marvelled that the duke seemed to enjoy the child's patter, but was grateful for the respite.

'Keep close,' Christian warned, as they crossed the lane near the front of the cottage and into a rocky field where lazy, horned cows were grazing with bells about their necks. The bells tinkled gently as they moved, but the great tan-coloured beasts were unperturbed by the invasion of their territory. Catherine looked about her as they walked, searching for anything familiar that could be added to her dwindling supply of medicaments.

At the end of the sloping field was a thick copse of trees, which yielded a fine patch of comfrey as they passed, and then opened onto a field of half-mown wheat.

Christian put out a hand to still her progress. 'Take care. There are peasants working this field today.'

Keeping to the shelter of the trees, they skirted the field where men, women and children laboured together cutting the hay and assembling rough stooks to allow the precious crop to dry. Their cheerful voices carried as clearly as the cows' bells on the still morning air and the rich earth steamed in the sunshine after the previous day's rain.

Beyond the wheat field lay an open meadow which sloped in undulating waves of green and gold down towards the river. Here the grass grew wild and tall, an abandoned crop field, Catherine surmised, for the tall grasses were scattered with bright red poppies whose nodding heads danced towards the sun.

They waded through the grasses, Catherine stopping now and then as something caught her eye.

'What purpose do the poppies serve?' Christian asked, as she stopped once again to pick handfuls of the elegant flowers.

She smiled. 'They make me happy,' she

replied. 'As to medicine, I fear they work best upon diseases of the soul.'

He looked down at her for a moment and she wondered if he would censure her for wasting time on their errand, but then he turned, taking her hand in his to steady her. His fingers felt warm and strong and she felt a little flush of pleasure steal into her cheeks.

'Come, we must not waste time,' he said, apparently not noticing. ''Tis dangerous to be out here.'

'But who could possibly see us? There's not a living soul in sight. Ah,' she said suddenly, spying some tall goldenrod waving in the breeze near a small outcropping of rocks. 'That is just what I need for Dominic's rash.'

Christian waited while she picked the precious leaves, looking about him all the while. 'What rash does he have?'

Catherine sighed as she tucked the herbs into her basket with the comfrey leaves and scarlet poppies. ''Tis from the rheumatic fever, I fear. But I am not a doctor, so I cannot be sure.'

Christian grimaced. 'You've seen more of this disease than many a doctor. Is it serious?'

She shrugged. 'Perhaps not.'

He made no reply, and she was grateful, for she did not care to speculate on the real significance of the rash, or of the abdominal

434

cramps she had witnessed that morning. They must get to America soon. He was still a young man. The doctors there could surely help him.

Christian helped her down a grassy bank, but she caught one wooden sabot in the half-hidden rocks and stumbled. His hands grasped her waist and she grabbed at him to steady herself. He lifted her safely down, but his hands lingered.

She looked up into his eyes, feeling the jolt of awareness that passed suddenly between them.

Christian dropped his hands and turned away. 'Do you need anything more? We must return to the cottage soon.'

'I need some hyssop,' she replied a little breathlessly.

She followed him across the field, aware of his frustration, for her progress was slow. She stopped to forage among the grasses, delighted to find a small patch of wild strawberries growing at the base of some bushes.

'Oh, Christian, we must have some of these!' She sat on the ground cross-legged, picking the berries, putting some into her basket and some into her mouth. She closed her eyes as the delicious tang melted on her tongue.

He crouched in front of her. laughing, 'I do believe you are like a child, sometimes, my sweet. They are only strawberries, and small at that. We have better in Paris.'

Catherine shook her head, for her mouth was full. She swallowed and held some out to him. 'Not like these. Open your mouth!'

He did as she ordered and she popped two berries inside, laughing as he savoured them thoughtfully.

'You see?' she said smiling. 'Are they not delectable?'

He bent his head and planted a kiss on her lips. Then he sat back on his haunches and considered her question. 'Hmm. Yes, I might say delectable.'

Catherine laughed, embarrassed by his *double entendre*. She gathered a few more strawberries for her basket and clambered up from the grass, following him down the hillside.

Far above in the endless blue sky a lark floated its ethereal song on the breeze. The sun warmed her back as she searched the meadow, stooping now and then to gather calendula and penny-royal as she went. She knew she was taking a lot longer than she might have, if only to enjoy the sheer joy of this glorious morning. She certainly had no wish to return to the confines of the dark little cottage any sooner than she must.

Suddenly, they heard voices from the top of the meadow, and the creaking of a wagon.

Christian growled a warning and she turned in time to see a fully loaded hay wain rumble down the cart track they had crossed sometime before. There were several peasants clinging to the heavy vehicle, including two small children perched precariously atop the mountain of loose-forked hay.

Catherine no sooner took all this in, than she felt herself being flung to the ground, her basket flying up from her surprised fingers and landing on top of her. Poppies and herbs flew everywhere, settling upon her clothes and face, but it was impossible to move for the weight that lay atop her.

Christian pressed a hand over Catherine's mouth, staring into her nut-brown eyes as he strained his ears for sounds of the hay wain's passing. She stared back at him like a frightened fawn but he made no move to release her. Her body squirmed beneath him as she struggled and her leg rubbed against him intimately, scorching him into awareness.

The sounds of the wagon faded away. Catherine fell still as if realizing what her movements were creating in him. Her cheeks flushed a telltale pink and he smiled ruefully as he lifted his hand from her mouth.

Still she stared at him. Then she giggled. 'You have a poppy on your head.' She reached up and gently pulled the offending bloom from his hair, dropping it to the grass.

Christian felt the blood pounding in his ears. He dared not move. The touch of her hand sent his senses reeling no less than the feel of her softly curved body beneath him on the grassy hillside. Her mouth was soft and pink from the wild strawberries and suddenly he was hungry for another taste of the fruit. Her eyes widened as she realized his intent and he paused for a heartbeat, giving her a chance to turn away, look away, give any sign that this was not what she, too, wanted.

With infinite slowness, she reached up and touched his cheek with one hand. He waited, mesmerized, as she trailed a finger down his cheek to the stubble of his jaw, then across his mouth. He opened his lips and captured the finger. She smiled, sparks of sunlight dancing in her eyes as she withdrew. She reached for his hand and drew it towards her, grasping his fingers and pressing them softly against her own mouth. Christian felt his groin surge into life as she opened her lips and enclosed them on his fingertips.

'Dear God,' he groaned, pushing her hand away. 'Maybe you are a witch, after all.'

He lowered his head to her, brushing his

lips across her mouth, tantalizing himself with the rush of sensation it brought. 'You are too tempting,' he murmured, moving his mouth to the sensitive spot behind her ear. and then down her neck beneath her chin, kissing every inch of her soft white skin. 'And I am so very hungry.'

He felt her fingers digging into his shoulders and heard the moan that issued from deep inside her throat. But he would not respond to her urging. His own need was too great. He needed time to find some self-control.

He moved back to her mouth, nibbling on the corners of her lips until she opened to him, then plunged deep into the strawberry sweetness within.

He thought he might explode. He wrapped his arms around her and rolled on his side, pulling her with him so they lay face to face in the grass. Her fingers dug into his scalp, pulling him deeper into the embrace. He obliged, freeing one hand to slide down the light fabric of her fichu and pull it from her bodice. The muslin whispered into the grass and he bent his head to kiss the milky expanse of her skin above the neck of her gown.

He rained kisses over that skin, hearing her sharp intake of breath as his hand brushed her breast through the cloth. He looked up. Her eyes were dark with desire.

'Don't stop,' she whispered.

'Are you sure?'

She nodded. Christian untied the string that held her bodice tight and pulled the soft cotton loose, watching as the sunshine caressed the soft mounds he exposed.

'You are so beautiful,' he whispered, bending to kiss her there.

Catherine was enflamed by the press of his lips on her breasts. She thrust herself forwards, yearning to feel more, knowing instinctively that she wanted him to touch her there. His breath heated her flesh, creating a pool of hot desire deep inside her body, and, when his lips closed over one nipple, she burst into a paroxysm of delight and cried out his name.

'Am I hurting you?' he asked, lifting his head sharply.

Catherine laughed. 'Indeed you shall if you do not continue,' she replied, then closed her eyes on a groan as she felt his mouth encircle her again. He tormented her breast exquisitely until Catherine thought she could stand it no more, and then without lifting his lips from her skin, passed to the other and repeated the sweet torture.

Catherine's head fell back as his palm

caressed her naked skin, her chest thrusting towards him as if begging his attention. She had never known it could be like this, had never dreamed the love between a man and woman could be so fraught with passion and joy. Suddenly she knew she wanted more. She reached for him, grabbing at his loose white chemise and tugging it over his head. She threw it into the tall grasses and ran her fingers through the light thatch of golden brown hair covering his chest. His skin was hot and slick, and she dared herself to lean over and kiss him there, as he had done to her. He seemed surprised by her boldness, but rolled obligingly onto his back and allowed her to press her lips to his shoulders and chest. Her long unbound hair flowed in waves around her, glinting with fire in the warm harvest sunshine, and he ran his fingers through it, then drew a sharp breath as her head began to descend towards his belt.

He grabbed her hands. 'Stop!' he moaned, 'or I shall not be able to control myself.' He rolled her away from him on the flattened grass, propped himself on one elbow and stared down at her. Her desire was as unmistakable as his own, if her swollen lips and swift breathing were any gauge.

His eyes locked with hers, engaging in some fierce battle of need. Christian reached down and with exquisite slowness slid off her sabots and ran his hand up her bare calf, pushing up the hem of her printed cotton gown as he went. He caught a flicker of alarm in her eyes, but as his fingers caressed her skin, it was replaced by a smoky hunger that set the blood to racing in his veins.

'I can't stay away from you, my sweet,' he murmured, as his hand reached her thigh. 'You drive me beyond distraction.' His hand slid up beneath the gown and caressed her hip through the fine silk of her pantaloons.

'I see you are still dressed like a lady beneath your peasant clothes,' he teased, kissing her softly as she smiled. With their mouths a breath apart, he watched her while he pulled on the string of her pantaloons. She lay as still as a bird. He slid his fingers beneath the band and inched the garment down.

Catherine nearly cried out with frustration. Why was he being so slow? She lifted her bottom to allow the slip of silk to slide down her legs, holding her breath as his hand returned, caressing the sensitive skin of her thigh as it slowly rose up her leg.

'Please,' she cried, reaching up to close the small gap that separated their mouths. She kissed him deeply and hungrily, leaving him in no doubt as to her need.

His hand smoothed the soft skin of her belly, then dipped lower exploring the curls that hid her womanhood. She squirmed under his touch and then gasped as his strong fingers found the very core of her desire and began slowly to caress that most intimate part of her.

She thought she would die. She gasped with the sensations that tore at her, trying to control them but knowing she could not. She lay back on the grass and closed her eyes, giving herself up to the explosion of pleasure he was wreaking inside her. But she wanted more, so much more. How could that be so, when she had always been so afraid —

'Christian,' she cried, unable to put her need into words. She clung to him as his fingers rubbed and teased and then gasped as a bolt of exquisite pleasure tore through her, spiralling from his fingers to her very soul. The sensation carried her to a pinnacle that she had never imagined, where all she could hear was the drumming in her ears and the humming in the depths of her body.

She fought for breath, sagging against him and burying her face in his naked chest as she rode the glorious spiral down to earth once more.

His voice came to her through the haze. 'Are you all right, my love?'

She laughed, delirious with the understatement. 'Oh Christian, what have you done to me?' She lay back on the grass and stared up at him, seeing the love and warmth in his face and knowing she had never beheld such a wonderful sight. 'You have given me so much, yet you — '

'Shh!' He silenced her with a kiss. 'That was just the *entrée*, my love.'

And with the same exquisite tenderness he had just shown, he gently lifted her gown over her head and threw it aside. Catherine lay as naked as the day she was born with the autumn sunshine caressing her skin. She watched as Christian kicked off his top boots and tore off his breeches. His skin was a rich gold, weathered by years at sea. but try as she might to keep her eyes firmly focused on his chest and face, the sight of him standing naked in the sunlight took her breath away and set her body throbbing into renewed desire.

She opened her arms as he came to her, thrilling at the erotic sensation of his muscle-bound limbs pressed intimately against hers. Slowly, he recommenced his exploration of her body, leaving no inch undiscovered or uncharted by his hands and mouth. Then, when she could bear it no longer, he lifted himself and slid inside her with exquisite slowness.

Catherine instinctively wrapped her legs about him, yearning to draw him deeply within her, to satisfy the rich ache that he had created. She felt him still as he filled her, caught a flicker of something in his eyes, but then she was lost, crying out from sheer joy as he plunged deeply inside her, filling her heart and soul and body until she called out his name and went spinning away with him into that place of blind delight.

* * *

Catherine awoke with a start as something wet landed on her stomach. She blinked in confusion, looking about her at the tall grasses and red poppies, then shivered.

Dear God, she thought as memory returned. She and Christian had made love, right here in the open meadow in broad daylight. She looked down at her utterly naked body, then at Christian who lay, as naked as she, with one arm flung across her belly.

She shivered, for the sun had gone. Another drop of rain fell on her, and then more.

'Christian! Christian, wake up!' she cried, pushing his arm away and grabbing for her pantaloons and gown. She tugged them on, careless of the bits of grass that clung to the fabric.

'What the devil . . . ?' Christian grabbed his breeches and tugged them on, jamming his feet into his top boots. 'It's almost dark.'

Catherine pointed to the western sky as she retied the string at her neckline. ''Tis that black cloud, and it's going to drench us for our sins.'

Christian paused in the act of putting on his shirt. 'Catherine?' He tugged the chemise down and grabbed her arms, none too gently. 'Are you ashamed of what we did?'

She looked away. 'Aren't you? You once told me you would never stoop so low.'

He pushed her away roughly, turning to pick up her discarded basket and gather the contents which lay strewn about on the ground, then striding away up the hillside without looking back.

Catherine tucked her fichu into her bodice and hurried after him.

Damn him for a fool, Christian thought as he trudged through the tall, unpleasantly wet grass. How could he have let such a thing happen? Had he so little control over his body? He could hear her trudging along miserably behind him, but he would not turn to help her. 'Twas she who had got what she so desired. Had it not been for her boldly stated desire, he would never have —

No, he reprimanded himself. You wanted her long before she put the actual notion of becoming lovers in your head. The truth was, he had thought of little else. It was only their confinement with Dominic that had kept them apart since they left Paris, he knew. Having his cousin constantly with them had helped keep Christian's thoughts on more important matters — like finding a way to get them out of France before it was too late.

And that was exactly what he should have been doing today, instead of gallivanting about in the countryside making love to his cousin's wife!

He heard her stumble behind him and turned swiftly, steadying her with one hand.

'Come,' he said gruffly, avoiding her eyes. ''Tis not far now.'

They crossed the lane where the haymakers had passed hours before, seeing no one, for the farmworkers had surely gone when the rain spoiled their work, and entered the field where the cows had been. The great beasts had taken shelter under a belt of trees and were contentedly munching the cud, their bells muted by the rain.

They found the cottage dark and gloomy. Young Giselle had clearly been home and returned with their evening meal, and the moment she saw them she jumped up from her stool, her eyes wide with anxiety.

'Oh, Captain, thank heaven. I was so afrighted — I thought you had been captured!'

Christian grabbed his cloak and wrapped it about his shoulders. 'We got lost, 'tis all,' he replied, giving Catherine a swift glance that he hoped Dominic would not see. 'Then the rain came and it got dark. Come, fetch your things and I shall take you home.'

Catherine watched them leave, then turned to her husband who lay propped up in bed glowering at her. 'I must change before I catch my death of cold,' she said, her teeth chattering. 'Then I shall get your dinner.'

She fled upstairs before he could answer and shut the door to her little attic bedroom, ripping off the garments and throwing them to the floor.

As she rubbed herself dry on a threadworn towel, she felt the salty sting of tears coursing down her cheeks and scrubbed angrily at them. 'I shall not cry! I shall not give him the satisfaction.'

She pulled a brown cotton dress from her supply of Martha's old things and pulled it on, grateful for the heavy fabric against the chill. But she still shivered, so she added a woollen shawl which she crossed over her chest and knotted at the back of her waist to leave her hands free.

Her hair was a mess, and she realized with dismay as she began to tug her brush through its length that it still bore bits of grass and poppy petals. She hoped Dominic had not noticed in the gloom.

She sighed, pausing to unravel a snarl from her hair. Why was life so cruel? She could no longer deny that she was in love with Christian. She probably had been since the day he rescued her in Paris. Yet making love to him did not change the fact that she was married to Dominic.

She tipped her head over and began to brush her hair underneath, wincing as the brush snared in the tangles. She had been away for hours, making love to her husband's cousin in a field like some common harlot when she should have been doing her duty as a wife and searching for medicinal plants to treat his ailments.

He will know, she thought miserably as she flicked her hair back and stood up, running her fingers through its length to settle the tresses on her shoulders. He must guess. He had already accused her of dallying with Christian, how would she bear it if he said such a thing again? Her face would instantly betray her.

She set down the brush, pressing her lips together. Well, she'd had her fun. Now she must live with the guilt that was her punishment from God.

Downstairs, Dominic watched in silence as she hung the herbs she had collected in little bunches from the rafter hooks, then opened Madame Luchon's food basket and withdrew a thick stew of beef and potatoes. Her mouth watered, for she and Christian had been away for the noonday meal and she was starving. She filled a plate for her husband, added a chunk of crusty bread and set it on his bedside table.

'I'm not hungry,' he said dully.

Catherine looked down at him in alarm. 'Are you ill?'

He attempted to laugh, but the movement merely set his teeth to chattering. Catherine laid a hand on his brow. It was cold and damp.

'You have a chill.' She fetched her cloak from the hook by the door and wrapped him in it, then went upstairs and took the blanket from Christian's bed. Dominic already had hers.

'Is that better?' she asked. The duke nodded, but she was still concerned. 'Did anything else happen while I was out? Did you have more pains in your stomach?'

He shook his head. 'Nosebleed.'

Oh no. Catherine sat on the stool Giselle had occupied. She must get him a doctor. As soon as Christian returns . . .

'You may be getting the tertian fever again,' she said, going to the mantel. 'Christian brought some quinine.'

'Don't want it.'

'But Dominic, you must!' Catherine was becoming truly alarmed. 'You are too weak to fight the ague as well as the rheumatic fever!' She ran to kneel at his side. 'Dominic, please!'

He looked at her, his eyes dull and cold. 'You'll be b-better off w-without me,' he said, beginning to tremble again.

Catherine glanced about her, but there was nothing else she could do to warm him. She looked longingly at the fireplace, wishing it were safe enough to light the fire and warm the chill cottage. Raindrops pinged into the cold soot, mocking her hopes.

Dominic groaned from the bed, and Catherine knew only one other course open to her. She slipped off her sabots and climbed into the narrow cot. Her husband was facing the wall, curled in a ball, but he started, turning to her.

'What are you d-doing, woman?'

451

'I must get you warm. You will not take the quinine and I cannot light a fire, so there is nothing else I can do, Your Grace.' She lay down beside him and placed one arm hesitantly across his chest. 'Try to relax and, God-willing, sleep will come and the fever will not.'

He was as tense as a trapped animal for a while, but Catherine lay very still, hoping the heat of her body would eventually soothe him, and was rewarded when she heard his breathing gentle. Eventually she, too, slept.

★ ★ ★

Christian took Giselle home, but did not return to the cottage immediately. He knew he could not bear to be under the same roof with Catherine and Dominic after the events of the day. He had to think, to calm himself.

He borrowed Madame Luchon's old nag and rode into Blaye, seeking solace at the inn where he could drink some wine and think amidst the rowdy tavern rats. They were used to seeing him from time to time, for he had told them he was a navigator waiting to enlist on a merchant ship. They knew him to be a gentleman, and were flattered that he chose to eschew the bordellos of Bordeaux for the rural pleasantries of Blaye on the north side of the river.

The ruse suited Christian, for he could move amongst the people of the village without arousing suspicion, and they respected him enough to leave him to his thoughts.

Tonight, he needed his solitude more than ever. He sat at the corner of a rough wooden table with a jug of dark red wine before him, letting the patter of voices flow over his head. He poured himself a mug of wine and sipped it slowly.

He was not in love with Catherine, there was no question of that, but he did make love to her — his loins still ached at the memory. He sipped his wine, trying to blot out the vision of her lying naked in the grass with the sun shining on her silky skin, staring up at him as he stripped in front of her. He blushed at his own arrogance. Yet she had not looked away, indeed the sight of him standing there like that had seemed to excite her all the more. He squirmed on his hard wooden bench.

No. He did not love her. He had simply *made* love to her to assuage the need that she created from the first time he saw her. It was a physical thing. He tossed back the wine and poured another. What man wouldn't be tempted when a woman as desirable as Catherine threw herself at him? Even though she was only doing it to get herself with child.

Child? His child? He gripped the battered pewter mug till his knuckles whitened, for the idea sent an almost physical pain through him. But he hardened his heart, frowning down into the drink — Christian Lavelle could have neither child nor wife. He was an explorer, a man as likely to disappear off the face of the earth as La Pérouse had done in '88, leaving a wife at home begging the authorities to send ships in search of him while she waited years for any news that he might be alive.

No, he could never be a family man. He, by his own choice, had outlawed himself from that felicity.

He ordered some food and ate hungrily but without taking note of what he was consuming. He must get them on a ship — any ship — and out of that accursed cottage before he went mad; for one thing was certain, he could not bear to sleep in that tiny attic room next to Catherine's night after night without going to her. How could he ever sleep knowing she was there, just a few feet away, her delectable body his for the asking?

And all the while, his own cousin — almost

a brother to him — was lying below stairs.

He threw some coins to the innkeeper, downed the last of his wine and wrapping his cloak around his shoulders went out into the chill night.

The rain had gone, but a cool wind blew. Christian took his customary path away from the inn towards the ferry, branching off at the last minute when he was sure no one was observing his progress, then doubling back to retrieve the nag from the cemetery behind the church. He rode off into the moonless night, making plans.

It was nearly midnight when Christian arrived at the cottage, having returned the old horse to Madame Luchon's field. He let himself in and latched the door softly, crossing to the bed to see how his cousin fared.

He leaned over, cursing the darkness and waiting while his eyes adjusted, for he could not quite make out —

Christian stepped back, his heart pounding. Catherine! Catherine, who only a few hours before had lain passionately making love to him, kissing his naked flesh, had run straight into the arms of her husband. The husband she had sworn did not wish to consummate their marriage!

He turned, white anger consuming him.

How could she do this? How could she betray him like this unless it was true — unless it *had* all been an utter masquerade?

She had used him. No doubt she didn't need to go out gathering herbs at all; 'twas just a ploy to entice him away from the cottage so she could work her charms on him.

He strode to the door, grabbing his cloak from the peg on which he had hung it not a minute before. No wonder she was no virgin, he thought bitterly, as he wrenched open the door and shut it behind him. That was one thing no amount of artifice could deceive him about.

So she had her duke after all, and who was to say she had not found some Paris fop to satisfy her appetites as well. But if she thought she could keep Christian Lavelle on a leash like some love-sick puppy, she had a great surprise in store for her.

He strode through the dark wood behind the cottage and headed for the crossroads. It was past time that he returned to Paris and found his uncle.

19

Catherine sat up with a start as the door to the cottage banged shut. She stared out the small window, and through the faded roses that partly obscured the panes saw Christian's silhouette as he stormed away from the house.

She ran across the room and pulled open the door. Too late. He was gone.

'Oh no,' she sighed, turning to stare at the bed she had just vacated, trying to imagine what he had seen when he walked in. Her, asleep in her husband's arms.

But it was not like that! It *wasn't* what it seemed. She dropped her face into her hands and stifled a sob. What must he think of her, to make passionate love to him in the afternoon and then take herself straight to her husband's bed?

How could she tell him?

She raised her head and stared out at the dark night, wondering if she could find him. No, she thought sadly, closing the door. She would have to save her explanation for his return.

But Christian did not return. At noon the

next day, Giselle arrived bearing a brief note.

Madame, it read curtly, *I must visit my uncle. Take care of your husband.* It bore no signature.

Catherine folded the scrap of paper with shaking fingers, tucking it into the pocket of her apron. She was aware that Giselle was watching her with a curious expression on her young face, so she gave her a small smile.

'When did he give you this, Giselle?'

'He didn't, ma'am. 'Twas brought to my mother by a young boy come from the tavern in Blaye.'

Catherine felt tears prick her eyes and turned away to busy herself with the herbs she was grinding in a mortar. She picked up the pestle and crushed it savagely into the dried leaves.

'Where's my cousin this morning?' Dominic asked from the bed. She had not known he was awake. Perhaps her attack on the herbs had awoken him.

Catherine went to him, straightening his blankets. 'He has gone to see your father,' she said, giving him a warning glance that the girl could not see. Dominic stared at her, then nodded.

'Perhaps you would like Giselle to sit with you,' Catherine said.

Dominic waved the idea away. 'I am rather

tired. Later perhaps.'

'Very good, sir,' Giselle replied with a little curtsy. She smiled shyly at Catherine. 'Is there anything else, ma'am? My mother needs me to go to the market. Perhaps there is something I can fetch for you or *monsieur*?'

'No, Giselle, but thank you. And thank you for bringing the note so promptly.'

When the child had gone, Dominic spoke again. 'Why did he go like that, without a word?'

Catherine turned back to her work, hiding the heat that had arisen in her cheeks. 'I have no idea, Your Grace. But no doubt he will return as soon as he has found your father.'

Dominic grunted noncommittally. 'And what of us? Are we to sit here in this draughty rat hole until he chooses to return?'

'Dominic,' Catherine said, coming to perch on the side of the bed. 'He said there were no ships yet. We must stay hidden and exercise patience.'

'Patience!' He snorted. ''Tis wearing exceeding thin.'

She looked down at him, suddenly noticing how high his colour was. 'Do you have a fever this morning?'

She felt his forehead and pulled back in alarm. He was hot, excessively hot. Quickly, she removed all but one of the blankets from the bed, leaving only the thinnest to prevent a sudden chill.

'Will you take some quinine today?' she asked.

He looked up at her with bloodshot eyes. 'What do you care, Catherine?'

She knelt by the bed. 'You are my husband.'

There was a moment's pause, then he said, 'Why did you marry me?'

Her eyes widened. 'Because I had promised.'

He shook his head sadly. ''Twas badly made. Our fathers were remiss.'

Catherine started to object, but Dominic stopped her. 'Bring me my cloak,' he said, pausing to cough.

She did as he asked while he struggled to regain control over his breathing. 'Cut the lining.'

Giving him a puzzled glance, Catherine fetched a sharp kitchen knife and sliced through the fabric. She felt around inside and was surprised to withdraw a sheaf of papers, pressed flat into the space between the layers of heavy cloth.

'What are these?'

'Take them. They are yours.'

She stared at the sheets. Bonds and

promissory notes, amounting to hundreds of thousands of *livres*.

Her dowry.

She looked up at her husband.

'I can't go on, Catherine,' he said in a whisper. 'Christian knows that. 'Tis why he won't let me speak of escape to Italy.'

'No!' she cried, tossing the notes on the bed and taking his hands. 'You will be fine once we get you to America. You will be just as comfortable there as you were in Paris. My house is not nearly as grand as your father's, but it is considered luxurious. You can rest and regain your strength and we can begin another life, without fear — '

'Catherine, I am dying. And no matter that I accused you of trying to poison me, I know you will not. In truth, perhaps 'twould be kinder if you did.'

She rubbed his hot hands with her cold ones. 'Please, Dominic, you are still a young man — '

'I can't, Catherine. If 'twill ease your conscience, I shall take your medicines, but — '

Catherine laid her face on their joined hands and wept, for she knew it was true, and although she had lost her heart to his cousin, she grieved deeply for a marriage that could end so quickly and so brutally.

They did not speak of America or of Christian again. October advanced, bringing cooler days and colder evenings. And, on the night when the spirits were said to walk, Dominic added his own soul to the parade and breathed his last.

Catherine stood at the small window in the dark cottage and stared out at the night. For the second time in her life, All-Hallows Eve had stolen something from her. Perhaps 'twas truly a cursed night bewitched by evil spirits.

Not even an owl hooted as she stood there. The silence was absolute. She had not noticed how quiet the cottage was at night, for her husband's laboured breathing had been her constant companion for many weeks. Now he was gone.

And Christian, too.

She took herself up the narrow stairs to the attic, eschewing the straw pallet she had brought down from her room and set beside her husband's cot so she might attend him if he woke at night. She opened the door to Christian's room and fell on to the bed.

Finally, tears came.

★ ★ ★

When Giselle brought the meal the next afternoon, she found Catherine sitting on the doorstep in the cool autumn sun, staring listlessly out at the forest.

'*Madame?*' she said, the alarm clear in her voice.

'He is gone, Giselle.'

'Oh, ma'am, I am so sorry.'

Catherine shrugged. 'I must see your mother. She will know how I can get him buried.'

'*Bien sûr, madame.* I shall go at once. I — ' the girl hesitated, looking from the dark room behind Catherine, to her face and back. Clearly, she had no wish to enter the room in which the duke's body lay. 'Perhaps I may leave the basket here.'

Catherine nodded. Giselle set the food down and hurried away, blessing herself as she went.

A few minutes later, Madame Luchon arrived. Catherine tried to pull her scattered thoughts together and greet the woman properly, but the widow was distracted, looking about her anxiously.

''Tis not safe, *madame*. You must leave here. Has the captain sent no word?'

Catherine flinched at the mention of Christian, despite the knowledge that she would not see him again. He had made clear

463

his abhorrence of her when he left so abruptly and penned so cruel a note.

'I am on my own now, Madame Luchon,' she replied. 'I must find my own passage back to America. But first, I must see that my husband is properly buried. He was a duke, you know.'

The widow's face paled. Clearly, she had no notion that Christian's relatives had been so highly ranked. But it scarcely mattered now.

Madame Luchon rubbed her hands together. 'I shall speak to the undertaker. Perhaps — But there is no doctor's certificate. I do not know — '

'Money speaks louder than paper in France, *madame*,' Catherine said with a shrug. 'So I am told.'

The woman's eyes widened, but she made no reply. 'I shall send Giselle at once.'

Darkness had fallen when Catherine finally heard the sound of a cart on the mud path outside. She peeked out the window, then opened the door for a man who looked more like an undertaker than she could have imagined.

He was tall and thin, dressed entirely in black and wearing a gaunt expression as though each of the bodies he dealt with was that of a member of his own family.

Catherine paid him twice. First, she asked his price to arrange the funeral at the local church, then gave him double what he asked. Then she paid him again, for his silence.

Not even that much gold in one evening could bring a hint of a smile to his macabre visage. He removed the body with the help of his son, who had remained outside with the horse and cart, and promised to send word.

Next day, despite Madame Luchon's begging her not to attend, Catherine walked openly into Blaye and attended her husband's funeral.

The tiny church held only the priest, the undertaker and his son, and Catherine, who stood beside her husband's coffin throughout the service. The celebrant was one who had sworn allegiance to the constitution, but she hoped Dominic would forgive her for not attempting to find a rebel priest.

Her husband, Dominic-Joseph Torignac, Vicomte de Montaltier and Duc de Charigny, had not been a bad man. Life had dealt him some vicious blows and while he might, as Christian had once said, have made more of himself, he did not deserve to be thrown in a pauper's grave. He would be buried as he had lived: as the Duc de Charigny.

She held her head high as she accompanied the casket to the small cemetery. The priest intoned the last words as the body was lowered into the ground, and Catherine dropped a faded rose and a handful of earth upon it.

Then she turned and left the churchyard.

'*Madame la Duchesse!*'

Catherine looked up automatically, and then froze. Blocking her path stood two soldiers with a man she did not know and one she had never been able to forget: Foscari.

He was smiling, an evil sneer that twisted his thin features and made her heart leap to her throat. She looked about her for a way to escape, but the soldiers stepped right beside her, their muskets pointed at her chest.

She stared at the Italian, knowing now that the shadowy figure she thought she had imagined had been none other than this evil man himself.

'Signor Foscari,' she acknowledged, trying to keep her voice calm, though her knees shook beneath her gown.

His companion responded. 'Are you Madame Catherine de Montaltier, Duchesse de Charigny?'

She looked at the official. He seemed a bit nervous, which gave her courage. 'There are no titles any more in France, *monsieur*,' she replied coldly.

'Allow me to phrase the question more accurately — are you the wife of the *ci-devant* Duc de Charigny?'

'No. I am his widow.'

The official's mouth twisted in a condescending sneer. 'You are wanted for charges of treason against the people of France. You will accompany me, please.'

'Treason!' Catherine gasped. 'I have done nothing against anyone — ' One of the soldiers prodded her with his musket and she stumbled. He glared at her, looking only too ready to repeat the act, so she was forced to gather her cloak about her and follow the official, who had marched away to a waiting carriage.

She was pushed inside and forced to sit opposite her accuser and the Italian, while the soldiers climbed up with the driver. Foscari sat contemplating her with a malevolent expression as the carriage bounced and swayed.

'Wh — where are you taking me?' she asked, looking only at the official, for she could not bear to look directly at Foscari.

'To gaol.'

Catherine thought she would have an apoplexy just as surely as her husband had done the day of his death. She squeezed her eyes shut against a torrent of useless tears.

Christian, she begged silently over and over, where are you?

When she was calmer, she again spoke to the man. 'I am an American citizen, and related to General Lafayette. I insist that you release me. You have no power over me.'

'On the contrary, *citoyenne*,' he replied blandly. 'You are the widow of a French traitor and an enemy of the people. You shall be tried.'

'In Paris?'

'In Bordeaux.'

She glared at him. 'I know no one in Bordeaux. Who shall represent me?'

'Something will be arranged,' was his only reply.

They continued in silence for some time, Catherine stiff with fright, staring unseeingly before her. With every jolt of the carriage her mind seemed to grow more numb as though she were slipping into helpless oblivion.

Suddenly Foscari signalled his companion and the official tapped on the roof of the conveyance. Catherine stared out the window in confusion. They appeared to be in a quiet lane overhung with trees.

'Where are we? Why have we stopped?'

Foscari ignored her, nodding to the other man, who climbed down and slammed the door. With the soldiers and the driver, he crossed to the other side of the road and squatted on a log, where they began talking among themselves.

'I have a proposition for you, *signora*.'

Catherine turned wide eyes to Foscari. Her blood turned to ice in her veins, for he was looking at her with an expression that put more terror in her than all that she had so far suffered.

He smiled, a cold, evil sneer. 'You are afraid of me.'

She made no reply.

Foscari reached across and stroked one bony finger down her face, twisting his hand and flicking the nail sharply across her cheek. She flinched, putting a hand to the wound.

She stared at her fingers, stained with blood, then back at him. 'You are an animal,' she hissed, slapping him hard across the face with her palm.

Catherine knew her life rested in this man's hands, yet she did not regret her action. Her fury would not be controlled. She had lost so much; she would fight for what little remained.

Foscari's eyes narrowed momentarily and then, to her dismay, he smiled.

'I do so love a woman of spirit, *Madame la Duchesse*,' he said softly. 'Will you not at least hear me out? It would be such a waste to lose you to the gallows.'

Catherine slid back against the seat, as far away from him as the confined space would allow. She contemplated grabbing for the door and trying to escape while the soldiers were distracted, but knew it was futile. She wasn't yet ready to risk a bullet in her back.

'I have done nothing. I am an American citizen.'

He laughed silently. 'So innocent. I told your husband that I liked innocence in women.' He sighed melodramatically. 'But he wouldn't share. Such a pity.'

Catherine felt bile rise in her throat, but clamped her mouth tight against it. Thank you for that much, at least, Dominic, she thought.

'My proposition is simple, *madame*. If you will agree to be my mistress, I shall speak to the judge. I am sure something could be worked — '

'Never!' Catherine's revulsion must have shown clearly on her features, for the Italian's face grew tight with rage. 'I would rather hang!'

There was a moment's silence in the murky air of the carriage. Foscari stared at her, his eyes assessing. Catherine stared back, knowing she had spoken the truth; she would rather die than be delivered into the

470

hands of this monster.

Finally, he reached across to open the door and signal the waiting men.

'Very well,' he said calmly. 'Then you will die.'

The remainder of the journey passed in silence. Catherine sat stiffly on the hard wooden seat and stared at her folded hands, feeling herself growing numb with shock. By the time the carriage came to another halt, she was scarcely aware of her surroundings. Someone led her inside a grim stone prison that smelled of rotting humanity. Other hands pushed her into a large room. She heard the grating of a key in the lock behind her as though it were happening to someone else, far off in the distance. She stood as still as a rock and stared blindly at the grimy stone floor in front of her. Soon she would wake up. Soon this nightmare would be over. She had only to wait.

Slowly, as time passed and the filthy floor did not fade into a dream, she became aware of others in the room. She looked up, encountering the curious stares of seven other women, most of them in rags, one clearly a prostitute.

Catherine looked at them for a few seconds and then turned away. Her gaze roved over the high barred window, the damp stone walls, the locked door.

She felt her eyes widen with fright as the room darkened. It began to close in, squeezing the air from her lungs. She gasped for a breath that would not come, searched wildly for a way through the swirling tunnel of claustrophobia that engulfed her, and finally closed her eyes and succumbed to total blackness.

★　★　★

November passed into December. Catherine used some of the money Dominic had given her to obtain the services of a Bordeaux lawyer, who promised to write to General Lafayette and ask him to intercede on her behalf. It consumed a considerable amount, but she spent more to ensure that none of the women who shared her cell would go hungry. She was grateful to her departed husband for making her sew the money into different sections of her cloak, so that she might appear to have less than she was actually carrying. She would need it to obtain passage on a boat for America when she was free of this dreadful place.

As the weeks passed, she had begun to think of the women as her sisters in despair. Occasionally one would be taken away to be tried and sentenced. Occasionally, another would arrive. Christmas came and went. Snippets of news were smuggled in. In this way, Catherine learned that the government had declared the property of *émigrés* forfeit to the nation. She wondered what had become of the beautiful Hôtel de Charigny and its priceless treasures. Looted no doubt, like the château belonging to Léonie at Béligny. As far as she knew, all that now remained of her father's dowry was what she carried on her person, still secreted in the lining of her cloak. And even that seemed worthless.

Catherine learned to control her claustrophobia with the help of the other inmates. At first it seemed impossible, but, as time went on and she began to despair of ever being released, she cared less and less. Her heart felt dead. She had given it to Christian in that sunny field in October and he had taken it away with him. She knew she would never see him again.

Finally, early in March, Catherine was summoned to the court.

It was all over in minutes. Her lawyer, it appeared, had been forced to withdraw from representing her owing to other pressing matters — Catherine wondered how much Foscari had paid him — and his replacement knew nothing of any petition to General Lafayette. Mention of the general's name did not assist her case either, she realized too late, for he was not as popular here as he had once been in Paris.

Her American citizenship was passed over, much as it had been months earlier when she had been arrested in Blaye. She was a French duchess, involved in a conspiracy to steal a traitor from beneath the noses of the gaolers at La Conciergerie. Despite Signor Foscari's appearance and his portrayal of the events, Catherine was pleased that he did not realize 'twas Catherine herself who had planned the whole escape. She kept her own counsel.

She watched the proceedings in a daze, puzzled by the rapidity of it all and the bored attitude of her own representative, who sat whispering to one of the clerks throughout most of the hearing.

She spoke briefly, answering truthfully, but offering no more information than was requested of her. Was she the Duchesse de Charigny? Yes. Had she been living in Blaye under a false name? Yes. Did she assist the Prince de Charigny to escape from the Conciergerie? Yes.

Forty minutes later, Catherine was found guilty and sentenced to death. She was to be executed the following day. The judge advised her to be grateful that as a noblewoman she would be spared hanging. Her rank entitled her to a more humane death by beheading.

She fainted in the dock.

★   ★   ★

When she returned to the cell that had been her home for four months and three days, she was too insensate even for tears. The other women hugged her and cursed the judge, but they did not seem surprised.

As night fell and the women settled to sleep, Catherine sat on her straw pallet and stared up through the grating at the starry sky a million miles away. She wondered what her father was doing, whether he had any notion what had befallen his daughter. She wondered whether her mother could see her. And in her heart, she pleaded for Christian to be safe.

Finally, she began to cry.

The torrent burst from her, spurred by self-pity and self-recrimination. Months of loneliness and sorrow, of regret at the poor decisions she had made, at the death of her husband and the disappearance of the prince — all these things poured in upon her, and she cried until not a tear was left.

But still, she could not sleep. What point

was there in resting a body that had less than a day to live?

She sat staring up at the window watching the stars fade and the sky grow pink. Red in the morning, sailor's warning, she thought, wondering if Christian had gone on his voyage to French India after all.

'*Madame?*'

She turned to see one of the older women, Babette Pichegru, who had been in this filthy cell longer than she, kneeling at her side.

'You must tell them you're pregnant,' Babette said in a low voice.

Catherine looked at her blankly. '*Pardon?*'

'You must say you are *enceinte!*' she whispered more loudly. 'They may think we are all enemies of the Revolution, but they are too squeamish to execute women who are with child!'

Catherine felt a tiny stirring of hope deep in her chest, but tamped it down deliberately. 'They would never believe me.'

'Of course they would!'

'And in a few months, when I am still as thin as I am now?'

'Then is then,' replied Babette. 'Now is now, and if you do not do this today, you cannot have a then, can you?'

There was some logic to that argument, however convoluted. 'But what do I do?'

'Easy,' said the woman, jumping up and running to the door. She hammered loudly, waking all the other women and causing loud curses to issue from other parts of the prison. '*Attention!*' she screamed, banging with her fists. '*Attention, les gens d'armes!*'

Seconds later, the door opened, and a guard stood there, none too happy to be summoned at so early an hour. '*Qu'est-ce qui a?*'

'*Madame la Duchesse est enceinte,*' Babette said, planting her fists firmly on her hips. 'She wishes to appeal.'

★   ★   ★

There was but one judge sitting on the high bench for the appeal held later that day. Catherine was led into the small panelled courtroom and made to stand, as she had the previous day, in front of two guards.

Trembling with fright, she stated her claim to immunity, as Babette had instructed her.

The judge observed her with disdain. 'You state you are with child, and yet your husband is dead. Pray tell the court how this miracle comes to be?'

Catherine flushed. 'My husband died on All-Hallows' Eve, sir.'

The judge considered this. 'And when did

you become pregnant?'

Catherine thought about her one day of real happiness, when she and Christian had gone searching for herbs and had made love in the meadow at Blaye. 'I cannot say for certain, but sometime in October.'

There was a sudden commotion, and then to her horror, Signor Foscari stepped from the crowd of gawkers at the back of the room.

'My lord, if I may cast some light upon this matter?'

The judge nodded. Foscari smiled, giving the justice a slight bow and turning to face Catherine, though his words were addressed to the judge and the gallery. Catherine began to shake.

'Indeed, this woman's claim is entirely impossible. Her husband the duke' — he emphasized the title with a sneer — 'was well known to me, and to most of Paris, as a man with not the slightest interest in women. In fact, he never consummated this marriage, which was made entirely to benefit this lady's desire to become a member of the oppressing nobility.'

'That is entirely false!' Catherine cried, appalled that such things should be spoken of in public, and most especially from the despicable mouth of a man like Foscari.

'Indeed,' the Italian continued almost

without a pause, 'the duke's interests lay far from the *female* sex. His personal preference was for catamites. I believe he kept a number of young boys for his own pleasure.'

There was a gasp from the crowded room, and Catherine felt the world begin to spin. She clutched the bench in front of her and squeezed her eyes shut. 'No, no, no,' she moaned, unable to bear another vile word.

Suddenly there was a shout from the back of the room.

All heads turned to observe a man push his way through the onlookers and stride towards the front of the courtroom.

'Your honour, Foscari is a liar and a lecher. I have proof. Here is a sworn statement signed by two officials of the Palais de Justice stating that this woman was in no way involved with the escape of the Prince de Charigny from the Conciergerie.' He tossed some papers to the table. 'There are other documents there, also, concerning Signor Foscari's activities as a blackmailer. You may find those of interest to the court.'

Catherine heard this voice as if from afar and lifted her head slowly. The man turned, his dun-coloured hair caught in a shaft of sunlight as he stared straight at her. Her heart gave a leap of unbelievable joy.

'Christian!'

Not a touch of emotion showed on his face, despite the tears of happiness that rolled down Catherine's cheeks just to see him standing there.

'My name is Citizen Captain Lavelle,' he said, addressing the court once more, 'and this woman is having *my* child.'

The courtroom buzzed again, and the judge frowned at Christian, but Catherine just stood staring into his eyes while tears shook her whole body. He was here. He had come back and found her at last.

Still he did not smile. The judge rustled through the pages Christian had dropped in front of him, then stared scornfully at Signor Foscari who was standing at the side of the room. The Italian looked decidedly uncomfortable, but was unable to leave due to the press of bodies intent upon this unexpectedly delicious scandal. He glanced about himself uneasily.

'Arrest that man!' said the judge, pointing to Foscari. The Italian broke into a torrent of babble in his native tongue, but the guards followed the judge's orders without concern.

Finally Catherine realized the judge was speaking to her, and she turned to face him. Whatever he said, she no longer cared.

'Citizeness, in the light of Captain Lavelle's evidence concerning the man who accuses

480

you of treason, this court believes you have been unfairly accused. As for the matter of the false documents found in your possession, your time spent in prison will, I trust, be sufficient to warn you of the dangers of impersonating others. You are therefore free to go.'

Catherine stared at him as though she had somehow fallen asleep and was dreaming. Then she felt the hand of her gaoler on her arm and realized she was being pushed towards the door.

Christian came to her side. His arm encircled her waist. The wooden boards beneath her feet began to swirl and she felt herself falling.

The crowds parted as Christian swept her up and carried her from the court. Catherine wrapped her arms around his neck and buried her head in his chest.

'There was a red sky this morning,' she murmured. 'I knew 'twould bring a storm.'

He made no reply, and she looked up in surprise as he bundled her swiftly into a small carriage, jumped in and slammed the door. The horses moved off immediately, making Catherine stumble. Firm hands grabbed her.

'Zamore!' she cried. But other than smile, he did not speak. She turned to Christian who was unfolding a large piece of sailcloth.

'Where are we going?'

'You will see soon enough. There is no time to explain. Lie down on this and put your arms at your sides.'

Catherine's brows rose. She looked from one man to the other, and something in their faces made her obey instantly. Once she was prostrate on the bumping floor of the carriage, they began to fold the cloth over her face.

'Stop! Christian, what are you doing? Have you forgotten that I am claustrophobic?'

She felt his hand on her shoulder through the canvas, and his voice was more gentle.

''Tis not for long, and you will be quite safe if you remain floppy like a rag doll. Can you do that, Catherine?'

'I . . . I suppose so . . . ' she replied faintly. It was certainly preferable to the executioner's axe.

They rolled her over, wrapping the canvas tightly about her and securing the bundle with a loose rope. Catherine found she could breathe quite easily, as the ends of the sack remained open and the canvas was stiff enough not to press against her face.

Through the thick wrapping, she heard Christian speak. 'Zamore will carry you. Make no sound.'

She wanted to ask more — a thousand

things — but there was no time. The carriage stopped, the door opened and she felt herself being hoisted over the blackamoor's shoulders like a parcel. She did her best to make her body slack, but every step he took jarred her ribs.

She strained her ears, but could hear only shouts and cheerful workaday chatter, none of it clear enough to comprehend. The smell of the canvas filled her nostrils and she thought if he did not put her down soon, she would surely be sick.

Finally, she heard his feet connect with something wooden and there came an added swaying to his movements. Then steps — narrow — for he bumped her from time to time against a wall as he hurried. She heard voices, then a door opening, and suddenly felt herself being dropped.

She bit her lip against an involuntary cry, but sighed with relief as she felt the canvas being untied and lifted away from her.

She opened her eyes to see Zamore standing over her in a small panelled room. She was on a ship!

'Are you all right, *madame*?'

She nodded, looking about her. 'Where are we?'

'Aboard the *Liberté*, *madame*. You must remain in this room with the door locked once I have gone. The captain will have a key and he will use it when he arrives. You must make no sound and speak to no one. It will not be safe until we reach the open sea.' He leaned down and removed her wooden sabots. 'You will not need these any more. They make too much noise.'

'Indeed,' Catherine said softly, matching her voice to his own, 'I shall be glad to see the last of them.'

He gathered up the sail and bundled it under his arm, indicating that she should follow him. She tiptoed in her bare feet to the door behind him and once he had left, locked it and withdrew the key. Then she turned and stared about her.

The room was small, but exquisitely furnished, with gleaming oak panels from floor to ceiling. The small bed, onto which Zamore had dropped her, was built into the wall. Beside it a chest of drawers with gleaming brass handles was bolted to the floor. Lanterns hung from the rafters, though they were as yet unlit, and a small-paned window gave out onto the stern of the vessel. Towards one side was a door which she suspected led to his private quarter gallery, and another door stood open to reveal a study, fitted with a desk and many small cupboards. Scientific instruments hung on deep hooks on the walls and a large map was spread upon the desk.

She heard a key in the door and stood still as it opened. Christian came in and locked it behind him.

Catherine's heart pounded. She longed to run into his arms, yet something about the hard set of his features held her back. She glanced down, realizing that after months in that abysmal prison, she must look and smell little better than a sewer rat.

He stood in the middle of the small cabin, tapping the key on his palm and staring at her. Catherine pressed her lips together, for they were trembling. Why did he stare at her so coldly, as though he despised her?

'I shall never be able to thank you,' she whispered. His eyes flickered, then he looked away.

He pointed across the room to a large trunk that sat on the floor near the bottom of the bed. 'You'll find something to wear in there. There is a toilet in the quarter gallery, and water in the jug.' He indicated the washstand, protected from heavy seas by a brass rail around its top. 'When you are ready, listen at the door. If you hear nothing, you may open it carefully and see if it is unoccupied. Go to the next door on your left and enter it swiftly. You will find yourself in the *grande chambre*.'

Catherine stared at him in dismay. He was so cold, so utterly aloof. Did he despise her so much?

'What kind of ship is this?' she asked.

'A navy frigate,' he replied, then turned and left, locking the door behind him.

Catherine's mind whirled. A warship? How could he be taking her aboard such a vessel? Surely he had lost his commission when the family had been accused of treason? And yet . . . She tiptoed to the study and pushed the door wider, staring at the map laid open on the desk.

The Atlantic. She lifted one edge, peering beneath, and her heart sank. Another map, complete with pencilled chartings, showed a route around the Cape of Good Hope and across the Indian Ocean.

She returned to the bedroom. So he was making his voyage to French India after all, and she would be his stowaway. She pulled off her filthy cloak — setting it aside so she could remove the documents still secreted in the lining — then discarded her grimy gown and dirty petticoats, piling them in a heap for burning. Despite the cold, it felt good to be free of the clothes. She poured some water into the wash bowl and began to scrub herself from head to toe. What she would have given for a bath! But she would make do — anything was better than spending another minute in that cockroach-infested prison cell. If she had to wait until they reached India for a bath, then she would wait, and be glad to.

She carried the filthy water into the quarter gallery and tipped it out, then refilled the bowl, and began to wash her hair, using Christian's sandalwood soap as she had on her body.

Finally, she towelled her hair as dry as she could and went to the sea chest. The heavy brass plate on the lid bore the initials C.L. Feeling strange to be invading his private things, she lifted the lid, expecting she would have to find something of his to wear, like the Léonie she had heard so much about who had disguised herself as a young naval officer on a voyage to the Pacific.

What she saw made her pause in surprise. This might be Christian's trunk, but these were certainly not naval clothes! Catherine nearly wept for joy as she lifted out some of her old American dresses and some of the elegant gowns she'd had made in Paris. She blushed to see petticoats and pantaloons and silk nightwear — everything she'd thought never to see again.

With trembling fingers, she dressed in a

soft gown of cherry-red wool, with a black redingote in velvet. The bottom of the trunk rendered up some black ankle boots and wool stockings, and she put them on, realizing how very cold she had been for many months, and wallowing in the warmth and comfort of her old familiar things.

When she was dressed, she took her cloak and returned to the adjoining study. Using a penknife from the desk, she cut the lining of the cloak and removed the treasures within. She looked about her. Where to hide them? On the desk beneath the maps lay a large leather-bound volume that seemed to be his captain's log. She opened it near the back, where the pages were still blank, and slipped the documents inside, hoping the prison stench that clung to the deeds would not taint the book. Later, she would ask him for a safer place to keep them. Wherever he was taking this ship, they would have need of funds.

She returned to the bedroom, tossing her cloak onto the pile with the other foul-smelling clothes. Then she tiptoed to the door. She pressed her ear to the wood and listened.

Voices, one young and another quite elderly. She strained to hear but they were cut off suddenly by the closing of another door, then there was nothing. She withdrew the key from her pocket and inserted it quietly in the lock. Listening again for a moment and hearing nothing, she opened the door a crack and peered out. There was a short hallway illuminated softly by a single lantern. It was empty. She slipped out, closing the door behind her and passed along the corridor to the next door. With a deep breath, she opened it and hurried in, closing it behind her.

There was a rustling sound, and Catherine turned, letting out a sharp cry.

20

'Catherine! My dearest!'

Catherine stared at the assembly of faces in the room, unable to take in the scene before her. She gave a cry of joy as Angé hugged her, then bent to wrap her arms around little Hélène and Alexandre. But she quickly disengaged herself and ran across the room to a tall, grey-haired man who stood leaning against the bulk of a cannon.

She threw her arms about the Prince de Charigny and buried her face in his black coat to hide her tears.

'Now, now, my dear, surely you did not think I would leave you in that foul prison?'

She looked up at her father-in-law. 'Oh, sir, I am so sorry. I could not save Dominic. His heart was so weak and with the tertian fever — '

'Hush,' he reproved her gently. 'I know all that. I knew it would be a miracle if you could get him to safety. You did your best and you buried him with honour. For those things — even without the efforts you made to save me from certain death — I shall be forever in your debt.'

Catherine bowed her head, but could not speak. She felt a handkerchief pressed into her fingers and smiled damply at him. '*Merci.*'

When she was better composed, she turned to the others. 'I cannot believe you are all here! How is this possible?'

Her attention was caught suddenly by a very old priest sitting beneath one of the deeply sloping windows at the back of the room. He smiled, getting up with the help of a cane and offering her a bow.

Angé introduced her. 'My dear Catherine, you must meet Father Cassel. He is an old friend of Christian's and has been at sea all his life. But he refuses to swear allegiance to the state, so he is coming with us instead. Is that not the most wonderful news?'

Catherine allowed the priest to kiss her hand, smiling at him, all the while feeling that he was examining her intently. It was as though the old pastor could see right inside her soul.

The door opened and Zamore entered. 'We shall be leaving at dusk,' he said. 'The captain says you must all move to the inner cabins for safety. Once we have cleared the coast of France, you may return here.'

'Tonight?' Catherine felt a touch of alarm. 'But Zamore, there was a red sky this morning. Surely that means we shall have a storm?'

The blackamoor grinned, his teeth flashing. 'The captain says 'twill make us harder to stop.'

Indeed, they could all feel the swell of the huge river beneath the decks as the winds chopped the water. Angé gathered the children close and followed Zamore as he led them away. Next, he escorted the prince and the old priest out, leaving Catherine alone.

She looked out the windows, observing the darkening sky and the heavy black clouds gathering there. She was an uneasy sailor, and the sight of that sky did nothing to reassure her.

When Zamore returned, she asked 'How long will it take us to get to French India?'

'India?' He frowned. 'We are heading for America.'

Catherine felt a flood of joy. She was going home. This day had brought so many good things, red sky or not.

She followed him in silence, sending up a silent prayer of thanks for her incredible good fortune. She looked up, surprised when he opened the door to Christian's cabin.

'I thought we were to have inside cabins.'

'The captain says *you* must wait here,' was the only reply. At least he didn't lock her in.

She sat upon the bed, listening to muffled shouts and footsteps from above, then suddenly the movement of the ship changed and she could tell they were out in the stream. She peered through the window and saw the dock receding. A few men stood with hands on hips watching the *Liberté* depart, and then a carriage drew up perilously close to the quayside. Two men in black leapt out and began gesticulating and shouting. Catherine frowned. The men hurried away, pointing towards another vessel, smaller than the frigate, that lay at anchor. It became too dark for her to see, then, and the *Liberté* was picking up some wind from the south-east, the sails snapping as they filled, pushing the spirited vessel out towards the sea.

Catherine lay down and tried to sleep. She made no move to light the lantern, for after so long in the prison in Bordeaux she was used to the dark.

She must have dozed, for suddenly she was awoken by some commotion. She hurried to the window.

Oh dear, she thought with dismay. The customs boat, for that was surely what it had been, had gained upon the *Liberté* and rode close off the stern. In the gloom, she could make out the hulking shape of the vessel clearly.

Without a moment's thought, she hurried from the cabin and up the stairs at the end of the corridor.

Rain lashed her face as she opened a door and came out upon the quarter deck. The wind howled across the ship, cracking in the ropes and snapping at the sails, and the sheep and cows tethered to the base of the masts moaned pitifully, in terror for their lives. If only they knew they were destined to be dinner, she thought, turning at the sound of voices over the storm.

Christian stood near the wheel, with Angé's husband, Gérard at his side. He wore a white shirt, open at the neck, and no coat despite the bitter temperatures. Suddenly, she realized that the smaller vessel had come perilously close alongside. The men she had seen earlier were shouting at Christian to stop the *Liberté* and be boarded. She heard Christian laugh, and them respond, picking up only snatches of words on the gusting wind. But she heard enough to know they were calling Christian a traitor.

Suddenly, she saw him raise his arm. His white sleeve flapped in the breeze as he brought it down.

'*Ouvrez le feu, les canons!*' he shouted. Catherine's cry of horror was drowned out by a deafening explosion as two of the *Liberté*'s

494

starboard cannons fired across the narrow space between the vessels.

The smaller ship lurched as the balls connected with the upper railings, tearing off a good portion of the planking.

Catherine looked back to see Christian and Gérard laughing as the other vessel veered away and dropped anchor. In seconds, they were alone in the river with the open sea only a short distance away.

Catherine saw Christian turn suddenly and felt his gaze fall upon her. Her blood ran cold. She turned and stumbled through the doorway and back into the safety of the ship, but no sooner had she entered the cabin, than she felt his hand grip her arm.

'I thought I ordered you to stay below!' he ground out, his voice cold with anger.

Catherine rounded on him. 'So you could keep your murderous intent secret from your passengers?'

'Murderous!' He released her arm and stared at her as though she had taken leave of her senses, his hands planted on his hips. 'That fool Piron wanted to come aboard and find out why we had sailed without letting him check our decks first. Why, pray, do you suppose he wanted to do that?'

She shrugged.

'So he could report that the *Liberté* was

smuggling enemies of the Revolution out of France!'

Catherine looked away. 'I did not know that.'

'And no doubt he saw you standing in the light of the companionway, so now he knows for sure.'

'You did not have to sink the vessel, all the same.'

Christian turned away, ripping his wet shirt over his head angrily. 'I did not sink it, Catherine. I barely gave the carpenters a day's work. He'll hobble back to port and be made a hero for his troubles, never fear.'

Catherine swallowed as he grabbed the same towel she had used only hours before and began to rub his chest with it. He turned and looked at her suddenly, casting his eyes up and down her person. He tossed the towel away.

'You have lost weight,' he stated, a slight frown on his face.

She shrugged, turning her back on his nudity, for it created painful longings in her and she had no wish to let him see how badly she was affected by his nearness.

She cried out as his arms encircled her, shutting her eyes as his mouth pressed a kiss on the top of her head.

'Thank God I was not too late.'

She turned in his arms and buried her face in his chest, sobbing with relief.

'Enough,' he said after a few moments. 'If I want to get wet, there's rain enough topside.'

She pulled away, dabbing her eyes with the prince's handkerchief which she still had in her pocket. 'I'm sorry. I seem to cry easily these days.'

He put a finger under her chin and lifted her face towards him. Catherine stared up at him, so familiar after months of inhabiting her dreams. She remembered every detail, every plane and contour, from the hard line of his jaw to the straightness of his nose.

She wanted him to kiss her, but his eyes held a hint of something she could not quite define and it held her back. He gazed down for a long moment, then dropped his hand and moved away, disappearing into his study. When he returned he was pulling a clean shirt over his head and his face had taken on an impersonal, shuttered look.

'I must go above. Gérard may need help clearing the coast in this storm.'

Catherine watched him go, feeling a chill colder than any Atlantic winter enter her heart.

★　★　★

She did not see him again that night. The small group of *émigrés* supped in the *grande chambre*, attended by Zamore and a young valet who turned out to be the son of Grimaud, the sailmaker. It was a happy meal, but an anxious one. Apart from Catherine and the old priest, Father Cassel, no one had set foot in America before, and Catherine was kept busy answering questions as best as she was able. She was made to promise that she would begin teaching them English the very next morning, for all were anxious to fit in quickly in their new country. The prince told her that the winter had been so bad not a single ship had set sail across the Atlantic for months. And all had harrowing stories to share of false papers and months spent hiding from the authorities.

She returned to Christian's cabin, expecting him to arrive and direct her where she should sleep, and sat up late trying to read one of the books she had found in his study while she waited. Eventually, she fell asleep on the narrow cot and slept more deeply than she had in months, lulled like a babe in a cradle by the steady rolling of the ship.

Morning came and reminded her that her stomach and the sea were not great friends. She was grateful for the proximity of the quarter gallery.

Afterwards, she felt better. She cleaned her teeth, having found her brush and tooth powders thoughtfully stored in her trunk, dressed in a warm, grey gown and hurried up to the deck for some fresh air, pulling her cloak about her. Sea sickness was not so hard to deal with, she had found, if she stood in the open air where she could keep a firm eye on the tossing waves.

She leaned against the portside rail and stared out at the thrashing sea. Gulls swooped and turned in search of morsels from the chef's slop buckets.

She turned as a dark figure approached.

'You are up early, *mon père*.'

Father Cassel smiled, his ancient face speculative as he settled his cane between gnarled hands on the railing.

'Are you a good sailor, Duchess?'

Catherine laughed shortly. 'I have none of my father's passion for the sea, Father. 'Tis an endurance for me, but one that I shall bear without rancour this time.'

'Ah. You are pleased to be returning to your home. Indeed, France did not proffer much of a welcome, did it?'

She shook her head. Then she turned and looked at him. 'Why are you leaving, Father, at your age, if you will pardon my impertinence?'

'I rather welcome impertinence, these days, my dear. Mostly, people treat me as though I am past such notions — a doddering old fool who needs to be helped up and down the stairs. Nothing more.'

She gave him a wry smile. 'You *are* quite advanced in years.'

'Less than I seem, my dear. The sea is the enemy of youth. As to my leaving France, 'tis something at which I am well practised. But I think this shall be my final voyage. I have an urge to throw myself upon the mercy of the Duc de Béligny. François and I go back a long time.'

'Léonie's captain?'

He smiled. 'I see you have heard that story. Yes. I miss them, and I have no family in France now. Home is where the heart resides, is that not what they say?'

'Indeed, it is,' she replied quietly, thinking that was perhaps why she felt so at home now that she was once again with Christian. Somehow, she had come to love that man, for all his strange moods: one moment stern and distant; the next, his eyes filled with laughter. He had saved her life, as well as that of all the *émigrés* aboard the *Liberté*, destroying his career at the same time. How many men would show such selflessness? How many were that brave?

'You have known the captain a long time,' Catherine commented, as she watched the ocean rising and falling about the ship like a hungry monster.

'Since he was a boy in officer's clothing.'

'He has destroyed himself, hasn't he? For me, even though he hates me.'

The old *curé*'s brows rose. 'He has told you this?'

'There's no need.' She turned her back on the waves and stared up at the mainmast, swathed in huge white sails that captured the breeze and flapped like wild things above their heads. 'He's a pirate now.'

The priest turned also, gazing up and down the ship's deck with an appreciative gleam in his eyes. 'Perhaps we all are, but what magnificent booty, do you not think?'

'Father!' Catherine was astonished. 'How can *you* condone such an action? Christian has stolen this vessel from the French Navy — along with its crew, no doubt. If we are not all murdered and thrown overboard before we reach America, 'twill be a miracle!'

'The crew are friends,' the priest replied easily.

'All of them?'

'Except you, perhaps.'

Catherine was beginning to get lost in this conversation. 'Father, I am scarcely a member of the crew, and I am most definitely not an enemy. If I were, why would Captain Lavelle have rescued me from my date with the executioner?'

'You know the reason.'

Catherine felt an upwelling of hope, but tamped it down. 'No,' she said sadly, turning back to share her thoughts with the churning ocean. 'He despises me.'

'Perhaps. But is there not a slender line between attraction and repulsion?'

Catherine ignored this. She could not possibly handle philosophy until after breakfast. 'He rescued me because I freed his uncle. And because he had promised the prince he would. There remains no further obligation.'

'Obligation? An interesting word.'

'And a true one, *mon pére*.' She turned to him suddenly. 'I sinned with Christian, you know, while my husband lay dying. 'Tis only God's retribution that he should hate me for it.'

There was silence for a moment, while a gull screeched past them and plucked a morsel from the waves. Others followed, wheeling and turning as though engaged in some macabre ballet.

'Actions of that nature,' Father Cassel said whimsically, as they watched the birds, 'usually require sinning in pairs, do they not?'

Catherine laughed, despite herself. ''Twould be difficult, Father, on one's own.'

★ ★ ★

She felt better after her conversation with the old priest. They went down to the *grande chambre* together and found Angé and the children breakfasting. Catherine's stomach was still uneasy, so she partook only of tea and took over the task of persuading young Alexandre to eat his pastries.

Angé was bubbling with excitement. She, too, had begun to think of them as pirates.

'But Angé, are you not concerned about your husband's future? He can never return to France, let alone to the navy.'

'*C'est vrai*,' the woman replied, but her blue eyes sparkled nonetheless, 'but he and Christian are speaking of buying ships and opening trade routes with the West Indies and Africa — even China, perhaps.'

Catherine's brows rose. 'How will they fund such a venture?'

Angé leaned across the heavy table and giggled conspiratorially. '*Monsieur le Prince* has promised them whatever they need!'

Catherine grinned wryly. Her dowry. She held part of it, but she knew there had been more. A great deal more. She was pleased that he had managed to escape with some of the fortune at least. 'My father will no doubt be delighted that his own money is being used to fund his competition.'

Angé frowned. 'Indeed, dearest, I had not thought of it that way. I shall speak to them.'

'No, no. Pray do not spoil their fun. They are excellent men and they will need a new career now they have destroyed their old ones. 'Twill do my father good to have a battle or two.'

But privately she wondered whether Patrick O'Donnell wouldn't welcome both young men into his arms as the sons he'd never had. She did not think she could bear that, having Christian involved on a daily basis with her father. How would her heart ever recover?

She excused herself from the table and returned to the cabin, opening the door quietly and feeling great relief that it was empty.

Then she was swamped by another bout of sickness and ran for the quarter gallery.

As she retched into the toilet, she felt warm fingers press against her forehead, a hand support her shoulders. When the biliousness passed, she stood up, accepting the damp cloth Christian pressed into her hand.

'Thank you.'

She allowed him to lead her to the bed and press her back against the sheets. Gently, he removed her boots and massaged her feet. It felt glorious and Catherine closed her eyes and gave herself up to his touch.

'Are you better?' he asked, finally coming to stand over her. She nodded, staring up at him. He was unshaven, his hair sticky with seaspray and dishevelled by the wind. His customary white shirt was untied and revealed a light thatch of hair on his bronzed chest. His legs were encased in fawn breeches that hugged his muscles like a second skin.

She closed her eyes. Looking at him did her no good at all. It fanned her hopeless desire and left her more miserable than if she never saw him. Somehow, when they reached America, she must find a way to keep him from any association with her father.

'Whose child is it?' he asked without preamble.

Catherine's eyes flew open. 'What do you mean?'

She saw a muscle flicker in his jaw, and he repeated the question, grinding it out between his teeth. 'Whose child are you carrying, Catherine?'

'No one's! I am not with child!'

He gave her a scathing look and turned

away, striding across the small cabin and back. 'Lies, lies and more lies!' he said in a venomous voice. 'Damn your lies.'

Catherine pressed her hands to her mouth to stifle a cry. 'Christian, I have never lied to you. Not ever. Why should I do such a thing, when I owe you my very life?'

He made no answer, nor would he look at her. Catherine climbed off the bed and steadied herself on the armoire as the ship rolled.

'Very well,' she said quietly to his back. 'I shall admit to one lie, though it was only to save my life. Babette — one of my fellow inmates — told me that they do not execute women who are with child, and that I should appeal that way. 'Twas just a ploy. I had written to General Lafayette, hoping he could intercede on my behalf. I needed time.'

He turned, staring at her, a picture of misery in a gown two sizes too big for her thin frame. Her eyes were dark shadows in her pale face and her wild hair fell around her shoulders in waves. He yearned to reach out to her, to take her in his arms and hold her close to him, to bring back that sparkle of joy and radiance that had lain engraved on his heart since that fateful afternoon in the meadow at Blaye.

But he stood still, remembering what else

he had seen that day.

'Does the child belong to your husband, after all?' he said coldly, cursing himself for the brute he was as he saw her face crumple in pain. 'Were you just looking to me as a plaything, as you once suggested?' He ran a hand through his hair, angry as he thought of the kisses they had shared near the little pond in his uncle's garden. 'You didn't need me to give you and Dominic an heir, did you? 'Twas a simple ploy to make me your lover, to while away the time.'

'Never!' She was appalled by his words, that he could even think such things of her. 'Christian, what poison is this? Who has given you such vile notions?'

'I know only what you told me, and what my senses told me. You claimed your marriage was never consummated, and I believed you, yet when we made love — ' He paused, his heart freezing around the words. 'I was not your first.'

'Oh, merciful God,' Catherine sobbed, falling to the floor.

He picked her up and carried her to the bed, setting her down. Her tears tore into him, but he had waited so long to say those words that his own anger was stronger than his pain. He turned away, going to his study and shutting the door between them.

Catherine heard the door close. She wiped her eyes and got up. It was no use. He despised her anyway, so he may as well know the whole of it, for it would scarcely chase him any further from her than his misconceptions would. She washed her face and cleaned her teeth again, the simple routines giving her a little courage.

Then she crossed the cabin and knocked on the panelled wood of the door adjoining the study.

It opened instantly. She looked up at him. His jaw was set, his eyes hard as flint.

'I do not deny that there was . . . someone before you,' she said quietly. 'And since you know that, you should know all there is about me. I do not expect compassion: understanding will suffice.'

Still he said nothing. She leaned against the doorframe, feeling light-headed, but determined to continue.

'When I was a girl, my dearest friend Amy dared me to an escapade on Halloween. There is a wood not far from where she lives, that is said to be haunted by the ghost of a young woman who was murdered there long ago. Amy said I was not brave enough to walk alone through the wood on All-Hallows Eve.' She clasped her hands together, looking down at her stockinged toes as she tried not to recall the night too vividly. 'So I did. As I neared the end of the wood, two men came along the path. They were drunk — '

Christian grabbed her shoulders and pulled her against his chest, cutting off her words.

'Stop!' he muttered brokenly into her hair. 'You do not have to tell me.'

'I do,' she mumbled into his shirt. 'Else however will you believe me?'

'*Nom de Dieu*,' he replied through clenched teeth. 'What kind of monster must you think me that I would put you through such an ordeal again?' He held her away from him, taking her face in his warm hands. 'Catherine, can you ever forgive me?'

She blinked. His face was no longer angry, but pleading, his eyes soft with concern. How could he not hate her for what had happened? 'I never made love to any man but you,' she whispered. 'My husband was as they said — he had no interest in me. There was only you.'

His eyes clouded with pain. 'But I saw you in his bed.'

'He was cold. The ague — I had wrapped him in all the blankets and cloaks, yet still he shivered. I thought he would die — '

'You did not make love with Dominic that night?'

'Never! Oh, Christian, how could I do such

a thing, when I had just given every ounce of my soul to you?'

He looked down at her, his eyes alight with pain and hope. 'Do you love me, Catherine?'

She laughed and cried at the same time. 'I always have, ever since the first time I set eyes on you — ' Her words were cut off as his mouth descended to hers, his lips crushing and demanding and taking what in his heart he had always known to be his own.

'Can you ever forgive me, Catherine?' he said, kissing her again. 'More importantly, will you marry me, even though I am merely a disgraced sea captain and not a duke?'

Happiness burst like an exploding star inside her. 'Of course I will, my dearest. I would marry you if you were a humble fisherman making his livelihood on the Seine.'

He drew back, remembering their escape from Paris. 'Then there is just one more thing I must ask of you, my sweet.'

'What, dearest?' she said, stroking his cheek with her hand and marvelling at how happy she could feel after all that had befallen them.

'You must stop denying my child.' He pressed a hand to her belly and Catherine gasped.

'But I am not — ' Her mind whirled as she considered whether in fact it could be true.

She had not had her monthly curse in the prison, but had put that down merely to the lack of good food — most women suffered the same fate.

She looked up as Christian's hand moved to cup her chin. 'How can you be so innocent, when you are so astute at the healing arts? You have been fainting and throwing up your meals in my quarter gallery ever since Bordeaux. It does not take a wizard to divine the cause.'

'But I am so thin. I have barely a swell — '

'You have been starving for months.'

She looked down at herself, smoothing a hand over her stomach, feeling the slight roundness there that she had never noticed before. Four months. Not so long. Was it possible? A small flame of joy unfurled in her breast.

'Could it truly be a baby, Christian?' she whispered, tears springing to her eyes. 'Our child? Our very own child?'

With a cry of sheer joy, she wrapped her arms about his neck and kissed him with all her strength. He answered her with equal passion, carrying her to his bed and showing her exactly how true it could be.

* * *

Catherine and Christian were married on board the *Liberté* by Father Cassel the next day. Three and a half weeks later, the frigate weighed anchor in the waters of the Delaware River and the *émigrés* finally got their feet onto American soil.

Patrick O'Donnell and half the city it seemed, were there to welcome the company of French settlers to their new home, and when he discovered his daughter was married and widowed and married again, he professed himself mighty confused. One thing he did understand, however, was that her gowns would soon need to be altered to allow for her growing belly.

As for Christian and Gérard, he took to them instantly.

'Two sea captains in one day!' he bellowed, grinning at his daughter as he wrapped his arms around the men's shoulders. 'My word, girl, you surely know how to bring your papa a useful souvenir! I need some good fellows like you. I've a mind to open a new route to the East to trade in spices — you're just in time!'

Catherine exchanged a smile with Christian as her father clasped their hands in welcome, then watched indulgently as he gathered up Angé's children, sitting them one upon each hip, and made for the waiting carriages calling out as he went, 'Come along, friends. America is waiting!'

She turned to Zamore, who was watching quietly at her side. 'There will be a place for you, too, Zamore. My father has struggled against bigotry all his life and beaten it — he doesn't hold with colour or race being used against any man.'

The blackamoor smiled. 'Then I shall learn to be an American too, like him.'

Catherine felt Christian at her side and turned to smile at her husband, feeling her heart fill with a love so deep it brought tears to her eyes. 'Thank you, my love, for bringing us all to safety.'

He leaned over and kissed her quickly, laughing when she blushed, for he had discovered that she was prudish in public.

'You will have to continue the English lessons you've been giving me,' he said as they followed the group down the quay. 'If I am to captain a bunch of colonials, I must learn to speak their language as well as they.'

Catherine jabbed him playfully in the ribs. 'Don't you dare call us 'colonials'! And if you have any notions that I shall teach you to speak like a sailor, then you are much mistaken. You may undertake your own research in the bawdy houses by the harbour.'

He feigned horror at such a suggestion and

513

they both laughed.

'But what of the *Liberté* and her crew?' Catherine asked, turning suddenly to look across the waters of the Delaware to the beautiful frigate lying at anchor. 'What will become of her?'

Christian gazed at his ship. 'I will find a crew willing to sail her back. I'm no pirate at heart.'

Catherine grinned impishly at him. 'You spirited us all out of France, absconded with a warship, fired upon a government vessel and as if that wasn't enough, stole my heart,' she said. 'I think that qualifies you as a brigand.'

'Indeed,' he replied, his eyes alight with laughter. 'And pray what does that make you, my dear?'

Then, without any consideration for the delicacy of her feelings, he took her in his arms and kissed her soundly, then picked her up and carried her towards the waiting carriage.

We do hope that you have enjoyed reading this large print book.

Did you know that all of our titles are available for purchase?

We publish a wide range of high quality large print books including:
Romances, Mysteries, Classics, General Fiction, Non Fiction and Westerns.

Special interest titles available in large print are:
The Little Oxford Dictionary
Music Book
Song Book
Hymn Book
Service Book

Also available from us courtesy of Oxford University Press:
Young Readers' Dictionary
(large print edition)
Young Readers' Thesaurus
(large print edition)

For further information or a free brochure, please contact us at:
Ulverscroft Large Print Books Ltd.,
The Green, Bradgate Road, Anstey,
Leicester, LE7 7FU, England.
Tel: (00 44) 0116 236 4325
Fax: (00 44) 0116 234 0205

Other titles in the
Ulverscroft Large Print Series:

STRANGER IN THE PLACE

Anne Doughty

Elizabeth Stewart, a Belfast student and only daughter of hardline Protestant parents, sets out on a study visit to the remote west coast of Ireland. Delighted as she is by the beauty of her new surroundings and the small community which welcomes her, she soon discovers she has more to learn than the details of the old country way of life. She comes to reappraise so much that is slighted and dismissed by her family — not least in regard to herself. But it is her relationship with a much older, Catholic man, Patrick Delargy, which compels her to decide what kind of life she really wants.

PAINTED LADY

Delia Ellis

Miss Eleanor Needwood was about to be married to a most unsuitable suitor when Philip Markham came to her rescue. He arranged for Eleanor to be in London for the Season, a guest of his sister, who decided that everyone would benefit if Markham married Eleanor. And thus the rumour started. The surprised couple decided to play along with the mistaken impression until a scandal-free way to end the betrothal could be found. But when Eleanor agreed to pose for a daring artist, the result was far more scandalous than any broken engagement.

IF HE LIVED

Jon Stephen Fink

Lillian is a woman who feels too much. As a psychiatric nurse, she empathizes with her patients; as a mother, she mourns for her lost, runaway daughter. Now suddenly she has a new feeling, that her house, one of the oldest in the small Massachusetts town where she lives with her husband Freddy, has been invaded, violated by some past evil. And then Lillian sees the boy . . .

A GOOD MAN'S LOVE

Elizabeth Harris

Hal Dillon and Ben MacAllister had been deeply affected by the appalling death of their university friend Laurie. Hal journeyed to Mexico to continue his anthropological studies, and there found distraction in his passionate affair with Magdalena. But was he inviting even more heartache? Ben became a wanderer. While working in Cyprus he had met English girl Jo Daniel, and, after a nomadic summer together, they travelled to England to embark on what promised to be a lifetime of marital bliss. But Jo discovers that promises don't always come true.

BLACKBERRY SUMMER

Phyllis Hastings

Debbie converted a wing of the old farmhouse into an Academy for Young Ladies. She hoped this would enable her to make provision for her children's future careers. But she could not foresee the disastrous fire or the regret and guilt she would feel for giving her youngest son to be reared by her twin sister Dolly. Next to the farm, Dolly's wealthy husband Christopher built an imposing mansion in the Gothic style, and planned to run a racing stable, but his schemes were doomed to end in tragedy.